HENRY VOGEL

THE LOST COLONY ADVENTURES

Published in the United States of America by Rampant Loon Press, an imprint of Rampant Loon Media LLC, P. O. Box 111, Lake Elmo, Minnesota 55042. "Rampant Loon Press" and the Rampant Loon colophon are trademarks of Rampant Loon Media LLC.

www.rampantloonmedia.com

Cover design by Miblart.com

ISBN: 978-1-958333-03-7 (ebook)

ISBN: 978-1-958333-04-4 (print)

Dedicated to the memory of Edgar Rice Burroughs and Leigh Brackett, and to everyone who encouraged me to follow in their footsteps.

SCOUT'S HONOR

1

ASTEROID FIELD

"WORMHOLE EJECTION IN ONE MINUTE," WARNED THE NAV COMPUTER.

"Acknowledged," I said. "Computer, verify the emergency message drone is receiving the sensor data feed and is ready to launch."

"Verified," the computer responded.

For the remaining few seconds, the computer was silent, leaving me to mentally prepare for as many wormhole endpoint hazards as possible. Unfortunately, there are some hazards you simply can't prepare for —exiting into the middle of an asteroid field is the worst one of those.

The collision alert began wailing at the same time my scout ship emerged from the wormhole.

"Computer, launch the drone," I said, firing thrusters to avoid an asteroid larger than my ship.

"Drone launched," responded the computer in its unflappable, calm voice.

"Tell me when the drone enters the wormhole," I said, diving under a rock the size of an aircar.

"Unable to comply," said the computer as I spun the ship starboard as fast as possible, barely sliding between two large asteroids.

"Unable to comply?" I asked. "Why?"

"Ship's sensors are blocked by the asteroid field," the computer told me.

"Acknowledged," I said for the hundredth time since my ship had first entered the wormhole.

Then I tuned out the computer and worked on staying alive. I almost made it out of the field without taking major damage, too. With the edge of the field only a short distance away, my scout ship shuddered from an impact. It was a small asteroid, just a few meters across, but it was more than large enough to breach the hull and damage internal systems. With air rushing out of the breach, my ship tumbled out of the asteroid field.

A planet lay just beneath me, far closer than one should be to an asteroid field. Out of control, the scout ship plunged toward the planet below.

The Airship

The ship spun and tumbled dizzily as the air in the cabin shrieked, leaking out into space. Strapped tightly into the pilot seat, there was nothing I could do to repair the hole in the side of the ship. Even if I were free to move, I wouldn't survive more than a few seconds of being tossed about the cabin.

"Abandon ship protocol initiated," the computer said inside my head, broadcasting directly to my implant to overcome the screams of my dying ship.

The pilot's seat dropped through the deck and into the escape pod, plugging itself into the control interface. The interface showed green and the escape pod launched itself from the ship. As it plunged toward the unknown planet, I had my first real chance to look around. I hadn't been in an asteroid field. The wormhole exit was inside a planetary ring.

My sightseeing was cut short when sensor readings started coming in. The readings cut off as the pod hit the atmosphere, but what I'd read looked promising. The planet should support human life, at least.

I held the pod's flight steady until it completed entry into the atmosphere, absently noted a fuel leak alert, then issued the command to deploy the wings and stabilizer. The expected whirring of the wings unfolding was replaced by a harsh grinding. That sound told me there was a major problem before the lights started flashing. I guess the asteroid impact had managed to damage more than just the escape pod's fuel tank. Fortunately, the designers had taken many possibilities into account when designing the escape pod, including fuel leaks and wing damage. The escape pod was a lifting body and could glide without the wings. More or less.

I worked the controls, slowly changing the angle of descent, waiting for the pod to begin generating some lift. At two hundred meters, with the pod finally leveling out, I found my glide path blocked. A primitive airship floated dead ahead. Instinctively, I dove beneath it—and the escape pod lost most of its lift.

The ground rushed up, ready to crush me.

Crash Landing

My eyes slid over the controls, desperately searching for a way to create some more lift. Almost on their own, my eyes slid back to the fuel gauge. The remaining fuel barely registered on the gauge, but it might be enough to fire the maneuvering thrusters for a few seconds. If I could nudge the escape pod toward level flight and add some forward momentum, maybe...

I fired the thrusters.

One second.

Two seconds.

Three-

The thrusters cut out, all of the fuel depleted. But the escape pod was moving forward again and slowly generating lift. I wrestled with the controls, trying to make the escape pod glide by force of will alone. The pod was leveling out slowly but it was losing altitude much too quickly for comfort. I yanked back on the controls, forcing the pod to nose up. If the nose of the pod hit first, it would cartwheel across the landscape, leaving pieces of itself—and me—scattered all over the place.

With a bone-jarring impact, the back half of the pod hit the ground. Skipped into the air. Hit the ground again. Skipped again. And suddenly, there was a small lake below me. The pod splashed into it and bobbed to a stop. With all the holes and rips in the pod's skin, I didn't think the pod would stay afloat for long. Slapping the harness release, I grabbed the standard issue survival pack. The pod was sinking even faster than I'd hoped, so I popped the canopy and dove into the water.

I struck out toward the shore, about fifty meters away. A couple of minutes later, I staggered out of the water. Scrub brush grew up around the water. Beyond that little ring of greenery stretched desert as far as I could see. From the other side of the little lake, I could hear something moving through the bushes. It sounded like something big, like something I didn't want to meet. Keeping an eye behind me, I struck out toward the desert.

At that moment, a man's voice cried out in pain and then cut off abruptly. The cry was followed by a woman's scream.

A Desperate Fight

Dripping from my swim to shore and clutching the emergency pack, I looked about for the source of the scream. A couple of hundred meters away, I saw a jumble of boulders. Now that I was alert to it, I could also hear the sounds of fighting going on beyond it—weapons clashing and voices shouting.

I ran to the boulders and quickly scrambled to the top. Below me, battle whirled between two human warriors, struggling to defend their position with swords, and about two dozen spear-thrusting wild...men? No, they were humanoid but not human, having squat, powerful bodies, blue skin, and sloping foreheads. Blood darkened the ground around bodies from both sides.

The warriors were backed against the boulders, forming a wall of flashing steel between the humanoids and a beautiful, raven-haired young woman. She moved restlessly behind her two guards, her sword poised to slash out should a humanoid come within her reach. As I took in the scene, one of her guards fell, a spear thrust completely through him. Even dying, the man found the strength to drive his sword into the stomach of the blue man who had thrust the spear. There was no scream from the young woman this time as she stepped forward to take his place.

Reflexively, I reached into the survival pack and grabbed the Onesie. The techs and quartermasters called it a Single-Shot Solar-Rechargeable Survival Blaster. All the scouts simply called it a Onesie because one shot per charge was all you got. Holding the Onesie over my head, I gave a wordless bellow. The fighting stopped as everyone turned their attention to me.

Brandishing the gun, knowing none could understand me, I yelled at the humanoids, "Leave or face the wrath of the Sky Wizard!" Then I fired the Onesie at the ground before the blue men.

I guess the blue men didn't like wizards. With guttural shouts, they charged at me.

Battling the Blue Men

Dropping the survival pack and the discharged Onesie—it would be hours before it could be fired again—I leapt to meet the charging blue men. *Boost*, I thought to my implant. Instantly, the implant flooded my body with adrenaline. Unless I could finish the fight quickly—not likely, given the odds—I'd pay a serious price for the abuse Boost put on a human body. But if I was going to save the man and the beautiful young woman, I was going to need all the strength and speed of Boost.

With adrenaline raging through my veins, I moved among the wild blue men so fast that none of them could land a solid hit. The blue men crowded around me, plunging their spears into each other as I dodged and wove among them. I felt no pain from the scrapes and cuts I picked up. When the blue men got too close, I used my enhanced strength to lift one of my attackers above my head and wielded him as a club, beating his fellows from around me.

Tossing aside the broken body, I scooped up a fallen spear and continued my dance of death among them. As the bodies of the blue men piled up behind me, the blue men still fighting with the man and the young woman realized the greater danger lay at their backs. They couldn't seem to decide whether to turn to face me or try to overwhelm the other two humans. Their hesitation doomed them, as the remaining guard shifted from defense to attack. We drove toward each other, cutting down all who stood before us.

Even as my spear plunged into the last of the blue men, I was turning to see if the man or young woman were wounded. My eyes met the flashing, green eyes of the young woman. She spoke in a language my implant's translator had not yet interpreted. I assumed it was some form of thanks.

I smiled and replied, "No problem. Glad I was able to help."

Having far exceeded Boost safety limits, my implant read the relaxation in my posture. Determining I was now safe, the implant cut off Boost. The adrenaline stopped flowing and pain from my abused muscles slammed into me. I fell into darkness even before I fell to the ground.

2

THE AIRSHIP RETURNS

"HIGHNESS, LET ME BIND THIS MAN," A GRUFF VOICE SAID. "HE COULD BE one of the raiders."

"He's not, Rob," said a lilting, female voice. "We'd never have escaped if he was. He's the best fighter I've ever seen."

"More reason to bind him," said the gruff voice. "We can always choose to release him after he wakes up. We certainly cannot bind him *after* he is awake."

The two must have been talking the whole time I was out. The translator in my implant had analyzed their language and was translating for me. Now that I was conscious, it would begin teaching me the full language, but I already had some words.

"He right," I said, sitting up and finally getting a good look at the man and young woman.

The man was probably in his mid-forties and looked like an experienced soldier. He had drawn his sword the second I spoke, moving with lethal grace.

The young woman was perhaps twenty, only a few years younger than me, with a tall, slender beauty that was breathtaking to behold. She was pointing my discharged Onesie at me.

"Who are you?" asked Rob. "Where do you come from?"

"Not easy to tell," I said. "Learn talk take time."

"That's another thing, Highness-" Rob began, cutting off as a shadow passed over us.

Looking up, I saw the airship I had nearly rammed. It was sailing a few hundred meters above us. I was drawing breath to shout to them when the princess gasped in dismay.

"Well, Highness, now we learn whose side this young man is on," Rob growled. "The raiders have found us."

Raiders

"Raiders chase you?" I asked, wishing my implant could imprint their language more quickly.

"Yes. We escaped yesterday," Rob replied. "Now, those who sacrificed themselves so we could do so have died in vain."

"No," I said, grabbing the survival pack. Above us, the airship was clearly venting gas to lose altitude.

"Ha," I said, pulling a large, thin cloth from the pack. "Safe now."

"Are you mad?" asked the princess, holding out the Onesie, "Drop the blanket and use this weapon to destroy them!"

I checked the Onesie's solar recharging unit. I'd been out longer than I thought because the gun would soon have enough charge to fire. But it would not be soon enough. Wrapping myself in the cloth, I dropped to the ground. "What see?"

The princess gasped, "Rob, did he just turn into a rock?"

"Well, Highness," Rob considered, "he *looks* like a rock."

"Chameleon cloth," I said, using the Terran term. I handed the cloth to Rob, "You two, under. Hide."

"What of you?" the princess asked as Rob wrapped the cloth around them.

"No room, Highness," I said. "I distract."

I handed the Onesie back to the princess and pointed at the controls, "Green good. Red bad. Point. Press button."

Taking the gun, the young woman gave a brief nod. Rob wrapped the chameleon cloth around them and they blended into the terrain.

Ropes dropped from the airship as it neared the ground. I began running toward them, waving my arms as men began sliding down the ropes. Seconds later, I was surrounded, half a dozen sword points pricking my skin.

Talk or Die

"Where is the princess?" a voice asked as swords pressed in all around me.

"Princess?" I asked in return, trying hard to feign confusion.

A tall, broad-shouldered man stepped into view from the left. A very recent wound slashed down his right cheek.

"Do not try my patience," demanded scarred-face. "My men saw you with her mere moments ago."

"She princess?" I asked.

"Yes, idiot, she is a princess. And if you don't tell me where she went, I'm going to have my lads poke several big, nasty holes in you." He smiled warmly, "Now, talk or die."

I pointed almost directly at Rob and the princess, "Go that way."

"South? Farther into the desert?" Scarred-face laughed jovially, "The idiot thinks I'm a fellow fool. We go north. Prod the idiot along, boys."

The raiders took scarred-face at his word. Every couple of steps, one of them poked me in the back with his sword. Soon, I was hopping forward with every other step, trying to stay just out of reach of the prodding. This drew laughs aplenty as my captors turned it into a game.

The game kept them so distracted that they didn't notice the two meter drop off until I hopped over it and vanished from sight. Shouts rose behind me as I sprinted toward a nearby tumble of rocks. Nearly there, I looked back and was surprised to see the raiders had stopped chasing me.

As I spun back to look forward, I heard a deep-throated growl. Looking up, all I could see was twin rows of long, sharp teeth.

Tammar

The raiders backed away, muttering "tammar." The predator—for it could be nothing else—stood two meters tall at the shoulders and was five meters long. My choices weren't good ones; die on the tammar's fangs or Boost and probably die overtaxing my body. Probably dead was better than definitely dead. I prepared to Boost.

The sound of a fully charged Onesie cracked through the air. The tammar's head disappeared in a spray of blood. Turning, the raiders and I saw the princess holding the gun. She was already turning the gun on the raiders.

"Run. Now," she commanded. "Unless you want to end up like the tammar."

All but scarred-face broke and ran. He stared at the princess, a smile crossing his lips, then he turned and walked after his rapidly receding crew.

"Nice timing, Highness," I said, joining Rob and her. "I'm in your debt."

The two stared at me in shock. Quickly, it dawned on me what was wrong.

"You're wondering how I learned your language so quickly," I said. "It will take some explaining, most of which you'll probably find unbelievable."

"What little we know about you—especially this weapon—is already unbelievable," the princess said, handing me the Onesie.

Taking the gun, I said, "You realize your threat was empty, Highness?"

"The raiders did not know-" she paused. "I do not even know your name."

"I am David Rice, Scout First Class of the Terran Exploration Corps," I said, bowing. "Let's start walking and I will happily tell my story."

The princess looked to Rob. "Northeast, Highness. I spotted a trading outpost during our escape from the raiders."

Carrying only the provisions in the survival pack, we headed into the desert.

3

PRINCESS CALLAN

We spoke little throughout the afternoon, moving too quickly to waste breath talking. At dusk, Rob slowed the pace.

"While we're hardly safe, Highness," he said, "following our trail will not be easy. Especially from an airship."

"Thank you, Rob," the princess replied. Turning to me, she said, "You promised us some unbelievable explanations, Scout First Class David Rice."

"First, please just call me David, Highness."

"Very well, David. This is Captain Robbill Vonsteader, captain of my personal guard. I am Her Royal Highness, Princess Callan Debah Lois Antrulta Ziliah Villas, daughter of His Royal Majesty, King Edwar of Mordan. You may continue to call me Highness, though Princess Callan is also correct."

"Thank you, Highness," my lips twitched up in a smile. "I'll start with the most relevant part of my story. I had never laid eyes on this planet, nor even knew it existed, until today..."

Princess Callan's eyes grew wide as I told of my wormhole exit and subsequent crash. "I told you I was a member of the Terran Exploration Corps. Terra is another planet, the original home of the human race. Thousands of years ago, humans began leaving Terra to settle on other worlds. These colonists traveled the vast void of space, many of them spending decades in transit. Some of those ships left no record of their destination. Some of them wished to withdraw from human civilization entirely, so recorded false destinations. And some of the records have simply been lost. The Terran Exploration Corps was formed, in part, to look for those lost colonies." I paused briefly, "Colonies such as your planet.

"Do your cultures have myths and legends telling of a great journey, Highness? Perhaps something along the lines of ships crossing the Sea of Night? Considering my experience earlier today the tales probably end with many of the ships being cast upon rocks and very few of the brave travelers reaching the new land alive."

"Yes, David, we do have such tales. They're almost exactly as you describe," replied the princess. "In certain scholarly circles, there is hot debate concerning those stories. Some claim the stories are based on true events while others are certain the stories are merely attempts to explain our presence here on Aashla. You say those tales are true?"

"Yes, at least in part," I said. "Is Aashla what you call this planet?"

"Every schoolchild knows that, David," Princess Callan said. Looking into my eyes, she continued, "Yet I believe you did not."

"Thank you, Highness. I know it will require quite a leap of faith to believe my story," I said.

"Is there no way to bolster my faith in your story? You could just be an adventurer with a fanciful imagination or simply insane. Can you offer proof, as well, David?"

I held out the survival pack, "Highness, you've used my weapon, heard me learn your language in less than a day, hidden beneath the chameleon cloth, and watched me fight while Boosted. I can offer no more proof than that."

"What of this ship you crashed this morning?" Callan persisted.

"It sank into the small lake," I said. "Yes, I know that sounds very convenient for my story, but it is true."

"Highness, all of this is quite fascinating," said Rob in a tone that belied his words, "but we must find a defensible place to spend the night. The tammar you killed was drawn out in daylight by the scent of blood from our fight, but they usually hunt at night."

"Of course, Rob," Princess Callan said. "But if danger strikes, at least we have David and his astounding Boost."

"Highness," I said, "do not depend on that. Boosting places an incredible strain on my body. Using it again so soon could kill me."

The princess appeared shocked at my words. Rob, on the other hand, looked surprisingly satisfied. Perhaps he was happy to learn just how mortal I was.

A site was soon selected and camp established. We ate a meal of tasteless survival bars from the pack then settled in for the night, Rob taking first watch. It seemed as if I had only just closed my eyes when Rob's hand clamped over my mouth.

"Wake up but make no sound or sudden moves," he hissed.

I opened my eyes and instantly knew what was wrong. A long, black snake-like thing was coiled on the princess's chest. It had hundreds of tiny legs along its body and a single fang bared in its open mouth. The thing's head was raised and ready to strike. The princess lay still, her eyes so filled with terror that I knew this snake-thing's bite must be deadly.

The Desert Creature

If the snake-thing was like Terran snakes, it was probably searching for warmth and found it on the princess's chest. Now aroused, it was nervous and looked likely to strike. Whatever we were going to do, it had to be done fast.

"Red or green?" I asked quietly.

"Red," Rob answered quietly, instantly knowing I referred to the Onesie. "This Boost of yours—does it make you faster?"

"Yes, but maybe not fast enough."

"But you must-" Rob began, breaking off as the snake-thing hissed and moved in agitation.

I waited, letting the creature settle a bit before answering, "I will. Now, give me your hat."

Without another word, Rob carefully handed me the hat to his guard's uniform. Slowly, I began moving the open end of the hat in front of the snake-thing. The thing swayed in agitation then struck at the princess—a fraction of a second *after* I Boosted. The creature's head plunged into the hat, its strike blocked. I grabbed it just below the head and pulled it off of the princess. Its legs wriggled disturbingly within my grip as I dragged it outside. Drawing his sword, Rob smoothly cut off its head.

Quiet sobs drew Rob back inside the tent to comfort the princess. I took up the watch in his place.

After a while, the sobs faded and, finally, were replaced by the deep, rhythmic breathing of sleep. When Rob looked outside, I motioned him back into the tent. The princess would feel safer if she awoke to a familiar face.

As dawn was breaking, I heard the raider's airship engine in the distance. Worse, I realized the airship was ahead of us. It was apparent the raiders knew of the outpost and knew it was our only hope for survival. They would be waiting for us when we arrived.

Giving My Oath

We broke camp immediately, hoping the outpost was close and we might reach it before the raiders could prepare for us.

"Highness, you know my story," I said, trying to distract her from the previous night's horror and from the raiders ahead of us, "but I know little of yours."

Rob gave a nod and she said, "Very well, David, it's not a complicated story.

"I was being escorted to my betrothal to Prince Rupor, heir to the throne of Tarteg. Ten airships of the Mordanian Navy escorted my own airship. Over unsettled lands, a large force of raiders surprised us. Three raider ships attacked my ship. When it was obvious all was lost, I ordered my men to surrender.

"The raiders locked us in one of their airship's holds and flew south. A few hours later, ten of my guards broke out of the hold. They attacked the raiders, sacrificing themselves as a distraction for the rest of us. In the confusion, Rob grounded the airship and we ran. Several hours later, you arrived."

"A harrowing tale, Highness," I said. "But why would the raiders come south? I would assume any ransom would be paid in the north."

"With her lineage and beauty," Rob said, "Princess Callan would fetch a very high price in the southern slave markets."

Slave markets? I knew primitive colonies had been known to revive the vile practice, but it was still shocking to hear.

Rob added, "I will die before allowing that to happen."

Unable to bear the thought of anyone—especially one so lively and lovely—being sold into slavery, I said, "As will I."

Rob stopped walking, "Will you swear to that, David?"

"Rob-" began the princess.

I interrupted, raising my right hand. "On my honor as a Scout First Class, I swear to protect and defend Princess Callan to the best of my ability, even at the cost of my life."

Rob smiled for the first time since I met him. "Nontraditional but quite satisfactory." He extended his hand. "Welcome to the Royal Guard, David."

"That was unnecessary, David," the princess said.

"Perhaps for you, Highness," I replied, "but it was essential to Rob."

Suddenly, a shout rang out. "The princess! She's over here."

The raiders had spotted us.

David the Distraction

The shout was taken up by other raiders and quickly echoed all around the trading post.

I turned to Rob, "You two use the chameleon cloth to hide while I-"

"It's gone, David," Rob said. "Lost when we threw it off so the princess could shoot the tammar."

"All right," I said, "new plan. I'll lead the raiders on a merry chase while you and the princess make your way around the trading post to the raiders' airship. They know where we are and are intent on surrounding us quickly. That will take most of the crew, so their airship should be lightly guarded."

"Right," Rob nodded. "After we take the ship, we'll wait for you for two minutes."

"Cast off immediately," I said. "Her Highness's safety is all that matters. Do *not* wait for me."

Rob nodded but the princess disagreed. "No! We all escape together or-"

"Highness, there are a very few times when your royal guards may disregard your orders," Rob said. "This is one of them. Your safety is paramount."

The princess shook her head in disagreement but did not argue. With that settled, I scuttled away from Rob and the princess. A moment later, I rose and dashed off in the direction opposite the path they would take. My appearance immediately drew another shout and the chase was on. I used rocks, bushes, low dunes, gullies, anything I could to pop in and out of sight. I couldn't draw the raiders off unless they saw me, but I couldn't give them too long a look or they'd realize they were chasing one person instead of three.

Perhaps a minute later, I came face to face with my first raider. I vaulted over a boulder and found him lurking behind it. I ducked his wild sword swing and ran him through with my own sword. He fell, screaming and twitching as life drained out of him. I popped up and ran out.

Behind me, someone shouted, "He killed Farley!"

Any raiders who hadn't been chasing me, would be after me now.

A moment later, I crested a small dune and saw the main building of the trading post before me. Gambling that all of the raiders were in the desert chasing me, I ran to it and threw open the door. Half a dozen raiders, led by scarred-face, stood within. They all had their swords drawn. Behind me, the raiders who had been chasing me charged up to the outpost.

I was surrounded by raiders. Again.

4

THE PLUNGING PRINCESS

I THOUGHT ABOUT BOOSTING, BUT KNEW I COULDN'T. I COULD ALWAYS trigger Boost if things got desperate, but until the princess was safe, I had to save it to use in her defense. With raiders all around me and no chance to survive a fight, I chose the only direction available to me. Up. Jumping, I caught the edge of the low roof and had pulled myself onto the roof before the first raider could react.

It was a mistake.

I had a great view of the raider airship. It was on the far side of the building and just lifting off. Now that they were looking up, the raiders outside the building could see the same thing.

"The airship," rose the cry. "She's loose and floating away!"

Raiders ran for the lines hanging from the airship, even before scarred-face began shouting orders at them. I pounded across the roof, hoping to grab a line and climb to the deck ahead of the raiders. That wasn't going to happen. Some raiders must have been near the ship and they were already scrambling up the lines.

Glancing at the airship deck, I saw Rob holding off three raiders while the princess sawed away at a dangling line with her dagger. There was no way she could cut all of the lines before the first raiders reached the deck. I *had* to get aboard the airship soon or all was lost. Casting aside caution, I sprinted to the edge of the roof and leapt off, aiming for a line dangling from the airship's starboard side.

I just managed to catch the end of the line. Even as I began the long climb, I saw several raiders reach the deck of the airship. The princess saw them and shouted a warning to Rob. She also saw a raider heading toward the line I was using. Princess Callan ran to defend my line against the raider, pitting her dagger against his sword. She whirled, dodged, blocked, and then tripped. I was halfway up the line when she fell against the railing, overbalanced, and fell from the airship!

Safe in My Arms

The princess plunged toward me, her eyes wide with terror and locked on mine. Wrapping my legs around the rope, I lunged out to intercept her fall.

Boost!

Her flailing hands would have been impossible for me to catch without the added speed and strength of the Boost. I caught her wrist, grasping it with both hands, but her momentum dragged us both down the line. A scream tore from the princess's lips, but I tightened my legs around the line and our descent stopped.

I pulled her up, wishing I could take the time to comfort her. "Wrap your arms around my neck."

She was shaking from terror but, mastering it, did as I instructed. "Hold tight, Highness, we're going up very fast."

With Boosted strength and agility, I swarmed up the line faster than any monkey. The raider at the railing had just enough time to realize the princess hadn't fallen to her death before we leaped onto the deck. Grabbing his shirt, I threw him off the airship. I sat the princess down, well away from the rail, then drew my sword and raced to Rob's aid.

I crashed into the raiders around Rob like a human battering ram, knocking two more over the rail and sending the rest flying across the deck. Rob, whose back had been to our ascent, stared at me in astonished relief.

"Her Highness-" he began.

"She's safe," I said, pointing behind me. Then I attacked the remaining six raiders. They were better fighters than the blue men I'd fought earlier—could it have just been yesterday?—but I also had Rob at my side. In less than a minute, the last raider fell to the deck.

Pain slammed into me as the Boost cut off, but this time I remained conscious. That meant I was entirely awake and aware when the princess—the *betrothed* princess—flew into my arms and began kissing me passionately on the lips.

Rebuked

I received a lot of training in the Scout Academy. None of it had covered my situation. When the princess's lips locked on mine, all rational thought fled, leaving instinct to take over. Placing my hand on the small of the princess's back, I pulled her close and returned the kiss. Enthusiastically.

"Ahem!"

We jumped apart like a couple of preteens caught necking in school, our eyes downcast and unable to meet Rob's stern gaze.

"Highness, go to the stern of the airship," Rob ordered.

The princess bristled at his tone, "Rob, you will not-"

"*Callan*, do as I say."

Chastised, she stalked aft.

Trying to head off the coming rebuke, I said, "Rob, I -"

"*Silence, boy,*" hissed Rob. "Less than an hour ago, you took an oath to protect the princess with your life. That includes protecting her from herself and her infatuations. That includes protecting her from your base instincts. *Do you understand?*"

"Yes, sir!"

His gaze bored into mine. Satisfied, he unbent slightly. "Many men develop strong feelings for those they guard, David, especially when their charge is a beautiful young woman. Burying those feelings is your duty."

"It will not happen again, sir."

He nodded and seemed to be satisfied. "Now, can that...thing...in your head teach you how to fly this airship?"

I checked and, to my surprise, my implant did have information on piloting airships. As Rob headed aft toward the princess, I concentrated on the airship controls. I tried very hard to ignore the discussion taking place at the stern, but it sounded like the "protectee" version of the speech Rob had just given to me.

I needed to figure out how to gain altitude so we could reach the prevailing winds. That meant forward speed and the right angle on the ailerons to generate lift beyond that provided by the gas envelope. A little experimentation with the controls showed me what I could do from the wheel. I'd have to set the ailerons by hand, but I could pilot the ship well enough to get the princess back to her country.

Looking up from the controls, I spotted a dark smudge on the horizon. Grabbing my survival pack, that Rob had brought aboard, I took out the binoculars and trained them on the smudge. Ice lanced through my gut as the smudge came into focus.

A sandstorm stretched across the horizon, bearing down on us.

The Sandstorm

The sandstorm drew visibly closer in the few seconds I watched through the binoculars. We needed a new course and a lot more speed or the storm would have us.

"Rob," I called as I turned the ship away from the onrushing storm.

Turning from the princess, brows drawing down in irritation at the interruption, he said, "Not now-"

"Sandstorm! It's closing fast."

Rob was standing next to me seconds later. I handed him the binoculars as I turned the ship away from the sandstorm.

"Look through—," I began.

"We have similar devices," Rob said, lifting the binoculars to his eyes. "Though none are so sharp or powerful as these."

Studying the storm, Rob added, "It appears you can fly this ship."

"Not well enough to fly through the storm."

"Can we outrun it?" he asked.

"Probably not, but..." I turned to the princess, "Highness, take the wheel and hold it steady. I need to show Rob something."

She took the wheel without a question. I led Rob to the engine room, below.

"Have you ever worked a steam engine?" I asked.

"Yes, years ago," he replied.

"If we're going to have a chance of outrunning the storm, I'll need as much steam as you can get me," I told him. "Even if the storm catches us, having our own power may help."

As Rob began feeding wood to the fire, I added, "I'll send the princess below. It will be safer for her down here, out of the storm."

The wind had risen considerably in the short time I'd been below. Taking the wheel, I told the princess to go below.

She gave me a sudden smile, "You kiss quite well, David. The woman who marries you will be a lucky woman, indeed. For her sake, whoever she is, do be careful."

She turned and went below, leaving me to wonder exactly what she meant.

Rob built up the steam quickly, powering the twin propellers to spin ever faster. Still, I doubted we could outrun the storm. It bore down on us, gaining no matter what I did with the airship's controls.

I fought the buffeting wind, scanning the desert for any place where we could land and take cover. Then the storm blotted out the sun and sand scoured the deck.

The storm was upon us.

Abandon Ship

The storm swept over the airship and visibility was cut to nothing. I wasn't sure if I could see the bow or was half imagining it through the swirling sand. I fought to keep us from being driven into the ground or being turned sideways to tumble keel over gas envelope. The ship danced on the wind, beyond my ability to exert much control over its course. I sensed more than saw a dune rise up before the ship and just managed to keep us from plowing into it. The airship's keel still scraped the top of the dune, jarring the ship.

Time vanished, leaving me with no idea how long I'd been fighting the storm. My implant told me it was mere minutes, but I felt as if it had been hours. Flayed by sand, my body taut with tension, I was on the ragged edge of exhaustion. So I did not notice that Rob was beside me until he grabbed my arm.

He was shouting but I could barely hear him over the storm, "Boiler pressure is rising too fast. Probably a clogged pipe, but there's no way to fix it before it blows. Not in this storm."

I shouted back. "You and the princess will have to abandon ship. I'll get us down close to the ground so you can jump safely."

Rob nodded. He understood there was no other way to insure the princess's safety.

"I'll blow the whistle when it's time for you to jump," I said.

"What of you, lad?"

Instead of answering, I shouted, "I'll find you once the storm passes."

"I don't doubt it for a moment, David." Though it was obvious he *did* doubt it. Clapping my shoulder, he went below.

I took the ship down until I was sure I saw ground beneath the airship, then blew the steam whistle long and loudly. Its wail rose above the roar of the storm and I hoped Rob and the princess had jumped safely. As the wind drove the ship up again, I heard the steam whistling again. For a moment, I thought the whistle had jammed, then I realized the sound was coming from below—from the boiler.

I dashed for the ship's railing but was too late. With a roar, the boiler exploded.

5

TRAPPED

I DRIFTED ON THE EDGE OF CONSCIOUSNESS, STRUGGLING TO STAY AWAY from it. For I knew pain lurked behind consciousness and I could not have one without the other. Better to float in mental limbo for a while longer, hoping the pain would get tired of waiting for me and go away.

"*David!*"

The voice reached to me, below the surface of consciousness, and pulled me upward. That voice meant something to me. It meant beautiful green eyes. It meant long raven hair. It meant a warm smile and a tall, slender body. It meant *Callan.* I came fully awake at the thought of her. With awareness came the pain, but also remembrance. Raiders. Escapes. The kiss. Her betrothal. My oath.

"*David!*"

I tried to respond but managed only a soft cough. Then I struggled to stand and found I could not. Prying my eyes open, I discovered I was buried under the debris from the wrecked airship—wood, rope, cloth. Experimenting, I found I could move one of my arms. I knocked on the wood as hard as I could.

"David? Is that you?"

I knocked again.

"Rob! He's over here. He's buried under the wreckage."

Footsteps approached and then a pair of eyes peered at me through an opening in the debris.

"I'm glad to see you made it, lad," said Rob. "I can't see much of you in there except your eyes, but I assume the rest of you is intact."

His arm reached as far into the opening as possible, "Here's a water skin. Drink, clear your throat, and conserve your strength. It's going to take a while for us to free you."

The water tasted heavenly and the sound of debris being cleared was music to my ears. And it lasted all of two minutes.

"Rob?" The princess sounded worried. "There are horses coming."

It was silent for a few seconds then Rob cursed.

"What is it?" I managed to croak.

Rob's reply was flat and chilling. "Slavers."

Martin Bane

"How far away are the slavers? Do you think they've seen you?" I asked.

"Half a mile, maybe," Rob answered, "and I doubt they've seen us yet. We should blend in with the wreckage at that distance."

"Then hide," I said. My implant told me half a mile was almost a kilometer. They could get clear if they left now. "When they get close, I'll call out for help. Maybe they won't look for anyone else if they think I'm alone. At the very least, they'll have fewer men searching for you."

Rob stood, "It's the best chance we've got, Highness. Let's go."

The princess's voice drifted down to me, "Take care, David."

I heard the two of them scrambling away followed by silence. Finally, I heard the riders approaching.

"Help!" I called. "I'm trapped under the wreckage."

The light was blocked and then voices began jabbering in a language new to me. It wasn't surprising, but it would make things more difficult until my implant could analyze and imprint the new language.

More jabbering came from the slavers, followed by the sounds of wreckage being moved. With horses to help drag larger, heavier pieces of the wreck, it only took fifteen minutes before hands were pulling me out. I put on my best grateful smile.

"I am so happy to see you! I'd never have gotten out on my own," I cried. "How can I ever thank you?"

The shadow of a rider fell across me.

"You can start by telling us where the princess is," said scarred-face. "And then you can explain what happened to my airship."

Time for plan B.

Boost! I snatched a sword from the slaver closest to me and leapt for scarred-face. All I had to do was take him hostage. That ought to be easy enough.

Moving impossibly quickly, scarred-face grabbed my wrist and threw me several meters from his horse. Then, he somersaulted off his horse and drew his sword, all before landing lightly on his feet.

Dropping Boost, I rolled to my feet and stared at him, "Who-"

"Ah, forgive my poor manners. We have not been properly introduced," scarred-face said, bowing. "I am Martin Bane, Scout Second Class of the Terran Exploration Corps."

Captured

"What-?" I began, but my thoughts stalled there. I tried again, "Why-?"

"You have quite a fascinating array of conversational gambits, my good man," Bane said, "but let's get back to the one important issue. Where is Princess Callan?"

That got through to me. "The princess and her bodyguard jumped off your airship during the sandstorm. Sand had clogged the boiler and pressure was getting dangerously high. I'd planned to follow them, but never could drive the ship close enough to the ground again."

"You flew my ship into a sandstorm?" Bane asked.

"No, I tried to run from it. The storm was too fast." I waved my hand toward the wreckage, "You can see the end result. But the princess is probably miles away from here."

Bane didn't believe me and called to his men, "Keep searching around the wreck. I'm sure those two are around here somewhere."

His men probably would find the princess and Rob unless I could distract them another time. Boosting once again, I leapt onto Bane's horse, slapping its flanks with the flat of my sword. Bane was caught by surprise, but his men ran for their own horses. The chase was on!

If I could get a dune between myself and the airship wreck, it would give Rob and the princess a chance to slip away from the site. I just had to keep the slavers busy for a few minutes.

The slavers were much better riders than me and came close to cutting me off before I topped the nearest dune. Two riders were racing to block me and it looked like they were going to succeed. Trusting to Boosted reflexes, I stood in the saddle, dove over them, and rolled down the far side of the dune. Whooping, the slavers chased after me.

At the bottom of the dune, I prepared to die fighting the slavers. Instead, they stayed well away from me and began twirling weighted ropes. Three riders threw their ropes at the same time. I jumped over one and ducked another, but the third wrapped tightly around my legs. Three more ropes followed, pinning my arms. Struggling against the ropes, I toppled over and could only watch as Bane strode over to me.

"We're going to find the princess," he said. "and you'll get to watch while she's sold at auction. Then I'll sell *you* at auction, too, and use the money I make to replace my airship."

Grinning, Bane bashed me on the head with his sword pommel and all went black.

Sacrifice For Naught

I awoke lying down, my hands and feet tied to a bed frame. Bane was there, watching me, a thoughtful expression on his face.

"How old are you, kid? Twenty-four?" he asked.

"Not quite."

"You must be the youngest Scout First Class ever," he said.

"Nope," I replied.

"Second youngest, then," Bane said. "And not by much, I'd bet."

"What makes you think I'm a Scout First Class?" I asked.

"There's no Master Scout with you," he said. "And since you're not mourning one's death, it seems obvious you were exploring alone. You can only explore alone if you're a Scout First Class."

"Does that mean your Master Scout—the one who was completing your training—is dead?"

"Yeah. We were hit by an asteroid right after our exit from the wormhole. She was killed instantly."

"How did you end up..." I wasn't sure how to complete that sentence.

"Like this? Raider, kidnapper, slaver?" he asked. "It's a long story and we don't have time for it."

"Have you got a pressing engagement somewhere?" I asked.

He shrugged and said, "I crash landed a day's walk from Morda, the Mordanian capital. I managed to walk to the city, but ended up in the worst part of the city. My implant picked up the gutter language spoken there, so I even sounded like one of the dregs of society. I went into the wrong bar, got into the wrong fight, Boosted at the wrong time, and killed a couple of thugs.

"That's usually not a big deal in the poorest quarters, but there was extra security because of a certain princess's fifth birthday. Someone had tried to celebrate Her Highness's fourth birthday by kidnapping her, so the city guard was being extra careful this year. No one in the city knew who I was and I couldn't give an explanation they were willing to listen to.

"I even tried telling them the truth, but even I wouldn't have believed my story if I'd been in their place. I'd usually have gotten time doing hard labor, but someone decided to make an example of me. I was sentenced to hang. Instead of hanging, another prisoner and I escaped. I've been working the other side of the law ever since."

He stood, "Some of us aren't lucky enough to crash on top of royalty, Wonder Boy. Some of us get stuck dealing with the seedy underbelly of a primitive civilization."

Bane was about to add something when the door flew open. Rob and the princess were pushed into the room by grinning slavers. My sacrifice had been for nothing.

6

THE MYTHICAL HERO

BANE BEAMED AT HIS MEN. "WELL DONE, LADS. WHO GETS THE BONUS FOR making the capture?"

"No one," Rob growled. "We came here on our own."

"You did *what*?" I said

Bane nodded toward me, "I'm with Wonder Boy on this one. Why would you give yourself up after you worked so hard to give us the slip?"

"Because we saw an army of trogs coming this way," answered Rob. "There are hundreds of them. Distasteful as it may be, this trading post was our only hope for survival."

Bane's expression grew serious and he said, "Rouse the men! Get spotters on the rooftops." Turning to Rob, "How much time have we got?"

"Thirty minutes, if you're lucky," he replied. "Highness, please release David."

"No, princess," Bane barked. "Wonder Boy is-"

"The best warrior here," Rob interrupted. "Let him help us."

Bane thought for a few seconds, nodded, then said, "Wonder Boy-"

"My name is David Rice," I said.

"Very well, Rice," Bane said, "give me your word of honor—as a Scout—that you will relinquish your sword to me after the battle."

I looked to Rob. He nodded.

"Yes, you have my word," I said.

As the princess untied my bonds, tears pooled in her eyes.

"Hey, Highness," I said, rubbing my wrists, "don't cry. We're going to get out of this alive, you know. Then we're going to escape from Martin Bane and get you home in time for your wedding."

Princess Callan wiped her eyes and tried to smile, "What makes you so sure of that, David?"

"I crossed the ocean of night and survived being cast upon the rocks," I said. "Then I found you in your most desperate hour. Isn't it obvious? I'm the mythical hero who rescues the beautiful princess."

The princess giggled, "But isn't the mythical hero supposed to marry the beautiful princess?"

"Shhh! Don't let Rob hear you say that," I said. "I don't want another lecture from him. These trogs—are they the blue men you were fighting when we met?"

Prince Callan nodded as I stood.

Bane said, "There are swords in the next room. Grab one." Then he asked, "Who has the Onesie? It could be useful."

"It's gone, lost when the boiler exploded," I said. "Besides, firing the Onesie just makes trogs mad."

"You'll forgive me if I don't believe you," Bane said. "I'll have to search-"

A shout interrupted him, "To arms! The trogs are here!"

Bane shot a look at Rob, "You said thirty minutes."

"I guess you weren't lucky," Rob shot back, as we grabbed swords and ran from the building.

As I'd expected, we were back at the trading post. From all around us, spears waving, blue figures charged toward us.

Into the Cellar

I took one look at the trog horde and knew they would overrun us with ease. Turning to Bane, I asked, "How well do you know this outpost?"

"What difference does it make?" Bane almost shouted.

"Does it have a storm cellar or a root cellar?" I demanded. "Some place underground with a single entrance?"

Comprehension dawned on Bane, "Yes."

Turning to his men, he ordered, "Recall everyone. We're going into the cellar."

We ran into the main building as his men spread word of the retreat. There was a trap door in one corner. It opened into a storage cellar, just as I'd hoped. I sent Rob and the princess into the cellar first.

"What of you, David?" asked the princess, concern in her eyes and voice.

"One of us guards you and one of us guards the entrance. Don't worry, I'll come down once everyone else is safely below," I told her, offering a confident smile.

After they had moved out of sight below, Bane gave me a sly grin. "Maybe Wonder Boy is the right nickname for you after all. Less than two days on the planet and you've already got the beautiful princess panting after you. You *are* a fast worker."

"Shut up," I growled.

I was saved further jibes as Bane's men began piling into the building. They wasted no time in jumping into the cellar. None of them showed a bit of concern for me as I waited for everyone to enter the cellar. By the time the last of Bane's men had jumped into the cellar, the howling of the trogs was deafening. Bane leapt down, leaving me to climb down the ladder and shut the trap door. I stayed on the ladder, sword in hand, ready to defend the door.

The doors to the building crashed open and heavy feet trod across the floor. A minute dragged past as we listened to the trogs searching the trading post. Then footsteps stopped above the trap door. It was flung open and a trog thrust his spear at me.

Boost!

I grabbed the spear and pulled. The trog tumbled to the floor below and Bane's men fell upon him. Above, two more trogs took his place.

Our battle for survival had begun.

Defense of the Door

Adrenaline blazed through my veins, giving me the strength and speed I needed to kill quickly. Our precarious position gave me the incentive to kill ruthlessly. Unless I could convince the trogs their attack wasn't worth the cost, I would fall. I'd suffer Boost Burnout or dodge left when I should have dodged right, and that would be it for me—and everyone else. The trogs would take the ladder when I fell. Once they controlled it, trogs could drop straight into the cellar. After that, it wouldn't take long for them to crush the remaining humans. There was no way around the terrible math of our predicament. If the trogs were willing to spend enough lives and take enough time, they would slaughter us all—even the princess.

Blood and snarls and screams filled my senses and time no longer had any meaning to me. I'd killed seventeen trogs and dragged four more into head-first dives to the cellar floor. Those four were killed before they could stand, but one of those trogs had still managed to kill two men despite lying on the floor. My implant said I'd been Boosting for nine minutes, three times longer than any known record. How long could I keep this up before I burned out?

Guttural shouting from above rose over the din of battle. A powerful voice cut through the shouts. Silence fell and the attacks ceased. I overrode my implant's safety protocols before it could turn off Boost. I knew I'd black out immediately after Boost shut down and I couldn't afford that. Besides, the attack could be renewed at any time and I had to be ready.

In the silence, we heard the sound of an airship engine above the trading post. Airmen could attack the trogs from above, never having to come within range of their spears. We waited to hear the cries of dying trogs. And we waited in vain. The engine droned on, fading as the airship passed overhead without stopping.

"Huuuuuumans," the powerful voice called. The faces below me went white, terrified by something I didn't understand.

"No warrior death for you," the voice continued. "You die, like beasts."

A trog slammed the trap door shut then we heard them piling heavy objects on top of it. A few moments later, the smell of smoke wafted down to us. The trogs had set fire to the building.

I dropped the override on my implant's safety protocols and it shut down Boost. I had just enough time to feel my heart stop beating before darkness overwhelmed me.

7

GOOD FORM

I WOKE UP. THAT WAS A SURPRISE. MY ACHING BODY HADN'T KILLED ME after all. I was lying on a dirt floor and, despite stiff, aching muscles, I felt comfortable. It was as if something was right in my world. Warm liquid splashed on my face. I opened my eyes and looked into the princess's tear-filled eyes. And now I knew what felt so right—my head lay cradled in the princess's lap. I smiled.

"Hi," I croaked.

Princess Callan's lovely green eyes focused and she gasped, "David? You're awake!"

A dazzling smile lit her face, drawing an answering smile from me. I would give anything, *do* anything, to keep that smile in place.

Rob and Bane stepped into view, towering over us both.

"Welcome back, lad," Rob said, smiling. "Good form, not dying."

Bane's eyes flicked to the princess, "Did you know your heart stopped when you stopped Boosting?"

I nodded. I'd remember that feeling for the rest of my life.

Bane continued, "My men performed a little CPR—something I teach everyone in my crew—while I fashioned a makeshift defibrillator using the Onesie. That's why you're still alive."

Bane held up the disassembled Onesie. "I don't know where she managed to hide it," his eyes roamed appreciatively over the princess's formfitting clothing, "but she did."

"After your heart started again, he said you shouldn't try to Boost again anytime soon," the princess said. "On this subject, at least, the raider and I agree."

"As you wish," I replied. Then another thought entered my head. It seems odd now, but at the time I felt as if it was the most important question in the world. Maybe it was my brain overreacting to my near death experience, but I asked, "Why did everyone look so scared when the trog leader spoke?"

The three of them exchanged glances, perhaps wondering if I had suffered some sort of brain damage.

"Trogs have never spoken human languages," Rob said. "It's generally assumed they're too stupid to learn it."

"Trogs have never organized an army, either. A hunting party is about the best they can do," Bane added. "Perhaps their leader is some kind of trog genius."

"When we get out of here, we've got to warn the northern countries," Rob said. "It's only a two day march to the border of Mordan."

"No, we don't," Bane said. "We've got a deal. You go to the Southern slave markets and you behave along the way. Just like your princess promised."

"*What*?" I cried.

"He was going to let you die, David," the princess whispered. "I couldn't let that happen. I promised him nothing he wasn't going to get, anyway. They outnumber us ten to one. We were going to the slave markets one way or the other. At least this way, you're alive."

"You don't think I destroyed that Onesie out of the supposed goodness of my-" Bane said, stopping as a deep thrumming sound reached us.

The airship was back!

Prince Raoul

We all looked up, as if we could see through the floor to the airship droning above us. No one spoke as our ears strained to catch any change in the engine's roar. We heard the engine shut down.

Minutes dragged by and we tried to make the airship crew find us by our force of will. Then we heard a thump from above. It was followed by another, and another after that. The sound of wood scraping against wood carried down to us. The debris of the trading post was being cleared.

"Hey!" I shouted. "We're in the cellar."

Two dozen voices roared as everyone else took up the shout. The sounds from above stopped, then renewed. More and more thumping and scraping came from above. More airmen were joining in the work.

Half an hour later, the sounds from above ceased. Footsteps stalked to the trap door. With the creak of hinges, the trap door opened and too-bright light burst upon us. Uniformed men began dropping into the cellar, each with a sword drawn and ready for action.

Princess Callan gasped, "Tartegian airmen."

"Your betrothed?" I asked.

Nodding, she rose to her feet, in the process transforming from the frightened young woman who had cradled my head into royalty. The regal bearing of a princess settled over her like a second skin. One of the airmen spotted her instantly.

"Prince Raoul," the airman called. "She's here."

"Raoul?" I asked.

"Rupor's younger half-brother," Rob answered.

More men dropped into the cellar, forming a wall of swords between Bane's men and the trap door. They were followed by a compact, energetic man about my own age.

"Callan?" he called.

"I'm here, Raoul," she said. "But beware, most of these men are raiders and slavers."

"I only want the princess, her companions, and your leader," Raoul said, his eyes sweeping the ranks of men. "If the rest of you surrender, you have my word I'll release you when we leave."

Bane must have Boosted, because he leapt over the line of Tartegian airmen and had a dagger at Raoul's throat before anyone could react.

"Coincidentally, I also only want the princess, her companions, and *your* leader," Bane said. "Surrender or your prince dies."

The Spare Prince

Prince Raoul's men milled about, uncertain of what to do. Martin Bane pressed his dagger against their prince's throat, nicking it.

"Do as I say or you'll be wearing the blood of your prince," Bane growled.

"No," Raoul gasped. "Don't risk our future queen's life. Not for the Spare Prince."

Bane laughed, "Bravely spoken, Spare Prince, but your men know what Mommy will do to them if they let you die. There's not a man among them foolish enough to cross the queen."

I filed 'Spare Prince' away for later and whispered, "There's got to be something we can do. If I Boost, maybe I can-"

"No," Callan responded. "I will not allow you to kill yourself for no reason."

"She's right, lad," Rob added. "The raider captain has your same abilities. If Boosting didn't kill you, he'd kill Raoul before you got close."

Within the circle of airmen, Prince Raoul stretched his neck, as if inviting Bane to slit it, then said, "Men, I order you to disregard any threat to my life and rescue Princess Callan."

"Belay that," commanded a voice from above. "If necessary, another woman can be found for Prince Rupor, but we cannot find another prince of the realm. Mister Bane, name your terms."

"No, Admiral Hamlan," said Raoul. "No terms. No surrender. The men must-"

"The men must follow my orders, Your Highness," said the admiral. "Mister Bane, I will accede to the following terms. You, your men, and your captives may leave unhindered, provided my men are unharmed and you release the prince safely."

"Agreed," said Bane, "though I've thought of one addition to my demands. I will also take your airship."

"You may take the airship's skiff, Mister Bane," Hamlan said. "along with my guarantee of safe passage."

"That's quite generous of you, Admiral," Bane said, "but how many men will your skiff carry?"

"A dozen."

"I have rather more than a dozen men with me," Bane said. "I don't suppose you have a spare skiff or two?"

"No, I do not," Hamlan said.

"And do you have a spare prince, Admiral?" Bane said. He flashed a grin at his men.

"Very amusing, Mister Bane," Hamlan said.

"I thought not," Bane said. "And that's why I'll be taking your airship."

The admiral sighed, "You leave me little choice. We have an accord."

Keeping his dagger at Prince Raoul's throat, Bane backed into a corner, then ordered the Tartegian airmen to ascend the ladder. Bane's men followed, took the weapons from the airmen, and established a perimeter around the trap door.

"After you, princess," Bane said. "Your guards will remain here, of course."

"I will not-" Rob began.

"I gave my word, Rob," Princess Callan said. "You will not gainsay it."

"Aren't you forgetting something?" I asked Bane. "You said you wanted to sell me at auction, also."

"That was when I needed to replace my ship. Thanks to the Spare Prince, I have a brand new Tartegian warship," Bane replied. "Princess, ascend if you please?"

Princess Callan gave Rob and me one last look, then climbed the ladder. Raoul and Bane followed behind her.

The trap door slammed shut and, with thumping and scraping, debris was piled atop it. The airship engines roared to life, then faded as Bane flew away with the princess.

Misjudging Raoul

As soon as the airship's engine faded away, we heard men begin clearing the debris from the trap door.

I asked Rob, "What's the deal with this 'Spare Prince' nickname of Raoul's?"

"Later," Rob said. "We have more important things to do."

"No, we don't," I said. "We can't make plans until we know the situation above. So tell me about Prince Raoul. It may be important, later."

"I suppose it might, at that," Rob said. "Do you recall me saying Raoul is Rupor's half-brother?"

"Yes."

"When Prince Rupor was three, his mother died of a debilitating illness," Rob said. "The Tartegian nobles gave their king little time to grieve before pushing him to remarry. For the good of the kingdom, of course. King Damon gave in, marrying the first suitable woman presented to him.

"Next, the nobles pressed Damon to have another child, to insure the succession if something happened to Prince Rupor. Again, he gave in. When Raoul was born, Damon is said to have told his advisors, 'Congratulations, you have your spare prince.' Alas for Raoul, the name stuck."

I contemplated what it would be like growing up with such a nickname as the last of the debris was cleared from the trapdoor. It was opened and we climbed out. A Tartegian airman led us to Admiral Hamlan.

Rob asked, "Where is Prince Raoul?"

"Still on the airship," Hamlan sighed.

"Bane lied? Shocking," I said.

"Actually, Bane didn't lie," Hamlan said. "He allowed the prince to slide down a line just as the airship was getting underway. A crewman called for Bane and he walked away just as the prince began sliding. I guess Bane assumed His Highness would continue down the rope. Unseen by those aboard, Raoul slipped into an open porthole."

"This is the man all of you call the Spare Prince?" I asked.

"Perhaps all of Tarteg has misjudged Raoul," mused Hamlan, "not least his father."

"It was bravely done," said Rob, "but Prince Raoul is only one man. He won't be able to take over the airship alone. Are there more Tartegian airships in the area?"

Hamlan shook his head, "No, our southern squadron is scattered, searching for your princess. Nor are there any animals to ride. I fear we'll have to walk out of here."

"If you'll loan me a dozen of your men, Admiral, we can build a vehicle," I said. "Rob and I can be pursuing Bane in just a few hours."

Hamlan looked at Rob, who said, "If David says he can do it, I believe him."

"Very well, but some of my men must ride with you," Hamlan said.

"There won't be room," I said. "Besides, you need to find a way to warn people about the trog army."

"Hardly an army, and they've been dealt with," Hamlan responded.

"You dealt with several hundred trogs?" Rob asked.

"Several hundred?" scoffed Hamlan. "More like two dozen."

"Their leader must have kept them under cover when the airship flew over the trading post the first time," I said. "Rob, fill him in while I get the men started."

I left Rob explaining the trog situation to the admiral and called the airmen together.

"Listen carefully," I said, and watched their eyes grow wide as I explained my plan.

It *had* to work. If it didn't, the princess would be lost to me forever.

Sand Schooner

Three hours later, Admiral Hamlan looked at the result of our work and said to Rob, "He's crazy, right?"

"Not at all," Rob replied with confidence. "I'm sure this... *What* is it, David?"

"I've been calling it a sand schooner," I said. "The wide wheels will allow it to ride on top of the sand and the sail will catch this desert wind and drive it forward."

"But that is hardly more than a frame with wheels, two seats, and a sail," protested Hamlan.

"It was important to keep the weight down, sir," I said. "And, with the wind that's been blowing for the last couple of days, it'll be fast."

Rob and I climbed into the seats on the frame, the sail flapping loosely in the wind. I trimmed the sail, it filled with wind, and the sand schooner began to roll. The airmen raised a cheer as the admiral shook his head in disbelief.

"Good luck," Hamlan called. "and do bring my prince back in one piece."

The sand schooner cleared the ruined buildings of the trading post and, catching the full force of the wind, picked up speed quickly.

Rob said, "Incredible! It *does* work."

I cocked an eyebrow at him.

"You didn't think I would express doubts in front of Tartegians, did you?" he asked.

Soon, the sand schooner was sailing along at a steady twenty to twenty-five kilometers per hour. At that speed, we might not gain on Bane's airship, but wouldn't lose much ground, either. I taught Rob how to handle the schooner, allowing us to take shifts at the helm and avoid having to stop for rest.

Racing over the dunes, we sailed beyond the sunset and into the night, steering as much by instinct as by moonlight and the light from the planetary ring. A few hours past midnight, our instincts failed us.

We crested a huge dune only to find the other side dropped off like a cliff. The sand schooner flew over the edge and plunged toward the sand a hundred meters below us.

8

A RICH MAN'S TOY

THE SAND SCHOONER ARCHING THROUGH THE AIR WAS FUN FOR THE second it took for my brain to remind me that we were falling. Neither Boosting nor training would get us out of this alive. Rob and I shared a helpless look. I was just considering if the sail could be a makeshift parachute when the sand schooner hit something soft—an airship's gas envelope.

"Jump!" we both said as the schooner began to slide down the envelope's side.

Rob managed to catch a line but my hands found only smooth fabric. I scrabbled to find something to grab—and only found it when Rob swung his leg to me. No longer sliding, I was able to grab a line of my own and we began to climb down to the deck below. My heart didn't stop hammering until, half a minute later, my feet were firmly planted on the airship's deck.

The moonlight illuminated a utilitarian, but still stylish, deck.

"This airship seems a bit small," I said.

Rob said. "I've seen the like before. It's a rich man's toy, nothing more."

"Oh, it's much more than that!" protested a voice. "But it's a bit of a toy, as well."

A large man, rounded with rich living and slowed by advancing age, stepped into view. His voice carried the tone of command, but there was an undertone of humor.

"Now, how did two gentlemen such as yourselves board an airborne ship?" he asked. Before either of us could answer, he said, "Come below. I rather expect this will be a long story."

He walked aft. Rob and I followed. We stepped on lines lying on the deck, quite out of place on the otherwise neatly arrayed airship. My brain raised the alarm too late. A net rose up around us, leaving us dangling from a boom. A smaller man rushed out of hiding and shoved the boom over the airship's side railing.

The old man spoke, "Oh dear, I have forgotten my manners and caught you in a net. I'll have my manservant release you immediately. Do enjoy your fall."

Tristan Agrilla

"Kill us if you must," I said, "but then you will be responsible for rescuing the princess."

"A princess! This gets better and better," said the older man. "Let me guess, she's been kidnapped and is on her way to the slave markets in Beloren?"

"Sir, were our swords drawn when you confronted us?" I asked.

"No," admitted the man.

"Did we reach for our swords or offer any threats when you discovered us?"

"Again, no," the man said.

"That's not exactly typical raider behavior, is it?" I pressed.

"True," the man said. "But why did you board my airship? Even better, *how* did you board my airship?"

"That story is even more improbable than our kidnapped, slave market-bound princess," I replied.

The man gazed at me for a moment, then said, "Pull them back over the deck, Nist, but don't release them."

With the deck beneath us again, the older man looked into my eyes. "Is there really a kidnapped princess?"

I met his gaze, "Yes. We're pledged to her service."

"I suppose she's radiantly beautiful, as well?" he asked.

"I've traveled quite extensively," I said, "and have never met her equal."

"And you're in love with her," he stated.

"How could I not be?" I replied.

The man nodded slowly, "Release them, Nist. I *must* hear this story."

"Hear it you shall," Rob said, "but could we bring up the steam and set course for Beloren? Those who hold Her Highness are several hours ahead of us."

"Quite right, my good man," the man said. "Nist, it's time we found out just how fast the *Pauline* can go. Full steam! Full power! Full speed!"

A grin creased Nist's face, "At once, master!"

"Master?" Rob frowned.

"That's just Nist's little joke," the man said. "My late wife, after whom this ship is named, and I bought him when he was quite young. We freed him and then adopted him. Even so, he always called us 'master' and 'mistress.' It always drove my wife to distraction.

"Allow me to introduce myself," he continued, leading us below. "I am Tristan Agrilla."

Below deck, Rob introduced us and then asked me to tell our story. Tristan's eyes widened when I told him where I came from, but he didn't interrupt. The ship had crossed the desert and the sun was rising before I finished.

Tristan turned to Rob, "Do you believe his story?"

"I've seen him do amazing things. If anything, the lad has been too modest describing his actions," Rob said. "Her Highness believes him, that is good enough for me."

"Master," Nist called from the deck, "we're approaching the city of Beloren."

Returning to the deck, we saw a huge city rising out of fertile plains. Hundreds of airships swarmed about the city.

How could we hope to find Princess Callan amid that teeming mass of people?

Beauty Never Passes Unnoticed

I gave voice to my concern, "How are we going to find the princess in a city that large?"

Tristan said, "Young people are so predictable—quick to anger, quick to love, quick to despair. And slow to think."

Rob barked a laugh, "So true, my friend. I assume you have a plan for finding Her Highness?"

"I *always* have a plan," exclaimed Tristan.

Nist added, "Sometimes, his plans even work."

"Bah. Ignore him, gentlemen," growled Tristan. "You told me this Martin Bane is flying a Tartegian naval airship, correct?"

I nodded.

"Finding it will be simplicity itself," smiled Tristan. "There are only two docks in the city capable of handling such a large ship. One is in the warehouse district and of no interest. The other, my friends, is near the slave markets."

Nist piloted the *Pauline* deftly through the airship traffic toward a dock on the far side of the city. Even before we docked, Rob spotted Bane's ship at the dock. We had found his ship, but there was no activity on its deck. It was obvious Bane was no longer aboard.

I leaned against the airship's railing and hung my head. Tristan clapped me on the back. "Fear not, my boy. We'll find your princess. The raiders will have had to escort her to the slave market and beauty such as you describe never passes unnoticed."

After docking, we left Nist with the airship and climbed down to the street. Tristan spoke with various acquaintances before setting off toward a central market.

"Your princess was brought this way no more than two hours ago," Tristan told us. "It appears you did not exaggerate her beauty, David. Her passage brought business to a standstill. Finding her won't be a problem, though getting her away from the sellers will be another matter."

That's when I spied Bane ahead of us. "Maybe not," I said. "I'll bet Bane would give her to us in exchange for his own life."

I began pushing my way through the crowd toward him, planning how best to take him. I was only a couple of meters away from him when one of his men rushed up.

"The prince and princess," he gasped. "They've escaped."

"Imagine that," said Bane, taking the news quite calmly.

"You don't understand, captain. During the escape, the prince led the princess into the old sewers beneath the city," said the crewman.

Bane's face drained of color, "That idiot! I warned-. Gather as many of the crew as you can and meet me at the Market Street square. Hurry! There's a chance they're still alive."

Bane, Again

Grabbing Bane's shoulder, I spun him around, "There's a chance they'll still be alive? What does that mean?"

Bane's eyes went wide, "Rice? How did you get here?"

"There's no time for that," Rob exclaimed joining me. "Answer the man's question."

Bane said, "The old sewers beneath the city are home to the most violent dregs of Beloren. The city guard only go down there in the most dire of emergencies. Then they go with at least a full squad, preferably three. The tunnel rats don't like outsiders and have nasty ways of dealing with those they catch. That's where the Spare Prince has dragged your princess."

Bane continued, "I've already summoned my men. We're going after them."

I didn't ask why, though I wondered. "We're coming with you."

"Suit yourself," Bane shrugged. "Just remember who's in command."

Tristan said, "That sounds quite exciting and dangerous, but an old man like me would just slow you down. What aid can I give from above ground?"

Bane was busy issuing orders to another crewman and paying no attention to us. I said quietly, "Can you gather armed men you trust? We may need to take the prince and princess from Bane when we return."

If we return.

"You can count on me, my boy," Tristan said, turning away.

"We'll wait for my men at the sewer entrance," Bane said. "Come on."

Bane set a fast pace through the market, but many people greeted Bane by name as he passed. I realized that he was a well-regarded businessman in Beloren. Rob and I would have to be careful if we were forced into a confrontation with him.

Moments later, we stood in a narrow alley, staring down into a dark hole. I wondered how long we would have to wait—how long we could afford to wait—for Bane's men. When the answer came, I didn't like it. Guttural voices roared up from below.

"That's not good," Bane said.

"That tears it," I said.

Without another word, I descended into the darkness.

Into the Tunnels

I slid down the ladder and dropped to the tunnel floor. There were widely spaced torches giving off just enough light to see by. Not waiting for Rob, I ran off toward the roaring voices. There wasn't a person to be seen in the tunnels, not even guards, until I was close to the source of the roaring.

The cheering crowd was deafening, but another sound rose above it —a sound that made my blood run cold. It was the cry of a tammar, the huge, fanged beast I had faced in the desert. A human screamed in terror, then in pain, and then was silenced. The cheering grew, crested, then returned to a steady roar.

I came to a branch in the tunnel and stopped to listen. The tunnels echoed with the sounds, but I thought the source of the sound came from the right. Glancing back as I sprinted into the right branch, I saw Rob was close behind me. The tunnel bent to the right and, ahead, opened out into a larger, far better lit room.

The entrance to the room was guarded by an ill-dressed man holding a sword. The guard wasn't paying attention to the tunnel. He was craning his neck, looking into the room. The noise from the crowd covered any sounds I was making. Lowering my shoulder, I charged.

The guard must have sensed something because he turned at the last moment. His eyes widened and then I crashed into him. The guard flew backward, his face contorting in terror and his arms flailing. Then he fell into a large opening in the floor and dropped, screaming, to the floor several meters below. He landed next to the tammar.

The tammar wore a leather harness with a rope fastened to it. The other end of the rope was tied to an iron ring driven into the floor. Screaming people thronged a couple of meters beyond the limit of the rope. More iron rings were driven into the ceiling of this upper room. Ropes were tied to several of the rings. Two of the ropes hung down into the tammar pit and had mangled corpses tied to them.

In the pit, the guard attempted to scuttle away from the tammar. I heard the guard scream as I turned my attention to the upper room. A large man stood across the opening from me, shock written on his face. Princess Callan and Prince Raoul stood next to him, each tied like the corpses below. I couldn't risk leaping across the opening. If I landed wrong or the man blocked me, I could fall into the pit. I started running around the opening to the princess and prince. The large man grinned, grabbed the princess, and shoved her into the opening. Terror filled her lovely face as she plunged toward certain death.

9

THE TAMMAR PIT

WITHOUT HESITATION, I JUMPED AFTER THE PLUNGING PRINCESS.

The tammar crouched over the body of the guard, ready to pounce again. The creature had not eaten any of its kills. These tunnel rats had obviously trained it to kill for pleasure—theirs and its. The tammar had locked its gaze on Callan, but its eyes shifted to me when I landed. Rising from its latest kill, the tammar looked between Callan and me. It decided I was the more dangerous prey and turned toward Callan. I shouted and waved, trying to draw the tammar's attention away from the princess.

Boosted, I knew I could kill the tammar. But after my extended battle with the trogs at the trading post, I didn't know what another Boost would do to me. With Callan's life on the line, I couldn't take that kind of risk. Normal human strength and reflexes would have to be sufficient.

Rob dropped to the floor behind the tammar as it slowly stalked toward us. At least I wouldn't be fighting alone. The crowd had gone silent at the change in the program, so I had no trouble hearing Rob's command.

"Keep it away from Her Highness," he called, hacking at the rope tying the tammar to the iron ring.

Tied, the tammar was only a threat to those in the pit. Loose, it could be the distraction we needed to escape. As Rob finished cutting the rope, the tammar crouched, ready to pounce on Callan. I roared a challenge and charged, but the creature ignored me. Rob grabbed the end of the rope and hauled on it with all his might. The tammar was pulled up onto its hind legs, unable to pounce. I reached the tammar and attacked. My sword sliced across its chest. The tammar roared in pain and spun away, searching for easier prey. It bounded at Rob, who still held the rope in his hands.

The tammar's claws slashed and Rob fell. The tammar kept going, leaping into the crowd of tunnel rats. Screams erupted as the crowd scrambled to get away from the wrath of the tammar. I cut the princess's bonds and we rushed to Rob. The cries of the crowd and the tammar faded to nothing when I reached Rob. The wounds were mortal and Rob knew it.

"Do something!" cried Callan, tears streaming.

"There's nothing to be done, Highness," Rob gasped. "You know it's true."

She turned to me, "There must be something you can do!"

I shook my head, "I'm sorry, Highness."

"You're the last of the princess's guard, lad. Take my sword," Rob said. "Use it always in her defense."

I nodded, taking his sword. Rob pulled Callan close and spoke softly into her ear. Louder, he said, "I love you like a daughter..."

Then the light faded from his eyes.

I Won't Leave Him

I tore my gaze from Rob's body, looking around the pit as Princess Callan wept. Echoing through the tunnels, I could hear the cry of the tammar and the screams of the tunnel rats scrambling to escape the beast. Listening to the panicked screams, I felt the tammar was dealing a kind of savage justice to the tunnel rats. Not one of them remained around the pit. It was time to make our escape.

I said, "Highness, come on. We've got to get out of here."

Cradling Rob's head and still sobbing, the princess shook her head.

"Highness... Callan, he gave his life for you," I said. "If we don't go now, his sacrifice will have been for nothing."

"I won't leave him in these awful tunnels, to have his body abused by the wretches who live down here," she said.

I sensed motion behind me and leaped to my feet, Rob's sword ready. Prince Raoul, his hands still tied, had managed to find a way to slide down the rope.

"Could I trouble you for a little help?" he said, holding out his hands.

I cut his bonds, saying, "I need you to carry Rob's body. I'm going to have to carry Her Highness and she won't leave without him."

A look of irritation flashed across Raoul's face. Perhaps he didn't like commoners giving him orders or perhaps he would have preferred to carry the princess, but he lifted Rob's body over his shoulder and I gathered Callan in my arms.

"We need to hurry," he said. "I'm pretty sure I saw one of Bane's men approaching the room as I was sliding down."

I nodded and set off in a direction I thought would lead to a way up. We ran, dodging panicked tunnel rats along the way. The tammar's cries receded as we ran, giving me one less thing to worry about. I made several wrong turns and we dodged three groups of tunnel rats—all armed and grim-faced—before finding a tunnel that sloped up. Forty meters further, it intersected with the wide tunnel Rob and I had run through bare minutes and an entire lifetime ago.

A few minutes later, we reached the ladder up to the alley. It took some encouragement, but I got Callan to climb the ladder. I took Rob's body from Raoul, sending him up next. I followed as quickly as my burden would allow. Seconds later, I was blinking in the comparatively bright light of the alley.

"It sounds as if you made quite an impression down there," said a familiar voice. "And you managed to fetch my property along the way. Well done."

Bane and his crew blocked our way to the street.

A Daring Escape

With the exit to the street blocked by Bane's men, our only hope was to head deeper into the alley.

"Run!" I said.

I heaved Rob's body at the crowd of men then ran off after Callan and Raoul. Her Highness might not approve, but Rob would have understood and approved. Even in death, his body was helping to guard the princess. The few seconds the raiders spent disentangling themselves from Rob could be the difference between capture and escape.

We dodged and dashed down the winding alley, but there were no branches, no side alleys, and no way out to the street. Rounding a bend, we found ourselves at a dead end. Walls rose up to the sides and ahead of us. But a set of stairs also rose up on the outside wall of one of the buildings.

"Take the stairs," I called. "Climb to the roof."

Raoul pulled Callan up the stairs behind him. I came up more slowly, ready to turn and fight if necessary. Behind us, Bane's crew charged around the bend and into the dead end. The narrow stairs slowed them down, as the men pushed and shoved, trying to be first up the stairs. We reached the roof a couple of flights ahead of our pursuers, but there my slim, final hope was dashed. There was no way down to the street. The building across the street was too far away for us to jump to it. The adjacent buildings were taller than our building, with no windows in the side walls. We were trapped.

"I'll hold them here," I said, taking position at the stairs. "Maybe there's a drain pipe on the front of the building that you can use to climb down."

"Wait, look up there," Raoul said, pointing.

A huge cargo airship moved slowly over us, a single line dangling to within a few meters of the roof. Sweeping Callan up in my arms, I lifted her toward the rope.

"Grab the rope and climb, Highness," I said.

As she did, I cupped my hands, "You next, Prince Raoul."

Raoul stepped into my hands and I lifted him. He caught the rope easily, but the airship was moving very slowly. With nothing to stop them, Bane's men might be able to catch onto the rope and recapture the princess and prince.

"Come on, David," Callan said. "Jump."

I called, "I have to stay and slow down Bane and his men. Drop down to the next roof and go to the docks. Find the airship *Pauline* in slip fifty-seven. They're friends and will get you home safely."

Bane's men rushed onto the roof, spreading out before me. I drew my sword, roared in challenge, and charged across the roof to meet them.

Respect

I expected some kind of answering challenge from Bane's men. Instead of advancing to meet my attack, they hung back, casting nervous looks between themselves. Maybe they were remembering my single-handed defense of the trap door against the trogs and didn't want to face me in a fight. If so, good. A few seconds of hesitation was all I wanted. In those few seconds, the prince and princess would be carried clear of the roof and make good on their escape.

One man plucked up the courage to come to meet me. Steel rang as our blades crossed, then Bane's voice rang out. "Stand down and stand aside."

Relieved, the crewman lowered his sword and stepped back. Bane stepped onto the roof. To my surprise, he cradled Rob's body in his arms. Rob's blood was staining his rich clothes, but the raider captain didn't seem to care.

"You dropped this," he said, gently laying Rob's body down at my feet. His eyes met mine, "I want you to know that I had true respect for him."

"As did I," I said, wondering what game Bane was playing now.

Bane saw my wariness and said, "You've nothing more to fear from me and my men. I've done what I was contracted to do. In truth, because of you I've ended up doing far more than that."

"Contracted? You mean someone hired you to kidnap Princess Callan?" I asked.

"You have no idea how hard it is to get raider airships to work together. Without guaranteed payment, it's almost impossible," he said. "Of course, if I'd known you were going to fall from the sky, wreck my airship, and nearly wreck my plan, I'd have charged double. You have been one big thorn in my side from the moment you first appeared."

"Who hired you? They've got to have deep pockets if they could afford to hire so many raiders at one time."

"Oh no, there's no chance I'll tell you that, Rice," Bane said. "Clients expect secrecy and pay well to get it. If you want to know who hired me, figure it out for yourself."

Glancing past me, Bane asked, "Didn't your plan involve the prince and princess dropping onto a nearby roof?"

I spun about and saw the airship was fifty meters away. Its line was now hanging twenty meters above the tallest rooftops. The unknown airship was climbing to cruising altitude and the princess and prince were being carried away with it.

10

PURSUIT

THE AIRSHIP CONTINUED TO CLIMB AS IT PASSED OVER THE CITY WALL. IT looked as if the princess and prince were shouting, trying to draw the attention of the airship's crew, but their cries were drowned out by the roar of the airship's big steam engines.

"Shouldn't you be running off to save them?" Bane asked.

"I will, but I want to make one thing clear. If anything happens to Rob's body..." I said.

"I told you, I'm finished with this passion play," Bane replied. "Go rescue your princess. Again. I'll see that Rob's body is properly prepared for a funeral."

Seeing the indecision written on my face, Bane added, "Scout's honor."

I looked into Bane's eyes and believed him. Looking over the edge of the roof, I spotted a drain pipe descending to street level. I climbed down the pipe and set off toward the docks at a run. As I entered the docks, I met Tristan leaving it, leading a band of armed men. His face creased in concern when he saw me.

"I gathered the men you requested as quickly as possible. Am I too late?" he asked.

"We've got to take off now," I said, slowing down but not stopping. "I'll explain in the air."

Tristan fell in behind me, lumbering through the crowds you can always find at a busy dock. His age and bulk took a toll. By the time we reached the *Pauline* he was red-faced and wheezing. I began casting off docking lines as Tristan stumbled aboard the airship.

"Nist, bring up the steam," I cried. "We've got an airship to catch."

Nist looked at Tristan, bent over at the waist and gasping to catch his breath. Tristan nodded and Nist began feeding the fire for the boiler.

Nist took us straight up while the pressure built. The little ship rose through the dockyard's traffic lanes and into the late afternoon sky. It had only been a few hours since we docked, but it seemed as if a lifetime had passed. A lifetime *had* passed for Rob.

The airship cleared the low altitude traffic and Nist set off in the direction I pointed. With the course set and Tristan's breathing returning to normal, I told them what had happened. They listened quietly, asking no questions. At the end, Tristan was briefly silent.

"I'm sorry, my boy. Rob struck me as a good man," he said. "For now, though, we have to concentrate on the living."

We said no more as the *Pauline* sped south in the wake of the cargo airship. The sun hung low on the horizon when we drew close enough to see the big airship clearly. The line still dangled from the ship, but the prince and princess were nowhere to be seen.

Slipping Aboard

Nist maneuvered the *Pauline* close to the other airship and I hailed it. The reply sounded like the same language spoken by the slavers who had pulled me out of the airship wreckage a few days ago. I didn't understand a word of it, but Tristan did. He took over the discussion. After several minutes of calling back and forth between Tristan and the ship's captain, Tristan signaled Nist to fly away.

"What did he say?" I asked.

"He says neither he nor his crew saw anyone hanging on the line," Tristan said. "He claims the ship's envelope developed a large leak about an hour ago. That's not uncommon in an airship this size. The airship dropped close enough to the ground for the line to drag on it before the crew finished patching the leak. He suggests the prince and princess dropped off then."

"Do you believe him?" I asked.

Tristan said, "No... An airship that size shouldn't have lost so much altitude from a simple leak. Besides, the captain had all his answers ready to hand. He didn't ask his crew any questions but was quite certain about what the crew did *not* see. I'd say he's hiding something."

"Yes, and it's probably the prince and princess," I said. "Nist, turn the ship as if we're searching back along the airship's flight path. I want to give the captain the idea that we believed him. Once it's dark, we'll head back to that ship."

Two hours later, Nist guided the *Pauline* into position above the cargo airship's envelope. He held us steady, out of sight from the other airship's crew. The larger ship's engines drowned out our own smaller engine.

I looped a rope over my shoulder, testing to make sure it would remain secure without getting in my way. I tied another rope to the bow rail.

"When this line goes slack, I'll be safely on the envelope. Drop away and below the cargo airship's stern. When I've got the prince and princess, I'll flash a signal to you with a lantern. I'll lower them to you, starting with the princess" I said.

I slid down to the envelope, finding plenty of handholds within the lines criss-crossing it. I took my time climbing to the deck below, descending into shadows along the starboard rail. I hugged the rail, staying away from the ship's lanterns and avoiding the small night crew.

A few minutes later, I found my way below deck. I had taken but a few steps when a door opened and a crewman backed into the passageway. He was balancing a heavily laden food tray and backed right into me.

Keeping his eyes on the tray, the crewman muttered something at me. I grunted in return and stepped away from him. The crewman kept his concentration on the tray and headed aft. Only one person on the ship would receive such careful attention—the captain. I slipped after the crewman. At the end of the passageway, the crewman knocked on a door then opened it. The cabin beyond the door was brightly lit. Within, the captain laughed, pouring wine for another man.

The other man was Prince Raoul.

What About Raoul?

I ducked into a doorway and out of the light spilling from the cabin. Peering around the door frame, I watched as the crewman placed most of the food on the captain's table. The crewman lifted the tray again, speaking to the captain. I understood the words "princess" and "food." My implant had begun to translate the language. There was no doubt the remaining food was for Callan.

When the crewman left the captain's cabin, I followed. He went halfway up the same passage before unlocking a door and stepping inside. I trailed behind him and looked into the room. He placed the tray on the foot of a cot. Princess Callan lay upon the cot, her eyes looking everywhere except at the crewman. Callan's eyes went wide when I entered, a tight smile forming on her lips. Then she kicked the crewman in the stomach. The crewman stumbled back, gasping for breath. I clouted him on the back of the neck with the pommel of my sword, laying him out.

Callan rose from the cot and flowed into my arms. Her embrace was unlike the impetuous, passionate kiss a few days ago. It was simply one person seeking comfort from another.

Callan laid her head on my shoulder and whispered, "I knew you'd find me, David."

I held her briefly, stroking her hair, then said, "Highness, we-"

"Callan," she said. "In private, the captain of my personal guard calls me Callan."

"As you wish, Callan," I said. "But I don't know how much time we have before this crewman is missed. It can't take very long to deliver a couple of meals. We've got to get you out of here now."

"What about Raoul?" she asked. "I haven't seen him since a crewman took him away a few hours ago."

What about Raoul, indeed, I thought, but said, "I can't risk having them capture you again. Once you're safe, I'll come back and look for Raoul."

And I'll have a few questions for you when I find you, Raoul.

It's more difficult for two people to move unnoticed than it is for one. It took several minutes longer to slip to the stern of the airship than I had hoped. Hiding Callan in a particularly deep shadow, I took a lantern that was hanging nearby. Shuttering all but a sliver of the glass, I flashed a signal to the *Pauline*, flying almost invisible below us. I waited but a few seconds before I saw the flashing reply. I motioned for Callan to join me. She blanched when she saw me tying my rope to the ship's railing.

"I can't climb down a rope, David," she whispered. "My hands still ache from gripping the rope this afternoon."

I would never have risked having Callan simply slide down the rope and was already tying the rope into a sling, "Don't worry, all you'll have to do is sit in the sling while I lower you."

She was nodding when we were blinded as lanterns snapped open around us.

Drawing his sword, the captain said, "Our prize is trying to escape, boys!"

Trapped

With a start, I realized the captain had spoken in the princess's language. His accent was thick and his tone was flat, almost as if he had memorized the words. Did he speak the princess's language? There had been no indication of that when we had hailed him during the afternoon. I thought I had a way to find out if he did.

"Highness, I hope I can get out of this without a fight," I whispered. "If I'm wrong, I'll guard this rope while you slide down to the airship below. They are friends. Trust them."

Eyes wide, Callan nodded.

I turned to face the captain, my sword sheathed and my hands up. I smiled and said, "You filthy pack of airdogs, I'll kill you all."

The captain smiled back, then spoke to his crew. My implant picked out "princess" again, but I couldn't get anything else.

Shaking my head as if in dejection, I said, "Are you ready to die?"

It took the captain a moment to realize I had asked a question. The captain studied me for a moment and then nodded. That settled the question of language. The captain was trying to read my body language and had no idea what I was saying.

Prince Raoul burst from the shadows and charged at the captain. The crew just watched as Raoul dashed past them and wrestled the captain's sword from him. The captain raised his hands as Raoul put the sword against the captain's throat.

Raoul spoke in the captain's language, one arm sweeping across the watching crewmen. My implant translated "princess" and "guard" this time around. How I wished I knew what Raoul was saying. When Raoul finished speaking, everyone but the captain turned and scurried to the bow of the airship.

Raoul took a quick glance at me, "Do you have a plan for getting Her Highness off of this airship?"

Thrusting aside nagging doubts about Raoul, I said, "I've got an airship trailing just off the stern. They're waiting for me to lower the princess to them."

"Then go ahead and lower Her Highness to safety," Raoul said. "I'll keep this rabble at bay."

Whatever was going on, ensuring Callan's safety was paramount. I put her into the sling and lowered Callan to the *Pauline*. Below, Nist and Tristan pulled her onto the deck and I breathed a little easier.

Drawing my sword, I said, "You next, prince."

"What?" Raoul said. "No, you must go. The princess is still a long way from home and will need your protection during the journey."

"Princess Callan is safely aboard a fast airship and with people I trust," I said. "As a prince of a neighboring realm and Her Highness's future brother-in-law, your safety comes next."

Raoul was not pleased with my statement. He watched me for several seconds—seconds during which the captain just stood there—then, eyes flashing anger, Raoul dropped the captain's sword and stalked to the rope. A moment later a shout from below told me he was safely down.

I heard the twang of a bow string and a quarrel buried itself in the railing next to me. The crew had crossbows! While I was distracted by the near miss, the captain scooped up his sword and attacked. I dodged before realizing I was not the target of the captain's swing. His sword sliced right through my rope and it fell into the darkness.

I was trapped on the airship.

11

BOOST OR DIE

Dropping into a dueling stance, the captain grinned in triumph. A crossbow bolt plucked at my sleeve, the second near miss. Unless I could find some kind of cover, it was only a matter of time before the crew skewered me. There was nothing on the deck for me to hide behind, so I rushed for the only cover available—the captain. If I engaged the captain, his crew would have to hold their fire or risk hitting him. He stepped forward to meet me. I blocked his swing and my sword vibrated from the force of his blow. The captain was far stronger than he looked.

Could Raoul possibly have taken the sword from that iron grip without the captain's cooperation?

Seeing the effect of his blow, the captain pressed the attack and drove me backward across the deck. In the bow of the airship, half a dozen men held cocked and loaded crossbows. They were ready to fire if I strayed too far from the captain. The rest of the crew had grabbed boat hooks and belaying pins and, careful not to block the crossbowmen's aim, were walking toward the stern. It looked like everyone wanted in on the kill.

I had precious few heartbeats left before the crew reached us. If I didn't get away before then, I never would. Blocking another of the captain's mighty blows, I fell back against the starboard rail. The captain roared in triumph, believing my end was near. He was right. I was about to die and had nothing left to lose.

Boost!

Adrenaline surged through my veins and it was as if time slowed to a crawl. The captain attacked again, but this time I dodged the attack with ease. I flicked my sword past his guard and into his wrist. Blood flowed and the sword flew from his hand. Surprise and fear flashed in the captain's eyes. Spinning past him, I smacked the captain's head with the flat of my blade. The captain fell and the waiting crossbowmen could fire without fear of hitting the captain.

The crossbow quarrels flew at me in a ragged line. My sword flashed as I blocked the first five shots. Feeling like showing off, I snatched the last bolt from the air by hand. The crew stared, mouths agape, as I flipped the quarrel over the railing.

I sheathed my sword and gave a sweeping bow. The captain had trained his crew well, though. Their slack-jawed amazement at my theatrics broke and, belaying pins and boat hooks raised, they charged at me.

I could feel the Boost taking its toll—my system hadn't fully recovered from the fight with the trogs. I had to get off the airship. I sprinted to the point along the stern railing where the rope had been tied and dove into the darkness.

Back to Beloren

Night-blinded by the lanterns on deck, I saw nothing but darkness below me. I had no way to judge how far out I'd jumped. Was it too far? Not far enough? Had the *Pauline* moved?

With a muted thump, I landed on the *Pauline's* envelope. Grabbing the first line I found, I squirmed and pulled until my body was underneath the line. Once I was secure from falling, I canceled Boost. I had Boosted for less than a minute, well under the safety limits. My muscles ached, but I didn't black out. It looked like I could begin counting on Boost again, within reason.

"David, that is you up there, isn't it?" called Princess Callan.

"Yes, it's me, Highness," I called back, "Please ask Nist to move the *Pauline* away from the other ship as fast as possible."

I watched the *Pauline* turn away from the larger craft. When we were clear of it and I was sure I wasn't suffering any after-effects of the Boost, I slid out from under the line and climbed toward the deck. A minute later, Callan and Raoul helped me onto the deck. Callan swept me into a tight hug.

"I knew you'd come for us, David," she said.

"It *is* the man's job, Callan," Raoul said, a frown making him look like a petulant child.

"Raoul is correct, Highness," I said. "And I expect my job to get a lot easier with you and His Highness safely aboard a friendly airship."

"Quite right, my boy," Tristan said. "It would be my honor to transport their Highnesses safely home."

Smoothing his face into a smile, Raoul said, "A generous offer, good sir. I will gladly accept, provided you agree to return Princess Callan to Mordan, first. Her parents must be worried sick about her."

"No, much as I want to go home, I can't yet," Callan said. Turning to Tristan, she continued, "I ask only that you return me to Beloren."

"Highness," I said, "why would you want to go back there?"

"Have you forgotten the trog army?" Callan asked. "They were but two days march from the Mordanian border. Our southern border was never heavily defended, as we rely on the desert to deter most invaders. With the navy mobilized to search for me, the border may be entirely undefended. Even now, the trogs could be attacking my people. I will not turn my back on them."

Tristan asked, "I understand your concern, Highness, but why stop in Beloren?"

Callan responded, "I need to speak with Martin Bane."

I Need a Fleet

"You need what?" Raoul asked.

"To speak with Martin Bane," Callan repeated.

Raoul said, "But he kidnapped you."

"I know," Callan replied. "You may remember that I was there when Bane did it."

"Yes, but- but-" Raoul sputtered.

"He kidnapped me," Callan finished for Raoul. "Please stop repeating yourself. I have to look beyond the kidnapping, Raoul. The safety of my people outweighs everything Martin Bane has done."

"What can Bane do for you, Highness?" I asked.

"If I'm going to defend Mordan's southern border, I'll need a fleet," she replied. "Martin Bane can provide one."

"I don't know the man, so please pardon me for asking this, Highness," Tristan said. "What makes you think this Martin Bane can procure a fleet?"

"He's already done it," she said. "When we were trapped in the trading post cellar—you were still unconscious David—Bane described how *he* had hired the other raiders, how *he* had molded that rabble into a fleet, and how *he* had devised the tactics to separate my ship from the rest. The man would not shut up about it. At the time, it was really quite irritating. Now...

"I need a fleet as soon as humanly possible. There simply isn't time to look for other options," she continued. "So, Martin Bane it is."

"Will raiders be willing to fight trogs for you?" I asked.

"They're a rather mercenary lot, as I understand it. If the pay is right, we should be able to hire a fleet," she said.

"What of the Tartegian navy?" Raoul asked. "If this airship is as fast as we've been told, we could fly to the nearest base and I could lead a squadron of trained airmen against these trogs."

"No, Raoul," Callan said. "We cannot have the Tartegian navy in Mordan before the wedding. There's been animosity between our countries for too long. The Mordanian people would not stand for it. Nor would the Tartegian people stand for it if the situations were reversed. It must be Martin Bane."

"If your kidnapping is any indication, Bane will honor a contract to the letter," I said. "No more and no less."

Callan was surprised, "Are you saying my kidnapping was contracted? But who would do-?"

She was interrupted by the rasp of steel as Raoul drew his sword.

In the Net

I stepped between Raoul and Princess Callan, grabbing his sword arm with both hands. He may have the nickname Spare Prince, but Raoul had received the full martial training a prince would be expected to have. Raoul dropped backward, pulled me off my feet, planted a foot in my chest, and flipped me over him.

I'd had martial training, too. Tucking and rolling, I drew my sword as I came to my feet. But that left Raoul between me and the princess. Unable to risk allowing him to turn away from me, I attacked. Raoul parried and then pressed an attack. Behind Raoul, I saw Tristan pull Callan away from us. At least she was safe for the moment.

Nist caught my attention and signaled toward a point on the deck. Once he was sure I had seen his signal, he ran toward the boom with the net. Of course. If I could draw Raoul to the net, Nist could drop it on us. Steel rang as Raoul blocked all of my thrusts and slashes. Hate blazed up in his eyes and he attacked me with cold fury. I was sure no one who called him the Spare Prince had ever crossed blades with Raoul. There was nothing "spare" about the lethal warrior before me.

Callan was calling for us both to stop fighting. I was willing, but I doubted Raoul would go along with the idea. I fell back again, stepping beneath the net, and smiled as Raoul pressed after me.

"Now, Nist!" I yelled.

The net dropped on top of the two of us. Nist pulled another lever. Raoul and I were thrown off our feet as one edge of the net swept along the deck and under us. Ropes from the boom hoisted the net off the deck. Immediately, Raoul began sawing at the net with his sword.

"Push us over the railing, Nist," I said.

Nist shoved the boom. Raoul froze as we swung over the railing. Fear replaced the hatred in his eyes as the net bobbed and swung, nothing but open space yawning beneath us.

"Tristan, will you take her Highness to her meeting with Martin Bane and safely home once the trogs are defeated?" I asked.

"You have my word," he replied.

"Nist," I said, "release the net."

12

THE REAL TRAITOR

"NO! DON'T DO IT," SHOUTED RAOUL.

Nist had never made a move. I had already seen how he and Tristan used the net to frighten potential criminals, so it was what I'd expected of him.

"You can pull them back over the deck, Nist," Tristan ordered.

I added, "But don't release us from the net until Raoul drops his sword."

Nist looked to Tristan, who nodded. Raoul looked to Callan, who nodded, too.

"You will not be harmed," she said. "You have my word."

"Provided he doesn't attack anyone," I amended.

Callan rolled her eyes, "Rob taught you too well."

The pain of Rob's death lingered in Callan's eyes, belying her light tone. But the issue of Raoul required all of her attention now. I could almost see her push the pain aside.

Raoul slid his sword through the net and dropped it to the deck. Nist grabbed it before freeing the two of us from the net. Callan glared at Raoul.

"You drew your sword for no reason. You must have known it would provoke David's reaction. Explain yourself," she demanded.

"May I add a question of my own, Highness?" I asked.

At her nod, I said, "Why were you wining and dining with the captain of that cargo ship?"

"I...was...negotiating with him," Raoul said. Seeing disbelief on my face, he continued, "I was. I offered him a reward if he returned us to Beloren. He's a merchant, not a slaver. All I had to do was make it worth his while to take us back."

"That sounds reasonable to me, David," Callan said. She turned her glare on Raoul again, "Of course, he could have told me what he was doing."

"It does sound reasonable," I conceded. "But on deck, the captain called to his crew in *your* language, Highness, and he does not speak it. I think Raoul taught the captain that sentence during his *negotiations*."

"I did no such thing," protested Raoul.

"I think Raoul had escape plans of his own," I said. "Plans that would make him appear to be dashing and heroic."

"That's the stupidest thing I've ever heard," Raoul sneered.

"How better to throw off the mantel of Spare Prince than to pull off a daring rescue of your future queen? And that's why he drew his sword," I said. "He had to kill me before I revealed just how pathetic he really is."

Raoul responded, "I drew my sword to protect Princess Callan from the real traitor among us. I drew it to protect her from *you!*"

Who Do You Believe?

Raoul's accusation hung in the air. Tristan, Nist, and, worst of all, Callan stared at me. Not one voice was raised in protest.

Sensing he might have an opening for attack, Raoul struck again, "It's obvious that he's working with Bane. Think about it, Callan. They both claim to be one of these Terran Scouts, whatever that means. They both have that Boost thing. Bane understood Rice's weapon *and* used it to save Rice's life when Bane had the upper hand. What kind of raider would risk losing such a powerful weapon merely to save an *enemy*?"

He looked at Callan, "Haven't you wondered why Bane just walked away after you shot the tammar with the Onesie? He knew it couldn't be fired again. Bane could have simply used the Boost to recapture you. He didn't because his *agent* was in place. Rice and Bane have been manipulating events from the beginning."

Raoul turned to me, "Who were you saving Callan from? Why, Bane and his men. It's easy to be the hero when the villain is planning your every move to make you look good. Go ahead, Rice, try to deny it."

I looked at the people around me. Nist was enthralled by the whole story, caught up in the excitement of heroism, villainy, and betrayal. Tristan looked thoughtful, as if considering Raoul's accusations. Callan looked torn between the undeniable logic of Raoul's charges and the emotional bond events had forged between us.

"Of course I deny it," I said. "Though I must say you've given a masterful performance, Raoul-"

"*Prince* Raoul," he said.

"Oh, shut up," I retorted. "I have sworn no oaths to you and owe you no allegiance. And, after *your* action in all of this, I have no respect for you. I will no longer grant you any unearned honorifics."

Ignoring Raoul's sputtering, I continued, "Raoul's words twist events to his benefit, Your Highness. But back on Terra, we have a saying. Actions speak louder than words. You've witnessed my actions and heard Raoul's words. Your Highness, I have a simple question for you."

Capturing Callan's eyes with mine, I asked, "Who do you believe?"

Rob Gave You His Sword

"You must believe me," Raoul said. "I am a prince of Tarteg. My integrity cannot be questioned."

"Sure it can," I said. "And after I question your integrity, I'll question your intelligence."

"You insolent, common dog! I'll-"

"*Be silent!*" Callan demanded.

It never occurred to me to disobey.

"Have any of you heard how Rob became captain of my guard?" Callan asked us.

"I... No," I answered.

"Just before my fourth birthday, there was a conspiracy to kidnap me. Several renegade nobles wished to use me as leverage to force my father to support something or other. I was too young to understand the details and, even now, cannot imagine how they expected to succeed," Callan said.

"Many among the palace guard were bribed, including the captain of the guard. Others cooperated because their families had been threatened. On the chosen night, no guards stood between the kidnappers and my room. Just past midnight, the door to my room burst open, frightening me terribly. I began to cry as my lone defender, a young guard recently assigned to my detail, leapt to defend me.

"That guard was Rob. He placed me into a nook in the room, one designed specifically for such a purpose, and drew his sword. Though there were five kidnappers, no more than two could attack Rob at one time.

As I huddled in the nook, crying, his voice rose over the ring of steel. He told me to stop my crying, that there was nothing to worry about. And then, out-numbered five to one, Rob began to tell me my favorite bedtime story. The familiar cadence of the story and his deep, reassuring voice calmed me as he spoke and his sword sang. One attacker fell. Then another. When the third man dropped, the other two ran.

"Rob sagged onto the floor, holding the worst of his wounds with one hand and cradling me on his lap with the other. Servants and other guards arrived, but he refused to leave my side until my parents were escorted into my room by their own guards. And he finished telling the story."

"A month later, as part of my birthday celebration, Rob was named captain of my guard. My father had his best smiths work around the clock to forge a special sword in honor of Rob's actions that night. As a special birthday treat, I was allowed to present him with the sword.

"In all the years he served me, I never saw him voluntarily part with that sword—until the day he died, when he gave his sword to David.

"*That* action spoke volumes. You ask who I trust, David?"

Callan raised her eyes, brimming with tears, to meet mine.

"Rob gave you his sword. How could I *not* trust you?"

It Was You

"Callan, you can't be serious," cried Raoul. "Some guard gives his sword to a man you barely know-"

"Rob dedicated his life to my service. He never married nor had children, because those kidnappers used threats against wives and children to suborn some of the guards," Callan said. "He was a mentor, a shoulder to cry on, the one person I could count on to always be there for me. He was like a second father to me. Rob was not just *some guard*!"

"I guess that settles the question of Raoul's intelligence," I said. "Though I still want to question his integrity."

Raoul started sputtering again as Callan said, "Have a care, David. Raoul *is* my future brother-in-law."

"Perhaps," I said, "but I'd like to know what else happened when he was in the captain's cabin."

"I have answered that question," Raoul announced. "I negotiated for our release. Nothing else."

"You didn't teach the captain to say 'Our prize is getting away' in the Mordanian language?"

"Why would I do such a thing?"

"I'll answer that once you've answered my last question."

"I taught the captain nothing," Raoul replied. "Ship's captains have been known to memorize foreign phrases for business purposes."

"Yes, they have. It's a common practice everywhere," I said. "But why would he memorize a line in Mordanian to use when he was talking to his *crew*?"

"You're asking me to explain the actions of a common sailor? I have no idea why the captain would do such a thing," Raoul said. "Callan, this indignity has gone on long enough."

"Princess Callan, do you understand the language spoken by the captain?" I asked.

"No," she said. "I never was very good at learning foreign languages."

"Am I safe in assuming Raoul translated for you on the ship?" I asked.

Callan nodded, turning doubting eyes toward Raoul.

"There's your reason, Raoul," I said. "That line was the perfect cue for your heroic entrance, but it only worked if its intended audience—the princess—could understand it."

Raoul protested, his voice filled with indignation, but I barely heard him. The events of the last few days cascaded through my mind and everything clicked.

"It was you," I said, interrupting Raoul. "Everything that's happened over the last several days—from the raider plot to kidnap the princess to the escape from the slave market to the fight on the merchant airship's deck. It was all staged to let you play the hero and rescue the princess."

Without conscious thought, the tip of my sword flashed, pressing against Raoul's neck.

I said, "*You* hired Martin Bane!"

13

LENIENCY

The silence stretched as all eyes regarded Raoul. Under the combined weight of those stares, Raoul broke.

"*I* did not hire the raiders," he said.

"Look at me," Callan commanded.

Raoul's eyes rose to meet Callan's.

"I believe you, Raoul," she said. "But I also believe you know who *did* hire them."

Raoul nodded fractionally, "I didn't find out until it was too late to warn you. Your airship was already on its way to Tarteg."

"And would you have warned us if you'd known in time?" Callan pressed.

"I...*think* I would have," Raoul said. As Callan shook her head in disgust, he added, "At least I'm being honest."

"Is that supposed to make it all better?" Callan asked.

"No, Callan-"

"You no longer have leave to use my given name."

"Yes...Your Highness," Raoul said. "It's just... Those Mordanian guards and airmen—it's not my fault they died."

"It's not your fault?" Raoul flinched at her tone. "Pray tell whose fault is it?"

Raoul hung his head but held his silence.

"An honorable man would have ended this whole thing at the trading post. One simple word from you and Bane would have left us behind," Callan said. "Not your fault, Raoul? Why don't you tell that to Rob!"

Turning away, Callan said, "Tristan, may I use your cabin? I would be alone, please."

Tristan showed her to the *Pauline's* cabin.

I said, "Tell us who hired Martin Bane."

Raoul's gaze turned defiant, "No."

"My boy, Raoul has already told us," Tristan said. "Only one person could conceive such a convoluted plan to reinvent the Spare Prince."

I was ashamed my emotions had kept me from realizing it sooner.

"I've known some mama's boys in my time," I said, "but never one so pathetic as you! Nist, would you please bind the Mama's Prince? We can't risk letting him have the run of the ship."

Once Raoul was secured, I asked, "Do you have any idea what we should do with him, Tristan?"

"Before retiring, Her Highness left instructions," Tristan said. "When we get to Beloren, we're to find a Tartegian registered airship and turn him over to them."

"That's more leniency than he deserves," I said.

"Perhaps that's true, lad," Tristan said, "but it's politically astute. It speaks well of Princess Callan's intelligence and training that she chose to do it."

We flew on through the darkness, each of us lost in our own thoughts. I had drifted into sleep when a shout from Nist roused me.

"Master," called Nist, pointing ahead of us. "Look!"

Across the plain, a wide-spread glow danced against the horizon. The city of Beloren was in flames.

Bane, Yet Again

Fire climbed into the night, raging across Beloren. Dark shapes moved against the flickering light as thousands of airships fled from the conflagration. The smell of smoke was in the air and, if the wind was just right, the smoke also stung our eyes. An ash floated down onto the deck of the airship. A minute later, another ash followed it.

"The city must have been burning for hours if ash has drifted this far," Tristan observed.

"What could have caused this? Is Beloren at war with someone?" I asked.

"The southern city states wage trade wars all the time, but those rarely involve more than import tariffs," Tristan said. "I haven't heard of anything that would provoke something like this."

"It seems too wide-spread to simply be a building fire that got out of control," I said.

"Master," called Nist. "We've got a ship bearing down on us. A very big one."

"See if you can get above it, Nist, but I don't think we need to run from it." Tristan turned to me, "Do you recognize the airship?"

"No, at least not in this light," I said. "Should I?"

"It's a common configuration for Tartegian naval vessels," Tristan said.

"You think it's Bane?" I asked.

"I would suspect so," Tristan responded.

"There's one easy way to find out," I said, cupping my hands. "*Bane*? Is that you making our pilot nervous?"

"I thought that little ship might be you, Rice. Yours is the only ship approaching the city," came the reply. "Permission to come aboard?"

"Why?" I asked, then remembered Princess Callan's plans to meet with Bane. "Never mind. Permission granted, though for you *only*. The rest of your crew stays on your ship. If any of them attempt to board, we'll kill your employer's only son."

A few seconds passed, then, "I have no idea what you're talking about, Rice."

"Since we both know you're lying, I'd suggest you just drop the act, Bane," I called. "We know the whole story."

"From what I've heard of intrigue in the Tartegian court," Tristan murmured, "I seriously doubt that's true."

Bane called, "Believe whatever makes you happy, Rice. But I agree, only I board."

Bane's airship maneuvered alongside the *Pauline*. I held my sword at Raoul's throat as Bane came aboard. True to his word, his airship moved away once he was aboard.

"Why were you looking for me, Bane?" I asked.

"I'm trying to keep your head from ending up on a pike on what's left of the gates of Beloren," Bane said. "The city government doesn't know your name, yet, but they blame you for the fire."

A Grand Pyre

"That's the most ridiculous thing I've ever heard," I said. "I just discovered the city was burning a few minutes ago. I couldn't have started the fire even if I'd wanted to—which I didn't."

"I didn't say they accuse you of *setting* the fire," Bane said. "I said they blame you *for* the fire."

"That's equally ridiculous," I protested. "I only spent a few hours inside the city. How can I be to blame?"

"The tunnel rats started fires all over the city in retribution for their fellow rats who died during your rescue of the princess and prince," Bane said. "And for forcing them to kill their tammar."

"Are you telling me that saving people from the tunnel rats is a crime?" I asked.

"You won't find any such law on the books," Bane said, "but the city and the tunnel rats have an unspoken agreement. The rats leave respectable, well-to-do citizens alone, preying on the poor and outcasts teeming throughout the city. The city's population of undesirables is kept in check without endangering anyone important. In return, the city leaves the tunnel rats alone.

"According to the unspoken agreement, the lives of the prince and princess were forfeit when they entered the tunnels on their own," Bane said. "By rescuing them, you broke the peace."

Glaring at Raoul, Bane added, "You also saved me from having to do the same thing."

Turning back to me, Bane said, "The debt I incurred for that is repaid with this warning. Keep clear of Beloren and you should be fine. Now, I'm going to recall my ship and-"

"Please stay a while longer," said Callan as she emerged from the cabin. "I have a proposition to discuss with you."

Callan strode toward us, her face calm and her eyes hard.

"But first, what became of Rob's body?" Callan asked.

"I'm sorry, Your Highness, I took his body to be properly prepared," Bane said, "but the fire changed everything. It was all I could do to escape the flames with my ship and crew."

Callan turned her gaze toward the city, "An entire city burns in response to Rob's death."

"It's as grand a funeral pyre as any man could ask," Bane said.

Callan watched the burning city for a moment and then nodded. Turning back to Bane, she said, "I have need of a fleet of fighting airships. Will you recruit and command such a fleet for me? If you will, how quickly can you recruit the fleet and how much will it cost?"

"The cost depends entirely on what you wish us to fight," Bane replied.

"Trogs," Callan answered.

"Ah, yes, the trog army did appear to be headed toward the Mordanian border. And the navy is sure to be spread far and wide, searching for the heir to the throne." Bane thought for a moment, "Standard mercenary wages for all ships. I'll need one day to recruit the ships."

"Agreed," Callan said.

"*And*," Bane said, "your father will issue a full pardon for one Martin Bane."

A Contract

"A full pardon?" I demanded. "For *you*?"

"You bring up a good point, Rice," Bane said. "Your Highness, change that to a pardon for me, my crew, and the officers and crews of all of the ships who sign up for this venture. After all, you can't expect men to risk imprisonment or execution at the hands of those they've come to aid."

"I am willing to grant a temporary stay of arrests and prosecution for all officers and crew, but only for the duration of their employment," Callan offered.

"Unacceptable," Bane countered. "Once the Mordanian navy has regrouped and we are deep within Mordan's borders, what keeps you from discharging us from your service and ordering your navy to attack us?"

"You have my word of honor as a princess of the royal house of Mordan."

Bane retorted, "That's very generous of you, I'm sure, but I prefer something tangible. Something in writing that I can show to, say, a naval ship's captain."

"What if my father refuses to honor my pardon?" Callan countered. "He is not bound to honor any agreements I make in his name."

"He may not be legally bound to honor the agreement, but if he doesn't he'll risk casting doubt on all documents signed in his stead by his diplomats," Bane said. "No, Highness, I have full confidence that he'll honor your agreement."

"You know I have little choice and you drive a hard bargain, sir," Callan said. "Very well, I agree to your terms provided we include one final condition. Upon completion of this contract, you leave Mordan and, on pain of death, never cross her borders again."

Bane's eyebrows arched, "Well, Your Highness, that addition was unexpected. Your father will be proud. With reluctance, I accept." Bane flashed a smile. "I suppose this means I'm off the invitation list for the wedding?"

Early morning light bathed the deck before the signing, sealing, and planning was complete.

Returning Bane to his ship, we gave Beloren a wide berth as we steamed north toward the rendezvous point where the fleet would gather. We spotted no Tartegian vessels along the way, leaving us with little choice but to keep the Spare Prince aboard.

Throughout the afternoon and into the night, a motley assortment of airships joined us. At dawn, we counted twenty-one ships flying north behind the *Pauline*.

A tight smile played across Callan's lips. "Let's go hunting."

14

THUNDER ON HIGH

It took us two days to cross the desert. Bane spent half that time on board *Pauline* planning strategy and tactics with Princess Callan. And, during a break in the planning, I had the chance to speak with Bane.

"You know, Raoul tried to convince Her Highness that I was in league with you," I said.

Bane arched an eyebrow. "Really? How did he do that?"

"He claimed you knew the Onesie was useless after Her Highness shot the tammar and only walked away because your agent—me, according to Raoul—was in place," I explained. "And, much as it pains me to admit it, Raoul has a point. Why did you walk away when you had the upper hand?"

"Yes, I knew the Onesie wasn't a threat. But you were a different matter," Bane responded. "My men had already run away, leaving me to face Rob, a trained warrior, and you, another Scout. Even Boosted, it was a fight I didn't think I could win."

"But I'd already overtaxed my Boost against the trogs."

"I didn't know that," Bane insisted. "Besides, there was only one place you could go if you wanted to survive in the desert. With an airship, I could get to the trading post ahead of you."

I nodded slowly. Bane's explanation made sense.

Finally, our mercenary fleet crossed Mordan's southern border and we began stalking our prey. It was not hard. The trog army had left a trail of devastation a blind man could follow.

Pain and anger warred in Callan's green eyes as we flew over slain people, burned buildings, and tortured land. Tristan, Nist, and I offered comforting words. Even Martin Bane, during our planning sessions offered tentative consolation. Callan would not be consoled, deflecting our words with discussions of tactics.

"We'll be within sight of Faroon within the quarter hour," Callan said, pointing to the horizon. "The city would be a perfect base of operations for the trogs."

"Why?" I asked.

"Faroon is a trading hub," Bane replied. "This time of year, with the harvests recently gathered, the warehouses will be filled with food from all over. The navy keeps a squadron there to patrol the border and deter smuggling. But, like the rest of the navy, they'll probably be searching for the princess. If the trogs have taken Faroon—which seems certain, at this point—we won't be able to force them out of the city."

"You're right," Callan agreed, "but we will control the skies. We'll be able to keep them pinned down in the city while we send airships in search of reinforcements."

Wind whipped around us, making the ship's lines sing, and clouds as dark as our mood scuttled above us. Bane nodded agreement with Callan as the first drops of rain hit the deck. "It will be difficult, Your Highness. The trogs will be free to do what they wish to the city's population. You must prepare yourself to endure it."

"With all the food in the warehouses, won't there be lots of airships docked in the city, as well?" I asked.

"I expect so." Bane said. "What of it?"

"Well, what if the trogs have captured merchant airships?" I asked. "Couldn't they mount an aerial defense of the city?"

"No," Bane said. "Trogs don't use airships."

An unbroken rumble of thunder sounded above us.

"Yes, but trogs don't form armies, either," I said.

Bane looked at me in surprise then turned to look up at the clouds.

"What do you-" I began.

"Quiet," Bane ordered. A few seconds later, he cried, "That sound isn't thunder."

Bane ran back to his own ship, shouting orders. "Emergency signal to the fleet. There are enemy ships above us!"

Lightning flashed and real thunder roared as airships filled with trogs dropped out of the clouds.

Trogs on Deck

As the airships drew nearer, it became clear that the trogs were not flying them. Men handled the airships, though they did not do so willingly. People—men, women, even children—were tied to railings, hostages to force the cooperation of those flying the ships.

Bane called across to me, "Rice, get away from the battle. You're not a warship and your crew is too small to repel boarders for very long. Besides, we can't risk losing our employer."

"You're all heart, Bane," I called back, but he had already turned his attention back to the coming battle.

Nist had heard Bane's instructions and was already steering away from the fight. I ran to Callan's side.

"We've got to free Raoul," I said. "We may need his sword if trogs try to board us."

"I'll go get him," she said, then added, "He's much more likely to listen to me than you."

The air battle began taking shape behind us. The trog airships outnumbered us, but our crews had their hearts and minds focused on the fight. The enemy airships were sluggish, as the trogs could only pass orders by pointing. Our ships maneuvered crisply as experienced crews sprang to obey orders from the ship's officers. The situation was dire, but victory *was* possible.

Nist shouted to catch my attention, then pointed back through the rain. Two trog ships had broken off from the main battle and were following us. We couldn't outrun them because we didn't have a full head of steam built up. We hadn't been expecting trouble—famous last words—so weren't able to simply fly away from the larger ships.

Nist spun the wheel and worked the ailerons with frantic intensity, bobbing and weaving, working to keep the trog airships from boxing us in. During one close swing by one of the airships, I saw one of the trogs plunge a spear into one of the hostages, all the while shouting at the crew.

Callan and Raoul stumbled out of the cabin, both of them clutching swords.

"David, what is Nist doing?" Callan called, trying to keep her balance. Then she spotted the trog airships and no longer needed an answer.

The trogs must have realized the *Pauline* was too agile and Nist too skillful for their airships to cut us off. The trogs began throwing things at Nist. Boathooks, belaying pins, anything solid they could lay their hands on rained down on the *Pauline*. It didn't take very long for something to hit him. Nist collapsed as a boathook smashed into his head. Without Nist working the controls, the *Pauline's* flight path straightened out.

I rushed to take the wheel but it was too late. With a thud, the first trog landed on the deck.

Take the Wheel

The airship rocked under the trog and he fought for balance. I kicked him in the chest. He stumbled backward and toppled over the railing. Raoul thrust his sword through the next trog to land on the deck. Two more trogs jumped down as Raoul pulled his blade free of the dead trog. I slashed wildly at each, driving both back a couple of steps, but three more of them jumped onto our airship.

"Princess," I called, "take the wheel. Steer as wildly as you can. It should keep the trogs off balance and make it harder for more of them to jump to the deck."

Raoul ducked under a spear thrust, cutting the trog's legs out from under him.

"Raoul, come over here," I called. "We need to fight back to back and defend the princess."

Callan took the wheel and spun it hard. The deck reeled beneath our feet. Raoul stumbled toward me and I caught him. We each grabbed hold of a ship's line with our free hand, using it as an anchor against the wild swings of the deck. Three trogs mistimed their jumps, plunging past the ship as the four remaining trogs lumbered toward us.

"I thought you were some kind of super swordsman, Rice," Raoul said. "Use your boost thing."

I drove my sword at a trog's face and he dove to the deck.

"I won't use the Boost unless the situation gets really bad," I said.

Raoul swung on his line, kicking a trog in the face.

"This isn't really bad?" Raoul asked. "How can it get much worse, man?"

The sound of ripping fabric came from above, answering Raoul's question. A trog had hit the airship's envelope rather than its deck. Trying to steady himself with his spear, the trog had torn a long gash in the airship's envelope. The unpredictable gyrations had thrown the trog off, but the damage had been done.

Hot air gushed through the gash and the *Pauline* lost altitude rapidly. I hazarded a look below. Our flight had taken us over the city of Faroon.

We were going down into a city full of trogs.

Downed in the City of the Trogs

I wrenched my attention back to the deck of the *Pauline*. Two of the remaining trogs had caught their balance and were advancing on Raoul and me. With Boost I could take all five trogs by myself, but the city was bound to be far more dangerous than this. I had no choice but to save my Boost. At least the two trog airships had returned to the aerial battle once it was obvious we were going down inside the city.

I dodged a trog spear thrust then sliced open the trog's arm with my counter. He dropped his spear and fell back, howling. Turning to face the other way, I ducked under Raoul's defense and thrust my blade through the chest of the trog he'd been fighting.

Leaving my sword in the dying trog, I charged the unwounded trog. His footing still unsure on the rolling deck, the trog managed to regain his balance just as I barreled into him. Legs churning, I drove him backward and over the railing.

As I returned to retrieve my sword, Raoul cut the throat of the last unwounded trog. The remaining trog, blood dripping from his wounded arm, jumped from the airship as we passed over a tall building.

Callan searched for a place to land the airship while Tristan tended to Nist. Running to the bow, I scanned the city for a defensible place to land.

"Callan," I said, pointing, "there's a walled garden over there. Can you land inside the walls?"

"I can try," she replied.

"But I can do it," Nist said, "if someone can help me stand at the controls."

Tristan easily lifted the smaller man and braced him at the wheel. Callan came to my side as Nist worked the ship's wheel and ailerons. Just when I thought Nist had overshot the garden, he twisted the ailerons. The little ship nosed up then dropped into the garden.

Guttural trog shouts came from streets all around us. We were stranded in the city of the trogs.

15

THE ALLEY

THE *PAULINE'S* DEFLATING ENVELOPE WAS STILL FLOATING ABOVE THE garden wall, visible to every trog in the area. We had bare minutes before the trogs found us. As much as I hated to leave it, we couldn't hide with the airship. Parts of its superstructure rose above the garden wall. Even after the envelope deflated, the ship would be easy to spot.

"Everybody out and into the house," I said. "We've got to find some sort of defensible location before the trogs find us."

The house wasn't what we needed—it was too close to the airship—but it was all we had at the moment. I'd see what we had to work with inside and then take it from there.

The calls of trogs sounded much closer as we ran into the house. Someone—probably the trogs—had been here first. Smashed furniture lay all around, dashing any hope of using the furniture as a barricade. The ground floor was too open for our small number, anyway.

"Upstairs," Raoul said, heading for the stairs.

"No," I countered, "we'd be trapped up there. The trogs could just starve us out or decide to burn the house down around us. We have to find another place to hole up."

I looked out the windows on the front of the house. The street before us was clear for the moment.

"Does everyone see that alley over there?" I asked, pointing out the window. "That's where we're heading. Raoul, take point. I'll take rear guard. Raoul, if you find a place to hide, do *not* wait for me. Go to ground and keep the princess safe."

"Leaving you to die at the hands of the trogs?" asked Raoul. "I can live with that."

"No, David," Princess Callan said, "we'll get out of this together or we won't get out at all."

"We don't have time for a debate, Highness," I said. "Please shut up and let me do the job I swore to do."

Callan's cheeks reddened—whether in anger or embarrassment, I couldn't tell—but she nodded. Then we ran for the alley.

We were halfway to the alley when five trogs rounded a corner and spotted us. The trogs began yelling and gave chase. We ran into the alley, finding it clear. Our hope for escape only lasted for a few seconds. Another trog patrol entered the far end of the alley. Behind us, the first patrol blocked the other end of the alley.

We were trapped.

Raoul Runs

Shouting and waving their spears, the trogs bore down on us from both ends of the alley. I looked for doors but found none opening into the alley except on the other side of the trogs. The only way out of the alley was to go through the trogs—or *over* them.

"Callan," I said. "can you climb to the roof?"

Before she could answer, a rope dropped in front of her.

"Climb the rope!" a boy's voice called. "Hurry!"

The trogs would reach us before everyone could climb to the roof, but with some teamwork, most of us could get away. I charged the trogs on my end of the alley, calling over my shoulder, "Raoul, hold off the other trogs while the rest climb the rope."

Grabbing the rope, Raoul sneered. "I do not die so commoners can survive. It is the place of commoners to die so I can survive."

I slashed at the leading trogs, slowing their charge, then ran back to the princess. I'd have to stay close to her so I could guard her from both groups of trogs.

"Climb, Highness," I said.

"No, David," she said. "I can fight. Just give me-"

"Dammit, Callan, if I'm going to die, let it be protecting *you*, not your corpse," I said, shoving the rope into her hands.

Callan's face fell and, without another word, she began pulling herself up the rope.

Nist held the rope out to Tristan, "You're next, Master."

"No, Nist, I'm too old, too fat, and too slow. I'll get us both killed if I go next."

I never heard Nist's reply.

Boost!

I rolled under the closest trog's spear, gutting him as I came to my feet. I charged into the trogs behind the one I'd just killed. Dodging, spinning, slashing, and thrusting, I drove the first squad of trogs away from the rope.

With these trogs on their heels, I rushed at the other squad. I passed Nist, who stood white-faced, guarding the rope as Tristan labored to climb it. On the roof, Callan and the boy heaved on the rope, trying to speed Tristan's ascent.

At least Callan was safely on the roof. Raoul was nowhere to be seen. I'd be lying if I said I was surprised.

The trogs before me lowered their spears, as if expecting me to attack from below as I had with the first squad. Instead, I leapt up and pushed off the wall, surprising the trogs. Their spears tangled as they tried to raise them. Taking that opening, I barreled into them, slicing a throat, slashing a shoulder, piercing an eye, forcing them to fall back.

Once again, I broke away from the squad I was fighting and ran back toward the rope. Nist was scampering up the rope just out of reach of the regrouped first squad. One trog drew his spear back, preparing to throw it at Nist. I drove into the trog at a full run, running him through before he could impale Nist.

"David," Callan called, "Climb the rope."

It was too late. Both squads of trogs had reached the rope. Spears jabbing, the trogs backed me against the far wall. I was cut off from the rope.

Keeping Trogs at Bay

Spear points bristled around me, jabbing and thrusting. I dodged and ducked, slashing and stabbing, keeping the trogs at bay. Even facing the unimaginative trog attacks, I knew I had little time remaining. I'd dodge when I should have ducked or, if I was lucky, hang on long enough to suffer Boost burnout, but the trogs would get me in the end. It would be worth it as long as Callan was getting away.

She wasn't, of course. Several people moved on the roof opposite me, manhandling something to the edge of the roof.

"David," she called, "we found a rain barrel. Be ready to climb the rope."

They shoved the barrel over the roof edge and it dropped on the trogs. Two trogs fell when, with a crack, the barrel burst on top of them. Water gushed, washing aside the trogs at the bottom of the rope. My path to the roof was clear. I leapt across the alley and pulled myself up the rope. A spear clattered against the wall as I rolled onto the roof. The boy yanked the rope up behind me as Nist dragged me away from the edge of the roof.

Safe for the moment, I released Boost—and didn't black out. It was a pleasant change of pace. The fight must have been shorter than I had realized. Or maybe I was adjusting to the Boost. That was a point for the techs to figure out, if they ever found a safe way to reach me.

Nist helped me to my feet and we moved away from the alley full of frustrated trogs.

"I don't suppose Raoul is off scouting for a hiding place?" I asked.

"Is he the jerk who came up the rope first?" the boy asked.

Astute lad. I liked him already.

"Yes," I said. "And thank you for your help. We would have been captured or killed without it."

The boy smiled, "Teach me how to fight like you do and we'll call it even."

"We'll talk about that later," I said. "Do you have a safe place to hide?"

"Yeah," he said, heading across the roof. "Come on."

There were so many twists, turns, ascents, and descents that I was completely disoriented by the time the boy led us into a small cellar. In the corner, a pale young woman lay huddled on a small bed.

"I need your help finding a doctor," the boy said. "I think my sister is dying."

The Desert Doctor

Tristan crossed to the bed, knelt beside it, and pulled back the blanket covering the young woman. He grimaced as he examined the deep wound in her side.

"Nist, I'm going to need my medical kit and supplies," he said. "Boiling water would be useful, too."

"Your supplies are on the *Pauline*, master," Nist said.

"The boy should be able to lead you back to the airship," Tristan said. "You'd do that wouldn't you, boy?"

"My name is Milo," the boy said, "and I'll do anything to help Kim."

Callan knelt next to Tristan, asking, "You're a physician?"

"I am."

"You never told us that," I said.

"My life has been rather busy since you dropped into it, lad," Tristan said. "Besides, you never asked. Would you please go with Nist and Milo and keep them safe."

"Highness, may I have your permission to accompany them?" I asked.

"Of course, David," Callan said.

Nist described the house where he had landed the *Pauline*.

Milo nodded, "I know where that is."

Once we were back on the rooftops, Milo asked, "Is that woman really a princess?"

"So they tell me—and I have no reason to doubt their word," Nist answered. "She is Princess Callan, daughter of your king. This is David Rice, her royal bodyguard."

"Yeah?" Milo said, looking at me. "I'd take your job in a heartbeat. I'd guard her royal body real close, if you know what I mean."

Based on his size, I'd originally estimated Milo's age to be ten. After this revelation, I revised it up to thirteen or fourteen. He must be quite small for his age.

Nist tried hard to smother a laugh, not succeeding particularly well, "Her Highness is quite beautiful."

Milo pointed across a several rooftops, "Is that the house where you landed." Nist nodded and Milo continued, "If we get these supplies, do you think Kim will be okay? Is the old guy a good doctor?"

"His skills are legend among the tribes of the desert," Nist replied.

Milo spun around, "He's the guy they call the Desert Doctor?"

"That he is," Nist replied. "Your sister is in excellent hands."

We moved parallel to a wide street, waiting to get as close to the house as possible before dropping to street level. Then I heard trog voices from the street below.

"Quiet!" I hissed, pulling Milo and Nist to their knees.

I crawled to the roof edge and looked down at the road. A squad of trogs prodded a man with their spears. The man's hands were tied behind his back and he faced away from me, but I'd have recognized him anywhere.

The trogs had captured Prince Raoul.

16

RESCUING RAOUL

Raoul jumped as a trog poked his backside with a spear. The other trogs wheezed. Laughter, I assumed. Another poke, another jump, more wheezing.

"The jerk got caught," Milo whispered. "Serves him right for running off."

"I should just leave him to his fate," I sighed. "It's what he would do to me."

"But you're not going to leave him," Milo said. "Because you're not like him."

"No, I'm not going to leave him," I said. "Rescuing Raoul should draw trog patrols this way. You two, get the medical kit then go straight back to the hiding place. Don't wait for me. I can find my way back there, I think."

"The Spare Prince doesn't deserve this," Nist said.

"I'm not doing this for him. I wouldn't be worthy to wear this sword if I just walked away," I said. "Get going."

Bent low, the two ran off. I stalked the trogs from above, waiting until Nist and Milo were long out of sight.

I jumped at the squad below. My slashing blade decapitated the rearmost trog. His head bounced off the street as I tucked and rolled with the landing. I ran another through as I rose to my feet in the middle of the squad. Whipping the blade around, I stabbed into the gut of a trog behind me. That was enough for the two remaining trogs. They ran, leaving Raoul standing above three trog corpses.

"*You!*" Raoul spat, his hatred of me battling across his face with his relief at being rescued.

I guess Raoul wasn't very happy to see me. His hatred won. Raoul's face turned red and he gave into his rage. Hands still tied behind his back, Raoul lowered his head and charged. I was really tired of dealing with Raoul. Stepping into his charge, I put all of my strength and weight behind a right cross. The pommel of my sword smashed into Raoul's temple and he collapsed at my feet. It wasn't very sporting to hit a man whose hands were tied, but it was *very* satisfying.

Cutting off a piece of a dead trog's loincloth, I stuffed it in Raoul's mouth, gagging him. Shouldering Raoul, I found stairs to the rooftops in a nearby alley. Twenty minutes later, I lugged Raoul into the hiding place.

Callan's and Tristan's eyes widened when they recognized Raoul, but I had other worries.

Nist and Milo weren't back.

Rooftop Confrontation

"Where are the other two?" Tristan asked.

"We had to split up," I said, dropping Raoul in a corner. "I thought my rescue of the Spare Prince would draw any trog patrols, leaving Nist and Milo clear to go after the medical kit."

"The trogs did that to Raoul?" Callan asked, eying the lump on the side of Raoul's head.

"No, I did."

Callan's left eyebrow arched, so I added, "Raoul took exception to being rescued by me and tried to attack. So, I smacked him on the head."

"Hard?" she asked.

"Very."

"Good," she said. "And now you're going back out to find Nist and Milo?"

“That’s the plan.”

Callan rose on her toes and kissed me lightly on the lips. “Be careful.”

“As you wish, Highness” I said. “Do you mind tying Raoul before he wakes up?”

Callan was happily pulling knots tight around Raoul’s wrists as I left. Soon, I was up on the rooftops, running back the way I had come. Trog shouts and calls echoed through the city, but none of them were anywhere near me. Had the trogs been frightened off by their losses in this area or were they stalking the area in silence? Whatever the reason, the silence allowed other sounds to carry. That’s how I heard Milo’s voice.

“Give that back,” Milo cried. “It’s not yours!”

A rough voice answered, “Anything I can take is mine, kid. This bag of medicine will be worth a fortune.”

“No. I need it for my sister. She might die without it.”

“Sister, eh?” said the voice. “Tell you what, boy, take us to her. I’m sure we’d all like to meet her. And if we like what we see, maybe we’ll give her some medicine. I wouldn’t want to lose my new plaything too quickly.”

Coarse laughter rose from several throats.

“Leave the boy alone,” Nist said. “You wanted the medicine and you have it. Take it and go.”

I came over a rooftop and saw them on the next roof. Four men surrounded Milo and Nist. Nist stood between Milo and the man holding the medicine kit. Nist also held one hand to his head as blood seeped between his fingers.

“I’m getting tired of his lip,” the rough-voiced man said to his men. “Kill him.”

Better Connections

There was no way I could reach Nist before the gang killed him, but there was also no way I was going to let Nist die.

“Kill him,” I called, running down the roof, “and you’ll answer to me.”

My arrival surprised the gang. Seeing me charge down on them, sword drawn, gave rough-voice's men pause. They turned to their leader for instructions.

Rough-voice motioned to the biggest and strongest of the bunch, "Sarn, teach that guy what happens to people who get in my way."

Sarn grinned and charged. The others grinned, too. I guessed Sarn was known for beating down anyone who displeased rough-voice. At least all of the attention was on me and no one was trying to kill Nist.

The way Sarn moved revealed everything to me. He showed no subtlety, no grace. He relied entirely on size and strength. Sarn was a brawler, not a fighter. I wouldn't need Boost to handle him.

As we drew together, I tucked, rolled, and came up at him with my fists together, driving with my legs. Sarn folded around my punch, his breath whooshing out. I flowed into a spin kick and Sarn reeled. He collapsed, gasping to draw breath, at rough-voice's feet. My sword was at rough-voice's throat before the others could react.

"Let. Them. Go."

The two thugs released Nist and Milo.

"Now the medicine kit," I said to rough-voice. His face darkened, so I added, "You can give it to me or I'll take it from your corpse. It's all the same to me."

"Don't think you've won," rough-voice said, tossing the medicine kit to Nist. "Once the trogs are run out of the city, I'll report you to the authorities. I've got connections in the guard. Who do you think they'll believe, us four citizens or some street urchin and two foreigners?"

The threat was so ludicrous I couldn't help it. I burst out laughing.

"Please do make that report. I'm willing to bet my connections are a tad bit better than yours," I said. Rough-voice's face went slack, unsure how to respond to my laughter. "You deserve a sound thrashing, but I've got more important things to do right now. If I see you again, though..."

I whacked rough-voice on the side of the head with the flat of my blade. He flinched, backed away, then turned and stalked away.

Moments later we were back at Milo's hiding place. Callan drew Milo away from his sister and, with a little prompting, got Milo to launch into a breathless and mostly accurate account of their exploits.

Nist gave the kit to Tristan and we joined him at the wounded woman's bedside.

"I've asked Her Highness to keep the boy distracted," Tristan murmured. "His sister has a deep spear wound in her side. The surgery will be tricky and she might not survive it."

Supply Search

I looked at Milo, somersaulting to demonstrate my attack on Sarn. Callan smiled, laughed, and gasped in all the right places, her attention seemingly riveted on Milo. Her eyes betrayed her true emotions—worry for her people, concern for Milo's sister, and sympathy for the boy capering before her.

Milo came to the breathless end of his story, adding, "Now that we've got the medicine, the Desert Doctor will save Kim."

"Such faith the young man has in an old man like me," sighed Tristan.

"He should have faith," said Nist. "But you are not an old man."

"I'm not?" Tristan raised an eyebrow.

"Not at all, Master. You are a *very* old man."

Tristan's lips twitched upward, "That's the final insult I take from you, scamp. I'm writing you out of my will."

Tristan turned to me, "I hate to send you out again, lad, but I need a few medical items for the girl's recovery. I've made a list."

"I can speak this language, Tristan. I can't read it," I said.

"Not surprising, considering how you learned the language. Take Milo. He shouldn't be here during the surgery, anyway," Tristan said. "And remind me to start teaching you to read when we find time to spare."

Milo scanned the list, relieved to have something to do other than sit around and worry about his sister.

"What do you need liquor for?" he asked.

"I don't have any anesthesia in the medicine kit. Drinking it will help Kim with the pain," Tristan said.

"It's not to calm your nerves? My Uncle Torm always said that, but I knew better," Milo said, looking hard at Tristan.

"It most certainly is not," Tristan replied in indignation.

Milo stared at Tristan for another moment. Whatever he saw satisfied him and we headed out. Our first stop was a nearby apothecary. It had already been picked clean.

"Gort and his gang probably took it all," Milo mused.

"Gort's the thug from the rooftop?" At Milo's nod, I continued, "Any idea where we can find him?"

"He'll be holed up in a bar somewhere," Milo said. "I think I know where to look. And liquor is on the list."

Milo led me across the rooftops for nearly a kilometer. It was dusk when he pointed to a bar across the street. I was about to drop to the street when I saw Sarn. He sprinted from an alley, crossed the street, and ran into the bar. That's when we found out we weren't the only ones who had spotted Sarn.

A dozen trogs ran out of the same alley and charged toward the bar.

17

TROGS AND THUGS

As if my day hadn't been busy enough already, now I was about to risk my life for Gort and his gang of thugs. Well, for their hoard of supplies, anyway. But rescuing the thugs would be a byproduct.

"Milo, stay here and stay hidden," I said. "If I'm not out in fifteen minutes, go report this to the princess."

"Report? That's it?" Milo asked.

"That will be enough. The princess must be told what has happened," I said. Callan would need to be told, but I also didn't want Milo getting himself killed trying to help me. "Can I count on you?"

Milo nodded as shouts rose from the bar. I cast a smile at Milo, jumped down, then dashed across the street and into the bar.

The fading daylight offered little illumination within the bar. Windows on the far side of the room silhouetted the chaos inside. Brawny Sarn swung two big clubs with enough force and wild abandon to keep four trogs at bay. Gort was behind the bar, cocking a crossbow, while the other two thugs stood on the other side of the bar swinging swords with great enthusiasm and little skill. The trogs before them had no more concept of unit tactics than any other trogs I'd fought, allowing the thugs' efforts to be more successful than they deserved to be. One trog lay within the door, a crossbow bolt through one eye.

I couldn't risk Boosting so soon after the fight in the alley. So, instead of charging into the center of the action, I stayed on the outskirts of the fight. A trog lurched back to avoid Sarn's wind-milling clubs. I ran him through before he even knew I was there. Gort fired his crossbow at the same time, the quarrel punching through another trog's chest and out the back. In the confusion caused by the sudden loss of two of their squad, I charged in among the trogs and slashed deeply into another trog's leg. Gort's eyes went wide when he saw me. The wounded trog's leg buckled and he yelled a warning to the others as he fell. Two trogs turned and came at me in a rush, driving me back toward the door.

One of the trogs looked past me to the doorway. Guessing that couldn't be good for me, I jumped to the left. The trog spear meant for my neck gouged my right shoulder. Pain flared from the deep cut and my hand spasmed. With a clatter, my sword fell to the floor, leaving me unarmed and surrounded by trogs.

Spears raised, the trogs closed in for the kill.

I Need a Doctor

With no weapon in hand, I was in big trouble. My only choice was to Boost and hope I'd stay conscious after the fight. I tried not to think how badly things would go for me if Gort and his crew had me at their mercy. Then I heard a *thunk* from behind me. Glancing over my shoulder, I saw the trog in the doorway topple toward me. I spun behind the falling trog, holding him between me and the two other trogs' attacks. The trogs realized their error too late. Two spears plunged into the chest of the trog I held.

Agony shot through my wounded shoulder as I shoved the bleeding trog into the other two. All three went down in a heap. Picking up my sword, I ordered my implant to release a pain killer and a fast-acting analgesic flowed into my blood stream. Agony receding, I finished off the three trogs then rejoined the battle.

A minute later, all of the trogs were dead. One of Gort's sword-wielding thugs was dead and Sarn sat against the back wall holding a deep leg wound. Milo stood at the door, a long, stout piece of wood in his hands.

"I told you to stay on the roof," I said.

"I saw another trog coming to the bar," Milo said. "Kim needs the medicine more than your princess needs a report. Besides, I saved your life."

"Those are all good points," I admitted.

"Ain't that sweet," Gort said. "Now, get out of my bar before I shoot you."

"You're welcome," I said.

Gort stared at me.

"For saving your worthless lives," I said.

"We didn't need none of your help," he said.

"Are you delusional?" I asked. "I killed six of the trogs and my friend took care of a seventh. You'd be dead or captured without us."

"Gort?" said Sarn. "I need a doctor."

Gort said, "We don't got a doctor."

"I do," I said. "The Desert Doctor is part of my group. I'll take Sarn to him in exchange for the supplies I need."

Gort shook his head, "Sorry Sarn, that cut ain't worth giving away any of my supplies. Time to prove how tough-"

A chair smashed over Gort's head. His eyes rolled back in his head and he crumpled to the floor.

"You really got a doctor?" the third thug asked.

"Yes," I said.

"You and the kid carry the supplies," he said. "I'll help Sarn."

Minutes later, Tal—the third thug—braced Sarn and we headed out into a city teeming with trogs. We were in no condition for any kind of fight. Darkness and luck were our only allies. I prayed they would be enough for us to get back to Milo's hiding place.

The Answer

We moved at a snail's pace. Crossing the street seemed to take forever, but it was fast compared to the climb to the rooftops. Unable to run for cover, we froze at every sound. The thirty minute trip to the bar dragged out to a two and a half hour trek back. Sarn was exhausted from blood loss and pain and the rest of us were all on edge by the time we got to the hiding place.

One look at Callan showed that I'd had the far easier task. She sat huddled in a corner, hugging her knees, her face drawn and pale. She was absently twiddling a thick leather strap. It was damp with saliva and had fresh bite marks ground into it. Without anesthesia for Milo's sister, the surgery must have been horribly painful for Kim and horribly unnerving for Callan.

Tristan took charge of the medical supplies, ordering Nist to prepare various concoctions for Kim's wound. While Nist was busy with the medicine, Tristan examined Sarn's wound and mine. Proclaiming mine to be a minor wound and not in need of immediate attention, Tristan selected a bottle of liquor. With a nod toward Callan, he gave it to me.

I crossed to where Callan sat and, sinking to the floor, offered the bottle to Callan, "Drink."

She didn't take the bottle, but her eyes widened when she saw my bloody shoulder.

"Tristan says it's not serious," I said, pressing the bottle to her lips and tilting it up. "Now, drink."

Callan swallowed. Her cheeks flushed and her eyes watered.

"Are you trying to poison me, David?" she gasped.

"Doctor's orders," I said, waving the bottle toward Tristan before also taking a drink. "Now, tell me about it or I'll give you another drink."

Callan leaned into me and I drew her close. From his corner, the trussed-up and now-conscious Raoul glared at me.

Callan looked at Milo's sister. "She was so brave during the surgery. She never cried out once, but she nearly bit through the leather strap."

Once Callan began, the words tumbled out. Callan told me of the pain reflected in Kim's eyes as Tristan operated, her crushing grip as Callan held her hand, her unending stream of tears, and how she held her body rigidly still so Tristan could operate.

"I felt so helpless," Callan said. "All I could do was stroke her head, hold her hand, offer empty words, and look her in the eye."

I wrapped my other arm around her, holding her tightly. Before I could offer my own empty words, Tal squatted down before me.

"The doctor said I should talk to you," he said. "He says maybe I got the answer."

"The answer to what?" I asked.

Tal replied, "Beating the trogs."

Beating the Trogs

"*You* know how to get rid of the trogs?" I asked.

Tal said, "The doctor says I do."

"Well?"

Tal's brow furrowed. It was easy to see how Tal had fallen in with Gort. Tal was a born follower, not particularly bright and generally happy to have someone else making his decisions for him. It made his attack against Gort all the more surprising. Sarn must be a really good friend for Tal to have taken such initiative.

"What did you say before the doctor sent you to me?' I asked.

Tal's face cleared, "I was talking to him about the challenges."

"What challenges?"

"The big trog has one every morning," Tal said. "At dawn, an old guy with the trog calls for a challenger."

"Guy? You mean a man?"

"Yeah, he's a man but he talks trog, too," Tal said.

"Tell me about the challenge," I said.

"Not much to tell," he replied. "Sometimes a prisoner volunteers, sometimes the trogs pull a prisoner out of the crowd. They fight, the man dies, and then the trogs all chant something."

"Is there anything else you can remember?" I asked.

Tal shook his head but Milo, who had been listening from his sister's bedside, nodded.

"Yeah, there's one more thing," Milo said. "When the trogs pull a challenger out of the pen, they just toss the body on a big fire when the fight is over. When someone volunteers to fight the leader, the trogs make a pyre and hold a short ceremony. It's like a trog funeral or something."

That was interesting and might even give some insight into trog culture.

"Do they fight with weapons or is it hand-to-hand?" I asked.

"People who volunteer get to choose weapons," Milo said. "The ones they pull from the pen have to fight hand-to-hand."

"Thank you, both. That's very helpful," I said.

Tal went back to Sarn and Milo turned his attention back to his sister.

"A lot of primitive cultures allow challenges to determine tribal supremacy," I said. "Holding a challenge each morning is a simple way for the leader to demonstrate his dominance over the humans in the city."

"You don't know if that's what the trog leader is doing," Callan said.

"It makes sense, Callan," I said. "Warrior cultures respect courage, so the bodies of those who volunteer to fight are treated with respect."

From the other corner, Raoul rocked back and forth, trying to talk around the gag I'd stuffed in his mouth.

"Tal," I said, "take the gag out of his mouth."

Tal did and Raoul spat, "There's no need to risk your precious royal guard, Callan. I will challenge the trog leader."

Request and Require

Let Raoul challenge the trog leader. That was such a tempting thought that I almost agreed to it. But no matter the appeal of the idea, it was one fraught with problems of its own.

"It has to be me," I said to Callan. "You can't allow Raoul to go in my place.

"How very noble of you," Raoul sneered. "This is your chance to save your lover, Callan. You can always send him off to be killed if I fail."

"Tal?" I asked. "Put the gag back in the prince's mouth."

"I forbid that, peasant," Raoul snarled.

Tal backed away, saying, "I don't think so. He might bite me."

"He's just desperate enough that he might," I agreed. "If he does, you have my permission to hit his head against the wall until he stops biting."

Tal brightened, "Thanks."

"You cretin!" Raoul said. "I'll see you hanged for-"

Tal stuffed the gag in Raoul's mouth, cutting him off. Raoul did not bite Tal. I was a little disappointed. I think I would have enjoyed watching Raoul's head bounce off the wall a few times.

"You keep insisting I shouldn't send Raoul. Why?" Callan asked.

"I think you know the reasons, Highness," I said. "First, he could run off. I know that's not very heroic, but Raoul isn't much of a hero."

That earned Raoul's nastiest glare yet.

"He could lose the challenge," I continued, "leaving you to explain to his family—including your future husband—why you allowed a Tartegian prince to die fighting Mordan's battle. And if Raoul won, you'd have to explain to the Mordanian people why a Tartegian prince fought to save them while a Mordanian guardsman stood by."

"Oh, David," Callan said, "losing Rob has been hard enough. I don't think I could bear it if I lost you, too."

"You're stronger than you think Callan. You can bear it," I said. "You *will* bear it if necessary. Your people need you to be strong enough to do that which must be done."

Callan sighed and pulled away from me. She composed herself and the tired, frightened young woman was replaced by the regal Princess Callan, heir to the throne of Mordan.

In formal tones, she said, "David Rice, Captain of my Royal Guard, I request and require you to save my people. At dawn, you will challenge the trog leader and defeat him in single combat."

18

ACCEPT AND ACCEDE

"Requeshed and require?" a voice slurred before I could answer. "Ish she some kinda prinshesh or shomething?"

"Kim," cried Milo, a grin splitting his face. "You're alive! And awake. And drunk."

Milo rushed to his sister, quickly followed by Tristan and Nist. Sarn and Tal appeared to have fallen asleep against the far wall. Only Raoul saw Callan take me by the hand and pull me outside.

She led me up to the rooftop and then melted against me. We just held each other and it was as if time no longer existed. All our worries faded into the background as we lived in the moment.

"David? Your Highness?" Milo's voice broke the spell. He came up onto the rooftop and saw us. "Whoa! Hey, sorry. I didn't mean to interrupt."

"What is it, Milo?" Callan asked, looking his way but staying wrapped in my arms.

"Tristan and I just wanted to make sure you two were safe," Milo said. Ducking back toward the hiding place, he added, "I'm glad you're taking your job seriously, David."

Callan cast a quizzical look at me, "What does that mean?"

"I'm, um, guarding your royal body," I grinned.

Callan clapped a hand over her mouth to stifle a giggle and her body shook as she laughed for the first time in days. It was good to hear her laugh. And it was good to feel her laughter, too.

When she was still again, I said, "I don't know the formal words to answer your question."

"I know your answer, David," Callan said. "But the formal phrase is *accept and accede*."

"What is it with royalty and alliteration?" I asked. "Request and require, accept and-"

Callan pulled my head down toward hers. "Oh hush and kiss me."

"I accept and accede," I replied.

Then time went away again.

Callan and I were dozing in each other's arms when Tristan and Tal came for me.

"It'll be dawn soon," Tristan said. "Time to go, lad."

Tal, my guide, was armed with a crossbow and a sword.

I gave Callan a last embrace then shook Tristan's hand. For his ears only, I said, "If anything happens to me, Tristan..."

"I'll see her safely home, lad," he said. "You can count on that."

I shared one last look with Callan, then Tal and I set off to challenge the trog leader.

Challenging the Great One

We made our way across the rooftops in silence. Only as we neared the center of town did Tal break the silence.

"This is gonna be easy for you, right?"

"Why do you think that?" I asked.

"Because you can do that boost thing. The kid, Milo, he told me about it," Tal replied.

"It's not as useful against a single opponent as you might think," I said. "A group never has the time to adjust to my quickness and that messes up their teamwork. Many times they end up hurting themselves more than I hurt them. A single fighter can adjust faster and better."

"If you say so," Tal muttered, unconvinced.

"I'll use it if things get really desperate," I added, "But I'd rather save the Boost in case I have to make a run for it after the fight. Like if the trogs attack me if I win."

Tal nodded, that last bit seemed to make sense to him.

By that time we had reached the rooftops overlooking the trog camp. It sprawled throughout the town square and into a small park next to the square. The sky was just bright enough for me to make out a few details. Trogs were everywhere; cooking, eating, sharpening spears, standing guard, or just sitting around doing nothing. On the edge of the park, a rough fence had been built. The human prisoners were packed inside the fence, many watching the lightening horizon with what I could only guess was apprehension.

"Stay hidden up here, Tal," I said. "If I have to make a run for it, cover fire from your crossbow will help a lot."

Tal hunkered down on the roof and said, "You got it." As I turned away, he added, "Whack that trog upside the head once for me."

I moved along the rooftop, getting far away from Tal while keeping an eye on the camp. I came to an empty alley and jumped down into it. I slipped to the mouth of the alley and waited for the challenge. It wasn't long in coming.

"Humans!" a man's voice called. "Once again, the Great One will allow one of you to issue challenge to him. Who will face him in single combat? Who will represent humanity against the greatest warrior who has ever lived?"

Stepping out from the alley, I called out loudly, "I, Scout First Class David Rice, will challenge the Great One."

No Weapons

There were four trogs loafing near the alley. They all jumped as if stung when my challenge rang out. Silence fell across the camp and all heads turned my way as I strode toward the man who spoke for the trog leader. I had expected a young man, maybe someone captured as a boy and raised among the trogs. This man was on the high end of middle-age, with thinning, gray hair, a full, white beard, and muscular build. It appeared he had done well for himself serving this Great One.

The penned humans stared at me in disbelief as I strode past. I gave them my brightest smile.

"Don't worry," I said, injecting as much confidence into my voice as possible, "Once I win this challenge, I'll have you out of there as quickly as possible."

The people in the pen began talking at once. Some of comments filtered out of the crowd. I heard "brave" several times and "foolhardy" even more often. I couldn't blame them. I'd probably have thought the same thing in their place.

Beyond the old man who spoke for the Great One stood a trog who must *be* the Great One. He was exceptionally tall for a trog—close to my own height—and looked like he was solid muscle. His body bore the scars of many battles. It was what I'd expected to see but would have been happy to have been proven wrong.

"You're the first man to come out of the city to issue challenge," said the man. "The Great One respects your courage and grants you the choice of weapons."

"Before I make that choice, could I ask some questions first?" I said.

"You may," he intoned.

"Do we fight to first blood, until one of the warriors concedes, or to the death?"

"The victor may show mercy if his opponent concedes. Do not count on receiving it," he responded.

"What happens if I win?" I asked.

The man laughed, "That will not happen."

"Humor me," I said.

"Should the impossible happen and you somehow defeat the Great One, you will be the new Great One, leader of all the trogs," he said.

"Prepare for new management, then," I said, loudly enough to be heard within the pen. "And what weapons do the trogs use in challenges among themselves?"

"They use only the weapons the gods granted them when they enter the world," he replied.

I unbuckled my sword belt and laid it on the ground.

I said, "Then I will fight the Great One as the trogs fight—hand-to-hand. No weapons."

Who Are You?

"Why fight no weapons?"

It was the first thing the trog leader had said since I had arrived, but I recognized his voice. I'd first heard that voice when we were trapped in the cellar of the trading post. It was deep, rasping, and inhuman—a perfect match for the hulking trog standing before me.

"I must win as you won or your people might not obey me." I said.

The Great One chuffed once—a short laugh, I guessed—then seemed to lose interest in further talk. His human translator, on the other hand, gave me a hard stare.

"Who *are* you?" he asked.

"Is there any more to issuing challenge than what I've already done?" I asked, ignoring the translator's question. "Do I have to beat my breast, brag about all of the men I have slain and the women I have wooed, stuff like that?"

"No, there is no breast-beating or bragging required," the man said. "The only thing left for you to do is fight and die."

The man leaned close to me, speaking quietly and with an authority absent from his public proclamations, "If you could, please die quickly. I have quite a lot to do today and this spectacle has already taken up far too much of my time."

Now my curiosity was piqued. There was a lot more going on between the translator and the trog leader than met the eye. Who was the translator and how had he ended up with the trogs? I no longer thought he was a trog captive who had been kept alive to serve the Great One. There was no subservience in the man's voice or manner. Was the Great One just a necessary figurehead for the translator? What complications would I face if I defeated the Great One?

Was every conspiracy on this planet Gordian in complexity?

"A challenge has been issued!" called the man, once again using the more subservient tone. "Is the challenge accepted?"

"Yes," said the Great One.

I wrenched my attention back to the challenge. I had enough problems without adding the puzzle of the translator to the mix.

The translator backed away from me and called, "Fight!"

The Great One hunched down, spread his arms wide and charged.

How Trogs Fight

I got the idea the big trog expected me to run from him. Instead, I went for the unexpected and charged at the Great One. I couldn't play it safe and hope to win. The trog slowed for just a second, letting me know I'd made the right choice.

Just outside of the reach of the charging trog, I dove head first. I spun in the air and landed on my back. The dew-soaked grass was slick and I slid fast. The Great One had been ready to grapple with me and couldn't adjust to my surprise move. I slid under his grasping hands and between his legs. Pulling my knees up to my chest, I threw my arms back against the trog's shins. His balance thrown off, the Great One toppled forward. As he fell over me, I kicked up with both legs. My feet caught him in the stomach and launched him into a flip.

With a grunt of pain, the trog landed hard on his back. I rolled to my feet. The Great One rolled over onto his hands and knees, struggling to regain his feet. While he was defenseless, I darted in and kicked him in the face. His head snapped back and a howl of pain burst from his lips. I skipped away as the Great One rose to a crouch. Blood dripped from his nose and anger burned in his eyes.

Again, the Great One opened his arms wide and advanced, but he was much more cautious this time. It looked like trogs fought up close, grappling with each other. I guessed that was his plan for me. I was sure he could crush me with those long, powerful arms. I had to wear him down with hit and fade attacks. That would take time and, as a bonus, interfere with the translator's busy schedule.

I charged right at the now-cautious trog, dodged right just before he could grab me, and landed a blow to his ear. Again, I was dancing away before the big trog could react.

I landed two more quick hits before the Great One lost his patience and came at me in a full out charge. Again, I dodged before landing a punch where a man's left kidney would be. The Great One roared in pain. He may not have a kidney where I'd hit, but whatever was there was vital.

I was feeling good. The Great One not only hadn't hit me, he was flailing about with clumsy sweeps of his arms. He had no idea how to react to my style of fighting. As long as I kept moving and avoided his sweeping arms, I was sure I could wear the trog down.

I feinted and skipped away, frustrating the Great One even more. His lips were pulled back in a snarl of rage. I was preparing for another furious charge from the big trog when I sensed someone behind me.

"You asked how trogs fight," the translator said quietly. "It's time to find out."

He shoved me toward the angry trog. With a roar of triumph, the Great One wrapped his arms around me and squeezed.

19

FOUL BLOW

ALL I COULD SEE WAS BLUE SKIN AS THE GREAT ONE CRUSHED ME AGAINST his chest and pinned my arms against my side. Hot, fetid breath assaulted my nose as the trog roared. I breathed in short gasps, the best I could manage while in the Great One's deadly embrace. My feet still touched the ground but I had no leverage. Without it, I couldn't lift the trog off his feet or force him to fall backward.

I pounded my forehead into the trog's face, breaking his nose and blackening his eyes. He roared in pain but his relentless grip never broke. I tried stomping his feet but, after my first attempt, he lifted me off the ground. Then I tried kicking his shins, but he held fast and even tightened his grip.

Spots swam before my eyes as I struggled to remember my academy training in xenozoology, but nothing useful came to mind. I was sure I must have learned *something* at the academy that would help me survive this fight. And then I recalled something the academy martial arts instructor had taught us.

"Nature works pretty much the same throughout the galaxy," he'd said. "All twelve of the sentient, bipedal races are vulnerable in nearly identical ways. There just aren't many protected places in a bipedal body in which to put vital organs. Just remember, any place your body is vulnerable, chances are an alien biped is vulnerable there, too."

Remembering my punch to the kidney, I rammed my knee between the trog's legs.

The Great One's eyes rolled back and a strangled moan escaped. His grip eased and I took my first good breath in what seemed like years. My arms were still pinned, so I rammed my knee into the trog's groin a second time.

The trog's grip relaxed further and I was able to wriggle free of it. Now that I was free from the Great One's crushing grip, I put everything I had into a last kick between the trog's legs. With a howl, he reeled away from me and dropped to his knees, hands protecting his groin. I drew several great breaths and considered how to finish the fight.

"Foul blow," cried the man who had shoved me. "This human has broken the rules of engagement!"

Rules of engagement? What was such a formal military term doing in the vocabulary of a desert madman? I put the thought aside for examination later—after I finished the challenge.

The man screeched something in the trog tongue before turning back to me. He said, "Your actions condemn you. The challenge is forfeited."

The trogs closest to me raised their spears and advanced.

What Are You?

Sometimes events reduce your choices so severely that there is only one thing to do. I did it.

Boost!

I was becoming quite used to the feeling of invulnerability as adrenaline flooded my system and time seemed to slow. The trog translator was bending to grab my sword. I flashed across the two meters separating us and drew the sword even as his hand wrapped around the scabbard. I slashed his chest in passing as I rushed the closest trogs.

I was among the trogs before they could react, a deadly blur who was too close for spear attacks. I broke a trog's knee with a kick, slashed the shoulder of a trog to my right, then punched another in front of me. Spinning, I hacked off the arm of one who had been behind me. Never stopping, I fell backward into a roll, came up in front of a fifth trog, and drove my sword into his gut. Yanking the blade free, I whirled to face the attack that I knew must be coming from the rest of the trogs.

There was no attack. All around me, the trogs backed away, pointing and muttering.

The translator, blood flowing down his chest, stared at me, agape.

"Y-you're the one from the alley yesterday," he said.

Dropping Boost before it dropped me, I nodded.

"And it had to be you in the bar last night," he continued.

"You're leaving out the trap door in the desert trading post and your scouting party the day before that," I said.

"I shouldn't have asked *who* you are earlier," the translator said. "I should have asked *what* you are."

"I'm just a man," I said.

"How many have you killed?" he asked.

"Just trogs, or should I count the men who got in my way, too?" I asked. "And, if you don't want that number going up by one, you'll keep your mouth shut unless I give you permission to speak."

The translator's eyes widened.

"As the new leader of this trog army-" I began.

"No!" rasped the Great One, staggering to his feet. "Have not yielded."

Didn't this Great One know when to give up? Anger washed over me, building with each step as I stalked toward the swaying trog leader. Dropping my sword so there could be no question that I had fought hand-to-hand, I slugged the Great One with an uppercut to the chin. His eyes rolled back and he fell backward, landing with a thud.

I glared at the trogs surrounding me and yelled, "*Now* he yields."

Fifteen Years

My proclamation was echoing from the buildings surrounding the park when the penned prisoners began cheering. That was a pleasant change from the translator's I-hope-you-die-screaming-in-agony glower. The trogs were silent, milling about, unsure how to respond to my unexpected victory.

Retrieving my sword, I walked over to the translator. I smiled broadly into his glower.

"Do you have any idea," he said, "how long it took me to insinuate myself into trog society? To learn their vile language? To manipulate them into this campaign?"

"Why, no, I don't know," I said. "You know what else? I don't care."

"Fifteen years, that's how long! Fifteen years feigning subservience to these brutes. Fifteen years of humiliation at their hands. All for *this* invasion of Mordan," he cried. "And you ruined all of my work in fifteen minutes."

"You're giving me too much credit," I said. "Our airship crashed in the city yesterday afternoon. So, really, it's more like fifteen hours."

The translator's face went purple with rage. With a bellow, he took a swing at my jaw. I stepped aside, grabbed his wrist, and flipped him onto his back.

Standing over the translator, I said, "As the new leader of this army of trogs, I order them to go home and disperse."

I waved toward the trogs, "Translate that order for them."

The translator stood and shouted something in the trog language. The trogs hefted their spears and turned toward the human prisoners. The cheering within the pen died as the trogs closed in.

I smashed the translator's head with the pommel of my sword. He fell in a heap as I ran toward the prisoners. I dodged through the trogs, ready to Boost if any of them attacked me or tried to block my path. None did. Maybe they thought I was leading the attack. Maybe they were too afraid of me to lift a spear against me.

Breaking through the ranks of advancing trogs, I held my hands up and willed the trogs to stop.

"No," I shouted, waving my arms. "I didn't order this. Go back!"

The only trog who understood human speech lay unconscious twenty meters away. The only human who spoke trog couldn't be trusted to speak to the trogs, even if he had been conscious. And the approaching trogs didn't understand a word I said. For all I know, they thought I was urging them on. Or maybe they thought I was crazy. But hundreds of trogs bore down on the captive citizens of Faroon.

An Unexpected Arrival

The screams of terrified people filled my ears. The advancing trogs, spears lowered, filled my vision. The threat of Boost Burnout filled my mind. The sorrow that I would never see Callan again filled my heart.

Above the screams, I could hear the roaring of my blood, ready for one last Boost.

A few meters to my left, a trog stumbled and pitched forward. One in front of me dropped his spear and clutched his arm. A third toppled backward.

All along the advancing line, trogs screamed and fell as crossbow bolts rained out of the brightening morning sky. The roaring I'd heard over the screams hadn't been my blood, after all. Vibrations shook my insides as I looked up.

A shadow fell across me as Martin Bane's airship rumbled overhead. Martin leaned against the rail, directing the firing of at least two dozen of his crew. They fired crossbows in rotating volleys, keeping a steady stream of quarrels raining down on the trogs. His airship was so low I could count the rings on Martin's fingers. His fleet flew in formation to either side of his ship. Each of the other airships also had rows of airmen firing crossbows.

Bane spotted me and sketched a salute, all the while keeping his attention on the firing line.

"Drive 'em back, lads!" he called. "And watch out for that young man waving the sword about like a fool. Her Highness will be quite put out if we damage him."

Confused, frightened, many of them wounded, the trogs were driven back by the aerial onslaught. The two outer flanks of airships pulled ahead of the others, encircling the trogs and driving them into a packed mass at the center of the park. One trog finally made a big show of throwing down his spear and dropped to his knees. Those around him followed his lead and it spread until all of the trogs knelt, unarmed, inside the circle of airships.

"Cease fire!" Bane bellowed.

The airmen stopped shooting but they all kept their crossbows cocked and trained on the trogs.

I ran over to the Great One. He was groaning but was still laying where I'd left him just a few minutes before.

"Get up," I said, grabbing his arm and pulling. "Now, tell your army to put their hands on their heads and wait for further orders."

The big trog spoke and the trogs did as I'd instructed.

I looked around, trying to spot the translator. I didn't see him anywhere. In all the confusion, the translator had escaped.

20

PUDDLE OF BLOOD

"You look like you've lost something, Rice," Bane called from above.

"Not some*thing*, some*one*. A man who was working with the trogs and speaks their language," I said. "He's got steel gray hair, a white beard, and was bare-chested. Can you see anyone like that from up there?"

Bane and some of his crewmen looked, but it was a futile hope. The park and town square were filled with people looking for loved ones, shouting thanks to the airship crews, jeering at the trogs, and crying for lost loved ones. Besides, it was probable the translator had run into the city. He could be hiding anywhere by now. I had no illusions that Bane would find him.

"No sign of anyone matching your description," Bane said, after a few minutes, "but I'll have my crew keep watch."

I had a feeling allowing the translator to get away would come back to haunt me, but I'd deal with him if he ever turned up again. I had far more things to worry about right now.

"Drop a line and come on down," I told Bane. "We've got some planning to do."

After Bane and some of his men were down, I said, "You cut it a little close there at the end. Did it really take you that long to defeat the trog airships?"

"It wasn't an easy job, Rice. We had to find ways to beat the trogs without harming the human crews on the airships," Bane said. "It took a while, but I thought it was what Her Highness would want."

"I can safely say Callan will be pleased with your actions, both against the airships and against the trogs," I said. "Mentioning Callan, I need to let her know everything worked out. I've got a crossbowman on a nearby rooftop who can take word to her. His name is Tal. Can you send someone to get him?"

Bane picked a crewman and I told him where to find Tal.

As the crewman ran off, Bane asked, "Have you got any idea what you're going to do with all those trogs?"

"Yes, tell now," said the Great One.

"I'm going to send them home and have them return to their tribes," I said. "They'll be unarmed and escorted by some of our airships."

"As long as the escorts will continue to receive the same pay rate, there won't be any problems," Bane said.

I turned to the Great One, "As for you, if you ever lead an army against humans again, I will personally kill you and have any who follow you hunted down like animals."

"Warrior's threat. You make good Great One," the trog said. He started walking toward the sitting trogs, "I tell them."

We were turning back to our planning when we spotted Bane's crewman returning at a run.

"I checked the roof," he said, gasping. "All I found was a puddle of blood."

The Return of Gort

Bane and some of his men came with me to check out the scene on the rooftop. The puddle of blood lay right where Tal had been kneeling when last I saw him. The blood had to be Tal's, but who had attacked him and why had they taken Tal with them?

"Everyone spread out and look for a club or something similar. It will have blood stains on it," I said.

"Wouldn't the attacker have kept his weapon?" Bane asked.

"Not if all he had was a club," I said. "Tal had a sword and crossbow, nice upgrades over a big stick."

One of Bane's crew found the blood-stained club on the ground below the roof and it told the whole story. It was one of the table legs Sarn had used to fight the trogs last night. Only one person had been in the bar when we'd left.

Gort.

"I know who attacked Tal," I said. "I'm sure the guy enjoyed clubbing Tal, but I'm his real target."

"You seem to make enemies everywhere you go, Rice. Maybe you should work on your people skills," Bane said. "What did you do to irritate this guy?"

"I ruined his little gang, which included Tal at the time. Then Tal whacked him with a chair and came over to my side," I said. "Tal knows where we've been hiding and Gort strikes me as the viciously persuasive type of thug. I've got to make sure Callan is safe. We can search for Tal after that."

"Want me to come with you?" Bane asked. "Or some of my men?"

"No," I sighed. "The situation between the trogs and humans isn't stable. All it takes is one person deciding to get a little revenge and we'd have a massacre on our hands. I need you to keep it under control."

Bane nodded, then surprised me by pulling my Onesie out of his pocket.

"If you're going to go alone, you'd better take this," he said. At my incredulous look, he grinned, "It wasn't ruined, just depleted. And in pieces. Yes, I lied. Raider, remember?"

Pocketing the gun, I ran off. As I got closer to the hiding place, I scanned for blood or signs of a struggle. I didn't see anything, but that didn't mean anything. I had to assume Gort had gotten here ahead of me.

At the door, I tapped out the signal we'd agreed on and then pushed the door open.

Gort sat against the far wall, Tal's crossbow aimed at me. Raoul was nowhere to be seen.

"It's him," Gort said.

Raoul's voice came from my left, probably from the corner nearest the door, "Shoot him!"

Got Him

The scene inside the hiding place seared into my brain. Tristan, Nist, Milo, Sarn, and Tal sat huddled against the far wall, hands bound behind their backs and eyes wide. Milo's sister Kim lay in the small bed beside them, her hands tied to the bed. She watched it all through heavy-lidded eyes. Gort crouched in the left corner, a feral grin splitting his face as the crossbow tracked toward me. Raoul was somewhere to the left of the doorway. I didn't see Callan at all. Raoul was probably holding a knife at her throat.

My sole advantage was that neither Raoul nor Gort had seen me Boost. Raoul had heard about it, but he'd run away before I Boosted in the alley.

Boost!

The *twang* of the crossbow stretched as time slowed. I fell backward, raising my hands as if to ward off the bolt. I caught the bolt just before it struck my head. I cried out as if I'd been hit, masking the sound as I snapped the bolt in two.

Dropping Boost, I lay on the ground, twitching and thrashing as if suffering the throes of death. The movement distracted Gort as I scraped the bolt tip across my forehead, just above my right eye. Blood welled and ran profusely, as head cuts always do, and I held the back end of the bolt over my right eye. I hid the bolt tip against my left forearm then let that arm flop to the ground. I kept my left eye open and stared at a spot on the ceiling.

"Well, what happened?" asked Raoul.

"Got him through the eye," Gort crowed, hopping up and capering about.

From the left, I heard Callan moan as Raoul said, "Stop celebrating and make sure he's dead."

Gort approached cautiously and saw just what he expected to see. He grabbed my foot and dragged me into the room. I kept my stare unfocused.

"*David!*" Callan shrieked.

Raoul had been holding a knife to her throat but he let it drop when he saw me. Callan broke free from his grip and dropped to my side. Perfect. She was blocking the view of both the prince and the thug.

I thrust the bolt tip into her hand and whispered, "Stab Raoul or Gort. I'll take it from there."

He Means Something Else

Raoul grabbed Callan's arm and pulled her back against the wall. Right next to him.

"That is enough, Callan," he said. "These histrionics over the death of a mere guard are beneath you. A woman of your station must stand aloof from the petty concerns of your subjects."

"You are an insufferable prig, Raoul. I will make you pay for all that you have done to me and mine," Callan said. "In pain and blood, I will make you pay."

Callan stabbed the crossbow tip into Raoul's thigh and then twisted the shaft after it had sliced through muscle. Raoul screamed as blood soaked his pants leg. Callan spun away from him and he fell to the floor.

Gort, who had cocked and reloaded the crossbow, raised it to take a shot. The whine of the Onesie echoed in the small room as I fired from the hip. My hasty shot hit Gort's crossbow and it exploded into a thousand pieces. Splinters ripped into Gort's face and neck. Gort opened his mouth to scream and blood gushed from it. He fell back into the corner, his body quivering as his life drained onto the floor.

Raoul was rolling back and forth holding his wounded leg, his face white with pain, when I pressed my sword to his throat.

A line of blood welled under my blade as I said, "Please, Raoul, give me an excuse to end this. Any excuse at all."

Raoul's knife clattered on the floor and I swept it away with my foot, sighing, "I guess you're not as stupid as I thought, Raoul. What a pity."

Callan picked up Raoul's knife and set to cutting the bonds holding our friends.

Tristan came straight over to tend to Raoul's leg. He was rubbing his wrists and shaking his hands, trying to get feeling back in them.

"Bring my bag, Nist. I'll remove the shaft once my hands stop tingling." Gesturing toward Gort's still-jerking body, he added, "Milo, cover the body with a spare blanket."

Once all the bonds had been cut, Callan ran to me and wrapped her arms around me. She pulled me close and kissed me hard.

"Don't you ever scare me like that again," she said, tears streaming down her cheeks and soaking into my shirt.

I held her tightly and said, "As you wish."

In a stage whisper, Milo said, "Kim, he keeps saying that to her but I think he means something else. Am I right?"

"Oh yeah, Milo, you're right," Kim replied in another stage whisper.

"Then why doesn't he just say what he means?" Milo asked.

Why indeed?

I looked into Callan's eyes, still shining with tears, and said, "I know very little about your country, Callan, but Mordan claims my heart because it claims your heart. Mordan holds my oath because you hold my oath. Mordan is my country because it is your country.

"Callan Debah Lois Antrulta Ziliah Villas, my life has no meaning without you. My heart has no purpose without you. I love you," I said. "Will you marry me?"

Wiser Advise

Leave it to Raoul to spoil the proposal I'd been rehearsing for the last two days.

"Idiot!" said Raoul through clenched teeth. "Callan is betrothed to a Tartegian prince. She would never give that up for the likes of *yargh*!"

"Oh, I am sorry, Prince Raoul," Tristan spoke in a monotone. "My hand slipped. It's probably because the ropes you used to tie us up cut off the blood flow to my hands. I do hope that didn't hurt."

"Raoul, your counsel is neither sought nor desired," Callan said. "I have already received far wiser advice on this matter than you could ever give."

"When could you have receive that?" I asked. "I *just* popped the question."

"Days ago, under the city of Beloren," Callan said.

I remembered Rob pulling Callan close and speaking softly to her just before he gave me his sword. "Do you mean Rob's last words to you?"

Callan nodded, "Yes, that's when he gave me his advice."

I said, "But he had already made his opinion *extremely* clear when we kissed on the airship, back before the sandstorm hit."

"He hadn't known you very long then," Callan said. "You'd been with us less than a day and had spent a lot of that time sleeping."

"That's true, but he hadn't known me very much longer when he died," I said.

"Rob always was a shrewd judge of character, David. You impressed him, and Rob wasn't a man who was easily impressed." Callan looked into my eyes. "What he told me was 'Marry Rupor if you must. Marry David if you can.'"

Out of the corner of my eye, I saw Raoul open his mouth. Tristan shoved a liquor bottle into Raoul's mouth and turned the bottle up.

"So, which is it? 'Must' or 'can'?" I asked.

Callan's lips spread into a smile and she said, "Can."

Our friends cheered so loudly we couldn't even hear Raoul's outraged sputtering. Not that I was trying to hear him. I was too busy kissing my future wife.

"David Rice?" a voice rose over the cheering.

One of Bane's men stood in the doorway.

"How did you find us?" I asked.

"I ain't deaf, son," he said, motioning at our cheering friends. "Cap'n sends his compliments and requests you join him at the town square."

"What's happening?" I asked, fearing riots or worse.

"Cap'n put ships out on scout duty after we won the air battle," the man said. "One of the scouts is steaming back to the city with a Tartegian warship on its tail."

21

TARTEGIANS

Damn the Tartegians. I didn't even get to finish kissing Callan.

"Tal, how are you feeling?" I asked, still holding my bride-to-be close.

"I'm okay," he said. "Gort didn't hit anything important—just my head."

"Then you're in charge of Raoul. You won't need brains for that; just keep him quiet and out of sight," I said. "I don't care how you do it, just don't do any permanent damage to him."

Tal grinned and gave a mock salute. Raoul sputtered with more outrage, which made me smile.

To Bane's crewman, I said, "Please get some more men and get rid of that body."

The crewman gave a much better salute than Tal and left.

"Tristan, do you need anything?" I asked.

"I'm fine, lad," he said, "though Nist could use some help mending my airship. We'll want the *Pauline* air-worthy so we can take Her Highness on the last leg of her journey home."

"I'll see how many men Bane can spare," I said. "Milo, come with us in case we need to send a message back here."

Milo grinned, falling in behind us as I took Callan's hand.

The park was bustling when we arrived. Bane had men guarding the trogs, men tending the sick and wounded citizens, and men patrolling the streets of the city.

"What news have you got for us?" I called.

Bane turned, his eyes immediately tracking to our clasped hands.

Arching an eyebrow, he said, "I suspect you're the one with the news. Am I correct in assuming congratulations are in order? Do you think her father will approve? And, of the utmost importance, do I get to kiss the bride-to-be?"

"When my father hears what David has done *for* me," Callan smiled, tilting her cheek so Bane could plant a kiss, "and what Raoul and his mother have done *to* me, I think he'll come around."

A shadow passed over us as the scout ship drifted up. It dropped lines to crewmen on the ground but the crew stayed at their stations, all eyes on the pursuing airship. The Tartegian warship came up close behind the scout ship, armed men crowding its rails.

An officer stood in the bow and, his voice booming, called, "We seek the man called Martin Bane. I hold a royal order for his arrest."

Shoot Him Now!

"Captain," Callan called, "why is a Tartegian warship attempting to enforce a Mordanian royal order? For that matter, why is a Tartegian warship in Mordanian skies at all? You are allowed in our skies to escort royalty, nothing more."

Murmurs of assent rose from the people in the park, all of whom had stopped to watch this drama play out.

"I am not in the habit of explaining my actions or my orders to random young women," the officer said, contempt in his voice. "Now, if you please, direct me to the *man* in charge, young woman."

Conversation in the park died away at this response. That meant my next words were heard by all.

"The proper form of address to this young lady is 'Your Highness.' Further, I will hear a proper tone of respect in your voice when next you speak or you will answer to my blade!"

Callan crossed her arms and did something I would have sworn was impossible if I hadn't seen it for myself. She looked *down* on a man floating twenty-five meters above her.

"That was a nice touch, David," she said quietly. "It's going to be fun having you around."

"Princess Callan?" the officer exclaimed. "Can it truly be you? You've been missing so long that some in the palace have begun to fear the worst. Prince Rupor, of course, is not among those."

Around us, voices rose again, this time in excited speculation and amazement. The kidnapped princess had turned up in their city and appeared to have had a hand in defeating the trogs. Listening to snippets of conversation, I could tell a legend had just been born. How long would it be before the story had Callan, sword waving above her head, leading the final charge against the trogs?

"You have not answered my question, Captain," Callan said.

"Of course, Your Highness," the captain said. I'll give him this, he got the tone right this time. "I'll be right down."

As the crew scrambled to lower their captain, Bane said, "What is your intention, Highness?"

"Have no fear, Martin," Callan said, "I will honor our agreement. You will not be turned over to this Tartegian."

"I had no doubts on that score, Highness," Bane said, "but if you expect a fight I must signal for my men to get into position."

"Forgive me for misinterpreting your concern, Martin. I do not expect a fight," Callan said.

The captain marched up to Callan and bowed. "Captain Hanral at your service, Your Highness. I am pleased to find you safe and well. To answer your question, we enforce the standing order of arrest issued by your father."

"And how long has that order been standing, Captain?" Callan asked.

"I am sorry, Your Highness," Hanral said, "I don't know exactly. I believe the order was issued the day after your abduction."

"Thank you, Captain Hanral. You may disregard that order," Callan said.

"I don't understand," Hanral said. "Don't you want those responsible for your kidnapping brought to justice?"

"More than you can possibly imagine, Captain," Callan said. Motioning to Bane, she added, "But Martin Bane has rendered invaluable service to Mordan and is no longer subject to arrest."

"This man is Martin Bane?" Hanral's eyes went wide.

Martin sketched a salute, "I'm so very pleased to meet you, Captain Hanral."

The captain jumped back from Bane and shouted to his crew, "Shoot this man. Shoot him now!"

Seeking Prince Raoul

My heart stopped as Callan jumped in front of Bane and shouted to the Tartegian crewmen, "You will do no such thing."

Then I jumped in front of Callan. To my immense relief, the Tartegian crewmen were already lowering their crossbows. Spinning to face Callan, I said, "Don't *do* that!"

Hanral, his face pale, added, "I must concur with your bodyguard, Your Highness."

"Well, *I* appreciate the gesture, Your Highness," Martin said. I glared at him over Callan's head and he added, "But it was rather ill conceived."

Callan, unflustered by all the commotion, turned her gaze back to Hanral. "Listen to me very carefully, Captain. I am countermanding the standing order for Martin's arrest. As of this moment it is null and void. Is that clear?"

"But Your Highness," Hanral said, "this order comes from your king. A princess cannot countermand her king."

"You *dare* to argue Mordanian law with *me*?" Callan's eyes blazed. Once again, she managed to look down upon a man who stood a full head taller than she. "You are in command of a foreign warship in Mordanian skies. Wars have begun over less. If you want to argue legalities, Captain, let's start with an explanation for that."

All thoughts of arresting Martin Bane appeared to flee from the captain's mind. Callan had neatly taken Hanral off the offensive and put him on defense.

"W-w-why I carry royal permits to sail Mordan's skies," Hanral stammered. "The permits, like the arrest order, are signed by your father. Our squadron escorted Prince Rupor to Morda and His Highness offered us to aid in the search for you, Your Highness. That is why we sail Mordan's skies."

"I see," Callan appeared to mull over the captain's answer. "You will fetch those permits when this conversation is over."

"Of course, Your Highness," Hanral replied.

"But that doesn't explain what you're doing here in Faroon," she added.

"Ah, that is easily explained, Your Highness," the captain beamed, apparently happy to have a ready answer. "We had returned to Morda to deliver a message to Prince Rupor and your father. While we were there, word came that Faroon may have been attacked. As the city was along the route back to the squadron, Prince Rupor suggested that we investigate the situation. Your father accepted his offer."

"Very well, Captain," Callan relented, "your explanation is reasonable. Have those permits brought to me and then you can be on your way to rejoin your squadron."

"Thank you, Your Highness," the captain said. "I do have one question for you, if I may?"

"Of course," Callan said.

"You are not the only person we seek," Hanral said. "We also seek Prince Raoul. Do you know where he could be found?"

A Loss For Words

"Prince Raoul was with us when our airship crashed in Faroon," Callan said. "I'm afraid we were separated shortly after that. Now that the city is once again under human control, the prince is our top priority."

Hanral's face fell, though he rallied to say, "I'm certain you will do your best, Your Highness."

"You have my word, Captain Hanral. We will not leave Faroon

without Prince Raoul," Callan said. "Now, please do not let me stop you from rejoining your squadron."

"Thank you, Your Highness," the captain said. "but that won't be necessary. All ships in my squadron have a standing order from Prince Rupor that overrides all others. Should any Tartegian ship find you or His Highness, we are to render assistance and provide escort to Morda."

I was cursing silently but Callan gave the captain a dazzling smile. "That's very kind of you and Prince Rupor. Now, could you fetch those permits you mentioned? It's important that my subjects see me verify their authenticity."

"At once, Your Highness," Hanral said.

After the captain was hoisted back to his airship, Bane asked, "What really happened with the Spare Prince?"

"He ran away the first chance he got," I said.

"And are you really going to take the time to search for him?" Bane said.

"Don't have to," I said. "We've got him tied up in a hideout not far from here. Tristan is looking after him."

"Isn't he a little old to be watching someone like Raoul?" Bane asked.

"Sorry, I wasn't clear," I said. "It turns out Tristan is a doctor. He's tending to Raoul's wounded leg."

"The trogs got him after he ran?" Bane said. "Good for them."

"No," Callan said. "I stabbed him."

Bane's mouth opened and closed twice but no words came out. It was the first time I'd seen Bane at a loss for words. Taking advantage of his silence, I told him the highlights of our time in Faroon.

"I've got no idea how we're going to keep the Tartegians from taking Raoul on their warship," I said, "but we most definitely do not want Raoul talking to any Tartegians before we get Callan home."

"Don't worry, darling," Callan said, "I've already figured that out. Milo? I want you to deliver a message to Tristan."

As Callan gave her message to Milo, I decided to have one last talk with the Great One. I wanted to ask him about the translator. By the time I returned, Milo had delivered the message and was back, also.

"Remember the human translator for the trogs?" I said. "The Great

One says the plan to form an army and invade Mordan was concocted by the translator."

"Does this translator have a name?" Bane asked.

"I only know what the trogs called him," I replied. "I had a hard time understanding what the Great One said, but it was something like Hard Hand Wind Low."

Callan cried, "Ardhan Windslow?"

Bane exclaimed, "It can't be. He's dead!"

22

WINDSLOW

"You both knew this man?" I asked. "Who is he?"

Bane bowed to Callan, gesturing for her to speak first.

"You remember the kidnapping attempt I told you about?" she asked. "When I was four and Rob earned the sword he gave to you?"

"Of course," I said. "Was Windslow one of the nobles behind the plot?"

"No, it's worse than that. Windslow was captain of the palace guard. At one time, he'd even been my uncle's personal bodyguard. My father trusted Windslow absolutely," Callan said. "The lords behind the plot bribed him to clear the path for the kidnappers. He changed guard schedules, moved guards to other positions, and bribed or threatened other guards.

"After the conspirators were discovered, those lords tried to lay most of the blame on Windslow. It didn't work and every one of them was executed, with the exception of Windslow. Somehow, he managed to escape the dungeon with the help of some petty criminal."

Comprehension dawned as another tale came to mind.

"Martin, are you the 'petty criminal' in Callan's tale?" I asked.

Callan whipped around in surprise, catching Bane's slow nod.

"We were kept in the same cell," he said. "Windslow had an escape plan, but it took two men. I was awaiting execution so of course I agreed to help. Once we were free, Windslow went to a bar in one of the poorest areas in the city. He told me he needed to arrange passage out of the country for the two of us. Windslow had me keep watch from an alley. After an hour of waiting, I went looking for him. I found his headless body in a back room."

"Are you sure it was him?" I asked.

"I didn't take time to investigate," Bane said. "The corpse had the right clothes and the right build. The head was missing, but I assumed it was Windslow and that he'd given himself away. It looks like I was fooled."

Callan said, "The lords always claimed Windslow recruited *them*, though no one believed it. I guess Martin wasn't the only one fooled by Windslow."

"Is it possible Windslow was working with Tarteg at the time?" I asked.

"There were rumors... Tarteg and Mordan have a long history of conflict," Callan said. "But I was too young to understand any of that. It was sixteen years ago, after all."

"Whatever drove Windslow to betray your family back then seems to still be driving him today," I said. "It can't be a coincidence that you were kidnapped just as Windslow decided to attack Mordan. But was Windslow working with Raoul's mother? Or does he just have a good spy network and decided to take advantage of the situation?"

Callan's face hardened, "Either way, all of this has only been possible because of my betrothal to Rupor."

Mostly Unharmed

"Everyone told me Queen Beatrice—Raoul's mother—was the one who suggested joining the kingdoms through marriage. It seems she waited until she had everything in place for her plot before making that suggestion," Callan said. "I thought the marriage would mean an end to war between our countries. Instead, it's caused more death and destruction."

"But why would she want the trogs to attack?" I asked. "How would that help turn Raoul into a hero?"

"Maybe her goal was to lure Rupor into combat," Bane said. "If Rupor dies, Raoul goes from Spare Prince to Heir Prince in the blink of an eye. That's one heck of a display of motherly love, don't you think?"

"This is giving me a headache," I said. "I'm changing the subject for a while. Martin, can you send some men to repair Tristan's airship? Milo can lead them to the *Pauline*."

"Consider it done," Martin said. He turned and began rounding up a repair team.

Callan said. "Milo, we need you to lead a repair crew to our airship. Head back to Tristan after that. Please deliver another message to him."

Callan whispered in Milo's ear for a few seconds. Milo grinned, saluted, then headed off with the crew. The salute wasn't bad for a kid who'd never given one in his life.

"Now what?" I asked.

"Now we're going to make Captain Hanral the happiest man in the city," Callan said. Raising her voice, she called, "Please tell Captain Hanral I've just received word that Prince Raoul has been found."

That caused some activity on the Tartegian airship. Within seconds, Hanral was lowered to the ground. Despite the excitement, the captain was carrying several pieces of paper. They must be the permits Callan had asked to see.

"You have news of His Highness?" Hanral asked.

"Yes, Captain. Raoul is alive and mostly unharmed," Callan said. "He's with-"

"*Mostly* unharmed?" Hanral interrupted. "What does that mean?"

Callan folded her arms and glared at the captain. Hanral had no idea why Callan was displeased. I decided to take pity on the guy.

"Pardon the Captain's *interruption*, Your Highness," I said. "I'm sure his concern for Prince Raoul's health and welfare overrode proper etiquette."

"Y-yes, that is exactly it," the captain bowed. "I humbly beg your pardon, Your Highness."

"Your dedication to Prince Raoul is commendable, Captain," Callan relented. "You need not concern yourself. Raoul has a leg wound, painful but nothing to worry about. We travel with a physician who is attending to Raoul's wound now."

"Please forgive me, Your Highness," Hanral said, "but I must insist my ship's surgeon examine His Highness."

A Fine Idea

"But of course, Captain. I'd expect nothing less from a dedicated officer such as yourself," Callan said, smiling. "I'm sure Dr. Agrilla will welcome a second opinion."

"Dr. Agrilla?" Hanral asked. "The man they call the Desert Doctor?"

"The very same," Callan said. "Is there a problem?"

"No. Not one bit," the captain said. "From all reports I've heard, Prince Raoul couldn't be in more capable hands."

"Splendid," Callan clapped her hands in delight. "Then you won't mind if Raoul stays on our ship, with his doctor?"

The captain was taken aback, "You won't be riding on my airship, Your Highness?"

"I began my return journey on Dr. Agrilla's airship," Callan said. "I'll finish it the same way."

Captain Hanral took a moment to think the situation through, balancing Tristan's reputation and a possible perceived insult to the woman he thought would be his future queen against the need to insure Raoul's survival.

"I'll defer to my surgeon. If he has no objections to His Highness riding with your doctor then I will allow it," Hanral said.

"That's a fine idea, Captain," Callan said. "Have your surgeon fetched and I'll take you to Raoul."

The captain turned to call instructions to his airship. I took a moment to pull Callan away from Hanral.

"Callan, we can't allow Raoul to talk to the surgeon or Captain Hanral," I whispered. "He'll tell them who stabbed him, for one thing, and-"

Callan placed a finger over my lips, "Raoul won't tell them anything. Milo is delivering instructions to Tristan to drug Raoul. He'll be incoherent at worst, unconscious at best."

"That's...brilliant. Our children are going to be smart *and* beautiful," I said. "But what are they going to get from me?"

"Courage, strength, conviction, quick wits, a level head in emergencies," Callan said. "I could go on, but the good Captain is looking our way."

We rejoined the captain and, soon, his surgeon joined us. Together, we set off for our hiding place. I only hoped Raoul was unconscious when we got there.

In Your Debt

Raoul's eyes were wide open when we reached the hiding place. When I walked in, his eyes swung toward me. Then they tracked past me to a spot on the wall. It looked as if Raoul was struggling to control his vision but not having much success. His eyes fluttered and then shut before Captain Hanral or the surgeon entered.

Tristan met the surgeon as he entered and the two quickly fell into a jargon-filled conversation. I got the gist of the conversation, if not the details.

"The surgeon seems impressed," I murmured to Callan. "It's good to know Tristan is as good as his reputation."

After exclaiming over the skill of Tristan's work, the surgeon asked, "Why is His Highness unconscious, Dr. Agrilla? I would have used a local anesthesia."

"As would I," Tristan said, "but Prince Raoul insisted I save that for the city's wounded. He put those people ahead of his own suffering. I gave His Highness a glass of liquor to help calm him. When he wasn't looking, I mixed a few choice drugs in with the whiskey. Knocked him right out."

"Very clever, Dr. Agrilla," the surgeon said. "Prince Raoul's bravery should be an inspiration to us all."

"I think I'm going to hurl," I whispered to Callan.

"You are so angry you wish to throw something?" Callan whispered back.

"Uh, no. It's old Terran slang, something I learned from my grandfather," I whispered. "It means to throw up, as if something were making you sick to your stomach."

"Hurl," Callan tried the word on for size. "It is much shorter than 'hugging the chamber pot.' I like it."

The surgeon addressed Captain Hanral, "Prince Raoul is in excellent hands, Captain. I see no reason why he shouldn't ride with the good doctor."

"All of Tarteg is in your debt, Dr. Agrilla," Hanral said. "Please let us know if you are in need of any medical supplies for the trip to Morda."

Hanral turned to Callan, "With your permission, Your Highness, I'll return to my airship and prepare her for escort duty."

"Of course, Captain," Callan said. "We'll leave once the *Pauline* is repaired."

Going Home

Once the Tartegians were gone, Callan addressed everyone, "Are you all ready for a trip to the palace? My father will want to thank each of you personally."

Milo was the first to respond, "Are there girls my age in the palace?"

"There are quite a few young ladies at court," Callan smiled. "I'm sure they will find a veteran of the trog war quite fascinating."

Milo grinned, "I'm in."

"I believe you already planned for Nist and me to accompany you," Tristan said, "and I wouldn't miss this for the world. But I must insist we take Kim, as well. She's still under my care."

"Of course Kim is coming with us," Callan said. "Tal? Sarn?"

"Nah," Tal said. Sarn elbowed him. "I mean, no Your Highness. Now that the trogs are gone, Sarn and me got to help get the city going again. And we got to tell a bunch of people that Gort won't be a problem no more."

Callan kissed each one on the cheek. "Take care of yourselves."

"Tristan," I said, "we'll send some crewmen over to help move Kim and the Spare Prince. Milo, stay with your sister."

As Callan and I headed back to the park, I asked, "Have you figured out what to do with Martin?"

"He has to come with us," Callan said. "The rest of the airships might cut and run if it looked like we were leaving their commander behind. Besides, I don't want someone shooting him for the bounty my father is bound to have set for him."

"You don't think it might be a bit, I don't know, startling to everyone at the palace for Martin to be on deck with us?" I asked.

"It will, but I'll be there to keep everyone calm and to explain the situation," Callan said. "Have I ever told you that you worry too much?"

"That's my job—it says so right in the description," I said.

Callan linked arms with me, "Then far be it from me to ruin your fun. Worry to your heart's content, darling."

Martin and Callan finalized their plans for the trogs and the disposition of the mercenary fleet, then Martin issued the necessary orders. He put his first mate in command of his airship and we went to the *Pauline*. Repairs were completed moments later and we all boarded the little airship.

Nist took the controls and the *Pauline* rose into the sky above Faroon. The Tartegian warship swung in front of us and the two airships set course for Morda.

The princess was finally going home.

23

APPROACHING THE PALACE

It was a lovely day for a flight, even if Raoul did wake up a few hours into the voyage. Callan and I stayed on deck, as far from Raoul as possible. More bothersome, with a Tartegian warship nearby, our behavior had to be circumspect. We could talk about anything we wanted, but we couldn't even risk holding hands. The last thing we needed was a Tartegian airman spotting us behaving in a romantic manner toward each other.

The sun lay close to the horizon when Morda came into view. The city sprawled across the horizon, far larger than any city I'd seen since my crash landing. Martin opened a small chest he'd left on deck and withdrew a flag.

Callan clapped her hands and said, "Wherever did you get that, Martin?"

Hoisting the flag, Martin said, "I spoke with the Lord of Faroon—decent chap, by the way—and he was happy to let me borrow one of the flags the city's naval squadron keeps on hand."

The flag showed Callan's family crest—a golden falcon preying on a green field—with a gold tiara above the hawk.

"I'm guessing that flag tells the world you're aboard this ship?" I said.

Callan nodded, giving Martin a dazzling smile.

Callan pointed to a vast and magnificent palace atop a low hill, directing Nist to land there. "But can you make the approach at low altitude and down that wide boulevard? It was designed with low flying airships in mind. I want my people to see that I'm safe. Martin, go below and get Raoul ready to leave the ship. I want him walking, so get him a crutch if he needs it."

Nist brought the ship in low, no more than fifty feet above the ground. Based on the cheering as we approached the city, Callan's flag had been spotted and word had raced through the city ahead of us. Heads poked out of windows and people thronged the street below. Callan, now standing in the bow, was visible to all. She waved and laughed and cried as her people welcomed her home.

Cheering crowds followed the airship up the boulevard, chanting, singing, and calling out good wishes to Callan. If her people loved her this much, I couldn't wait to see her reception at the palace.

Captain Hunter

At the palace docks, guards hurried to form ranks and palace functionaries ran about, preparing for the return of the princess. Our arrival was so unexpected, Nist docked the airship before the king and queen arrived on the scene.

A uniformed man bounded up the docking stairs, meeting Callan with a broad smile and a snappy salute. A dozen guards followed him.

"The whole country rejoices at your safe return, Your Highness!" he said.

"Thank you, Captain Hunter," Callan replied. "Are my parents on their way?"

"They should be here any second," Hunter said as gaze swept across those of us on deck. "Where is Captain Vonsteader?"

"Rob gave his life protecting me," Callan said. "This is David Rice, my new captain of the guard."

Hunter frowned, "I don't recall that name among your guardsmen, Your Highness."

"David was not a member of the guard. He saved Rob and me when trogs set upon us in the desert," Callan said.

Hunter's frown deepened.

"Rob personally took his oath," Callan said, "and David has saved my life half a dozen times since."

Hunter's frown did not change.

"And with his dying breath, Rob gave his sword to David," Callan continued.

The frown vanished and a hand shot out to grip mine, "Welcome to the Royal Guard, Captain Rice."

Two horns sounded a fanfare as a middle-aged couple entered the dockyard. A much younger man walked behind them. I felt certain the younger man was Prince Rupor.

"Nist," Callan said, "have our guest brought on deck."

Shortly, Raoul hobbled on deck, somewhat roughly aided by Martin. Captain Hunter's eyes widened.

"It's Bane!" Hunter shouted. "Cover him."

Half of the guards on deck leveled crossbows at Martin. Raoul let out a squeak and stopped moving.

"You've caught the man responsible for your abduction," Hunter said.

"Yes," Callan said, "but things aren't quite as you might think. Martin, turn Raoul over to Captain Hunter."

Martin propelled Raoul toward the guard captain. Raoul tried to dig in with his feet but his wounded leg buckled. Martin pulled Raoul up just as Raoul flailed his crutch for balance. The crutch struck a crossbowman's arm.

The guard's crossbow swung toward Callan, who had stepped forward to speak with Captain Hunter, and his finger jerked on the trigger.

Boost!

In terrible slow motion, I saw the crossbow string snap forward. With Callan between me and the quarrel, I couldn't deflect it or snatch it out of the air. So I did the only thing I could do. I flung Callan to the deck. The quarrel plucked her sleeve in passing. Then it struck my chest.

Shot

I was still Boosting, so everything around me continued in slow motion.

Captain Hunter waved to his guards to lower their crossbows.

Martin pushed Raoul aside and moved toward me.

Callan looked up from the deck. Her eyes were wide and she was screaming something I couldn't quite make out.

Maybe it was the Boost distorting sounds. I didn't think Boost had ever done that to me before, but what else could it be? Then my implant canceled Boost and I felt a terrible pain in my chest.

The world returned to normal speed. Suddenly, my legs felt wobbly. Something had caused that, if I could just remember what. Oh, right—I'd been shot.

Martin caught me before my legs gave out. He lowered me to the deck and shouted "Tristan! David's been shot!"

Callan's face appeared above me. "No no no no no," she said, shaking her head with each word.

Tears rolled down her cheeks. I wanted to raise my hand and wipe away her tears but for some reason my arms weren't working.

Callan caught my head in her hands, "David, don't you dare die on me! Do you understand? That's a royal order. You're the captain of my guard and you have to obey my orders!"

From a long way away, I heard Tristan shouting, "Get out of the way! I'm a doctor! Let me through!"

To my right, I saw Raoul watching me from where he'd fallen. He smiled wide and said, "Die Rice! Die in agony!"

Martin dropped onto Raoul's chest, grabbed Raoul's throat, and began choking him while also pounding Raoul's head into the deck. I hoped that hurt.

My view was cut off as Tristan dropped to the deck next to me. He was saying something, but I couldn't hear him.

Then everything faded to black.

24

GO TO HER

"David?"

A voice came out of the darkness. It was a voice I recognized.

"Come on, lad," the voice said. "You need to pay attention."

The voice seemed to be right in front of me. I was sure my eyes were open, but I couldn't see anything.

"Enough malingering, boy!" the voice commanded. "I expect better of you than this."

"Rob?" I asked. "Is that you?"

Rob popped into view right where I thought he should be. He looked a lot better than the last time I'd seen him. His uniform was crisp with no sign of blood anywhere.

"Of course it's me, lad," Rob said. "Who else do you think they'd send to guide you?"

"But you're dead," I said. "How could anyone send you to guide anyone? Unless... Am I dead, Rob?"

"Not yet, David," Rob replied, "but you're not in very good condition. Tristan says you could go either way."

"So, are you really here or am I delusional?" I asked.

"What difference does it make?" Rob replied.

He had a point. If I died, it wouldn't matter. If I lived, I'd convince myself it was a dream.

"So, if you were sent to guide me into the afterlife, why are you here before I'm dead?" I asked.

"Remember when you came up out of the tunnels in Beloren and threw my body at Bane's men?" Rob asked.

"Yeah, about that-" I began.

"That was brilliant, David," Rob laughed. "It was almost worth dying just for that. I got to protect Callan even after I was dead."

"I'm glad you approve," I said.

"That's why I'm here before you've died, lad," Rob said. "I've been given another last chance to protect Callan."

"I don't understand," I said. "Callan isn't in danger."

"I'm not talking about physical harm, David. Callan has lost a lot of people in the last couple of weeks," Rob answered. "It's a heavy burden to have men die for you. I know, because I carried that burden myself before I died. And my death just added weight to her burden.

"You are the reason Callan's burden didn't overwhelm her," Rob continued. "Your bravery, your compassion, your dedication, and—most of all—your love eased Callan's burden."

"I just thought I fell in love with her and she with me," I said.

"You did. And she did," Rob said. "But you showed her a future beyond her burden. You showed her the way past her grief. You gave her love and she found life again. But now her new life with you is threatened. If you die, David, she may never recover."

"No. Callan is too full of vitality, too full of life for that to happen!" I insisted.

"I wouldn't be so sure of that, David. Did you know she hasn't left your side since you came out of surgery three days ago?" Rob said. "Sometimes she talks to you, sometimes she cries for you, sometimes she just sits with you. But she's always there. Always waiting for you. Listen to her, David. She's talking right now."

I concentrated. From far away, Callan's voice came to me. "Did I ever tell you about the time Rob let me get drunk? I was sixteen and..."

My concentration broke and Callan's voice faded.

"David," Rob said, "from the moment you burst into Callan's life, you've been there for her. And now she needs you more than she's ever needed anything in her life. Go to her, lad. Be there for her again."

Rob faded from view and I found I could hear Callan quite clearly.

"...first hangover. And my last," Callan said. "Later, I realized the hangover was Rob's plan all along. Sometimes, it seemed like he was some kind of evil genius."

I opened my eyes. Callan was holding my hand, her eyes red and swollen. Tear tracks ran down her cheeks. Yet she still looked beautiful. I squeezed her hand.

"Hi honey, I'm home." I said.

"David!" Callan cried. "Oh, I was afraid I'd lost you forever."

I smiled, "No, I'll always be here for you."

Blessing

It was another day before Tristan allowed me to have visitors—besides Callan, I mean. Tristan suggested she leave and get some rest. He even tried the old stern-doctor-issuing-orders approach. Callan let him escape with his life, but it was a close thing.

My first visitors were Callan's parents, King Edwar and Queen Elaina. Callan's mother took one look at her daughter and led her off for a bath and some food. Callan tried the same refusal that had worked so well with Tristan. Her mother just overrode it and had Callan out the door in under a minute. Tristan, who had shown them in, could only watch in stupefaction as the queen bundled Callan past him.

"How did she do that?" Tristan asked.

"I have no idea," the king replied. "I'm just glad Elaina is on my side."

As soon as Tristan left us, the king said, "Callie tells me you want to marry her."

"I do," I said.

"Why?"

"Because I love her," I replied.

"Why?"

"She's feisty," I said without hesitation.

He wasn't expecting that answer and, after a brief silence, asked, "What do you mean by that?"

I smiled, "Callan is intelligent, courageous, strong-willed, and compassionate. She can even be practical, if you yell at her loud enough."

The king said, "You left 'beautiful' off your list."

"Your Majesty, neither of us is blind," I said. "I rather thought 'beautiful' was a given."

"Yet it's the first—many times the only—thing men notice," the king said.

"If I'd met Callan at court, perhaps I'd have been like other men," I said. "Even so, possessing beauty simply makes one beautiful. Callan's other qualities make her compelling."

"Did Callie give you those answers?" King Edwar asked. He must have seen me preparing to respond because he waved me down. "No, don't answer that, David. It wasn't a serious question. But I must steer this conversation toward a different matter.

"We've been holding Prince Raoul under house arrest while we wait for King Damon to arrive from Tarteg," King Edwar said. "This whole situation is a political nightmare of colossal proportions. Callan has already told me the story, but I'd like to hear it from your perspective."

Callan and her mother returned as I was wrapping up. Callan sat next to me on the bed and rested her head on my shoulder.

"Daddy, have you finished interrogating David?" she asked.

"I'd hardly call it an interrogation," her father protested.

"David, did Daddy start off by asking why you want to marry me?" Callan said.

"Well, yes," I said.

"Interrogation," Callan pronounced. "And how did he do, Daddy dear?"

"His answers were...unexpected," King Edwar said, "and quite good."

"So we have your blessing to marry?" Callan asked.

"Would it matter if I said no?" the king growled.

"Of course not, Daddy," Callan said. "But I really do want your approval. I want you to walk me down the aisle and give me away."

"Well," the king mused, "I must admit you'd be quite a bit safer if you and your staunchest defender were sleeping together..."

I felt the heat rise in Callan's cheek as she gasped, "Daddy!"

"Blast, I didn't mean *that* and you know it," King Edwar said.

"Well, we *do* want grandchildren and an heir, Edwar," Queen Elaina said. "That's never going to happen if they don't sleep together."

"Mom!" Callan cried, hiding her face in her hands.

"Good point, Elaina," King Edwar said, "but only *after* they're married."

Callan pulled her hands from her face, "So we have your blessing?"

"Of course you have our blessing, Callie," her father smiled. He turned to me, "Welcome to the family, David."

Recovery

After the king and queen left, I had a steady stream of visitors. Milo, Kim, and a girl about Milo's age visited. The girl didn't say much, but she sat close to Milo and held hands with him.

After they left, I asked Callan, "Milo already has a girlfriend here at court?"

"No, it's more like he's holding auditions for the post," Callan laughed. "Milo is quite the hero around here. The guards respect the courage he showed helping us in Faroon, the pages are in awe of his accomplishments behind enemy lines, and all the younger ladies swoon and hang on his every word. His dating schedule is so complicated, I believe Kim has taken to keeping an appointment book for him."

"I hope he can keep their names straight," I said. "Hero or not, young ladies are not amused when you call them by the wrong name."

"And how would you know this?" Callan folded her arms across her chest.

"I have been to seven settled worlds besides this one," I said. "I've met my share of women and even dated a few of them. But you're the only one I've wanted to marry."

Martin entered as Callan was rewarding me with a kiss. "If I'm interrupting something, I can come back later."

"You are," I said. "Begone foul raider."

At the same time, Callan said, "Of course not, Martin. Please stay."

So Martin pulled up a chair and told me a most amazing story.

"David, did you know you have magical powers?" he asked.

"I-. What?"

"Yes, indeed. You are so pure, just being around you can cleanse the soul of the even the most foul villain," Martin said. "Yes, David, you brought the wretched raider, Martin Bane, back from the darkness with your purifying light of truth, goodness, and the Mordanian way."

"That's crazy," I said. "Who makes this stuff up?"

"No idea," Martin said, "but I added the bit about Ardhan Windslow turning my soul toward the darkness in the first place. I was just an innocent Terran Scout before his foul influence drove me to become a raider."

"Until I saved you from the darkness and all that bunk?" I asked.

"Exactly, oh shining light in my darkness," Martin laughed.

"Callan, would you hit Martin for me?"

"It's actually a useful story, darling," Callan said. "It makes it easier for some of our subjects to accept Martin's heroism in Faroon and the pardon my father granted."

"And," Martin added, "everyone wants to hear the story straight from the devil's mouth. I haven't had to pay for a drink in days."

"As long as no one asks me to make blind men see and lame beggars walk, I suppose I can live with it," I said.

We chatted for a while longer, then Martin said, "That's your third yawn in five minutes, David. Either I'm boring—which I know isn't true —or you need some rest. I'd best be going."

As he rose, I said, "One more thing, Martin. Now that you're all purified and everything, I have a request for you."

Martin hesitated a second, then said, "Name it."

"Strange as it may seem, you're the best friend I've got on this planet. Scratch that. You're the best friend I've got on any planet. Would you be the best man in our wedding?"

For the second time since I'd met him, Martin Bane was at a loss for words. After several attempts to speak, he just nodded.

As One

The next day, King Damon of Tarteg arrived. The situation had been tense enough with just Prince Rupor around. It got worse with his father on hand. Prince Raoul was released into his father's custody, but he was restricted to the chambers set aside for visiting royalty.

For once, I was happy to be restricted to bed rest. It allowed me to avoid most of the difficult diplomatic wrangling. Not even doctor's orders could save me from being called upon to tell my tale to King Damon. He was escorted to my room and spent three hours grilling me. No detail escaped his notice and I was exhausted by the time he was finished with me.

"Do you think he believes us?" I asked Callan when we were alone.

"Yes," she answered. "He wishes he didn't and who can blame him? But he knows Queen Beatrice and he knows Raoul."

"What about Rupor? How is he taking all of this?"

"I think Rupor is embarrassed and ashamed of Raoul," she said. "Rupor is also not very fond of you. I think it has something to do with stealing his woman. According to Milo, the Tartegian royal guards are upset, too. He says they were looking forward to watching my backside."

Callan heaved a theatrical sigh and wiggled her backside, "When the Tartegians leave, who will I get to watch my backside?"

A slight gurgling sound came from the door. Tristan was standing in the doorway, his eyes wide and his face red.

"It appears Tristan is already watching it," I said. "Problem solved."

Tristan turned brighter red, "You seem to have survived your royal interview in fine fettle." Backing out of the room, he said, "Well done, my boy."

Callan collapsed into my arms and we laughed long and hard.

The next day, the Tartegian delegation left. Raoul would be given an airship and sent into exile. Queen Beatrice was to spend the rest of her days in a convent. Callan and I were just glad to put the whole affair behind us.

The day after that, Tristan allowed me to get up and walk. Callan was there, helping and encouraging me. A short walk left me gasping, but I had begun to hate lying around in bed. I pushed myself hard to make sure I was ready for the wedding and all of the festivities that would follow the ceremony.

Five weeks after I was shot, I stood next to Martin before the gathered nobility of a dozen countries. My heart was hammering as the cathedral doors were thrown open and I beheld my bride. Callan was radiant, more beautiful than I could ever have imagined. I'm told her father looked splendid, as well. I never even noticed him.

The ceremony passed in a blur. We gave our vows and had our first kiss as husband and wife. Then it was down the aisle and into a waiting carriage. We paraded through the streets of Morda, cheered by thousands of subjects who had turned out to see their beloved princess and her new husband. At the end of the parade was the wedding reception, with dancing and dining.

It was late before we were allowed to escape the festivities. An honor guard, led by Captain Hunter, escorted us to our chambers. Captain Hunter held the door as I carried Callan across the threshold and closed it once we were inside. At long last, we were alone.

We fell into each other's arms, time went away, and we were as one.

SCOUT'S MERIT

1

LATE NIGHT INTERRUPTION

Callan and I lay entwined in each other's arms. Moonlight shone through the windows, casting the room into a harsh contrast of deep shadows and silver light. My gaze was drawn, as always, to my wife's face and the soft curve of her shoulder. I felt anew the wonder that this beautiful princess had fallen in love with me—a crash-landed Terran scout with no lineage and no family within fifty light-years of her kingdom.

Her beauty so captured my attention that I did not consciously notice the murmur of conversation outside our door until it stopped. We rarely had anyone come to our rooms at this late hour. My curiosity piqued, I carefully disentangled myself from Callan, pulled on some pants, and padded to the door. More out of habit than worry, I grabbed my sword before opening the door.

The guard in the hallway turned an inquiring look my way. "Yes, my prince?"

I didn't recognize this guard, but there were quite a few new faces in the Royal Guard. Captain Hunter had to replace the brave men who gave their lives defending Callan when she had been kidnapped just a few months before.

"I thought I heard voices, Corporal...?"

"Evans, Your Highness."

"Pleased to meet you, Evans. And it's just Captain Rice or, when it's just the two of us, David," I said. "I'm the prince consort, not an actual prince."

"Yes sir." Evans said nothing about voices.

"Voices, Corporal?"

"Oh, yes sir! It was nothing. Just my superior officer checking in on me." Evans flashed a smile, his eyes not meeting mine. It was obvious he didn't want to talk about it any further. Perhaps he'd gotten a bit of a dressing down.

"Very well, Evans. As you were."

Evans released the breath I hadn't realized he'd been holding. "Sorry to have disturbed you, sir."

After locking the door, I stared at it for a few seconds. I couldn't put my finger on it, but something didn't feel right.

"Are you going to stare at that door all night, prince consort," Callan said, "or come back to bed and consort with the princess?"

"The things I do to insure the royal succession..." I heaved a theatrical sigh.

"Mordan appreciates your unstinting dedication to duty."

"Only Mordan?" I asked, slipping into Callan's arms.

Callan kissed me deeply, giving me all the answer I needed.

Distracted as I was, I wouldn't have heard the door to our balcony open if it hadn't had a squeaky hinge. But the squeak drew my attention.

Someone was sneaking into our room.

Unexpected Visitors

I rolled out of bed, drawing my sword from the scabbard hanging on the bed post. My arm was back, ready to swing at the small figure slipping into the room when I realized who it was.

"Milo? What do you think you're doing?"

Milo put his finger to his lips. "Shhhh. Get dressed, David. Something's not right in the palace."

Behind me, I heard Callan get out of bed. Milo's eyes went wide.

Stepping in front of Milo, I said, "Callan, you're giving Milo an eyeful."

"Pish, David. Milo lived with his sister in a single room for years. I'm sure he's seen a woman's bare backside before."

Milo leaned to his right, trying to look around me. "I have, you know."

I stepped to my left to block Milo's line of sight again. "Seeing your sister's backside is not the same as seeing my wife's backside."

The rustle of clothing came from behind me. "I'm wearing a shift now, darling. Stop worrying about what Milo is going to see and start worrying about what he is going to say."

I reached for my clothes, nodding at Milo to fill us in.

"Things are too quiet in the palace, even for this time of night," Milo began. "And I don't recognize any of the guards."

That got my attention. As a court page, Milo was expected to know all of the guards.

Milo continued, "When I tried to come up here to talk to you, the guards at the ground floor door to the stairs wouldn't let me pass and ordered me to go to bed. I had to scale the palace wall to a third floor window to get around them."

Certain of the answer, I asked, "Was that you talking to the guard at our door a few minutes ago?"

"Yeah. He wouldn't let me knock on the door and threatened to have me beaten if I didn't clear off. I acted all scared and pretended to go away. Then I slipped through a door, onto a balcony, and got here jumping from balcony to balcony."

"Milo!" Callan gasped. "It's a hundred-foot drop from those balconies. What if you'd missed a jump?"

Milo shrugged. "I didn't."

Our hushed conversation was interrupted by the sound of a key being inserted into the lock of our door.

Keep Callan Safe

Whoever was outside the door was taking it slowly, trying very hard to minimize noise. Unlike the squeaky door, I doubt I'd have heard the key if I still lay within Callan's embrace.

Safe rooms had been built adjoining each of the royal bedrooms after an unsuccessful attempt to kidnap Callan when she was four years old. The doors, designed to blend in with the walls, were quite sturdy. It would take ten to fifteen minutes for a band of determined men to break one of them down. Under normal circumstances, that was far longer than it would take the alarm to be sounded and the royal guards to arrive. From what Milo had said, I suspected the situation was far from normal. I had to assume we were on our own.

"Callan, Milo, get into the safe room," I whispered.

Callan touched a spot on the wall and a door popped open. "What about you, David?"

"I don't think we can count on the palace guards arriving any time soon," I replied. "I've got to stay out here and drive the attackers off."

"I can help." Daggers appeared in Milo's hands. He looked like such an innocent kid it was hard to remember he'd grown up on the streets.

"No, Milo," I said. "If something happens to me, I need you to keep Callan safe."

The boy stood a bit straighter. "You can count on me."

"I know I can. Now get into the safe room, both of you."

For once, Callan didn't argue. The safe room door clicked shut just before the lock in the hallway door clicked open.

I took three quick steps and pressed against the wall next to the hinges of the hall door. In the moonlight, I watched the door knob slowly turn and then the door inch open. I expected light to shine through the widening crack but none did. Whoever it was obviously hoped to slip into the room unnoticed and catch Callan and me unawares.

Five sword-wielding shapes glided silently in through the door, fanning out at the foot of the bed. One of the men carried a tightly shuttered lantern. It looked like they hoped to blind us by opening the lantern just as they made their move. Their plan probably would have worked, too, if it hadn't been for Milo. I no longer begrudged the boy his look at Callan's bare backside.

One of the men held up his hand, fingers splayed. He tucked in his thumb, then his little finger. It was a countdown to insure all five acted at once and with absolute surprise.

My lips curled up in a smile. Time to crash their surprise party.

Boost!

On the count of two, I stepped forward, grabbed the assassin with the lantern and threw him into the leader. The two men went down in a heap. The lantern rolled free, a small puddle of flaming oil pooling on the floor. I spun to my left and kicked one of the other assassins under the chin with all of my Boosted strength. His head snapped back with an audible crack. Neck broken, the assassin fell twitching to the floor.

I had hoped my sudden attack would scare off the others. It didn't. The two assassins still standing moved toward me with skill and deliberation. Backing toward the safe room door, I readied my sword and waited for their attack.

As the assassins attacked, it was obvious they had worked and trained together. They pressed their attack with a level of coordination I'd never faced in my short time on this planet. From the first cross of our swords, I was on the defensive. I was so busy parrying their attacks I was unable to mount any attacks of my own. Behind them, the leader and the lantern bearer were rising to their feet. I was hard pressed fighting two on one, I'd have no chance at all fighting four on one.

Gambling that I had learned the rhythm of the two assassins facing me, I went on the offensive. I parried an attack from the assassin on the left then lunged at the assassin on the right. My unexpected and reckless attack slipped past his guard. The point of my sword pierced his eye and drove into his brain. The assassin reeled back, screaming. The other assassin kept his attention fully on me and I just managed to jump back ahead of his next attack. Before I could take advantage of the one on one situation, the other two assassins joined him.

The three men fought with the same attention and coordination I'd been facing from two men. I was sorely pressed keeping these three assassins at bay. My sword flashed and I danced back and forth just ahead of their blades. I found no openings for attack and knew I'd never get away with the surprise attack I'd used seconds before.

The leader sized up the situation and grinned. "Just be patient, lads.

He can't keep this up for more than a few minutes. He'll tire and then we'll have him."

Devilishly Hard to Wind

The leader of the assassins was right. I might hold these men off for several minutes, but one of them would get past my guard or I'd eventually suffer Boost Burnout. My only hope was to take as many of them with me as possible. I prepared to attack, planning to ignore defense entirely and concentrate on killing these three men. I fully expected to die from the wounds they would inflict.

Then I heard the door open behind me.

"Callan," I said. "That door is going to be your only protection in a minute or two. Shut and bar it!"

"Don't be daft, darling," Callan said, her voice rock steady. "And could you stand in one place for a second or two?"

I had no idea what she had in mind, but the eyes of the assassin leader had gone wide as Callan spoke. I did as she requested.

I heard a sharp snap over my shoulder and a crossbow bolt buried itself between the eyes of the assassin leader. The confident grins vanished from the faces of the remaining assassins.

"Don't let those two escape," Callan said. "This crossbow is devilishly hard to wind."

"Try this, Your Highness," Milo said.

"Oh, well done, Milo," Callan said.

I heard the crossbow hit the floor then Callan said, "Darling, duck."

I dropped to one knee. The assassins looked perplexed. Then the Onesie whined and the assassin who had pretended to be a guard flew back against our bed. The gun had punched a fist-sized hole through his chest.

I'd hoped the remaining assassin would run, giving me a chance to capture and question him. I had no such luck. The sudden reversal of fortune unnerved him. He panicked and attacked wildly. Unable to disarm him, I ran the man through.

I dropped Boost then swept Callan and Milo into a fierce hug. "I'd have died if it weren't for the two of you."

"I picked the Onesie out of your pocket when you stood in place so Callan could shoot the crossbow," Milo said. "I hope you don't mind."

"You did fine," I said, tousling his hair.

"Winding the crossbow took so long," Callan said, her calm beginning to unravel now that the fight was over. "I was afraid I wouldn't be-"

I interrupted her with a kiss, "That was quick thinking, dear. I didn't even know there were weapons in the safe room."

The assassin I'd run through groaned. He wasn't dead.

Dropping next to him, I caught his head in my hands. "Who hired you? Were you trying to kill us or capture us?"

"W-water..."

Milo ran to our bedside table and grabbed the water pitcher kept there. I poured a trickle of water into the man's mouth.

"T-thanks." He licked his lips. "K-kill you. Capture princess. Already have parents."

Callan gasped at that. Her parents had been out of the country on a diplomatic mission. They were expected back tomorrow afternoon.

"Who hired you?" I asked again.

The man shook his head, refusing to answer. He'd just given up what he had to see the anguish on our faces.

"We don't need him to tell us anything else, David." She looked into the eyes of the dying man. "It can only be Ardhan Windslow. This kidnapping attempt is just like the one he planned sixteen years ago. Tell me I'm wrong, assassin."

I glanced from the assassin to Callan. The rising emotions of a moment ago were gone. Her face was hard and her eyes were as cold as the depths of space. Under her glare, the assassin nodded.

Without another word, Callan stood. "Milo, find Martin and bring him up here. Tell no one else what has happened."

Milo nodded and dashed out the door.

"You're not going to summon the guards?" I asked.

"No," she said, striding to her wardrobe. "My parents lives may depend on secrecy. Having a couple of dead assassins found in our room will help, too."

2

ROB THE TREASURY

"I'M SURE YOU'VE COME UP WITH A GREAT PLAN," I SAID, "BUT COULD YOU explain it to me?"

Behind me, the dying assassin convulsed, gurgled, and breathed his last.

"Windslow hired these men to kidnap me," Callan replied, "so I'm going to let him think his men got me. We leave a couple of bodies in the room—testament to your abilities—then we slip out of the palace without letting anyone else know we're leaving. The logical assumption will be that we've been kidnapped. We'll have a day or two before Windslow figures out what really happened. We've got to use that time to find my parents."

"Won't that leave the country in chaos?"

"That's why our first stop is going to be my uncle's fief. I'll send him back here to take the throne until we get my parents back. It's a long shot but Windslow hasn't had a lot of time to plan or prepare for this. If we put our minds to it, I think we can figure out where he's holding them."

"What's Martin's part in all of this?" I asked.

"The same as it was when the trogs took the city of Faroon," Callan responded. "I need a fleet for the search and involving the navy would tip our hand to Windslow. Besides, I'll need to be directly involved if this plan is going to work, and the navy would insist on keeping me out of harm's way."

"I want to keep you out of harm's way, too."

"I know, David. But I won't have to argue with you like I would the admiralty." She tilted her head and batted her eyelashes.

I sighed. "Which bodies do you want to leave in our room?"

Callan and I spent the next several minutes setting the scene in our room.

"My but you two have been busy," Martin said as he and Milo slipped into the room. Martin winked. "And you've killed five assassins, too."

Callan didn't even crack a smile. "I need you to gather a fleet for me again, Martin."

"Um, correct me if I'm wrong, but aren't we in the palace? Don't you have a whole navy at your command?"

"Did Milo fill you in on the situation?" Callan asked. At Martin's nod, she continued, "What do you think will happen if I go to the Royal Navy with this?"

Martin grimaced, "Hours wasted while the naval brass debate and dither and make plans. You'd be placed under heavy guard and end up trying to command a search of the north country from the palace."

"Right. Windslow would see the navy coming from miles away. He'd cut his losses, kill my parents, and disappear." Callan's voice flattened. "I won't let either one of those things happen."

"If you want it kept quiet, I'll need hard currency to hire the ships. Money buys silence—credit, not so much." Martin glanced around the room. "Have you got much money in here?"

"I don't have any money," Callan replied. "That's what the exchequer is for."

"I'll have to remember to get an exchequer of my own when this is all over." Martin smiled without humor. "But that's going to make it a lot tougher to hire ships quietly."

I shook my head. "No it won't."

"Care to enlighten a poor Scout Second Class, Rice?" Martin growled.

"It should be obvious to a former raider like you." I turned to Milo. "Are you interested in robbing the Mordanian treasury, kid?"

I've Caught a Thief

Milo's eyes went wide, a grin split his face, and his head began nodding so fast I was afraid it might come loose.

"David, that's brilliant," Callan beamed at me.

"Yeah, brilliant," Martin groused, "until Milo gets caught breaking into the treasury. He's a talented pickpocket, David, but you're asking him to break into one of the most secure rooms in the country."

"He won't need to break in, Martin." Callan sat at her desk and began writing. "This note will get him inside."

Martin read the note over Callan's shoulder. "I've seen your tiara, Callan. It's a lovely antique but it doesn't have enough gems to cover the ships we'll need."

"The tiara is just Milo's excuse to get into the treasury." Callan folded the note and sealed it with her signet ring. "Once he's inside, Milo gets to prove to us just how good a thief he is. There are plenty of jewels to choose from, Milo. We'll have to trust your professional judgement."

Milo took the note from Callan. "Are there cut gems in the treasury?"

Martin clapped Milo on the shoulder. "Smart thinking, lad." Seeing our confusion, he said to Callan and me, "Jewels are distinctive, that makes them harder to sell and worth less money. Gems are easier to carry, easier to sell, easier all around."

Callan nodded her understanding. "I always wondered why the spymaster kept all those loose gems down there. How much will we need to hire the ships?"

"Err on the side of excess, Milo," Martin advised. "A big fistful would be perfect."

"Speak to Nist and Tristan before you rob my treasury," Callan said to him. "If he can, I'd like Nist to fly the *Pauline* to my balcony in two hours. I don't want to risk anyone catching sight of us as we leave the palace. I want Tristan along in case my parents need medical attention after we rescue them."

Milo nodded and slipped out the door.

Martin moved to follow him. "I'd best get started hiring ships. I'll come back on the *Pauline* to pick up the gems."

The waiting chafed on both of us. We ended up staring at a two hundred year-old framed map of Mordan hanging on the wall of our room, trying to remember where modern cities stood and guess where to concentrate the search. It was almost a relief when someone knocked on our door.

Almost.

Motioning Callan out of sight, I drew my sword and opened the door a few inches. Outside stood Captain Hunter, the man in charge of the royal guard. One of his big hands gripped Milo by the neck.

"Captain Rice," Hunter said, "I must speak with Her Highness. I'm afraid I've caught a thief."

It Wasn't Easy

"You may leave the boy with me, Captain Hunter," I said. "I'll see that he's suitably punished. What was he stealing?"

"Gemstones." Hunter craned his neck, trying to see past me into the room. "Where is Her Highness?"

"Indisposed. We were sleeping when you knocked."

"You sleep with lanterns lit? And where is your guard?" Suspicion clouded Hunter's face. "I must insist upon seeing Her Highness. Now."

"You'd best let him in, David," Callan said, stepping next to me. "But before you enter, Captain, I must request and require that you remain quiet and do nothing until I have a chance to explain what you will see."

Hunter's eyes widened, but he never hesitated. "I accept and accede, Your Highness."

I swung the door open and Captain Hunter stepped into our room. If his eyes had widened before, they fairly bulged out at the sight of the blood and the bodies.

"I must alert the guard!" Hunter exclaimed. "I must-"

"Do nothing until you hear my explanation—as you swore just seconds ago," Callan's voice was a whip crack.

Hunter straightened to attention, "My apologies, Your Highness. It's just..." He waved his hand around the room.

"I understand your reaction, Captain, but I cannot allow you to follow your first impulse," Callan said. "My parents' lives may depend upon you doing the exact opposite."

It took but a moment for Callan to bring the captain up to speed.

"My apologies for suspecting you, Captain Rice," Hunter said.

"Never apologize for making Callan's safety your priority," I replied.

Hunter nodded once. "But I am not sure about this plan, Your Highness. It seems very risky."

"That's because it *is* very risky, Captain," Callan said. "But I believe it's the best chance we have to save my parents."

"And what does your husband think of your involvement?" Hunter asked.

"My husband hopes to convince me to stay at my uncle's fief," Callan replied.

I hadn't said any such thing, but Callan's assumption was correct.

"Am I going to succeed?" I asked.

"It's doubtful."

"You know I'll have to try anyway."

"Yes, darling. I'd be hurt if you didn't."

"Best of luck with that, Captain Rice," Hunter interjected. "But, Your Highness, you indicated I had a part to play in this plot of yours. What did you have in mind?"

"I'd like you to be the one to raise the alarm, Captain Hunter," Callan replied. "Having the captain of the Royal Guard discover my supposed kidnapping will add just the right touch of veracity to our deception. Though you must wait until we're long gone from the palace before doing so."

"If you think that's best, Highness, I shall do just that."

"Thank you, Captain," Callan said. "Return to your normal duties. Give us two and a half hours, then come 'discover' our disappearance."

Captain Hunter saluted, started for the door, then paused. Fishing a small bag from his pocket, he handed it to Callan. "I suppose you'll be needing these gems the lad was...I suppose *stealing* isn't the right word here."

After Hunter was gone, I looked at Milo. "What happened? How did Hunter catch you?"

"It wasn't easy." Milo pulled a second small bag from his pocket. "I had to be really blatant before he finally realized what I was doing."

"Wait, you got caught on purpose?" I asked. "Why?"

"Because we needed Captain Hunter to do exactly what Callan told him to do," Milo replied. "Like Callan said, it'll be more believable—especially to Windslow and his goons."

"Why didn't you mention that earlier? I could have added it to my note," Callan said.

"I didn't think about it until I was in the treasury. Captain Hunter is too duty-minded to leave his post at my request—even in your name, Callan—and I couldn't just explain the situation to Captain Hunter because he'd have raised the alarm."

"So you gave him a reason to come up here," Callan said. "Very clever, Milo."

Milo was still basking in Callan's praise when the *Pauline* drifted up to our balcony. Martin and I loaded three of the assassins' bodies onto the airship—we planned to dump them overboard once we were well away from the city—and we boarded the little airship.

Callan looked at each of us. "Let's go find my parents."

3

HOSTAGE

Two hours had passed since our rendezvous with Martin Bane's mercenary fleet. Martin, Callan, and I had devised search patterns for each of the airships involved in our hunt for Callan's parents. Each airship's captain had been paid in advance for his assistance in the search.

"I have to wait here for one more ship," Martin said as the airships left to begin the search. "It'll be here soon, but there's no reason you two should stay."

"Good," Callan said. "I need to warn my uncle about Windslow and send him back to the palace. After that we'll join in the search."

Callan's uncle, Lord Garrett, was the kingdom's designated regent should anything happen to Their Majesties before Callan's twenty-first birthday. He'd been spending more and more time in his fief as Callan's birthday drew closer. But that was before Their Majesties were taken by Windslow.

"Once Uncle Garrett is on his way to the palace to establish his regency, I'll be able to concentrate fully on my parents," Callan added.

"Did you check with your usual information sources before we left?" I asked Martin.

"Yes, David," Martin said. "I've done this before—former raider, remember? No one had heard anything about Windslow."

"What about news out of Tarteg?" I asked. "Is Raoul's mother getting back into the family business, maybe?"

"No. It's been over a month since anyone heard anything from either of them. The last news had Raoul living and traveling among the city states to the south. His mother is living quietly in a convent."

We settled a few more details, boarded the *Pauline*—fast becoming known as the princess's unofficial airship—and set course for Pingor, home to Lord Garrett. Four hours later, the dim lights of Pingor came into view. Callan answered the challenge from the airship on patrol and we were escorted directly to Garrett's palace.

As we landed, Garrett's wife, a pale and delicate-looking woman, hurried from the palace and wrapped Callan in a hug.

"Callie, what are you doing here?" she said.

"Aunt Michelle," Callan said, "my parents have been kidnapped!"

Michelle grew even more pale, "Kidnapped?"

"Where is Uncle Garrett?" Callan asked. "I must speak with him immediately."

"You can't," Michelle said. "Garrett is being held hostage in the mine!"

Be Careful

Callan pulled Michelle back into a hug. "What are you doing to get Uncle Garrett back?"

"Whatever Garrett's advisors suggest, which seems to be little more than waiting and hoping." Michelle shook her head. "I wish Rob were here. He'd know what to do."

Callan's face clouded for a moment as the pain of Rob's loss returned in full force.

"Oh, Callie, I'm so sorry. That was thoughtless of me." She took Callan by the hand and drew her toward the palace. "Come inside and tell me what's going on."

Callan told the tale in a cheery sitting room. Michelle's eyes flashed when she heard of the attempt to kidnap Callan and slay me.

"I hoped to send Garrett to Morda to establish a regency while I led the search for my parents," Callan concluded.

"If Windslow has your parents and tried to kidnap you, he's probably behind Garrett's capture as well," Michelle said.

"The timing is too convenient for it to be anything else," Callan said.

A young girl's voice came from behind a tapestry, "See? I told you Callie would bring David to rescue Daddy."

"Ann, come out here this minute," Michelle said. "Ellen and Brolan, that goes for the both of you, too."

Three children came out. Ann, who was four, carried a teddy bear under one arm, wore a big smile and ran to Callan. Ellen, eight, looked as if she wanted to do the same thing but was trying to act grownup. Brolan, all of eleven, was somber, as if he was trying on the mantle of man of the house and found it heavier than expected.

"That's why you're here, right Callie?" Ann turned big eyes on me. "To rescue Daddy?"

"That wasn't why I came," Callan said, "but of course we're going to help now that we're here."

Taking a knee beside Callan, I said, "Lady Ann, you have my oath to do all in my power to rescue your father."

"I should be rescuing Da- Father!" Brolan's voice broke, ruining his pronouncement.

Michelle sighed. "David, could you talk some sense into my son?"

"Brolan doesn't suffer from a lack of sense, Lady Michelle, merely from a lack of experience." I turned to the boy. "A wise ruler delegates important missions to the person best suited for the task."

Brolan crossed his arms and looked me in the eye. "Then why are you and Callan trying to rescue the king and queen? Isn't the Royal Navy better prepared for that?"

"Yes, the Royal Navy is well equipped for search and rescue operations," Callan responded. "But there's more to consider than airships and men."

Brolan didn't back down. "Like what?"

"Brolan, how dare you take that tone of voice with Callan," Michelle scolded.

"He's right to question me, Aunt Michelle," Callan said. "All right, Brolan, what would the Royal Navy do if I had gone to them?"

Brolan looked thoughtful for a moment. "They'd have gathered airships and made plans for the search. They'd have sent a squadron here to check on us. And they'd have put you under heavy guard."

"Very good," Callan agreed. "And what would Windslow have done when he heard about that?"

Brolan's eyes went wide. "Oh."

The two girls looked confused but Callan and Michelle gave the boy an approving nod.

"Now that we've settled that," Callan said, squeezing my hand, "promise me you'll be careful, David."

"Careful? Doing what?" Michelle asked.

"Careful in the mine," I said. "Time is a luxury we don't have right now, so I'm going down to fetch Lord Garrett."

Delaying Tactics

Michelle gaped at me, "Don't be foolish, David. There are ten men holding Garrett. Callie, talk some sense into your husband."

"A few minutes ago, you wished Rob were here to offer advice. What would your response have been if Rob had said that?" Callan asked.

"I'd have asked what he needed," Michelle sighed. She turned an inquiring gaze on me. "So, what do you need, David?"

"To start with, I'll need maps of the mine and an explanation of how Lord Garrett was captured," I said.

Michelle sent for maps, then gave the explanation.

"The day before yesterday, a group of former military engineers arrived in an airship and requested an audience with Garrett. They said they'd come to demonstrate a new steam drill. Callie, you know how your uncle is when he has a new mining toy to play with."

Callan nodded and rolled her eyes.

Michelle flashed a smile that never reached her eyes. "Of course, he insisted on seeing the drill in action as soon as possible. The engineers told Garrett they were sorry, but they had to wait for their mechanic to join them because they didn't know enough about assembling steam engines. They gave some story about the mechanic having to pick up some tools in another city, insisting the mechanic should catch up with them in three or four days.

"A new drill and a steam engine to assemble? It was like dangling raw meat before a starving dog. 'I know all about steam engines!' Garrett assured them. 'I can assemble it for you.' Whoever planned this was very clever. It took fifteen minutes before they agreed to let Garrett handle the assembly.

"Garrett worked all night putting that infernal engine together. When it was finally ready, the engineers asked everyone to leave the mine. It was all for safety, they said. They'd do a test run and then call everyone back to view the results. Garrett ordered the mine cleared but insisted on staying down there himself, just in case they had trouble with the steam engine. Once Garrett's guards were clear, they took Garrett hostage. They claim to have an armed man with Garrett at all times. If we storm the mine or try to sneak in, they swear they'll know and will kill Garrett."

"How do they communicate with you?" I asked.

"The mine has speaking tubes, just like you'd find in a large airship," Michelle answered. Tears began sliding down Michelle's cheeks. "Installing them was Garrett's idea."

Callan moved next to Michelle and put an arm around her. "We're going to get him back, Michelle."

Michelle sniffed, smiling bravely. "You know that's the first time you've addressed me without 'aunt' in front of my name?"

"You'll always be Aunt Michelle to me," Callan said, "even if I just call you Michelle."

"And you'll always be the little flower girl from my wedding, Callie, even if you aren't a little girl any more."

I waited a moment while Callan and Michelle hugged. When they pulled apart, I asked, "Have they made any demands?"

Michelle snorted. "Oh, yes. They want royal pardons and more money than our fief has."

I mulled over that for a moment. "Agree to the demands."

"We can't do that, David. They'll kill Garrett when we can't deliver," Michelle protested.

"I don't think so," I said. "If I'm right, they'll change their demands."

Michelle looked thoughtful. "I don't follow that. Please explain."

"All of their demands are nothing more than delaying tactics designed to keep you off balance and thinking about anything except rescuing Garrett," I said. "These men don't care about the ransom. They're waiting for a signal of some kind. When they get it, they'll just leave. I'd guess they're even using the steam drill to dig their own escape tunnel."

"In that case, can't we just wait for them to leave?" Michelle asked.

"For one thing, we really need Garrett to assume the regency while we search for Callan's parents," I said.

"What's the second thing?" Michelle asked.

I met Michelle's gaze. "When they don't need Garrett any more, they'll probably kill him."

Jim

Lady Michelle was digesting what I'd said when a map of the mine was brought to me. I began studying the map, looking for something the kidnappers hadn't thought about. An hour later, I found what I was looking for.

"Lady Michelle, do you know if there are any retired miners among the staff?" I asked.

Michelle relayed the question to her majordomo. Ten minutes later, the husband of the head cook was ushered in. At my prompting, he introduced himself as Jim.

"Jim, do you know anything about the silver mine just north of the city?"

"Where them men is holdin' Lord Garrett?" he asked. "Yeah, I worked it some. Worked the copper mine t'other side o' the mountain more."

"That's what I was hoping to hear," I said. I pointed at the map. "This copper mine shaft looks like it gets very close to the silver mine—close enough for me to break through the wall. The thing is, I don't know anything about mining. Without a good guide, I'll probably just get lost."

"Copper mine's been shut up fer nigh on twenty years. Timber's prob'ly rotted out in places," Jim said. "Be dangerous."

"If I don't do something, Lord Garrett will probably die."

"Then I's yer man," Jim said. "What kinda supplies you got?"

"You tell me what you think we'll need and I'll make sure we've got it."

Jim rattled off an impressive list of items. Half an hour later, with the requested supplies loaded on the *Pauline,* Nist flew us to the entrance to the copper mine.

Swinging a heavy pack onto my back, I said, "Nist, I'll send Jim back once he shows me the shaft I'm looking for. Wait here for him, then the two of you head back to Garrett's palace."

"What about you?" Nist asked.

"I'm planning on coming out through the main entrance to the silver mine," I said as Jim and I set off for the boarded-up entrance to the old mine.

Prying the boards from the entrance proved easy—several were rotten, as Jim had predicted—then we headed in. Every inch of that mine was familiar to Jim until we came to the sinkhole blocking our path.

"Sorry, son, ain't no other tunnel goes where you wanna git." He turned toward me. "Boy, what you think yer doin'?"

I dropped the last of my gear to the ground and tied a rope around my waist. "I'm going to jump across."

"You crazy, boy? Tha's gotta be thirty foot."

"Just find a place to tie this end of the rope, in case I don't make it," I said.

Once Jim had tied off the rope, I grabbed a pick and stepped back. *Boost*! I charged toward the sink hole and leaped out over the impenetrable darkness of the sinkhole.

4

LEAD ON

My foot slipped on some loose stones as I jumped. It wasn't much of a slip, but it was enough. I knew immediately I wasn't going to make it to the far lip of the sinkhole. Worse, if the bottom of the sinkhole was closer than my rope was long, I was in for a world of hurt. Halfway across, I realized I was going to make it to the other side of the sinkhole, just not to the lip.

Maintaining Boost, I pulled my pick arm back and then drove the pick into the wall of the sinkhole. I crashed into the wall and put all my weight on the pick. It held, but I didn't want to put too much trust into such a blind swing and began looking for handholds.

"Yee ha!" Jim called. "You got guts, son. Scramble on up and tie off the rope fer me."

Yeah, that was easy for Jim to say, but I found I could dig out hand and foot holds without too much effort. Feeling more secure, I dropped Boost and climbed the wall. A few minutes later, I tied off the rope, Jim pulled himself across the sinkhole, and on we went.

Jim got talkative after my jump, filling our walk with tales of the mines and the miners. The man knew a story for every foot of that mine. A lot of them were funny and a few were tragic. It filled the time until, at last, Jim pointed to a tunnel.

"This 'un here's the one you want."

"Thanks," I said. "You head on back to the airship, now."

"Nah, I gotta see how yer gettin' through t'other mine. 'Sides, I knows where you oughta make yer hole."

I wasn't about to turn down expert advice. "Lead on, Jim."

Ten minutes later, Jim and I used our picks to dig out a two foot deep hole in the tunnel wall. Then I pulled out the Onesie. Jim watched, curious, as I broke down the gun and set the power supply to overload. Believe it or not, the power supply overload is a design feature. Sometimes a Scout just needs to blow something up, even if it turns the Onesie into a high tech decoration. The whine of the overload was building as I placed it in the hole and scooped dirt in behind it. Grabbing Jim by the arm, I ran back up the tunnel.

A couple of minutes later, the power supply blew. Impatiently, I waited for the dust to settle. Had we blown a back door into the silver mine?

Words to Live By

Through the settling dust, I saw the hole we'd dug was almost man-height and, when I brought a lantern to it, was relieved to see it opened into the silver mine.

"I couldn't have done this without you, Jim. But now it's time for you to go back to the airship and head home," I said. "Tell Lady Michelle to wait for me to call on the speaking tubes."

"You sure you don't need no help, son?" Jim asked. "They's got ten men."

"I've faced worse than that before, Jim, and I'm still breathing. I appreciate the offer but it's best if I go on alone from here."

"If'n you say so. But you be careful, son." Jim winked, "I 'spect that purty princess be right riled up if'n you gets hurt."

"Trust me, *not* riling my wife is always one of my top priorities," I said.

"Them's words ta live by, lad," Jim gave me a thumbs up and started back to Nist and the *Pauline*. I strode through the new connecting tunnel and into the silver mine.

The first thing I did was shutter my lantern until it gave off the narrowest beam of light possible. Once my eyes adjusted to the near-total darkness, I started toward the main tunnel. And almost immediately tripped over a rock. I just managed to catch myself with my free hand before the lantern could be smashed on the rocks. After that, I reined in my desire for haste and opened the lantern's shutter a bit more. Better to go slowly with a little more light than to break the lantern and be forced to crawl with no light.

I probed the darkness ahead with my ears, hearing being the most useful sense available to me. After fifteen minutes of hearing the periodic drip of water and scuff of my boot on rock, I heard the steam drill. Five minutes later, I reached what my mental map told me should be the main tunnel. The engine sounds came from the right, farther into the mine, but the speaking tubes were to the left, closer to the surface. Where would they be more likely to be holding Garrett? I decided they'd want communication most and turned left.

Another ten minutes of careful walking and listening—the last two minutes with the lantern completely shuttered—and I was looking into the kidnappers' camp. I only saw seven of the ten men Michelle had said were down here. I assumed the other three were tending the steam drill. Garrett was tied to an iron ring driven into the left wall. As I'd hoped, he was on the end of the camp farthest from the mine entrance—the same end I was on. If luck was with me, I thought I could free him before the fighting began.

Luck was most definitely not with me. My recently sharpened hearing picked up the sound of two voices drifting up from behind me. I'd reached the kidnappers' camp just before shift change on the drill.

Surrender!

If I charged into the camp, I'd be silhouetted against the camp light and easily visible to the men behind me in the tunnel. It would only take one shout to alert their comrades and put Garrett's life in peril. Instead of acting rashly and charging, I rolled to the left side of the tunnel, where Garrett was bound, rose into a crouch, and slipped along the tunnel wall.

The camp's sentry faced away from me, toward the surface entrance where Garrett's men at arms were just waiting for the order to charge into the mine. The rest of men sat talking, paying no attention to anything around them. I decided to try to let Garrett know what was about to happen.

"Garrett, it's David. Rescue time is at hand," I hissed. Garrett's face sharpened into concentration. "Pull the rope taut, it'll be easier to cut. I don't have a spare sword, so run for the surface once you're free. I'll be right behind you. Do *not* wait for me."

Garrett gave a bare nod and stretched as if trying to loosen stiff joints. The rope pulled taught. I moved to within five feet of Garrett and quietly drew my sword.

Boost!

Jumping up, I sawed on the thick rope binding Garrett to the iron ring. The rope parted, but not before a shout rose from down tunnel. Two of the men in the camp reacted quickly, drawing swords and charging toward Garrett and me.

"Get going, Garrett," I shouted and I ran to meet the two who had reacted so quickly. They hadn't expected me to come to them so I was able to roll under their hurried swings. I slashed at the man on my right as I came out of the roll, cutting a leg out from under him. Whipping my sword around to the other man, I thrust the point into his throat. Blood fountained as I ripped my blade away. The man's hands flew to his throat and his eyes widened in horror. Gurgling, he fell away from me.

The swift brutality of my attack gave the five men within the camp reason to pause. Then we all heard the sound of running feet coming from the direction of the steam engine. Emboldened by the thought of reinforcements, the men advanced.

Charging had taken the first two men by surprise, so I figured it wouldn't hurt to try again. I ran toward the closest three men, calling, "Surrender or die!"

No one surrendered. Instead, the three men spread out, their swords held ready. From the corner of my eye, I saw a fourth man angling to get behind me. I had charged at the man in the middle, but it was time to throw off their maneuvering. I planted my right foot and dove to the left. All three men froze at my unexpected change of direction. I took advantage of their confusion and swung my sword at the man standing before me. My sword bit into flesh, opening his belly from right to left. The man screamed and clutched his gut, trying to keep his organs from spilling out. Spinning around, I found the other three men backing away.

"Surrender," a voice called, "or your lord dies."

I turned toward the sound of the voice. Garrett lay on the ground, pinned down by a foot on his back. The sentry stood over him, his sword at Garrett's neck.

5

WHAT NOW?

I MOVED MY SWORD TO MY LEFT HAND AND HELD IT WITH TWO FINGERS. Spreading my arms wide, I concentrated on looking as non-threatening as possible. I knelt down slowly and laid the sword on the ground. As I'd hoped, all eyes were on the sword. No one saw me pick up a rock with my right hand. I raised my left arm, again using it to keep the men looking the wrong way. With a sidearm delivery, I hurled the rock at the sentry. It hit him hard on the forehead. Cursing in pain, the sentry stumbled back, freeing Garrett.

I snatched my sword from the ground and was on the sentry in an instant. Knocking his sword from his hand, I placed my sword against his throat, and dropped Boost.

"All of you, stay back or I'll kill him," I snapped. The men stopped, stunned at the sudden reversal of their fortunes. "Garret, please get going. Michelle and your children are waiting for you at the mine entrance."

Rising, Garrett asked, "What about you, David?"

"I'll be along shortly. Send some of your men at arms when you have the chance," I said. "Oh, and tell Callan I'm fine. She's probably starting to worry."

"I always thought Callan was exaggerating when she told stories of your fighting prowess. It looks as if I owe her an apology." With that, Garrett turned and ran toward the mine entrance.

Turning back to the kidnappers, I asked, "What now, gentlemen?"

The men exchanged puzzled looks.

"I can't afford to waste any more time on you—not even the time it will take for Garrett's men at arms to arrive," I said. "Thirty minutes ago, I blasted a hole into this mine from an old, abandoned copper mine. Take it or don't. It doesn't matter to me."

"You're not going to execute us?"

"I'm tired of killing people," I said, "but I'm sure Garrett's men will be happy to oblige you. They'll be along soon."

"What about our steam drill?" one asked.

"On behalf of Lord Garrett, I thank you for donating it to his mining operation," I smiled. "Do you have any more stupid questions?"

They shook their heads.

"One more thing," I said as they started to turn away. "If any of you ever tries something like this again, I will hunt you down and kill you. No appeal. No mercy. Do we understand each other?"

They nodded, then the man who'd been on sentry duty asked, "How do we find the way into the copper mine?"

"I'm giving you a chance to get away and now you want directions?" I waved my hand down the mine shaft, "Find it yourselves."

The unwounded men ran down the tunnel, ignoring the pleas of the man with the wounded leg and the groans of the man I'd gutted.

I ignored them as well and headed after Garrett. I met his men at arms along the way and told them the kidnappers were trying to get away through the copper mine. Unlike the kidnappers, I gave the soldiers precise directions to the connecting tunnel I'd created and they set off in pursuit.

Callan threw herself into my arms and kissed me soundly when I emerged into the morning light. Her public display caused lots of murmuring and a few disapproving looks from those gathered at the entrance. I guess that kind of thing isn't considered proper for a princess, even if she is kissing her husband. I pulled Callan close, returned her kiss with equal fervor, deciding I couldn't care less what the watchers thought of that.

As we broke off, a smudge in the sky drew our attention. I realized it was Martin Bane's airship trailing smoke as it limped toward the city.

Firing Range

"What's a Tartegian warship doing here?" Garrett asked.

"That's not a Tartegian ship," I said. "It's the one Martin Bane acquired as part of his deal with the Tartegian admiral."

"You're sure it's Bane?" Garrett asked. When I nodded, he pointed toward three of his patrol craft moving to intercept Martin's ship. "Then we could have trouble. After the Tartegians orchestrated your kidnapping, Callan, my men have been itching for a shot at one of their ships. They don't know Bane nor will they see much beyond the Tartegian design. I'm afraid they'll attack as soon as they're within range."

"No!" Callan cried.

"Nist!" I yelled. "Is the *Pauline* ready to fly?"

At Nist's nod, Callan sprinted toward the airship. Following her, I called over my shoulder to Garrett, "Come on."

"I'm right behind you, David," Garrett said.

I bounded over the airship's railing and then pulled Garrett aboard the *Pauline*, "Is there any way to signal your airships?"

"I'll try, of course, but all of their attention is going to be on their target."

Grabbing a couple of colorful flags, I handed them to Garrett. He positioned himself in the bow of the *Pauline* as the little airship rose into the air. Nist brought the engines to full power, worked the ailerons, and put the ship into a steep ascent. Over the roar of the engine, Callan filled her uncle in on the attack against us, what little we knew of her parents, and who we believed was behind everything.

His arms still waving frantically, Garrett said, "It appears you've accrued another debt of thanks that my family owes you, David."

"Uncle, David is part of your family, too. He has been for nearly a month," Callan smiled and slipped an arm around my waist.

"Forgive me, my boy," Garrett said. "I'm still adjusting to the idea that the niece I spoiled so horribly is a married woman, now."

Callan rolled her eyes. "You and Daddy, both."

Nist called, "The airships are in firing range."

I could see Martin trying to get the attention of the patrol ship captains, but they were too busy maneuvering to pay him any attention. His ship too damaged to maneuver, Martin began a rapid, controlled descent. Surprised by Martin's move, the patrol ships' first few shots flew harmlessly over the stricken airship. If Martin could hold out for another few seconds, we'd be in among the patrol ships. We were no more than a hundred yards away from the battle when a ballista bolt hit the airship's envelope at just the right angle. Instead of punching straight in, it sliced along the edge of the envelope, ripping a gaping hole in it.

Gas poured through the rip and the envelope began to crumple.

He's Not Working Alone

"Nist, find the fastest way to get me to Martin's ship!" I cried, rushing to a coil of rope on the *Pauline's* deck. "Garrett, you've got to find a way to call off your patrol ships."

"How?" Garrett demanded.

"Keep waving the flags. Shout. Jump up and down. Whatever it takes. Just get it done," I said, tying one end of the rope to a docking cleat. "Nist, does the *Pauline* have enough lift to help Martin land safely?"

"Not at the rate he's losing gas," Nist replied, "but if we can get the patrol ships to stop shooting and help, I think we can do it."

"Then do whatever you have to do to make sure those patrol ships see Garrett."

Nist grinned and began making course corrections. Seconds later, Nist squeezed the *Pauline* through the narrow gap between two of the patrol ships. With the *Pauline* steaming just feet from both patrol ships, Garrett—waving, jumping, and shouting—finally got the attention of the crews. Those two airships broke off their attacks as Nist dove toward Martin's flailing ship.

The third patrol ship finally spotted the *Pauline* and, more important, Garrett in the bow. The ship broke off its attack, too, leaving a clear path to Martin's airship.

"With the envelope flapping around, this is as close as I can get," Nist called to me a few seconds later.

We were twenty feet above the deck of Martin's ship and ten feet from its railing. It was farther than I'd have preferred, but I clutched the rope and took a running jump from the rail. Eight hundred feet of empty space yawned beneath me, then I crashed onto the deck of the stricken airship. Crewmen took the rope from me and rushed to tie it to an envelope mooring cleat.

Through all the commotion, I could hear Garrett shouting orders to his patrol ships, instructing them to render all aid to Martin's airship. I hoped they had some kind of procedure for aiding damaged ships, perhaps something similar to what I had done?

Half a minute later, I had my answer. Patrol ship crewmen began jumping to the deck, each holding the end of a rope. Lines were tied off and our descent began to slow. It finally stopped about a hundred feet from the ground.

Martin was kept busy directing the three patrol ships, the *Pauline*, and his own crew during the short flight to Pingor. Only when his ship was docked, did Martin come talk to me.

"I've got bad news, David," he said. "Not only is Callan right about Windslow being behind these kidnappings, I discovered he's not working alone."

"Who's working with him?" I asked, certain I knew the answer already.

Martin grimaced. "Raoul."

6

HE WASN'T LYING

Before I could ask Martin for more information, the voice of Tristan Agrilla, well known as the Desert Doctor for his work among the southern desert tribes, rose from below deck.

"Martin! I need stretchers and stretcher bearers for the wounded." Climbing onto the main deck, Tristan's eyes focused on me for the first time. "Good to see you, lad. Could you please nip off and arrange a room for my patients?"

"How many have you got?"

"Too many. Twenty-two," Tristan replied. "None of them are very serious, though, so there's no need for an operating theater."

"I hear and obey, Mighty Healer," I sketched a bow.

"Bah. You sound just like that scamp, Nist," Tristan replied. "Begone, boy."

"Once the wounded are taken care of, you'll need to tell us what happened," I said to Martin, then dodged through the crowd to find Garrett.

Moments later, a line of stretchers was headed into Garrett's palace. Callan and I watched them pass, our worst fears ameliorated when Milo walked off the airship. His head was bandaged but his stride was steady. Milo gave us a smile that took on a strained quality when Callan pulled him aside and started checking him over.

"I'm fine, Cal— um, Your Highness," Milo protested. "You know Tristan would have me on a stretcher if I'd taken more than a bump on the head."

"Just stand still and let her satisfy herself, Milo," I said. "It'll be easier for us all in the long run."

Callan had just finished giving Milo the once-over when Martin joined us. The four of us went to join Lord Garrett in his sitting room.

Garrett was busy reuniting with his family, one arm around Michelle's waist and the other holding Ann. Ellen was hugging one of Garrett's legs, a big smile on her face. Brolan stood nearby, looking like he wanted to join in the hugging if only no one was watching.

"Now that I've had a chance to think about what's been happening," Garrett said, "what on earth do you think you're doing, Callie?"

"What do you mean, Uncle?"

"I understand why you engaged this ex-raider," Garrett pointed at Martin, "to fight the trog army, but the Royal Navy is no longer scattered to all points of the compass searching for you. So why isn't the capital fleet escorting you?"

"Ask Brolan," Callan replied. "He figured it out."

"Did he?" Garrett looked at his son. "Well, my boy?"

Brolan bit his lip and then blurted, "Because the admirals would still be making plans and keeping Callie under guard and the king and queen would be dead before the navy could find them."

"I think you do our naval commanders a disservice," Garrett said, "though I suppose there is some truth to your reasoning."

"But?" Callan asked.

"But by now the navy is bound to be mobilized and starting another search for you, Callie. So your objections to dealing with the navy are no longer valid," Garrett responded. "Now it's time for you to return to the capital and let the navy handle this matter. If you apologize for the insult to the navy brass, I can persuade the admirals to chalk all of this up to the impetuousness of youth. No lasting harm need come of it."

"No lasting harm? The navy excels at many things, Uncle, but subtlety is not one of them," Callan said. "Windslow would see the navy coming from miles away. He'd have plenty of time to kill my parents and make good his escape before the navy even knew where Windslow was hiding."

"That's another thing," Garrett said. "Your only evidence of Windslow's involvement is the confession of a dying assassin. What if he was lying?"

"He wasn't lying, Lord Garrett," Martin said. "The damage to my ship occurred when we were attacked by Ardhan Windslow and Prince Raoul."

Martin's Report

"Remember the airship I was waiting for yesterday?" Bane asked. "Apparently Windslow and Raoul convinced—or bought, more likely—the loyalty of the ship's captain. I expect it happened sometime after I worked with the captain in Faroon. He was probably already working for them when I put the word out last night that I was hiring ships."

"A raider who sells out to the highest bidder?" Garrett sneered. "I'm shocked at his disloyalty."

"Perhaps he simply took after the sterling examples of loyalty shown by some of your royal commanders," Martin shot back. "There's the example of the western squadron captains thirty years ago, handsomely paid to sit idle and watch while a Tartegian fleet sailed across the border to attack. Or raiders could emulate Windslow, himself. How much does one have to pay the captain of the Royal Guard to mastermind a plot to kidnap a four year old princess?"

"Stop it, both of you," Callan commanded. "Uncle, you will stifle your opinions and work with Martin. If you cannot do that, I'll take my leave of you right now and make do without the benefit of your advice."

Callan glared until Garrett nodded.

"As for you, Martin," she whirled to face him, "despite your obvious change of heart and your heroics at Faroon, you were a raider for fifteen years. It's going to take time to convince people you've changed. Learn to deal with it."

"As you command, Highness," Martin said, flourishing a bow that was, for once, devoid of irony.

"Good. Continue with your report, Martin."

"As I said, I was waiting for one more airship, the *Kestrel*, before heading north to coordinate the search. When he arrived, Captain Stubb and a few members of his crew came aboard for their briefing. Once we were below decks, the crew of the *Kestrel* swarmed aboard and had my men at sword point before they even realized what was happening," Martin said. "That's when Windslow and Raoul showed themselves. They wanted to know where they could find you. Stubb incidentally, wanted to take all the valuables we had onboard."

"Wait," Callan said. "They knew I hadn't been kidnapped?"

"They suspected it," Martin said. "I tried to lead them astray, Your Highness, telling them I had been hired by David to find you."

"Didn't they wonder why I wasn't with you?" I asked.

"Indeed. Alas, you were severely wounded defending Her Highness," Martin said. "You sent your trusted page, Milo, to me with instructions to find your wife."

"And they believed you agreed to help out of the goodness of your heart?" Garrett interjected.

"No, they believed I agreed to help because Princess Callan is my one and only patron among Mordanian royalty," Martin said. "No offense, David, but Raoul seems to think your good will is of no consequence without Callan."

"In that respect," Garrett said, "they are sadly mistaken."

Callan rewarded Garrett with a smile before nodding to Martin to continue.

"I told Stubb where to find our valuables and told my men to cooperate. Stubb's crew didn't appear eager to put us to the sword and I began to hope we were going to get out of the situation without a fight," Martin continued. "That's when Milo came up on deck. Tristan had sent him to see what was going on. I guess seeing Milo reminded Raoul of everything that happened in Faroon. Anyway, when Raoul spotted Milo, he lost all of his composure. Raoul drew his sword and attacked Milo."

Raoul

Garrett looked at Milo. "Raoul is a grown man. The lad can't be any older than Brolan."

"I'm fourteen," Milo said, with the vehemence of a teenager accused of being younger than his true age

"Even so, it's still not very noble of Raoul to attack such a young lad," Garrett growled.

"As David has observed in the past, Raoul isn't particularly noble. Besides, 'tried to attack' is a much more accurate description of events," Martin said. "Raoul's leg buckled before he could reach Milo. I'd say that stab wound you gave him still hasn't fully healed, Your Highness.

"While Raoul struggled back to his feet, Milo darted below deck. Once he was on his feet, Raoul hobbled after him. With all the attention on Raoul, I elbowed Stubb in the stomach and ran after the prince," Martin said. "Raoul chased Milo into the surgery, hitting Milo on the head with the pommel of his sword. Tristan stepped between Raoul and the boy then tried to talk sense into Raoul. As most of you know, that's a waste of time, words, and breath. Raoul looked as if he was about to attack Tristan when I tackled Raoul from behind.

"I put a dagger at Raoul's throat just as Windslow and Stubb reached the door. They were backed by a couple of crossbowmen, so we had a bit of a stand off. Raoul makes a good bargaining chip—that's the one thing he's proven to be good for—and it's apparent Windslow doesn't want to risk upsetting the Tartegian royal house," Martin continued. "I ordered Stubb to pull his men back to his ship and to take Windslow with him. I promised Windslow I'd release Raoul once they were off my ship. In return, Windslow promised to leave in peace once they had Raoul. I kept my part of the bargain. Stubb, encouraged by Raoul, broke their part and attacked after our airships separated.

"My ship and crew weren't prepared for battle, so I took a page from your playbook, David. I Boosted and jumped across to Stubb's ship." Martin smiled, "You know, it's rather fun to be the dashing hero every now and then—even if there isn't a beautiful princess to rescue. I ran Stubb through before he could draw his sword—not very sporting of me, Lord Garrett, but Stubb *did* break his word. I slashed two crossbowmen who were taking aim at my crew and then had a clear run at Raoul.

"Raoul, meanwhile, had a clear run below deck. He took off as fast as he could hobble. I chased the coward into the captain's cabin and was ready to kill him right there. I thought I might get a medal from the Tartegians for taking care of their embarrassing Spare Prince. But I'd forgotten about Windslow. He followed me into the cabin, hit me on the head with a belaying pin, then shoved me over the railing of the captain's balcony."

A Navigational Chart

"The only thing that saved me from a very long fall was the flagpole for the Beloren flag Stubb flies from the stern of the *Kestrel*," Martin said. "Since I was still Boosting, I was able to catch the flagpole, swing around it, and pop back up onto the balcony. Windslow was just looking over the rail to watch me fall, so I plowed into him, knocking him backwards into Raoul. The two of them crashed to the deck and were just lying there helpless. I would have taken the opportunity to finish them off except a bunch of Stubb's crewmen piled into the cabin.

"Even Boosted, those were odds I just didn't like. I jumped from the balcony to the railing above and pulled myself onto the main deck. During the confusion, my ship had separated from the *Kestrel* and pulled away. They were circling nearby, waiting for me. The *Kestrel's* port ballista crew was watching my ship, just waiting for a chance to fire on it. I charged into them and knocked two of the crew overboard. That was too much for the remaining two crewman and they ran. I spun the ballista around to aim at the *Kestrel's* port engine and fired, blowing away the propeller. Then I took a running jump to my ship.

"The second I landed on the deck, the helmsman swung away from the *Kestrel* and we made a run for it. Despite the confusion on board, Stubb's crew managed to get off one good ballista shot. It nearly destroyed our steam engine. With Stubb wounded and the airship down to a single engine, the crew of the *Kestrel* didn't press the attack." Martin wrapped up, "We made what repairs we could then limped here for full repairs to the engine. And, thanks to the fine welcome we received, my ship also needs repair to its envelope."

"Don't go there, Martin," Callan warned.

Martin raised his hands in acquiescence, then said, "There is one more, rather important bit to the story. I think I know where Stubb is taking Raoul and Windslow. Unless I miss my guess, it's to wherever they're holding the king and queen."

"What makes you think that?" I asked.

"Stubb had a navigation chart laid out on the table in his cabin," Martin replied. "I only got a brief glance at it, but instructed my implant to record the image. If Lord Garrett has charts for the mountains northwest of here, I think I can show you where they're going."

Moments later, Martin selected a chart from those Garrett had ordered brought to us. Martin's finger pointed into the mountains. "Here. Stubb's chart had a mark right here."

Garrett leaned closer, "Of course. I can't believe it didn't occur to me."

"*What* didn't occur to you, Uncle?" Callan asked.

"They're headed to the Aerie, a long-abandoned mountain fortress," Garrett said. "That's got to be where Windslow is holding the king and queen."

7

THE AERIE

"I ADMIT IT'S COMPELLING EVIDENCE AND AGREE IT'S THE FIRST PLACE WE should check," I said, "but why would Windslow use any place on Mordanian soil, much less an old Mordanian fort?"

"The Aerie was Windslow's first post after he joined the military," Garrett said. "The fortress was built centuries ago to guard the only mountain pass between Tarteg and Mordan. The Tartegians have a similar fort at the other end of the pass. When airships came along, the fortress became obsolete. Who needs a mountain pass when you can just fly over the mountains? It was kept manned out of force of habit until my father closed the place. I was quite young when it was abandoned, but my personal guard told me all about the place."

"Was Windslow your personal guard?" Callan asked.

Garrett nodded. "The Aerie has been abandoned for forty years, it's hard to reach without an airship, and well fortified. It would be perfect for hiding royal hostages. If you'd had this information last night, Callie, you could have gotten there long before Windslow and Raoul. There's no chance of that, now."

"That's not necessarily true," Martin said. "They'll have to repair the port engine or limp along at half speed. Either way, a small, fast ship like the *Pauline* might get there before them, if it could make the entire run at full speed."

When I explained the situation to Tristan, he readily agreed to let us borrow his airship again. "You know Nist and the *Pauline* are available any time you need them. But you must take me along, too. Their Majesties may need medical care, especially if Windslow's men have been treating them roughly."

I agreed, adding Tristan to our team of Nist, Martin, five of Garrett's men, and me. Garrett wanted to volunteer as well but Callan refused.

"You must go to Morda and keep the kingdom running smoothly," she said. "Someone from the family has got to sit on the throne and I won't be of legal age for another three months. There's no other choice —it's got to be you."

"Callie, you don't understand how quickly a hostage's perception of reality can be subverted," he protested. "Hunger, thirst, and sleep deprivation can take a toll very quickly. If Windslow is also using drugs, which wouldn't surprise me, your parents may have a badly distorted memory of the last few months. They'll need to see a face they've known for years or they may not trust their rescuers. You need someone in the rescue party your parents will trust instinctively."

"I know, Uncle," Callan said. "That's why I'm going with them."

On My Honor

"You're going to do *what*?" Martin asked.

"My wife says she's going with us on the rescue mission," I said.

"And you don't have anything to say about that?" he asked.

"I must admit I share Bane's curiosity," Garret said.

Callan crossed her arms, "Choose your next words with care, darling."

"Garrett, you have already raised an excellent point. A familiar face may be necessary to get through to Callan's parents. Callan, you have raised the excellent point that someone must take the throne. Legally, that person must be Garrett. That means Callan should be the one to come with us," I said. Turning to Callan, I added, "But when we are inside that fortress, you have *got* to follow my orders. If you don't do that you could get someone killed."

"I understand," Callan said.

"Good, so you won't mind swearing to do as you're told?" I asked.

"Swear, David?" Callan's voice went flat.

"Callan, would you accept a man into your service if he said he'd guard you with his life but wouldn't swear an oath to that effect?" I asked. "It isn't a perfect analogy, but I'm trying to impress on you just how serious I am about this."

Callan shook her head and sighed. "On my honor as a princess of Mordan and heir to the throne, I swear to obey your orders on this rescue mission."

"If I hadn't seen it with my own eyes, I wouldn't believe it." Garrett turned to Callan. "Who are you and what have you done with my willful niece?"

"If she has enough close brushes with death, Uncle, even a willful niece can change," Callan said.

I wrapped my arms around Callan and kissed her. "Thank you, my dear. Your husband and the captain of your guard both appreciate your understanding. Now, let's gather supplies and get going."

It didn't take us long to get ready. Garrett placed the five-man squad he was sending with us under my command and the squad ensured the *Pauline* was well supplied. Light-weight camouflage netting was spread over the little ship's gas envelope, making it more difficult to spot from above.

As the mooring lines were cast off, Garrett said, "Bring her back safely to us, David."

"Count on it," I replied. "I've sworn an oath, too, after all."

Then the *Pauline* was free and rising rapidly into the late morning sky. Nist flew faster than I would have thought possible for the little ship. The main reason Nist could fly so fast was because the five man squad took shifts feeding the fire, keeping the boiler pressure up. Martin handled navigation, using wind charts to plot the fastest course. He was able to direct our course so we picked up a tail wind, adding to our speed.

Having nothing to contribute to the operation of the airship, Tristan, Callan, and I spent the time studying an old floor plan for the Aerie. It was something Garrett had found in his library while our provisions were gathered. I could see three areas in the old fortress that seemed like secure places to keep prisoners. We'd have to hope for some sign to identify which of the three areas held the king and queen. Without something to point the way, we'd end up having to search through half of the fortress to find them. I doubted we'd have anywhere near that much time.

After a while, the plans to the fortress began to blur. I called for a break, suggesting we all get some rest while we could. It looked like we had a long night ahead of us.

Conversation waxed and waned as the little airship sped on toward the Aerie. One of the men served dinner as the sun sank below the horizon. We were lounging in the cabin, struggling against boredom, when Martin called us up on deck. Nist had brought the ship down to about fifty feet above tree level. A full moon bathed the night in soft, silver light.

Martin motioned us to the port rail and pointed off into the darkness. "Stubb's airship is over there, five or six miles off. We've caught up with them."

The North Face

I looked in the direction Martin was pointing and saw nothing but dark sky. Even with the light from the moon and the planetary ring, I was clueless as to the other airship's location. Since I don't have Martin's experience, I wasn't really surprised by that. Besides, a raider who couldn't spot a nearby airship in the dark probably ended up having a very short career.

"Do you think they can see us?" Callan asked the question on everyone's mind.

"I doubt it," Martin said. "We're flying at a much lower altitude than they are. Between the darkness and the camouflage netting over the envelope, the *Pauline* should blend into the background. I think we'll slip past them safely enough."

"It sounds like there's a 'but' in there somewhere," I said.

"There is. The *Kestrel* is making better time than I thought she would. We won't have anywhere near as much time to spare when we reach the Aerie as I had hoped," Martin said. Scratching his chin, he continued, "I'd guess we'll have an hour at most, and we'll spend a lot of that sneaking up to and into the fortress." He turned to me, "How goes the planning for sneaking into the Aerie?"

"It's going great, with one exception. I've identified three places that are secure enough to hold the king and queen," I said. "Unless you can offer some insight I haven't thought of, it could take us a lot more than one hour to find Callan's parents.

Martin thought for a moment, "Is one of the areas you found on the north face of the fortress?"

I had my implant recall the image of the map. "Good guess, Martin."

"It wasn't really a guess. Anyway, you should make your plans with the north facing area in mind," Martin said.

"Why do you think they'll be on that side, Martin?" Callan asked.

"The land north of the pass is nothing but mountains—and inhospitable ones at that. They can burn lights on that side without worrying about some farmer or a passing airship spotting the light and getting curious."

"This occurred to you because—and I'm just taking a wild guess, here—that's what you'd do," I said.

Martin just grinned in reply.

Callan and I went below and began planning our landing and entry into the Aerie from the north face of the fortress.

Three hours later, the Aerie came into view. It squatted atop the tallest mountain in the region, a huge, hulking fortification that commanded all that lay below it. It also looked like the perfect set for one of those horror vids my parents didn't want me watching when I was a kid. All it lacked was a howling wolf and dark clouds scudding across the face of the moon.

Nist kept our airship close to the ground and reduced speed, keeping our engine as quiet as possible. It wouldn't do for our engine noise to alert those within the Aerie. Slowly, Nist piloted us around the mountain.

When the north face swung into view, I said, "Callan, we'll have to tell your uncle that sometimes it very definitely helps to have a reformed raider on your side."

Light flickered from four of the north-facing windows.

8

CALLAN'S PLAN

It took Nist twenty minutes to complete his approach to the fortress, drifting in with the wind, only using the propellors to improve steering and maintain his heading. Despite the darkness and the cross-winds, Nist landed the *Pauline* in the exact spot Martin had selected when we were floating half a mile away from the fortress. Nist set the airship down on the wall in deep shadows, with a tower between us and the lit windows.

We climbed out onto the fortress wall as Martin issued instructions to Nist. "If Stubb's airship gets here before we're back, slip away as quietly as possible and go get help. If you have to sacrifice quiet to get away safely, do it. The map I gave you shows where all of my ships are and the search pattern they're following. Make for the closest pair of ships and send them back here. If you spot the Royal Navy along the way, send them instead."

Nist nodded his understanding and the rest of the team entered the tower. We descended the stairs within the tower until we reached the same level as the lighted windows. We didn't have to worry about the stone stairs creaking, but the ancient, rusted iron hinges on the doors were going to be a different matter. I'd been prepared to risk the squeal of rusted iron, but Tristan had a better idea.

Using chisels from the *Pauline*, we dug into the rotted wooden door and freed the door from its hinges. Three of the soldiers pulled the door from its frame and leaned it against the wall. It was quiet but took five precious minutes. I fervently hoped we wouldn't come across any more doors.

Slipping from hallway to hallway, we kept watch for patrolling guards. Whoever was in charge in the fortress wasn't expecting company, because we didn't see a single guard making the rounds.

Eight long minutes later, we got our first indication of life since we had spotted the lighted windows. The sound of metal banging on metal began echoing through the hallways. As the sound grew louder, we were able to discern a man's voice yelling over the sound.

"Wakey wakey, Your Majesty. I've got strict orders—no sleeping for you!"

I peered around a corner and saw a lantern burning at the far end of a long hallway. A lone man stood next to the lantern, banging an iron rod on the bars of a cell door. He cradled a cocked and loaded crossbow in his free arm. As I watched, he stopped hitting the bars in the door and peered into the cell.

"Yes, sit up. There's a good king. It's time for your medicine."

"What's happening?" a slurred voice asked. "W-where's my wife?"

Behind me, Callan gasped in dismay at that question.

"Oh, don't you worry none about the queen," the cell guard said, the smirk obvious from his tone. "She's gone to a fancy ball. The lads at the party will give 'er the time of 'er life."

"David, we've got to hurry. I don't know what they're doing to my mother-" Callan's urgent whisper broke as she choked back a sob.

I scanned the approach to the cell. There were no closer cross corridors, so anyone approaching the guard would have to walk down a hundred feet of hallway in plain sight of the guard. He could sound the alarm long before we reached him. And, of course, anyone in the hallway would be an easy target for the crossbow.

I described what I saw to the others. "Boosted, Martin and I can dodge the crossbow bolts, but the guard could kill the king before we got close to him. Does anyone have any better ideas for approaching this guy?"

"I have one," Callan said, "but you're not going to like it."

That was an understatement. I *hated* it.

An Extra Guest

Martin, Callan, and I marched around the corner and into the long hallway. Martin walked ahead of Callan and me, his stride full of purpose and confidence. I held Callan's arm and walked a bit ahead of her, like I was pulling a reluctant prisoner along with me. Callan held her hands behind her back as if they were tied.

We were gambling that the guard would assume we were part of the team sent to kidnap Callan. There was a chance the man would recognize Martin or at least know him by his reputation, but Martin had that covered. If the guard got suspicious about Martin's change of allegiance, Martin was prepared to spin a story about gaining Callan's trust so he could aid in the kidnapping. With the airship carrying Windslow and Raoul bearing down on us, we had no time to come up with a plan I liked better—it was Callan's idea or a headlong charge.

When the guard noticed us, Martin raised his hand in greeting.

"We've got an extra guest for you," he called.

"Bane? What are you doing here?" the guard called.

"Horst, good to see a familiar face," Bane said. "After my contract ended, your employer made me an offer." He motioned back to Callan. "He wanted the full royal set, I guess."

A haggard face peered through the bars in the door next to the guard.

"Callie?" cried the king, his voice still slurred. "No, not my little girl, too," The eyes shifted to Martin. "I know you! I'll-" the king grabbed the bar with both hands and tried to shake the door.

"You'll what? Take a firm tone with me?" Martin sneered. He turned to the guard, "Give my lad the key and walk with me for a moment. I've got new instructions."

Horst's eyes roamed appreciably over Callan's body as he handed me the keys. As he walked down the hall with Martin, Horst said, "It's gonna be fun having *her* around to party with."

When Horst and Martin walked out of earshot, the king stared at me through heavy-lidded eyes and whispered, "Do I know you? I feel like I should." He shook his head as if trying to clear it. "No matter. You look like a smart young man. If you help us escape. I'll reward you handsomely."

Unlocking the door, I whispered, "That's what I'm here to do, Your Majesty."

A thud sounded behind us. Martin had knocked out Horst.

Callan rushed into the cell and hugged her father. "Come on, Daddy, let's go find Mom."

Martin returned and whispered, "We've got to hurry. Horst told me the other guards have vile plans for the queen."

First Dibs On the Queen

A fist hit Martin on the side of the head and he reeled against the wall. King Edwar followed it with a punch to Martin's stomach. As Martin doubled over, I caught the king's raised fist.

"The situation is not as you think, Your Majesty," I said.

"I know all I need to know," King Edwar snarled, the drug-induced stupor pushed aside by his rage.

Callan placed her hand on his arm, "No, you don't, Daddy, and we don't have time for explanations. Martin is here at great personal risk with no wish other than to help us."

"Martin?" King Edwar asked. "You call this criminal scum by his given name?"

"I call him friend," Callan replied.

"What has happened to you, Callie?" her father asked.

"Nothing happened to me—that is why I know we can trust Martin." Callan took her father's hands and look into his eyes. "You've been beaten, deprived of sleep, drugged, and probably starved. I know what I'm doing and who I can trust."

"But you're just a little girl," my father-in-law said.

"No, Daddy, I'm a married woman who'll be twenty-one in a couple of months," Callan told him.

A puzzled look crossed Edwar's face. "Married?" He looked at me. "To you? Is that why you look familiar?"

"Yes, Edwar, it is," I said. "But right now we have to find the queen."

Martin straightened, wincing, "Horst told me the other men have gotten bored just sitting around. They're off gambling for first dibs on the queen."

The color drained from the faces of Callan and her father.

"Do you have any idea where they've taken her?" I asked.

"Horst didn't want to have to listen—though more because he was on duty and unable to join in the fun than through any sense of decency—so he sent them to the far end of that side passage," Martin said, pointing at a passage back beyond where we'd first spotted Horst.

Callan started down the hallway toward the passage, the king on her heels.

"Stop, Callan," I said. "I'll get your mother. You and your father must go to the airship."

"I'm not going to run to safety while my mother is in danger."

"Yes, you are," I said. "The kingdom comes first. That means ensuring the safety of the king and his heir."

"But-"

"I'll rescue her, Callan."

"And I'll help," Martin said. "With two scouts-"

"No, Martin," I said. "You're the only person I can trust to fly off and leave the queen and me behind, if necessary. And that is exactly what you will do if the *Kestrel* arrives before I get back to you."

Martin nodded, "I'll keep them safe, David."

Callan kissed me. "Be careful, darling. I don't want to lose you or Mom."

I nodded and took off down the side passage to find the queen.

9

A BIT OF FUN

As I neared the end of the passage, I heard raucous voices and rough laughter. Cries of excitement rose, followed by disappointed curses and one yell of triumph. The sounds all came from behind a closed door, one without a barred little window cut into it. The raised voices died down and the men launched into some kind of bantering discussion. I desperately wished I had some idea what was happening behind the door but I couldn't afford the time it would take to figure it out by listening through the door. Even if the queen wasn't in immediate danger—which didn't seem likely—the other airship could arrive at any time. I needed to get the queen to the *Pauline* so we could make good our escape.

Without giving myself the chance for second thoughts, I opened the door and strode into the room. I swept a critical gaze over the room. To my right was a large table around which sat five men. Dice were scattered across the table, along with several empty bottles of wine. The men were drinking from goblets and their eyes shone with excitement. The object of their attention stood to my left. A sixth man stood before the queen, looking her up and down. He wore a disturbing smile and was casually tossing a knife from hand to hand.

The queen's arms were spread wide, each wrist tied to an iron ring driven into the wall. Strips of cloth, which I suddenly realized were the queen's slashed clothing, were piled on the floor next to her. The queen was left wearing only her shift and the underclothes beneath it. Worst of all, my proud mother-in-law sagged forward, only kept up by the ropes around her wrists. Head hanging down, her dull eyes were open but were not focused on anything. Queen Elaina ignored all within the room. She didn't even look up as I entered the room.

The six men were so enthralled with their entertainment, they hadn't noticed me yet, either. That couldn't last long and I thought my act would be more believable if I announced myself before they saw me.

"What is the meaning of this?" I demanded.

The heads of the five men at the table turned my way. The man standing before Queen Elaina gave a start before spinning to face me. To my considerable relief, the queen's head turned slowly toward me, as well.

Pointing at me with the knife, the man before the queen asked, "Who are you and what are you doing here?"

The men at the table rose from their seats and drew their swords.

It had been too much to hope the men would just accept that I had authority to match the tone of voice I'd used. Still, I did the only thing I could do at this point. I continued with my act.

"Our employer was afraid you cretins would do something stupid like this. You were under strict orders to keep the prisoners secure and unharmed." That last bit was a complete guess, but it seemed like a reasonable one.

"Aw, we ain't harming 'er. We's jest havin' a bit of fun."

"You're not being paid to have fun, you idiot. It looks like our employer was wise to send me to insure the prisoner's safety." I held out my hand. "Give me that knife and get away from the queen."

Keeping my left hand outstretched, I continued toward the man. He looked to one of the men at the table. I'd instilled doubt but the man wasn't ready to take orders from me yet.

"Your word don't cut it around here," one of the men at the table said. "Unless you got some written orders from the boss, you can just turn around and leave."

"Written orders? Just how stupid can you be?" I snarled. "And worse, just how stupid do you think our employer is? You don't honestly think he'd put anything about this in writing, do you?"

I'd kept walking during this exchange and was now within reach of the knife wielder. Drawing my sword, I slashed the man's forearm and the blade fell from his hand. He retreated away from me toward his friends at the table.

"The six of you stay here." I put all the derision I could muster—which was a lot, considering what I'd seen—into my voice. "I'll be back to deal with you after the queen is back in her cell and safe from the likes of you."

At a signal from the apparent leader of this crew, a couple of men moved to block my way to the door.

"Tell you what, boy, what say you stop throwing around orders and answer a few questions for me?" the leader said. "Let's start with something easy—just who do you think you are?"

My bluster had gotten me farther than I had hoped it would, but the time for play acting was over.

"You want to know who I am?" I asked. "I am David Rice, prince consort and protector to Her Royal Highness, Princess Callan, heir to the throne of Mordan. I am the man who fought the trog leader in the city of Faroon and defeated him in hand-to-hand combat. I am the man who defeated the five assassins Ardhan Windslow sent to kill me and kidnap my wife. As far as you are concerned, I am death incarnate. Surrender now or die."

Kill Her

My speech had very different effects on those who heard it.

Queen Elaina lifted her head and struggled to focus on my face. I hoped she could push through the drugs and sleep deprivation to recognize me. After King Edwar, though, I didn't have much hope.

I also hoped my reputation would lead the six men before me to surrender or, at the very least, back off and let us leave. It didn't. Instead, they laughed.

"Look, men, it's David the Pure—and the stories are true. I can feel his amazing powers of goodness driving the evil from my soul," the leader said to his men. "We'd better do something before we all end up all noble-minded like Martin Bane. Do me a favor, men, and kill this idiot."

"I don't know, Nars," said the one whose arm I'd slashed. "You ever listened to them songs about Rice? He's s'pposed to be real good."

Nars rolled his eyes. "You're not telling me you've started believing tavern songs, are you Jon?"

The four other men looked at their companion and laughed.

Jon smiled nervously, "Nah. I— I was jest funnin' with you, Nars."

Jon's concern had been my last hope that Queen Elaina and I could just walk away from this. As I had expected, there was only one way I was getting us both out of this alive.

Boost!

While the men were all distracted laughing at Jon, I charged. The move surprised all six of them. Instinctively, they all took defensive stances.

One of the men held his guard much too low. I didn't hesitate, attacking him with a slash aimed at his throat. Suddenly aware his guard was out of place, the man brought his blade up to block my swing. With Boost-enhanced speed, I changed direction and brought my attack down low. Before the man even registered what I had done, his sword passed harmlessly above my blade. I drove two feet of steel into his gut. Withdrawing my now-crimson blade, I threw the screaming man at the closest man to my right. The two of them went down in a tangle of limbs and blood. I kept moving.

Despite his song-induced concern about my reputation as a warrior, Jon jumped into cross blades with me. He made a surprisingly neat move and caught me in a bind. My survival depended on constant motion, so I rammed my knee into his groin. Jon's eyes rolled up and he doubled over, breaking the bind. As I spun past Jon, I cut his sword arm to the bone. With a metallic clatter, his sword fell to the floor. Jon dropped to his knees, cradling his arm and trying to stop the bleeding.

I had broken through the line of men, leaving two to my right and two to my left. I leapt onto the table and spun to face the room. Two men were already out of the fight. The other four looked stunned at the speed of it all. The smiles and the laughter were gone, replaced by smoldering anger. And festering fear.

"As you can see, the tavern songs didn't exaggerate my abilities," I said. "This is your last chance to surrender."

"You're a quick one, boy, and good with that sword. I'll give you that," Nars said. "But you're not a real smart fighter. It seems to me you're way over here, standing on the table, and the queen is way over there, tied to the wall. Lon," Nars singled out one of his men, "go over to the queen. If this boy doesn't throw down his sword, kill her."

Smart Man

The man closest to the queen—Lon, I assumed—raised his sword and stalked toward the queen. In the old adventure vids my father and I used to watch, there would have been a chandelier that I could use to swing over my enemies to protect my mother-in-law. I had a knife but it was simply a blade for cutting. It was too poorly balanced to throw effectively. So I threw the only other thing I had to hand.

My sword spun and flashed in the torchlight before burying itself between Lon's shoulder blades. His back arched and a hand scrabbled over his shoulder, trying to reach the sword. The other men gaped, their eyes locked on my blade. While they were distracted, I hopped from the table and grabbed one of the chairs.

Recovering his composure, Nars was just turning back toward me when I smashed the chair over his head. The chair splintered and the guard leader reeled under the blow. I delivered a spin-kick to Nars' head and he collapsed. I was left holding two pieces of the chair back. Armed with those sturdy clubs, I charged at the man nearest to me.

Eyes wide, the man slashed wildly at my neck. I blocked the swing with one piece of the chair then smashed the wrist of his sword arm with the other. Bones snapped and the man's sword fell from his hand. I cracked him across the head with one of my clubs. The man's eyes rolled back in his head and he dropped to the floor. I never stopped moving toward the queen.

The third man broke and ran toward the queen. There was no way I could get to her first, so I hurled one of the pieces of the chair at his head, then threw the second piece at his legs. He ducked and the first piece missed, but the second piece hit a shin, tripping him up. That slowed him down long enough for me to dash to Lon, who was still flailing and trying to reach the sword stuck in his back. I rammed the blade through him up to the hilt.

Putting my foot against Lon's back, I shoved him away and yanked my blade free. I spun to face the man I'd tripped up with the thrown chair pieces. He stopped his stumbling charge toward me, arms windmilling wildly. His eyes went wide in terror and he dropped his sword.

"I surrender."

"Smart man," I said.

I clouted him over the head with my sword pommel. As he fell unconscious, I dropped Boost.

As I cut the queen free, she asked in a slightly slurred voice, "You said you were Callie's guard? You're not Rob."

"Yes, Your Majesty, I'm Princess Callan's guard," I said. "And no, I'm not Rob. But let's discuss that later. Her Highness is not far from here. She's with her father. And we need to join them before a raider airship arrives."

That Was the Plan

Rubbing her chafed wrists, the queen peered at my face through heavy-lidded eyes. "You look familiar. And you said you were a prince consort? I didn't catch your wife's name. Is she known to me?"

"I believe so, Your Majesty." I helped Queen Elaina step into her shoes and then, taking her by the arm, led her from the room. "But as I said before, we must hurry."

"Yes, there is a raider ship on the way." The queen came to a sudden halt. "It's not that raider Martin Bane, is it? He's taken my baby before, you know."

"I do know, Your Majesty," I replied, struggling to keep my voice calm and soothing. "But the man I'm worried about is most definitely not Martin Bane."

I started walking again, giving the queen little choice but to stumble after me.

Unable to maintain focus, Queen Elaina's attention wandered yet again. Her head swung back and forth as she watched the sword I held in my other hand. Despite the drugs, she proved quite capable of recognizing the blade. "Why do you carry Captain Vonsteader's sword, young man?"

I didn't have the time or the creativity to craft a believable story on the spur of the moment. "I'm afraid Rob lost his life defending Princess Callan. He gave me the sword before he died and ordered me to use it in defense of your daughter."

The queen bowed her head, "Poor Callie. She must be devastated."

Three months had passed since Rob's death, but Callan still mourned her long-time companion and guardian. "That she is, though she tries to hide it."

Queen Elaina came to a sudden stop yet again. "Wait a moment, young man. You said you were a prince consort *and* protector to a princess. And you say Rob ordered you to defend Callie."

I could almost see the wheels turning in the queen's mind as she struggled against the drugs to make connections. I most definitely did *not* want to discuss my marriage to Callan right now.

"Let's keep moving, Your Majesty," I said, once again nearly dragging Queen Elaina down the hallway. "Princess Callan will explain everything once we're aboard the airship."

"That would mean *you* married Callie," Queen Elaina mused. Shaking her head, she continued. "But that can't be right. Callie is marrying Prince Rupor, isn't she?"

"That was the plan," I said, walking faster. "We've got to hurry, Your Majesty. Time is short and we don't want the airship to leave without us."

Elaina continued to stumble along behind me and we moved more slowly than I'd have preferred, but at least we were moving. Soon, I could see the corridor where we'd first seen Horst, the cell guard. We were no more than thirty feet from the hallway when I heard voices.

Putting my finger to my lips in the hopes of keeping Elaina quiet, we stopped and listened. There could be no mistaking the voice.

"I thought you said there was a guard in this hallway?" Raoul said, his tone short and peremptory.

The queen's face lit up. "Why that's Raoul, Rupor's brother. He'll have a whole ship full of men with him. Those raiders you're so worried about are in for a rude surprise."

"No, Your Majesty," I said, grasping for the only idea I could think of. "It's a raider trick to lure us out."

"Pish and tosh. I'd recognize Raoul's voice anywhere." Queen Elaina waved my objections aside. Raising her voice, she called, "Raoul! We're down here."

Boots clattered on stone as our enemies rushed toward us.

10

IS THAT WINDSLOW?

I WAS STAGING ONE HECK OF A RESCUE. ADDLED BY DRUGS AND SLEEP deprivation, the queen had asked all the wrong questions and, based on my answers, made all the wrong connections. She might not be suspicious of me yet, but Raoul would turn her against me if he had a chance to speak with her. I could only begin to imagine how she would react if I tried to convince her that Raoul wasn't the friend her memory told her he was. Unfortunately, I had to try to convince her of just that.

Light and shadows flickered on the wall at the intersection of the two hallways. The heavy tread of boots pounded closer to our passageway. Much as I wanted to explain the situation, I simply didn't have the time to do so. I had hoped I could get Queen Elaina to Callan and the king. Their presence would have calmed the queen. Rest and time would restore her memory and the queen would remember I was the good guy. Right now, we needed to run.

I lifted the queen and threw her over my shoulder. Or I tried to do that. The queen held her body rigid, refusing to bend over my shoulder. I couldn't outrun anyone with the queen throwing off my balance like that. It was time to improvise. I lifted the queen's legs, balancing her over my shoulder like a wooden board. It was still awkward, but at least I could run.

Realizing holding herself stiff hadn't slowed me down, the queen suddenly went limp. The sudden shift of weight threw me off balance again and I stumbled. As I fought to regain my footing, the queen beat and scratched at my back and began screaming, "Help me, Raoul! A raider has me!"

Our pursuers rounded the corner just in time to see me lurch into a side hall.

"There he is!" Raoul yelled. "Save the queen, men!"

Raoul didn't sound believable to me, but the queen kept shouting.

"Stop shouting, Your Majesty," I said. "Raoul is not the friend you think he is."

"Foolish man, do you really expect me to believe that? Raoul is the brother of my daughter's betrothed."

"He wishes!" I said. "Look at our pursuers, Majesty. Do you see an older man with wild, gray hair?"

"Yes, I see him. What of it?"

"Look at him more closely. Don't you recognize him?"

"I can't-" The queen gasped, "Is that Windslow?"

"Yes, it is," I said. "That's extremely strange company the prince is keeping, don't you think?"

I came to a side passage, the first I'd seen in this hallway. Without hesitation, I turned into the hallway. I immediately saw that the hallway ended in a door, but it was too late to turn around.

"I don't know. It's so hard to think!" the queen moaned

"Then I suggest you trust me," I said. "I promise you Princess Callan does."

Raoul, Windslow and their men charged into the side passage as I reached the door. Hoping to find stairs, I turned the knob and pushed. Nothing happened. The door was stuck fast.

Block Their Escape

The queen hung limp over my shoulder, no longer beating and scratching my back. I hoped that meant she had decided to trust me. I was afraid it meant she had been overcome by the stress of her ordeal and the stress of seeing Windslow.

Seeing my struggles with the door, Raoul and his men slowed to a walk. "You can't escape, Rice. Return Her Majesty to me unharmed and I'll make sure you get a fair trial."

I had to give Raoul top marks for sticking to the script. If I had the opportunity, I would cut those marks into his forehead with my sword.

"Drop the play acting, Raoul. Her Majesty has already spotted Windslow and now knows you're not to be trusted," I said. "It wasn't very smart bringing him with you, but intelligence never was your strong suit. In truth, I'm still trying to figure out what your strong suit is."

"Do not try my patience, Rice," Raoul cried, his eyes narrowing in anger. "Your fate hangs by a very narrow thread. Anger me further and I'll cut that thread without compunction."

"Well, I'm impressed, Raoul. I didn't realize you knew such big words," I said. "Or did you say 'without compunction' when 'without courage' is what you meant to say?"

Raoul's face went red and he sputtered incoherent curses. Entertaining as that was, it was time to make my getaway. While bantering with Raoul, I'd considered my options. There was but one option and in other circumstances it wouldn't have been an option at all. If the Terran Exploration Corps ever found me, I was going to be quite the case study on the effects of Boost on the human body. At least I'd only Boosted for a minute or so when dealing with thugs guarding the queen.

Boost!

I spun and kicked the door at the end of the hallway. The latch held firm, but the rusted hinges groaned and that side of the door moved an inch. Raoul shouted to his men to charge as I gave the door another kick. The hinges broke and the door pushed open a couple of feet. Releasing Boost, I ran through the door.

"After them! You stay with the men, Raoul," Windslow shouted at him. "I'll get back to the airship and take off. Aloft, I may be able to block their escape."

Beyond the door, I found just what I needed—stairs going up. I kicked the door shut in the face of Raoul's charging men and then sprinted up the stairs. I hoped the next door I came to would open on the first try. Two flights up, the stairs ended at a landing with a door. The hinges squealed like dying animals but the door opened.

I charged through the door and onto the top of the fortress wall. It stretched out before me, bathed in silver moonlight. Silhouetted against the moon, I saw something that buoyed my spirits even as it doomed Queen Elaina and me. A dark shadow moved away from the Aerie—it was the *Pauline* flying away.

Callan and her father were safe—but the queen and I were trapped in the Aerie.

Can You Run?

The queen stirred and attempted to straighten up. Perhaps the cold, fresh air was breaking through the drugs and fatigue affecting her mind.

"You can put me down, David," Queen Elaina said.

"You remember me, Your Majesty?"

"Yes, or at least some things about you," she replied. "I remember your name and know that I can trust you."

That would be more than enough for now, especially when I heard the door I'd kicked shut just a moment ago crash open.

"Can you run, Your Majesty?" I asked. "I am going to need to keep my sword arm free."

"Yes, I can," the queen answered. As I swung her to her feet, she continued, "You're more than Callie's bodyguard, aren't you, David?"

"I'm her husband," I said as I took her hand and began running along the wall toward the next tower.

"And Edwar and I approved?"

"Yes ma'am. You and His Majesty have been very kind and welcoming to me."

"Good for us," Elaina said, beginning to pant at the exertion. "That little airship you were watching—Callie and Edwar are aboard? I assume it was also our way out of this fortress?"

"It was, but only if we reached it before Windslow and Raoul arrived," I said. "If we didn't, my orders were for them to leave us behind."

"Why would you give such orders, David?"

Shouts erupted behind us as Raoul's men spotted us.

"A kingdom must have a monarch and an heir," I said, running faster and pulling Elaina with me. "That airship carries both."

"I can see why I approved of you, David. You're a very practical man," the queen said as we reached the door into the tower.

To my relief, the door opened easily and we ran inside the tower. To my consternation, there was no way to bar the door from the inside. Drawing my knife, I jammed it under the door. Perhaps it would slow down our pursuers for a few extra seconds.

The tower had stairs, but they only went up to the top of the tower. That was out of the question. We'd be trapped at the top of the tower and make easy targets for airborne crossbowmen. Even worse, there was no other door out the other side of the tower.

"I'm afraid this is where I must make my stand, Your Majesty," I said.

"After watching you fight, I have full confidence in you," the queen said.

I sighed. Boost was our only hope—and likely my death sentence. "You must run from the tower as soon as I clear a path for you."

"And what of you?" she asked.

"Chances are I'll be dead."

The tower door shook from a sharp blow. I raised my sword and prepared to defend my new family one last time.

11

YOU WILL OBEY MY COMMANDS

THE DOOR RATTLED FROM ANOTHER BLOW. ON THE OTHER SIDE OF THE door, Raoul exhorted his men to try harder.

"David, I'd rather not lose my son-in-law before I've had the chance to remember him." Elaina said. "Would you mind being a bit more practical and little less heroic?"

"Uh, sure," I replied.

"Good. Come over here with me." She backed up to the wall next to the door hinges. "When the door swings open, it will block us from view. We can hope the men will see the stairs and assume we climbed them. That will give us a chance to run out the door."

I joined her as the door shook again. "What happens if they don't take the bait? I mean, it is one of the oldest tricks in the book."

"Either you'll get your chance to die heroically or, more likely, I'll choose to surrender," the queen said. "Whatever I decide, you will obey my commands."

I lifted my sword in salute. "As you say, Your Majesty."

Another blow struck the door. My poorly balanced knife was holding much better than I'd hoped, but now I needed the door to swing open. I wrenched the knife from under the door, standing up just ahead of the next blow. The door jamb broke and the door was flung open. We were hidden from sight by the door, but it threatened to smash into my face as well. I caught and held the door handle, saving my nose in the process.

Raoul's men charged into the tower and their footsteps continued toward the stairs. We waited for the men to reach the far wall before slipping around the door and out onto the fortress wall. I felt just like one of the heroes in the adventure vids from my childhood. Unfortunately, one of Raoul's men followed the same script and looked toward the door as we ran through it.

"Your Highness, they're behind us," the man shouted as he set off after us.

And just like that the chase was on again, with Raoul and his men trailing us by no more than thirty feet. I pulled the queen along with one hand and sheathed my sword with the other. I could draw it again if need be, but expected I would need a free hand to open a door before I would need to swing my sword again.

Coming from the courtyard of the Aerie, I heard the roar of steam engines driving an airship into a climb. Windslow must have reach Stubb's airship and was bringing it to join the chase. Her Majesty and I had to get off of the wall soon. If we didn't, we would be easy targets for Stubb's airborne crossbowmen.

Leave Me

The roar of the airship's engines deepened and I could detect movement in the darkened castle courtyard. The *Kestrel* rose from the shadows and powered into the moonlight.

"You can't get away from us, Rice," Raoul called, as he chased Queen Elaina and me across the wall. "Our airship will cut you off before you reach the other tower. Even if it doesn't, our crossbowmen will cut you down."

"Do you really want to be responsible for starting a war between Tarteg and Mordan?" I called back, picking up speed in the hopes of proving him wrong. "Callan's uncle, Lord Garrett, knows you are working with Windslow. If we don't return, you can count on Tarteg paying the price for your actions."

"Why would I care what happens to a country that turned its back on my mother and me?" Raoul shot back.

"What did you expect would happen after your role in Callan's kidnapping was exposed?" I asked over my shoulder. "You'd be welcomed back as the unconquoring wannabe hero?"

"I'm going to rip your heart out with my bare hands, Rice!" Rupor screamed over the engine noise from the approaching airship.

"Is it wise to taunt Raoul like that, David?" Queen Elaina asked between gasps for air.

"Most definitely. Raoul makes his worst mistakes when he lets his emotions get the better of him," I replied. I decided not to mention just how much fun it was, as well.

Screaming in wordless rage, Raoul put on an unexpected burst of speed and pulled away from his squad of men. The men sped up, trying to keep up with their enraged leader.

Unfortunately, the queen slowed down, unable to keep up the pace I'd been setting. Her chest heaved and her breath was ragged.

"I can't keep going," she gasped. "Leave me. Escape and return to Callan."

The *Kestrel* swung up over the castle wall, little more than a hundred feet behind us. The helmsman steadied the airship ten feet above the fortress wall. The massive vessel bore down on the two of us, already flying twice as fast as we could possibly hope to run. Windslow was perched at the bow of the ship, pointing at me with his sword and directing the *Kestrel's* crossbowmen.

Our eyes locked over the distance and a grin stretched over Windslow's face. "It's the end of the line, bodyguard. Prepare to die!"

Rice Must Die By My Hand

I tensed, ready to risk Boosting again. I had kept my Boosts short so far today, but between the fight in the mine and the fight in the fortress, I was pushing my body harder than I had in months. Even Boosted I doubted I could block the two-dozen quarrels that would be flying at us shortly. I could, however, put my body between the crossbowmen and the queen. Windslow raised his arm. No doubt, dropping it would be the signal to fire.

"Stay behind me, Your Majesty!" I said, stepping in front of her. "I'll protect you as best I can."

Raoul and his men had stopped their pursuit, not wanting to put themselves in the line of fire. Windslow grinned, nodding in approval. Raoul's head swung between Windslow and me, his eyes wide in frenzied rage.

"Don't kill him, Windslow!" Raoul yelled. "Rice must die by my hand."

"Don't be foolish, boy," Windslow called back. "It doesn't matter how Rice dies—just that he ends up dead."

Windslow raised his arm a bit higher—for added effect and drama, I suppose—and posed for just a second, his eyes locked on mine.

With a roar, the *Pauline* crested the outer wall and struck the bow of the larger airship. Windslow and his crossbowmen staggered as the deck heaved beneath their feet. Ragged twangs sounded as the crossbowmen's fingers twitched and they fired involuntarily. Unaimed quarrels flew in all directions. One quarrel pierced a crossbowman's leg. Another one of the quarrels slammed into the shoulder of one of Raoul's squad. The rest of the squad dove to the ground, leaving Raoul the only one of them standing.

Nist worked the *Pauline's* controls and flew straight along the wall toward us. In the little ship's wake the helmsman of the *Kestrel* fought to bring the larger airship back on course. I could see Martin and the soldiers standing at the rail, ready to toss ropes to us.

"Lovely to see you again, Raoul!" I shouted as the *Pauline* passed over his head. "As always, I've enjoyed watching your plan fail in such a spectacular fashion."

Raoul broke into a run, waving his sword and shouting curses I couldn't hear over the *Pauline's* engines.

On the *Pauline*, Martin yelled, "Are you ready?"

"Yes," I shouted, wrapping an arm around the queen. "Throw me a rope."

I saw a subtle change in Martin and his movements became more fluid and graceful. He was Boosting to make his throw more accurate.

"Hold on tightly, Your Majesty," I said, pulling the queen close against me with one arm. Her arms wrapped around me, careful not to interfere with my free arm.

Martin threw the rope and it landed right in my free hand. I grabbed hold of the rope and we were yanked into the air.

The next tower on the wall was less than a hundred feet ahead of the airship. Having little choice, Nist spun the wheel and steered the *Pauline* over the edge of the Aerie's walls. A two-thousand-foot drop yawned beneath us as Martin and the soldiers hauled on the rope. Queen Elaina buried her head against my chest, unable to bear to watch as we were pulled to the ship. The few seconds we dangled in the air seemed unending, but end they did.

Hands caught us as we reached the airship and the two of us were pulled to the safety of the deck. Right after we reached the deck, a crossbow quarrel struck the airship. Looking back, I saw Raoul climbing on board the *Kestrel* with Windslow. Ropes had been thrown to him and his squad on the wall.

Raoul, rage still written on his face, was giving chase.

12

DEATH FROM ABOVE

THE AIR HUMMED AS ANOTHER QUARREL FLEW PAST ME, DRIVING DEEP INTO the deck with a resounding thunk. Several other quarrels missed the airship entirely, their passage marked by sound alone.

"Your Majesties, Callan," I said, "you need to get into the cabin, now. That goes for you too, Tristan."

Tristan shepherded Callan and her parents below deck and out of immediate danger from the crossbow fire.

"Everyone find something to hold onto," Nist yelled. "I'm going into a steep dive."

"Good idea, Nist," I said. "Raoul has a lot more men and firepower than we do. What can Martin and I do to help?"

"I'm stuck at the wheel and can't dodge incoming shots. Can you put up something to block them, instead?"

Nist hadn't finished talking before Martin and the soldiers began piling supply crates up behind Nist. The wall was only a few feet high when one of the soldiers cried out as a quarrel buried itself in his chest.

"Carry that man below deck," I told two of the soldiers. "If Tristan needs your help to setup a surgery, stay below and help him."

The two soldiers nodded and ran to carry their wounded comrade to our doctor.

Then the deck tilted under us as Nist put the *Pauline* into a dive. The engines roared and the little airship began picking up speed. Caught by surprise, the *Kestrel* was slow to respond to Nist's maneuvers. We began to pull away from the larger airship, but the other ship's altitude meant they could continue firing down on us. The next two volleys missed us entirely, but by then the *Kestrel's* helmsman had pointed the ship's nose down. We had gained a few hundred feet, but Raoul and Windslow were back on our tail.

"They're following us, Nist," I yelled over the whistling wind and the roaring engines. "Have you got any idea how to get out of this?"

"If we can get the pressure up in the boiler, we can just outrun them," Nist said. "We used up a lot of pressure coming up to ramming speed back at the wall. And until now, everyone has been busy pulling you and Her Majesty safely onboard the *Pauline*."

"Martin-" I began.

"I'll deliver the orders to the men below, David," Martin called as he ran toward the cabin door.

A crossbow quarrel hit one of the boxes piled up behind Nist. Another quarrel clanged off of a brass fitting. It looked like Raoul's men were getting a feel for the range and elevation.

I went back to dragging crates close to the wall we were building to protect Nist. The crates were heavy. I'd definitely need Martin's help to add any of them to the stack. And just like that, Martin returned and we lifted the crate together, adding it to the wall protecting Nist.

Meanwhile, Raoul's crossbowmen were getting organized, firing in rotation and, now that they were getting the range, keeping us under a near constant barrage of crossbow quarrels.

Martin and I rushed to finish building a wall for Nist before Raoul's crossbowmen really got the range figured out. Then it was too late. The next volley rained down on us and one of the quarrels struck the crate between the splayed fingers of my left hand. In a rush, Martin and I added the crate to the stack then leapt over the wall of crates, seeking shelter from the crossbowmen.

Midway through our leap, Martin grunted in pain. When we landed on the deck, I glanced at Martin, who was still lying on top of the crates. A quarrel had buried itself in his shoulder. I pulled him down behind the crate wall, propped him against it, and started to examine his shoulder. With a sigh, Nist collapsed next to us. Despite the wall we had built, a quarrel stuck out from between his shoulder blades.

With no one to man the controls, the *Pauline* leveled off and slowed down. Raoul's airship, still under the control of her helmsman and emulating the bird of prey it was named for, dove toward us from above.

A New Pilot

"Do something, David," Martin gasped. "You need to find a way to keep them off of us for a few minutes while the boiler pressure comes up."

Another rain of crossbow quarrels fell around us. If I stood in at the wheel for any length of time, I was sure to be shot. I thought I might be able to pilot the airship while crouching low enough that the wall of crates would protect me. It was worth trying, at least.

I scurried to the airship's controls, grabbed the wheel with one hand and the aileron controls with the other. Keeping my head down, I worked the ailerons and put the *Pauline* back into a dive. I was sure we were at least a thousand feet from the ground, but I couldn't both keep my head down and see what was ahead. At some point, I'd have to stand up to look and risk ending up like Nist.

"Martin, what are the chances you can get Nist down to Tristan?"

"Absolutely none," Martin said through gritted teeth.

"I didn't think so," I said. "Different question—can *you* get below deck and send someone back for Nist?"

"Yeah, I can do that," Martin said. "What about you?"

"I'll stay here, pilot the ship, and hope we get out of crossbow range before we crash into a mountain."

"Aren't you the cheery one?" Martin asked.

Another volley of crossbow quarrels hit the deck and the crates piled up behind us. The sound of the last quarrel striking wood hadn't faded when Martin jumped to his feet and ran for the cabin door. He threw the door open and dove through a split second before the next volley clattered on the deck where Martin had been standing.

Right after the next volley, two of Garrett's soldiers dashed through the door and up to join me on the deck.

As they carefully lifted Nist between them, one of the men asked, "What can we do to help you, sir?"

"Go back to stoking the fire," I said. "Outrunning the other airship is our best chance of survival."

"Yes, sir!" the soldier said, waiting for the next volley to pass. When it did, the two soldiers dashed off with Nist. Despite their burden, they were through the cabin door and safely under cover before Raoul's men could take any further shots.

At the same time, I risked popping up from concealment to see what was ahead. It was a good thing I did. The side of a mountain was no more than two hundred feet ahead of us.

What's the Plan?

I spun the wheel, changing our course away from the looming mountain, and worked the ailerons to level off. As a result of Nist's piloting, we had been at long range for the crossbows. And if Nist were piloting the ship right now, we'd be farther ahead than we were and probably pulling away from the other airship as well. But I was piloting and I just wasn't as skilled as Nist. In avoiding the mountain and leveling off, I overworked the ailerons and the *Pauline* nosed up twenty degrees. Too much hard won speed bled off before I could level off again. I looked over my shoulder to find the *Kestrel* looming large and closing.

Another volley of crossbow quarrels clattered all around me. Raoul certainly had his men firing without pause. Maybe we'd get lucky and they'd run out of quarrels before they hit anyone else. It wasn't likely, but hoping for that seemed the most useful thing I could think of to do.

Light spilled onto the deck as the cabin door opened then vanished as the door shut again. Light footsteps pattered across the deck. Even before she threw herself behind the makeshift barrier, I knew Callan had joined me on deck.

"What are you doing out here, Callan? You should stay below where it's safe."

"Safe from what? If we don't find a way to get the *Kestrel* off our tail, Raoul and Windslow are going to catch all of us," Callan said. "Better I take a risk to help you than stay below and wait for us to get captured—or killed."

I couldn't find fault with her argument, but that doesn't mean I had to like it.

"Well, darling," Callan asked, "what's the plan?"

"I'm trying to think of one, dear," I responded. "And in case you're wondering, my masculine pride won't be bruised in the least if you have any suggestions to offer."

"Until the boiler pressure builds, we can't outrun them," Callan mused, "so maybe you should give up on speed and rely on maneuverability."

It was worth a try. I spun the wheel hard to starboard and our airship turned quickly to its new heading, off at right angles from the old course. We lost speed and the *Kestrel* drew closer, but now we were on a completely different heading than they were. We heard a volley of quarrels pass behind us as the crossbowmen lost their aim.

Within seconds of our course change, the *Kestrel's* helmsman was bringing the big ship around to our course. Worse, I had picked a course that allowed the bigger ship's crew to bring the starboard ballista to bear on the *Pauline*. With a deep thrum of springing wood and rope, a massive bolt was hurled across nearly two hundred feet. With a horrific crash, the bolt smashed into our airship's rudder. The tension went out of the wheel as the cables running to the rudder were snapped.

The *Pauline* still flew, but I no longer had control over the airship.

13

THE SPARK OF AN IDEA

"I WISH I HADN'T MADE THE SUGGESTION TO TRY TO OUT MANEUVER them," Callan said in a small voice.

"It wasn't the suggestion, Callan, it was the course I chose," I said. "But let's worry about recriminations after we figure out what to do next."

I looked about the moonlit deck for something—anything—I could use to defend us from the rapidly closing *Kestrel*. Nothing I saw sparked an idea.

Spark. That was it!

"Callan," I said, "can you light a lantern with a flint and tinder?"

"Of course. That was one of the skills Rob made sure I learned," Callan replied. "But won't a lit lantern make it easier for the cross-bowmen to hit us?"

The latest volley struck all around us. As soon as the last quarrel had hit, I dashed from behind our makeshift cover, grabbed the *Pauline's* stern lantern, and then snagged a mooring line as I dove back behind cover. Three quarrels struck where I'd been just a second ago.

"They don't seem to be having any trouble hitting us in the dark," I said. "So please light this."

"Are you sure?" Callan asked.

"Trust me."

Striking the flint, Callan said, "Always."

Holding the mooring line, I jumped off the airship's port side and swung around toward the bow. The *Pauline* blocked me from the sight of Raoul's men as I swung forward, though I think I'd have been a tough target to hit even without the cover. Landing at the bow, I snatched the lantern hanging there and was swinging back to the stern before Raoul's men even knew where I was.

The stern lantern was burning brightly when I ducked behind the crates again.

"Nice work, my dear," I said, swapping lanterns. "Light this one while I'm gone."

"Gone where?" Callan asked.

Perhaps I should have answered her, but I was in too much of a hurry. The latest volley of quarrels struck the ship and I charged out from behind the makeshift wall and toward the stern. By now, the pursuing airship loomed no more than eighty feet behind us.

At the rail, I flung the lantern at the *Kestrel*. It arched into the night as I ran back for the second lantern. Shouts erupted behind me as I dove back behind the crates. Once again, Callan had the lantern burning brightly. I took the second lantern and ran back to the stern. The first lantern had hit on the bow of the *Kestrel*. The dry wood of the airship's hull had caught fire quickly. The flames were spreading fast as the crew tried to figure out how to fight a fire they couldn't reach. Windslow, Raoul, and a man I assumed was Stubb were at the bow, directing the efforts to quell the blaze.

I aimed for the knot of crewmen on deck, hoping to hamper their efforts to put out the fire. The second lantern struck Windslow full on the chest and shattered. Burning oil splashed all over Windslow and he was engulfed in flames. Screaming in agony and fear, Windslow flailed at all around him. Rope, wood, and crewmen's clothing caught fire and panic flashed through the crew.

Raoul cast one baleful look toward the *Pauline* before doing the only thing he possibly could do about Windslow. Lifting a foot, Raoul kicked Windslow in the back. The fiery form toppled over the *Kestrel's* railing and dropped, flaming and flailing, a thousand feet to the valley below.

Ardhan Windslow would never again threaten the royal family of Mordan.

I Never Will

Working the ailerons allowed me to steer the *Pauline* somewhat. Keeping her speed low, I moved us a couple of hundred yards away from the dying *Kestrel.*

Screams floated across the distance from the flaming airship, along with the twang of taut lines as they weakened and snapped. The airship began dropping as the crew raced to land the ship before they burned to death or lost too many support lines, allowing the hull to break free from the gas envelope and plummet to the ground.

Now that we were free from pursuit and out of range of the other airship's weapons, I released the controls and ran to the cabin. Callan was right behind me. Tristan was tending to the soldier with a leg wound, aided by Queen Elaina. Nist was resting on his stomach, eyes shut and breathing evenly. Martin leaned against the wall, the crossbow quarrel still stuck in his shoulder, drinking brandy and chatting with King Edwar. A blanket covered the body of the guard who had been hit in the chest.

Spotting us, Martin called out, "Tristan says Nist will survive. Further, though my wound is dire indeed, the good doctor sent me to sit in the corner without even giving me a bottle of brandy."

"And yet you have somehow managed to get your hands on a bottle," I noted.

"His Majesty was kind enough to fetch one for me," Martin said. "You'll be pleased to know I've been helping him and Her Majesty sort through their memories and to circumvent the effects of the drugs. They seem to recall thinking rather highly of you, David."

"Well I should hope so," Callan said, taking my arm. "It's a little late for second thoughts."

"I assume your presence down here means we are safe from pursuit?" King Edwar asked.

I nodded and then Callan launched into an explanation of what had happened to the *Kestrel.*

With no threats looming, I was suddenly exhausted. I laid down and Callan cradled my head in her lap. In seconds, I was asleep.

Daylight was streaming in the portholes when I awoke. Shouts rang all around us and I started to jump up to investigate. Smiling, Callan bent over and kissed me so soundly I knew we must be safe.

“A pair of Martin’s ships found us just before dawn,” she said. “They’ve almost finished repairing the rudder. We’ll be underway and heading home shortly.”

“Oh, well, if there’s no need for a gallant hero, I’ll just stay here with you,” I said. “Assuming you aren’t getting tired of cradling my head.”

“I never will.” Callan bent over and kissed me again.

Ardhan Windslow was dead and there was a lot of work waiting for us back at the palace. But my family and friends were safe. I put everything else out of my mind and went back to kissing the most beautiful woman on eight planets. As always, time went away and all was right in my world.

SCOUT'S OATH

1

OLD MR. HART

DAVID IS SEVEN

"IT TOOK ME TEN MINUTES TO FIGHT MY WAY THROUGH ALL OF THE Warlord's minions," Old Mr. Hart said. "I hacked left and right with my sword and a minion dropped with every swing."

"That's the sword the king gave you the first time you saved the princess?" I asked.

"Of course! It was my most treasured possession, my boon companion, ever sharp and ever ready! It was in my hand for every fight and at my side for every kiss."

"Yuck," Billy said. He was only five and hadn't learned that kissing girls was something a hero sometimes had to suffer through if he was going to have adventures.

"My boy, there might come a day when you won't mind smooching a pretty girl or two." Mr. Hart rocked back in his chair, laughing. He looked off over our heads, something he always did when he was trying to remember something. "Now, where was I?"

"Hacking and slashing your way through minions to get to the Warlord," I said.

"Right you are, David." Mr. Hart rocked forward and then leaned even closer. "I fought on, but it seemed like the Warlord had a never ending supply of minions. For every one I cut down, two more popped up in his place. But I gained a step with every minion I killed until, at last,

I finally broke free of all those underlings. Leaving them for the king's men to handle, I looked for the Warlord. Good ol' Roy was just a few seconds behind me and his sword was stained just as red as mine was.

'Where is the Warlord, my Captain?'

'Looks like he's scarpered off, Roy.'

"What's 'scarpered' mean?" Billy asked.

I hoped Billy learned all this important stuff soon. The rest of us were getting tired of him interrupting the story with stupid questions. But Mr. Hart never missed a beat.

"Good ol' Roy gave me a puzzled look.

'Is that another of your colorful Terran words, my Captain?'

"I laughed as we ran down a corridor we had just discovered, hidden behind the Warlord's throne.

'Indeed it is, old friend. It means the Warlord has run away.'

"Good ol' Roy boomed his famous laugh.

'And so you have enriched our language yet again! Truly, is there nothing you cannot do, my Captain?'

"Then we ran out the back door of the Warlord's palace and spied the evil overlord not thirty meters ahead of us."

"Did he have Princess Audrey with him?" I asked. "Was she fighting him?"

"You got it, David. The Warlord had one huge hand wrapped around her slender wrist and was dragging her toward a boat waiting on the river. She was fighting him like a heckcat!"

"You said 'hellcat' last time," I reminded Mr. Hart.

"Last time your mother wasn't outside tending to her garden and close enough to hear everything I said," Mr. Hart said in a low voice. "Language like that is best kept for when it's only us men, don't you think?"

We all nodded. You couldn't expect girls, even if they were also moms, to understand guy talk.

"So, the beautiful Princess Audrey fought against the Warlord with every fiber of her lovely being, but the evil man was too strong for her. He dragged her closer and closer to the boat. More of his minions were on the boat, preparing to cast off. I knew if he got onto that boat, he would vanish into the jungle and the princess would be lost to me forever!"

"What did you do?" three of us asked in unison.

Mr. Hart smiled and leaned even closer. "What do you boys think I did?"

"I know," Billy said. "You shot him with your Onesie!"

The rest of us rolled our eyes. Billy really needed to start paying attention to important details.

"I already used up the gun's single charge shooting the Shaman," Mr. Hart reminded him.

"Oh, yeah."

"Anybody else got a guess?"

All us older kids knew the answer, but it was Art's turn to say it. "You Boosted."

Mr. Hart beamed at Art. "That's right, lad. I Boosted. I got a jolt as adrenaline poured into my blood stream. The pain from all the scrapes and stabs I'd gotten fighting the Warlord's minions disappeared and my fatigue was washed away."

"What's that mean?" Billy whispered to Art.

"It means he didn't hurt any more and he wasn't tired," Art whispered back.

"With renewed strength, I bounded toward the Warlord."

'Unhand the princess and fight me, Warlord!'

"At the sound of my voice, Audrey's eyes met mine."

'I knew you would come for me, my love!'

"Her spirit was unbowed and, knowing I had come for her, Audrey struggled even harder to break free of the Warlord's iron grip.

"The Warlord realized he couldn't get to the boat before I caught up to him. With a sneer, he shoved the princess away from him and drew the huge sword he wore over his shoulder. The song of steel sliding free from its scabbard was music to my ears. At long last, after countless adventures, the Warlord and I were going to go toe-to-toe, blade-to-blade, man-to-man. It was our destiny and we knew only one of us could survive the battle."

The five of us who were sitting on Mr. Hart's front porch gasped and scooted closer. We'd been listening to Mr. Hart's adventures all summer and *this* was the moment we'd all been waiting for!

"The Warlord was swinging his mighty sword even before I reached him. He knew his stuff, I'll give him that. The Warlord had timed the attack perfectly. I was charging right into the path of the blade. I heard Audrey cry out in fear as I brought my sword up to block the powerful blow. Steel met steel with a resounding clang. A lesser blade might have broken, leaving the man wielding it to be cut in two. A man whose heart was not fueled by the love of a beautiful woman might have crumpled under the awesome force of that blow. But my blade was great and my love was greater! The Warlord's blade was blocked.

"I rolled away, slashing at the Warlord's chest as I came back to my feet. My sword bit flesh–"

We all cheered.

"But the Warlord wasn't just strong, he was quick. He jumped back at the last second and my blade did nothing more than scratch his chest."

"Aw, no," we moaned.

"But I was the first man to ever draw blood against the Warlord. He stared at the scratch as if I had cut his belly wide open. When he looked back at me, I saw fear in his eyes.

'No man cuts me.'

'There's a first time for everything, Warlord. And I aim to cut you again and again until you've been whittled down to nothing!'

'Perhaps I have underestimated you, Hart. It is a mistake I will not make again.'

'There won't be a second time.'

"Through all the talk, our blades had clashed again and again.

"Then the Warlord did the unexpected, the unthinkable! When we spun apart after a flurry of blows, he drew his dagger and hurled it right at the unprotected heart of Princess Audrey!"

"No! He can't kill the princess," I cried. "Not after all you went through to save her!"

"He was the Warlord, David. What he could not possess, he destroyed. He knew the princess was mine, heart and soul, just as I was hers. He might have her, but he could never have her love. And at that moment and in that fight, he knew he could not defeat me. So he threw the dagger, hard and true, to kill the woman who meant everything to me."

"Did– Did he kill her?" I asked in a voice barely above a whisper.

"I was afraid he had. I heard the knife bite flesh. I heard Audrey cry out. Fearing the worst, I turned toward her. The sight that met my eyes was seared into my brain, never to be forgotten. I can see it now as clearly as I did on that day so many years ago. A body lay crumpled on the ground, the dagger protruding from the body's chest. Blood welling up around the blade, turning everything around it crimson."

A far away look came into Mr. Hart's eye, as if he really was seeing it all over again.

"Oh no," I breathed.

'Do something, my love!'

"Tears streaming from her eyes, Princess Audrey cradled the limp form of good ol' Roy in her arms.

'He leapt in front of me and took the blade meant for me. Hurry, my love, you must save him!'

"I looked around to see where the Warlord had gotten to. He was jumping into the boat as his men cast off.

'We will meet again, Hart. And when we do, you will die.'

"The Warlord got away?" Art asked.

"I'm afraid so," Mr. Hart said.

"But what happened to good ol' Roy?" I asked. "Did he die?"

"That's a story for another day, boys," Mr. Hart said, leaning back and starting to rock in his chair.

We protested, but once Mr. Hart went back to rocking there was no changing his mind. Story time was over for now. The other boys and I got up quietly. Mr. Hart's head was already drooping and the first snore came shortly after.

"That was the best adventure yet," Art declared as we walked away.

There was no doubting that Art was right. Just as there was no doubting what I planned to do when I grew up. I was going to have adventures. I was going to fight evil warlords. I might even kiss a girl.

I was going to be a Scout!

2

HE KICKED ASS

CALLAN IS ALMOST FOUR

My room was messy. I knew Mommy wasn't going to like that. I would tell her that the mess wasn't my fault, but I'd tried that before. She never believed me before, but maybe she'd believe my new guard, Rob.

He could tell her about the bad men who came into my room. Maybe it would help that three of them were in here, lying on the floor. Two of them were really quiet. The third one was making a bubbly sound when he breathed. I wished he would stop because it sounded really creepy.

I cried when the men kicked open my door. It scared me *and* they'd knocked my dollhouse over. I spent all day getting the house just right and the bad men had ruined it.

Rob put me in my safe corner. Then he drew his sword and started fighting the men. My guard made me proud because he was a very good swordsman. Of course, Daddy only let good swordsmen guard me, so that wasn't a surprise. The worst thing was the fight was so loud it scared me even more. I covered my ears and cried louder.

It took a minute before I realized Rob was talking to me. I took my hands from my ears to listen. He was telling my favorite bedtime story, the one about the princess who fell in love with a hero from nowhere. Rob told the story better than any of my other guards, even though he was my newest guard. Rob did voices for everyone in the story and that made it sound a lot better. Listening to the story over the sound of the fight, I should have still been scared. But I had Rob fighting for me *and* telling my favorite story, so I wasn't scared at all. Or not as much, anyway.

When the third man fell down and started the bubbly breathing, the last two men ran away. Rob sat down in my safety nook and pulled me onto his lap.

"Are you all right, my princess?"

"Finish the story."

Rob smiled as if I had answered his question. And, as I wondered what Mommy would say about the mess, he finished the story.

Then Mommy and Daddy came running into my room. Mommy didn't say anything about the mess, she just ran to me and hugged me tight. I knew she was going to notice the mess sometime, so I brought it up.

"It's not my fault my room is messy, Mommy."

"What?" Mommy held me out so she could look at me and I saw she was crying.

"The mess isn't my fault. And it's not Rob's fault, either. Not really. Those men on the floor started the fight. Rob just fought back. And that's what he's supposed to, right? And he told me my favorite story. So the mess isn't my fault *or* Rob's fault."

Mommy's face got that funny look you get when you want to laugh and cry at the same time.

"Oh, Callie, I'm not worried about the mess. I'm worried about you!"

"Why? I had Rob with me and he kicked ass."

The funny look on Mommy's face got funnier.

"*Where* did you hear that, young lady?"

"It's what the guards say when someone does a good job, Mommy."

"I see. I believe I shall have to have a word with your guards. Several words, in fact."

Rob cleared his throat. "If you'll permit me, Your Majesty, I shall convey your displeasure to the rest of Her Highness's guards. I will make your will crystal clear and in no uncertain terms, even if I have to kick them in the..."

Rob had forgotten the word, so I helped.

"Ass."

"Thank you, Your Highness, but I was going to say 'seat of the pants,' instead."

"Oh. Is that what I should be saying, Mommy?"

"It would be a good start, Callie."

I gave a big yawn.

"And we should get you to bed. How would you like to sleep with your father and me tonight?"

I laid my head on Mommy's shoulder. "Will Rob be there, too?"

"Tonight, I will be right outside your parents' door. But if you need me, I'll be there for you, Little One. I'll always be there for you."

I decided then and there that I was going to marry Rob. Or maybe the hero from nowhere. But I knew I was going to marry a hero.

3

ENVOY FROM BELOREN

DAVID

Life settled down after Windslow's death. Raoul vanished, abandoning the crew of the *Kestrel* to the less than tender mercies of the Mordanian judicial system. Martin spent hours in the dungeon visiting with the crew. I don't know what he said to them, but I got the distinct idea the crew preferred Mordanian justice to whatever Martin had in mind.

Meanwhile, during the day I learned about the myriad duties expected of the consort to Her Highness, Princess Callan. Apparently, there's more to the job of prince consort than rescuing the princess and foiling kidnappings. Who knew?

At night, well, let's just say I learned other important things. It was a happy, busy, Boost–free life.

Four months after Callan's twenty–first birthday, harsh reality intruded on us again. Finding ourselves with a rare morning free of appointments, Callan and I had decided to enjoy some private time together. We'd given the servants the morning off and enjoyed a languorous few hours entwined in each other's arms. We had only recently arisen when a knock came at the door. Callan threw on a robe and padded to the door.

A page bowed when she opened the door. "I beg pardon, Your Highness. His Majesty summons you and Captain Rice to his council chambers."

"Thank you, Michael," she said. "Please tell my father we'll join him shortly."

As Callan shut the door, she said, "I wonder what this is all about?"

"Perhaps your father simply forgot we were going to stay in this morning," I suggested.

"Don't I wish. No, he and mother were all smiles when I told them our plans." Callan rolled her eyes. "Daddy, bless his heart, made some offhand remarks about an heir and pining for the patter of little feet."

I chuckled at the thought of how that conversation had gone.

Callan glared at me. "You only laugh because you weren't there when my mother added her advice."

"Oh? What did she suggest?"

"Mother was not subtle in the least." Callan shuddered, but then followed that with a wicked smile. "Based on your reaction this morning, though, her advice was spot on."

My mouth dropped open. "Dare I ask *which* reaction you're grinning about?"

Callan leaned in close and whispered in my ear, "No."

My plan to pursue this line of inquiry further was interrupted by the arrival of our servants. Other pages must have been sent to alert them at the same time Michael was sent to us. To my surprise, the servants dressed us in formal court clothing rather than our less elaborate daily clothing. Callan's ladies-in-waiting spent an hour fussing with her hair and make-up before declaring her fit for court. Even then, they only stopped when Michael returned to find out what was taking us so long.

"What is this about, Daddy?" Callan asked when we joined her parents in the council chambers adjoining the court.

"An envoy from the city-state of Beloren has arrived and requested an audience," the king replied. "He specifically requested the two of you be present, as well."

I didn't care for the sound of that, nor did Callan. She took my hand in both of hers.

"What does he want?" she asked.

"I have no idea," her father replied, "but the navy reports he was escorted across the desert by a fleet numbering at least two hundred airships. All twenty-seven of the southern city-states are represented in the fleet. They stopped ten miles south of our border, allowing the envoy's ship to sail on by itself. Those ships are still there, holding position and, we assume, waiting for the envoy to return. The admiralty is understandably concerned about this. They are mobilizing every serviceable airship they can find."

Further conversation was cut off when a court functionary knocked and entered. "The envoy from Beloren awaits, Your Majesty."

We were announced to the formal court session and the chamberlain presented the envoy.

"Thank you for acceding to my request with such alacrity, Your Majesty." The envoy bowed deeply. "I shall come directly to the point of my visit. I have been sent seeking justice for the people of Beloren, justice for crimes most foul. The lords of the city request the extradition of the heinous criminal David Rice."

4

A MORE PRECISE WORD

CALLAN

My heart raced and my chest constricted as the envoy's words registered. I gripped David's hand tighter. He squeezed my hand once, letting his calm strength flow into me. As always, it worked. My heartbeat slowed and I found I could breathe normally again.

"I have no reason to believe your accusation is valid, envoy, especially when one takes into consideration *why* David Rice was in Beloren," my father said.

Daddy always chose to be diplomatic, if possible. If I had been sitting on the throne—a seat I was in no hurry to assume—I'd have told the envoy where he could stuff his accusations and then have had him thrown out of the palace on his ear. A quick glance at Mom's face showed she felt the same way I did. Daddy probably did, too, but he was speaking for the kingdom rather than himself. That is just one reason it's not so easy being the monarch.

The envoy turned and looked David in the eyes. Then he turned and looked me *not* in the eyes. I've only met one man whose eyes met mine the first time we met. I married that man.

The envoy turned back to Daddy. "While I understand your reluctance to accept the truth, the facts are plain for all to see. They leave no doubt as to the guilt of your son–in–law."

"We have a busy schedule today, Envoy," Daddy said. We didn't, which the envoy probably knew, but niceties must be observed. Daddy continued, "If you have facts of which we are not aware, then present them to us now."

"Of course, Your Majesty. Since that fateful day several months ago, numerous witnesses have come forward with stories of the attacks David Rice initiated against Beloren citizens," the envoy said.

My patience broke. "Come now, Envoy, why call them 'stories' when a far more precise word—'lies'—is available?"

Daddy frowned at me but Mom gave me an approving nod.

"Further more," the envoy raised his voice, "David Rice loosed a dangerous beast—a full-grown tammar—within the city walls. More than a dozen citizens were slain by the tammar. The resulting panic led to the ignition of a devastating fire. Many more citizens died in the fire, which eventually destroyed half of the city."

"Only half?" I said. "That is rather disappointing news. David, shall we go back and finish the job?"

The envoy's voice rose a second time but his tone remained mild. I began to wonder if this speech was nothing more than a performance. "I am appalled at your callousness, Your Highness. You jest over death and destruction on a massive scale. King Edwar, have you spent no time training your heir in the art of diplomacy?"

Daddy had been keeping his temper in check, but that was the last straw. His face a mask of cold fury, Daddy rose to his feet and glared down at the envoy. "Those tunnel rats you call Beloren citizens are nothing more than a nest of criminals your government is too weak-willed to clean out. They planned to feed my daughter to that tammar for their own macabre entertainment, a point I notice you conveniently ignore. David did what your own city guards refuse to do—he entered that rat's nest to save an innocent life. Without David's 'unprovoked attack,' my daughter would be dead and, in the wake of my wrath, there would be nothing left of Beloren other than a few scribbled lines in dusty, unread history books.

"Now, Envoy, I strongly suggest you scurry back to your pathetic little city-state before I *really* lose my temper," Daddy thundered.

"Should you have the misfortune to witness such an occurrence, you will think my daughter a model of tact and decorum in comparison."

"There is one last detail I must mention, Your Majesty," the envoy smiled thinly. "If I do not return with Captain Rice in my custody, that fleet off your southern border will immediately attack Mordan."

5

INSANE THREATS

DAVID

"Do not make absurd and meaningless threats, man," King Edwar said. "Our navy is much larger, much stronger, and our crews much better trained than anything your motley collection of city-states could hope to send against us. Your fleet cannot possibly win a war with Mordan."

"Everything you say is true, Your Majesty. And yet the fleet *will* attack if I do not return with Captain Rice in custody," the envoy said.

"But why would you throw away lives and airships without even the hope of victory?" King Edwar betrayed his bafflement at the envoy's intransigence. The same look was reflected on the courtiers present and, I'm sure, my own face.

The envoy cast a furtive glance around the court then lowered his voice. "Perhaps I could shed some light on this matter if we spoke privately."

"I have no secrets from those present in these chambers. You may speak freely before them."

The envoy's voice remained low. "If word of what I wish to tell you reaches the wrong ears, my family will be endangered."

"You show precious little concern for *my* family. Why should I be concerned for yours?"

"Please!" The envoy bowed in supplication.

My father-in-law glared at the envoy for a good fifteen seconds. The man held his bow the whole time.

"Clear the chamber," the king said to his chamberlain. A moment later, we were alone with the envoy.

"I have acceded to your request, Envoy," King Edwar said. "Now explain what is behind this insane threat of yours."

"The lords of the twenty-seven city-states have no desire to wage war against Mordan. Unfortunately, they fear the aftermath of a war with Mordan far less than they fear a threat within their own city walls," the envoy told us. "What do you know of those we call the tunnel rats?"

Callan spoke, "They are a murderous rabble your lords are too uncaring or too weak-willed to eradicate."

"I understand why you hold that opinion, Your Highness, but it is far removed from the truth of the matter," the envoy said.

"Then explain it so we may understand," the king said.

"The tunnel rats have been a problem among the various city states for generations. Any city with long-abandoned sewers and catacombs has some criminal element who find safety and shelter in such places. Even Morda, your own capital city, is said to have criminal lairs hidden beneath its streets. But the city-states stood for centuries before men settled this far north. The network of tunnels beneath Beloren dwarfs Morda's catacombs. The same holds true for the other city-states.

"For centuries, the lords of the city-states attempted to drive out or destroy the tunnel rats hiding beneath our streets. Traditional military units fare poorly underground. Their training and tactics are ill-suited to such missions. Invariably, they fail to eradicate the tunnel dwellers, losing too many men in the process," the envoy said.

"If it was just a matter of training," I said, "why not devise proper training and create an elite unit to combat the tunnel rats?"

"Because the tunnel rats, while irritating, did not cause sufficient trouble to be worth the extra expense of such training," the envoy replied. "In retrospect, it was short-sighted of them."

"Really? What was your first clue?" Callan's tone was thick with sarcasm.

"Are you implying what my daughter went through isn't considered 'enough trouble' to be worth the attention of the lords of Beloren?" King Edwar's tone matched that of his daughter.

"No, Your Majesty, I most assuredly am not implying that. That rationalization ended twenty years ago. The lords of Beloren, wishing to be viewed as 'doing something' about the tunnel rat problem, hired a mercenary named Vraal to take care of the criminal infestation in the tunnels.

"Vraal led his band of violent, ruthless men into the abandoned sewers and killed the leaders of the tunnel rats. I must assume Vraal liked what he found in the tunnels. Instead of claiming the balance of his fee from the lords, he declared himself King Rat and took control of the city-state's criminal element," the envoy said. "Over the next ten years, he has found ways to extend his control beyond Beloren's walls and into the tunnels under the other twenty-six city-states. For the last ten years, he has wielded enormous power throughout all of the southern city-states. It is true the lords administer the city-states, but they do so at the forbearance of King Rat.

"Over the years, King Rat has expanded the tunnels, building new underground passages throughout each of the city-states. His messengers can pass unseen into the most secure rooms in Beloren. His assassins do so, as well," the envoy said. "Vraal wants Captain Rice and doesn't care how much blood must be spilled to get him. The lords would rather have thousands of their subjects slain in a war with Mordan than have their families slain in their beds."

Thousands dead? How many of them would be Mordanian? I could not allow death on such a scale when it was within my power to stop it.

I stepped forward. "You may call off your fleet, Envoy. I will surrender myself to you."

6

ANNOYINGLY NOBLE

CALLAN

As David's announcement echoed in the vast court chamber, the envoy from Beloren and my parents stood there and blinked in astonishment. I'd had a feeling he was going to say something noble and selfless. That meant I was the first to react to his words. My reaction was going to be emotional, but I was unwilling to start crying before the odious envoy. So I chose to react with anger and punched David in the arm.

"Ouch!" he said, rubbing his arm.

"Before you make such a bold pronouncement in the future," I said, "I strongly suggest you discuss it with your wife, first."

"There wasn't anything to discuss, Callan, because I had only one honorable choice," David said.

He can be *so* annoying when he decides to be noble.

"How can you stand there and tell me—your wife—that there was nothing to discuss?"

"The day after we met, I swore an oath to you and to Rob, pledging to protect your life with mine," David said. "When we were married, my oath to you extended to your family and your kingdom. If I stand firm against the envoy's ludicrous claims-"

The envoy found his tongue. "Ludicrous? Now just-"

"Shut. Up." I snarled at the envoy. "Ludicrous is far too polite a word to describe the charges you have presented to us. I was raised to behave as a proper princess should behave, otherwise I'd have used a long string of single–syllable words instead. I was surrounded by guardsmen from the moment I was born. I learned quite a collection of improper words from them, all of which are far more appropriate to this situation than my husband's innocuous choice of words."

I only realized I had stalked into the envoy's face when David caught my arm and gently pulled me into his embrace.

Then David looked me in the eyes and said, "My love, thousands of men will die if we go to war with the city–states. Parents will lose sons. Wives will lose husbands. Children will lose fathers.

"In a war to defend the entire country against another nation's attacks, such losses are necessary. In a war to defend a single man, such losses are," and here he gave me his infuriating, irresistible smile, "a string of single–syllable words inappropriate for a proper princess to use."

What could I say to that? Dozens of men had died attempting to defend me from the kidnapping plot of the former Tartegian queen. I would always bear the burden of their deaths. How could I wish a far heavier burden on David? I leaned my head against his chest, let go of my anger, and let my tears flow.

"David," my father said, "you do not need to do this. To a man, our military will defend you and Mordan against this rabble from the city–states. To a man, they will *want* to defend you, son."

"I know they will, Your Majesty," David said, "but I cannot allow sacrifices on such a massive scale for a single man. Even if I were willing to allow the men to fight and die for me, it makes no sense from a military or political point of view. While I have no doubt our navy would rout the city–states' fleet with comparative ease, it would distract and weaken us at a time when tensions remain high with Tarteg."

Daddy gazed at David for a moment and then nodded his head. "Very well. I will defer to your wishes in this matter."

Still holding me in his embrace, David spoke to the envoy. "We will depart tomorrow morning, Envoy. I would spend a last night with my wife."

Then David took my hand and led me back to our chambers for our final hours together.

7

I WILL BE BACK

DAVID

Even in a royal palace, you'd think it would be possible for a man to retreat to his chambers to spend a few hours alone with his wife. This should be especially true when the man is going away for who knows how long the next morning. I was fortunate enough to have an entire palace full of people eager to show me just how wrong I was.

The first knock came no more than a minute after we'd shut the door. I had just pulled Callan into an embrace and was leaning in to kiss her when knuckles rapped on the door. Unable to ignore her royal training, Callan tried to pull away to answer the knock. I tightened my embrace, pulling her even closer.

"Ignore the door, dear," I breathed into her ear. "After a few minutes, whoever is out there will figure out that we don't want to be disturbed and go away."

Our prospective visitors not only didn't go away, they called through the door.

"Callie? David? Please let us in."

It was Callan's parents. I know they wanted to comfort their only child and her husband, but I also knew they wanted a grandchild and heir to the throne. You'd think they would give us a chance—perhaps our last chance—to try to provide one for them. Callan looked toward the door and when she pulled away this time, I released her.

Callan's mother swept her daughter into a hug, speaking soft words of comfort to her. My father-in-law surprised me by wrapping me in a fierce hug, as well.

"Like most fathers, I was certain no man would ever be good enough to marry my daughter—not even Prince Rupor," Edwar said as he released me. "You proved me wrong when you rescued Callan. You proved me wrong again when you rescued Elaina and me. And now you've proven me wrong a third time. Do me a favor, lad. When you get back from Beloren—and I'm certain you *will* get back—stop trying so hard to show me the error of my ways."

"If you can get the rest of the planet to cooperate, I'll be more than happy to do as you ask," I replied, flashing my first genuine smile since we received the king's summons to court.

"I shall bend every ruler and diplomat to my will in an attempt to do as you ask, David." The king gave me a knowing smile. "Callie and Elaina will expect no less from me."

Once again, the king and queen offered to wage war against the city-states. Then they traded back and forth, offering words of comfort and concern. What they did not do was offer to leave us alone. By the time the king and queen finally ran out of words and hugs and took their leave of us, word of my decision had spread throughout the capital. Our friends dropped everything to visit and offer their deepest consolation in this difficult time.

What I found most difficult about the time was finding some way to spend it with Callan. But I was polite and kept that thought to myself.

Don't get me wrong, I love my friends and family dearly. I very much wanted to say goodbye to Tristan and Nist. I wanted to tousle Milo's hair and to make sure he and Kim knew that, with or without me, they would always have a place in the palace. I wanted to ask Martin what he knew about Beloren's tunnel rats. But I planned to arise early the next morning and do all that before leaving with the envoy. Other than those few people, I could have happily gone without seeing anyone else from the palace.

I grew heartily tired of hearing visitor after visitor tell me how selfless and heroic I was. My arm grew tired shaking all of the proffered hands. My facial muscles felt as if they had frozen into the perpetual smile I wore for Callan's sake. It took all of my self control not to shout at everyone to go away and leave us alone. And it took hours to clear our chambers of all of our unwanted well–wishers. Only then did I have Callan all to myself.

I locked the door to our chambers and then kissed Callan deeply. As always when I held her in my arms, time went away and Callan and I were as one.

The next morning, Callan and I walked hand in hand to the palace docks. With an honor guard before us and most of the palace population behind us, I kissed Callan one last time. I tilted Callan's head back and gazed deeply into her eyes.

"I *will* be back, my love."

"You had better be," she whispered fiercely.

As I turned away from my wife, light flashed from polished steel as the blades of the honor guard snapped up into a sharp, silver arch. Passing beneath the crossed swords, I looked straight ahead. A moment later, I boarded the Beloren airship and left behind all I had ever known and loved in this world.

8

ARE YOU WITH ME?

CALLAN

I PROMISED MYSELF I WOULD NOT LET DAVID SEE ME CRY. I KEPT THAT promise until the honor guard formed up along David's path. When their swords flashed, forming the arch beneath which he walked, tears welled up in my eyes. My vision blurred and I found it impossible to see clearly. I blinked the tears away, only to have them return immediately. I refused to wipe them away, just in case David looked back. His last sight of me must not be that of a girl, weeping for her lost love. It must be that of a woman, determined to be reunited with her husband.

Perhaps David suspected what he would see in my eyes if he looked back at me. Perhaps he struggled to control tears of his own. Perhaps he refused to give the Beloren envoy the satisfaction of an emotional reaction. Whatever the reason, David strode forward, head held high and faced forward.

Only when he stood on the deck of the Beloren airship did David cast a final look at me. By then, he was too far away to see my tears, which flowed like rivers down my cheeks. Two Beloren airmen took him below deck while the rest of the crew cast off. The airship's engines roared to life. Through my tears, I stood and watched the airship rise from the courtyard. Through my tears, I watched as the airship turned to face south. Through my tears, I watched the airship steam over the palace rooftops and pass from sight.

Turning back to the palace, I wasn't surprised to find my parents standing a few paces behind me. Without a word, they gathered me into their arms. I released my grief and sobbed as I had not done since I was a little girl.

Some moments later, I kissed my parents on their cheeks and offered them a brave smile. With my eyes dry, I walked back to the chambers David and I shared. Everyone I met along the way bowed or saluted, each of them showing respect for my grief and respect for David's sacrifice. I offered a smile and a nod to each of them and felt immense relief when I reached our chambers.

Entering my room, I found Martin leaning casually against the balcony door, his arms folded. Tristan, Nist, and Milo were arrayed along the wall beside him.

"He's gone," I whispered.

Martin said, not unkindly, "Your Highness, you didn't ask us to meet you here just to tell us what we could see with our own eyes."

"No, Martin, I didn't," I said. "I asked you here because I need a fast airship and the most daring of pilots. I need a doctor who knows the desert. I need a young thief who knows life on a city's streets. And I need a reformed raider who knows Beloren's darkest secrets."

I looked them each in the eye, "I am going to Beloren to get my husband back, but I cannot do that without your help. Are you with me?"

"You don't even need to ask, lass," Tristan said.

"But just in case there's any doubt, I'll give you our answer," Martin added. "Damned right we're with you."

The Crown Jewels

The problem with secret rescue plans is you have to spend time making the plans. I didn't want to spend hours discussing how best to slip into Beloren unnoticed or how to get one of us down among the tunnel rats. I wanted to board the *Pauline* and fly off after David *right now*.

I could see it all in my mind's eye. We would catch up with the Envoy's airship. Nist would bring the *Pauline* alongside the airship.

Then Martin would Boost, we'd all storm aboard, and...probably all die grisly deaths.

I have never been good at this kind of planning. I prefer to skip all that tedious thinking ahead stuff and get straight to the action. That's why my father has always surrounded me with thoughtful guards and advisors. In the past, Rob kept me focused and forced me to plan my actions. David had done it since Rob's death and, I hoped, would do it for me again when we came home. Today, I counted on Martin and Tristan. They were thorough—painstakingly, mind numbingly thorough.

"Milo," I asked, when I was no longer able to concentrate on their endless discussion, "when will Kim be here?"

"She said she would come right up after completing her etiquette lesson with Lady Andrea," he said.

"Very good. And you told her what I'm asking you to do?" I asked. "She must give her permission for you to come along.

"Yes, Your Highness, I have her permission to go," he said, rolling his eyes. "She knows you'll do everything in your power to keep me safe, blah blah blah." He grinned, "Kim did show real concern when I told her about the rescue—but only when I told her Nist was going to be your pilot."

Nist's eyes went wide. "Your sister is worried about *me*?"

"I told you he'd never figure it out, Milo," Tristan sighed. "Nist has spent too much time flying me around on that airship and too little time courting the fairer sex. The lad claims he can see the wind but he can't see the love written on a pretty girl's face."

Nist's face went crimson at his adopted father's words, but Tristan was right. Nist was the only person in the palace who hadn't a clue about Kim's feelings.

A complicated knock came from the door—the signal Milo had given Kim. Milo opened the door and his sister slipped into the room. One glance at Nist told Kim everything.

Blushing to match Nist, Kim whirled on her little brother, "You told him!"

"Of course I told him. I'd have been an old man in my twenties if I waited for Nist to figure it out or for you to make the first move," Milo said.

Martin gently shoved Nist toward Kim. "Why don't you take the blushing beauty out on the balcony. Perhaps the two of you could *talk* to each other for while?"

Milo flashed a mischievous grin. "Nist, as Kim's only male relative, I grant you permission to kiss my sister if you want."

Both of them blushed even deeper, but they went out onto the balcony. Nist even took Kim's hand just before pulling the balcony door shut behind them.

Martin turned serious. "Tristan and I have worked out a plan, Callan."

"Tell me," I said.

"Remember when we robbed the treasury to pay for my airships?" Martin asked. When I nodded, he continued, "We need to rob the treasury again. No, it's more like *I* need to rob it. And I need to 'steal' more than a fistful of cut gems."

"Spill it, Martin," I said. "What do you have in mind?"

Martin drew in a breath, as if preparing to deliver bad news. "I need to steal the Mordanian crown jewels."

You Poor Dear

Steal my country's crown jewels? Was Martin insane? I opened my mouth to ask that very question—and then shut my mouth again. Martin was many things, but I had no doubts about his sanity. Besides, Tristan had helped concoct this plan. The good doctor is a romantic, but, as my father frequently says, he is also quite a sober, sane, and sensible man. If Martin and Tristan thought we needed the crown jewels, I would hear them out before offering an opinion.

Before I could ask Martin to explain further, a knock sounded on the door to my chambers. Who could it be? Everyone in the palace must know I had shut myself in my room to mourn for David.

"Callie?" It was my mother. Of course. Who else would come knocking at a time like this? "May I come in, dear?"

After I had waited so long for Martin and Tristan to conceive of a rescue plan for David, Mom had to show up and delay their explanation further. My mother certainly had great timing. I shooed Martin, Tristan, and Milo out to the balcony while also calling out in an emotion–laden voice, "Just a minute, Mother."

I only called her 'Mother' when I was upset. I felt a tinge of pride at that added touch. Then I remembered I truly *was* upset. It hadn't even crossed my mind to call her 'Mom.'

"Keep quiet out there," I hissed to my conspirators, closing the balcony doors.

On my way to let Mother in, I mussed my hair and worked up a few tears. Planning the rescue had pushed the grief into the back of my mind, but it came rushing back as soon as I tried to look grief–stricken. Hanging my head, I opened the door.

"Y–yes, Mother?"

Mom shook her head, tutting. "Look at you, shut up in here and crying your eyes out. You poor dear."

Mom raised her eyebrows, wordlessly asking why she was still standing in the hallway.

"Come in, Mother."

Mom breezed in and made a beeline for the balcony. "It's so dreary in here, Callie. A little light and a little fresh air will make you feel better."

"I don't want light. I don't want fresh air. And I don't want to feel better," I sounded like a petulant child, even to myself.

"Pish and tosh, dear," Mother said, reaching for the door handles.

In a rush, I slipped between Mom and the doors and threw my arms around her. Burying my face in her shoulder, I tried for the same wracking sobs I'd had in the courtyard. My mother spun me around as effortlessly as she had when I was five. She ended up facing me and with her back to the balcony doors. Reaching behind herself, she turned the knobs and threw the doors open.

"Martin," Mother said, still watching me, "why don't you and the others come inside? After that, I'd like my daughter to tell me what is going on."

Releasing my mother, I looked her in the eye. "What do you think is going on, Mother? We're all going after David. Everyone except Kim.

She's going to stay in these chambers and pretend to be me. With a little luck, she can keep it up long enough for us to rescue my husband."

Much as I hated it, the next thing I said came out in the wheedling tone of voice I used on her—to little effect—when I was a young child. "Please don't try to stop us."

"Dearest daughter, I wouldn't dream of trying to stop you."

Who was this woman and what had she done with my mother?

"You wouldn't?"

A slight smile played across Mom's face. "Whether I like it or not, you're not my little girl any more. You're a newlywed young woman, forcibly separated from your husband by cruel events beyond your control. You'd never forgive me if I did anything to interfere with your plans. And you would be quite right to do so."

"So, you're not going to place me under guard or lock me away in a tower or anything like that?"

"Goodness gracious, no, Callan. Where do you come up with these ideas?"

"So why are you here?"

"I came here to ask you a question."

"What question is that, Mother?"

"What can I do to help?"

Without a Second Thought

"You want to help us?" I asked.

"Yes, Callie."

"With our plan to rescue David?"

"Well, I certainly didn't come up here to help you with your embroidery."

To my surprise, I laughed. I hated embroidery with every fiber of my being, something Mom knew all too well.

"Why are you so surprised, dear? David is a member of our family, now, and we *always* take care of family. Besides, your father and I are quite taken with the young man." The corners of Mom's mouth quirked up. "On top of that, you're quite smitten with him, as well. Those grandchildren your father and I want will arrive all the sooner if you're, shall we say, *enthusiastic* about spending time with your husband."

I felt a blush climb my cheeks. Who knew my mother had such a bawdy imagination? Well, I suppose my father knew. And I stopped *that* line of thought before it could go any farther. There are some things a child simply shouldn't know about her parents.

"Rescue before reunion, okay Mother?" I turned to my friends. "Martin, how can my mother help us?"

Martin didn't beat around the bush. "It would be much easier to get our hands on the crown jewels with your mother's help."

"Why, pray tell, do you need our crown jewels?"

Mom's tone of voice was curious rather than accusatory. Was it possible she would be willing to risk the crown jewels in the hopes of getting David back?

"There are a lot of people—many of them within this very palace—who have been waiting for me to revert to my raider form," Martin said, "I thought I would live down to their expectations in a big way. I'll use my new found status as a friend of the royal family to move freely about the palace, take callous advantage of the distraction David's surrender has caused, and steal the crown jewels. Having completed this nefarious deed, it would surprise no one if I fled back to my old home port of Beloren. *Stealing* the jewels should get me back in the good graces of Beloren's criminal class. *Having* the jewels should allow me to gain an audience with King Rat."

"With an eye toward trading the crown jewels for David?" Mom said.

"Some of the crown jewels, yes. Most of them, even. But there must be some profit for me. After burning my Mordanian bridges so thoroughly, no one would believe me otherwise."

"You've fought tooth and nail to show all Mordan that you're a changed man. Would you really risk ruining your hard–won, barely–rehabilitated reputation just for the chance to rescue David?" Mom asked.

"Yes, Your Majesty, and without a second thought."

"I rather suspected that would be your answer. David is a truly remarkable young man and, if you ask me, quite deserving of such loyalty." She got that far away look that meant she was thinking. "Would you be willing to have a naval squadron chase you south? Just among ourselves, we will know it's an escort for Callan. As an added bonus, with you and the crown jewels inside Beloren's walls, the squadron will have an excellent excuse to stay nearby."

Martin nodded. "That's a *very* nice touch, Your Majesty."

"Raiders aren't the only people who can be devious, Martin." Mom turned to me, "You said you were leaving Kim behind?"

"Yes, she's going to stay in these chambers and pretend to be me. The distraught princess who has shut herself away in the bedroom, just like in the fairy tales you used to read to me," I said. "With luck, no one will even know I'm gone until after we have David back."

Mom nodded, "I can help Kim with that. I'll be the doting queen trying to comfort the distraught princess, also just like in the fairy tales."

Mom turned to Martin and Tristan. "Gentlemen, let's discuss the details of this plan. I want to make sure we've done everything possible to insure my daughter's safety and my son-in-law's safe return."

I groaned. Knowing how thorough my mother could be, I began to suspect it would be long past dark before we got under way.

Sometime in the afternoon, Mom sent for Daddy. He had more than a few suggestions for improving the plan. Most of those suggestions involved keeping me safely in the palace. The fifth time he made such a suggestion, I lost my temper.

"Daddy, that's enough. I'm going on this mission, whether you like it or not. And if you suggest I stay behind one more time, I swear I won't name my first born son after you."

My father laughed. "That's not much of a threat, Callie. Everyone in the kingdom knows you're going to name your first born son after Rob."

He was right, blast him. So I just crossed my arms and turned the full force of my princess glare on him.

Daddy heaved a dramatic sigh. "Very well, Callie, I shall limit my suggestions to the course of action you've already chosen."

Finally, as the clock struck midnight, Nist piloted the *Pauline* to my balcony.

Climbing aboard the airship, I looked south. “Hang on, David. We’re coming.”

9

GOING TO BELOREN

DAVID

As soon as I boarded the envoy's ship, two crewmen led me below deck and locked me into a small cabin. My cabin faced the palace, but the porthole was closed and locked. I wasn't even allowed one last look at Callan as we flew away. This pettiness was at odds with the near-pleading tone the envoy had taken when speaking privately with the royal family. It also proved indicative of my treatment while aboard the envoy's airship.

Crewmen intentionally dropped my food then kicked it across the deck with filthy bare feet. They'd spit into my water or drink it all while standing before me. It was the kind of casual cruelty displayed by the powerless when they are given dominion over some small aspect of another man's life. As a refined member of a royal family, the crewmen expected to horrify me with such behavior. They expected me to choose noble privation over accepting such tainted food and drink. I ate and drank everything I was given and relished the disappointment displayed by the crewmen at each meal. Had they seen what I had eaten during academy survival training, they'd have thrown up their hands in despair—right after throwing up their last meal.

Just as the sun was setting, the envoy's airship rejoined the vast, motley fleet from the southern city-states. The shouts between airships, the dull roar of boiler fires, and the wail of whistles blowing off steam were my first clues we were among the fleet. This cacophony served as my constant companion for three days as the fleet crossed a thousand miles of desert. The calls of the crewmen served another purpose, as well. My implant assimilated and translated the language of the city–states by the end of the first day of the trip.

The implant imprinted the language before the sun rose on our second day of travel. By the time we reached Beloren, I understood everything the crew said and could have conversed with them, had I chosen to do so. I kept that fact to myself, pretending ignorance as crewmen laced their commands with vile insults. Language fluency was one of the two advantages I had over the tunnel rats. Boost, which I hadn't used the first time I was in Beloren, was the other.

To pass the long, hot days, I catalogued everything I knew or could guess about King Rat. The list was short, depressingly so. Based on the Envoy's statements in his private audience with the royal family, King Rat exerted complete control over his people. There was no sympathy to be found among the tunnel rats. Even without King Rat's iron rule, I was an outsider entering an insular and paranoid society. Once in the tunnels, I would be on my own.

To what I had been told and what I had guessed, I added what I had seen in my brief time in the tunnels. King Rat went in for over–the–top execution spectacles. No doubt, the blood and terror served multiple purposes—entertainment for tunnel rats, reinforcement for the us–versus–everyone–else sense of isolation, and a warning to any subjects who chafed under King Rat's rule.

Gruesome as it was, the man's love of spectacle was my primary source of hope. I had no doubt King Rat planned a brutal death for me, but my execution would be a special occasion. It had to be. When I rescued Callan and Raoul from the rat king's tammar pit, I dealt a serious blow to his pride and weakened his grip on this people. King Rat would make an example of me, but that example would be the main event in a day filled with blood and slaughter. No doubt, he would begin with a warmup act of lesser executions. After all, a proper spectacle requires a lot of pleading, a lot of blood, and a lot of corpses. With filled prisoner cages and the tunnel rats boiling over with excitement, what else could the rat ruler do but bow to the will of his people and stage his carnival of carnage?

I had a few days to find a way to kill King Rat. And I concluded I had no choice but to kill him. Left alive and still in power, King Rat would simply intimidate the lords of the city-states again. In short order, we'd be right back where we currently were. Maybe there would be some tunnel rat tradition I could call on, some way of forcing him to fight me. Maybe I could find an ambitious underling whose yearning for power exceeded his hatred of outsiders. Maybe I could do a lot of things, but I wouldn't know what those things were until I was underground.

At last, we docked in Beloren. The crewmen bound my hands and, led by the envoy, took me to the slave market. Silent crowds lined the streets, watching their official deliver me to the tunnel rats. It was yet another spectacle. It was yet another demonstration of King Rat's power over the city. The envoy led me directly to the entrance to the tunnels and, without ceremony, ordered me lowered into the darkness.

King Rat

Hands rose out of the darkness and caught me. They untied the rope binding me and dragged me along the tunnel. As my eyes adjusted to the darkness, I recognized the tunnels through which my captors led me. They were leading me toward the tammar's arena, to where I had almost lost Callan and where Rob, her personal bodyguard and the most courageous man I had ever known, gave his life to save hers.

Could my guesses about King Rat have been wrong? Was it possible he cared more about revenge than spectacle? Could he consider me so dangerous he would choose a quick execution over a blood-soaked lesson for his subjects?

Then my captors led me past the tunnel that went to the arena and down a different one. Perhaps my assessment of King Rat had been correct, after all. At the end of the new tunnel, two guards stood before a door. One guard threw open the door as we approached and the other stepped inside ahead of us.

"The prisoner has arrived," the guard announced.

In my first visit, the arena was bright with massed torchlight. The throne room, if that's what this was, was the opposite. Lanterns spread dim pools of light every twenty feet or so, hiding the size of the room and providing deep shadows to mask the identity of those who attended the court of King Rat. The crowd was large but quiet, nothing like the frenzied mob I'd seen in the arena many months before. On the far side of the room, surrounded by the only bright lanterns in the room, stood a large chair. On the throne, for that was obviously what it was intended to be, sat a man no more than a few years older than Martin.

The two of us regarded each other with interest. The man before me was lean and smoothly muscled. He looked wiry and quick. I had no doubt he'd be a wily and capable fighter. I'd expected a brute of a man, tall and broad and starting to go fat. King Rat was nothing like I expected. The feeling appeared to be mutual.

"You're not all that impressive, now that I see you close up. And you're shorter than I remember," he said, speaking in accented Mordanian. "Of course, you're standing still this time, so it's easier to get a good look at you."

"I didn't notice you at all, last time," I replied, also in Mordanian. "I was rather busy and, truth to tell, not interested in sight-seeing. Not that your little kingdom would be a tourist high point, anyway."

"Ha," He slapped his knee. "And you're not scared of me."

I affected a puzzled look. "I must admit that you've lost me. As a member of one of the most powerful royal families on Aashla, why should I be scared of you?"

"I sent for you and here you are." King Rat leaned back in his throne, a satisfied look on his face. "*That* is power, little princeling."

"It's prince consort, not prince and certainly not princeling."

"Do not banter semantics with me, boy. You have been given to me and are now mine to do with as I wish."

"You are sorely deluded if you think I was given to you," I said. "You live and breathe because I convinced my father-in-law your ragtag fleet, this half-destroyed city, and this pathetic sewer kingdom of yours were not worth destroying. I came here of my own volition, *not* because a rat pretending to be a king sent for me."

"Is that so?" sneered King Rat. "Pray tell, why are you here?"

"I have come to challenge you, before these witnesses, to a duel to the death for that ratty throne you're sitting on," I said.

"You are a well-spoken young man. I'll give you that," King Rat said. "You must have been working on that challenge for hours."

"Yes, I'm a traditionalist to the core. Mentioning that, I notice you haven't answered my challenge. Do you accept?"

"Of course not."

"What's the matter?" I asked. "Are you too afraid to face me, Vraal?"

"No, boy, I'm too smart to face you without need." Vraal turned to the men who'd brought me into the throne room. "Throw him in the cell with the other one."

Vraal's men dragged me from his presence. I'd had no expectation the man would accept my challenge. There had been the slim hope I could make him lose his temper, though. I hadn't managed that, but I had not come away from our discussion empty handed, either. A blind man could see the rat king thought highly of himself. He rightly believed he wielded power beyond his tunnels, but he was sadly mistaken just how far his power extended on the surface world. Well, when you rule in an echo chamber, it's easy to fall prey to your own propaganda.

The guards led me through dozens of twists and turns and then walked me up and down hundreds of stairs. Disorientation was the intention behind the twists and turns, the climbing and descending. Without my implant, the plan would have succeeded admirably. Instead, I had my implant start recording a map of the rat kingdom's tunnels. Nearly thirty minutes later, we stopped next to a heavy door. A guard fished keys from a pocket and unlocked the door. The lantern-bearing guard shined just enough light through the door for my captors to chain me to the wall. The door clanged shut and absolute darkness cloaked the room.

"Hello?" called a voice from the darkness. "Who's there?"

"Well, my sins really are coming back to haunt me," I said. "What are you doing down here, Raoul?"

The Spare Prince

"Rice?" Raoul asked, his voice rising in the darkness. "Is it really you?"

"Of course not. King Rat held a David Rice sound-alike contest and I won," I said in a monotone. "The prize was a stay in this cell with you."

"Oh," Raoul replied, his voice dropping. His voice was so filled with dejection, I could imagine his head hanging and his shoulders drooping.

"For God's sake, you moron, of course it's me," I snapped. "What's the matter with you?"

Raoul gave a shuddering sigh, "I've been down here for a long time and had given up hope that anyone would come to rescue me, much less someone such as you."

"Rescue you? Are you out of your mind?" I wouldn't cross the street to rescue Raoul. There was no way I'd cross a desert to do it. "Have you forgotten the time you tried to get an airship captain and his crew to kill me? Or how about when you abandoned Callan, my friends, and me to the tender mercies of the trogs? Or kidnapped Callan's parents and–"

"Forget I said anything, Rice," Raoul snarled. He did sound much more like his usual self, at least.

"I'd love to forget you, Raoul, but you keep horning in on my life," I said. I took a deep breath, reining in my temper. "But that doesn't matter right now. I'm as much a guest here as you."

"So you got captured, too?" Raoul asked. "I'm sure Callan is worried sick for her missing lover."

"Husband, as you well know," I corrected.

"I had held out hope that King Edwar would regain his senses after taking the time to think through the prospect of a commoner for an in-law. I have no doubt my father and brother would have given all due consideration to renewing Rupor and Callan's betrothal if approached diplomatically."

"What a brilliant idea, Raoul. After all, only *half* of the Tartegian royal house conspired to kidnap Mordan's princess and heir to the throne. After you add in an unknown number of your mother's accomplices concealed within the Tartegian court, you have quite a strong argument in favor of Callan marrying into your family. It's all so clear to me now. I cannot imagine why you were the only one to see it with such clarity."

Raoul lapsed into silence. My ridicule had, no doubt, hurt his prickly little feelings. I most assuredly hoped that was the case. Raoul's steadfast refusal to recognize just how thoroughly he and his mother had screwed up Rupor's betrothal never ceased to amaze me. But Raoul was the least of my worries.

Freed at last from listening to Raoul's nonsensical blather, I turned my attention to more pressing concerns. I pondered my options for escape, fantasized about what I'd do to King Rat if given the chance, and waited for something to happen.

An hour after Raoul stopped talking to me, I found another reason to dislike the man. He snored. Raoul's deep–throated roar did not quite bring the walls down around us, but it made it nearly impossible for me to sleep.

According to my implant, twenty–two hours passed before a guard arrived to take me back to the throne room. As I was led away, Raoul begged the guards to leave him a light. The guards laughed at the exiled prince and mocked his desperation. In spite of myself, I felt a twinge of pity for Raoul. It was no more than a twinge, mind you, but it was the first time in months I felt anything beyond loathing for the Spare Prince.

The guards led me up and down stairs and through a new set of twists and turns. Smiling to myself, I added this new information to the map being built by my implant. Entering the throne room, the map and the last few twists and turns were driven from my mind. I could not believe what I saw.

Martin Bane stood before King Rat.

10

SEARCHING FOR A HERO

CALLAN IS TEN

I LEANED MY BACK AGAINST A SUPPORT BEAM IN THE LOFT OF THE BARN. My arms stretched around behind the rough column of wood, my shoulders aching from the discomfort. I looked to the ladder on the far side of the loft. Where was my hero? Why had he not come? Why had he forsaken me in my hour of need?

This waiting was intolerable. My nose itched and I had straw tangled in my hair. What kind of champion would leave his princess in such distress?

I sighed and pulled my arms from around the beam. The pain in my shoulders eased as my right hand scratched the tip of my nose. I ran a hand through my hair but found it so tangled my fingers caught and pulled at my hair. Well, ladies–in–waiting had to have something to do when I got back to my room, right?

I'd just have to make Mom understand I made a mess of myself out of deep concern that the ladies–in–waiting would be released from service if they had nothing to do. Maybe Daddy would be there instead of Mom. If he was, I could just whip up a few tears, he'd melt, and so would my problems. Of course, all was lost if Rob was on duty tonight. He always saw through my schemes.

A high–pitched voice rose from below.

"Boy, why isn't my saddle properly polished? I should be able to see myself in it."

Lovely. It was my least favorite palace prat, Squire Bertram. I peeked down into the barn and saw just what I expected to see.

Bertie boy and two of his lackeys had my hero backed into a corner. Poor Tim, the stable boy, tried to hide the practice sword, which I'd brought to make him feel more heroic, behind his back. What was Tim's problem? Why didn't he use the practice sword to whack Bertie and his bully boys?

"I– I'm sorry, sir," Tim stammered. "I t–tried to shine your saddle b–but something c–came up."

"Oh, well, that's different, boy. I mean if *something came up...*" Bertie smiled and clapped Tim on the shoulder. "Hey, is that a practice sword you've got there, Tim?"

Tim nodded, knowing what was coming next.

"That's wonderful, Tim. I guess this means you'll be joining us squires at sword training soon." Bertie grinned over his shoulder at his followers. "You know, I've just had a great idea! Why don't I start your training right now, Tim?"

"N–no, sir, I've got to f–finish p–polishing your saddle."

Bertie lost his false look of congeniality. "It's a little late for that, *boy.*"

My temper flared and I jumped from the loft into a pile of straw behind Bertie and his friends.

"That's enough of that, you stupid bullies."

Bertie whirled, his face red with anger. "Milk maid, you will regret interfering with your betters."

Bertie's eyes went wide when he realized who I was. His face paling, the stupid squire dropped to one knee. His bully boys quickly followed suit.

"A thousand pardons, Your Highness! I did not realize it was you who had spoken."

Bertie cringed and bowed even lower. This was more like it!

"You have offended me, Squire Bertram. I order you and your little friends to go run around the palace from now until dinner time."

"But Your Highness, dinner is not for another two hours."

"Do you think I need you to tell me the time?" I did, actually. I thought dinner was three hours away. Oh well...

"Of course not. I beg your pardon, yet again, for my temerity, Princess Callan."

I cast my best look of disgust upon Bertie and his boys and waved a hand toward the stable doors. "Begone from my sight at once."

The three squires bowed their heads in acknowledgement and then beat a hasty retreat from the barn.

"Ha! Look at them run," I grinned in triumph. "You're safe from them now, Tim."

"Don't be foolish, Your Highness. They'll simply come back after you're gone. And the beating Tim receives will be much the worse after he witnessed the way you treated those louts."

It was my turn to cringe, for Tim had not spoken.

I spun about. "Rob, it's not my fault! I–"

"Of course it's your fault, my Princess. *You* took Tim away from his duties. *You* gave him the practice sword. *You* embarrassed the sons of nobles before a defenseless stableboy."

"Don't be silly, Rob. I saved Tim *from* a beating. Tell him, Tim."

"Her Highness is right, of course, Sir Robbill," Tim mumbled.

"See, Rob? Tim admits it."

"What do you expect him to do, Princess? You just *ordered* him to support your claim."

I rolled my eyes. Rob was being *so* unreasonable.

"Don't be daft, Rob, I'm–"

"The princess and heir to the throne. And as such, your words have power. To someone of Tim's station, your least comment can destroy his life, which is exactly what you have done today." Rob turned to Tim. "Go and gather your things, lad. It's no longer safe for you to work in the stables."

"B–but, sir, I love working here! I knows all the animals and they knows me. Who will mix water in Molly's oats so her old teeth can chew them okay? And nobody 'cept me knows the right place to scritch the king's charger after a hard ride."

"They're not your concern any more, Tim. I'm sorry. I'll do my best to find a similar position for you somewhere else."

Tears spilled down Tim's cheeks as he stumbled away to do Rob's bidding. I felt one tear roll down my cheek, too.

"I didn't mean to do it, Rob," I whispered. "I was just trying to find my hero."

"I know, Little One." Rob put an arm around my shoulder. "But, as I've told you a hundred times, you never find a hero if you go looking for him. But when you least expect it and most need it, a hero will rise to the occasion."

"But what kind of man will that hero be, Rob?"

"God only knows, Your Highness, but, if the hero must save *you*, then I pray the Lord sends us a man of strong will and stronger character."

I punched Rob's arm, but my heart wasn't in it. I felt badly for what I had done to Tim. And, as I heard Bertie and his bullies run past, I fervently hoped my hero wouldn't turn out to be someone like them.

11

CAST OFF!

CALLAN

We made good time crossing the desert. Despite the sixteen hour head start enjoyed by the Envoy's ship, the speedy little *Pauline* docked a mere four hours behind the Envoy. Milo slipped into the crowd around the dock, searching for any information concerning David, the tunnel rats, and the plans King Rat had for David.

"You don't speak the language of the city–states, do you, Milo?"

Milo just shook his head as he checked his inventory of...of whatever it was street thieves carried, I guess.

"Then how can your plan succeed if you cannot understand what these people are saying?"

Milo rolled his eyes. What is it about teenagers and eye–rolling? I recall doing it a lot myself—Mom said daughters are particularly prone to it. I'm only twenty–one, but I cannot remember why I thought it was such an effective response to questions from adults. David said it was due to something he called hormones.

"I grew up in a shipping center, Callan," Milo said. "Airships from all over the world docked in Faroon. That meant the docks were filled with tempting targets for thieves. I had to be able to understand bits of a whole bunch of languages if I wanted to find the richest, easiest targets."

"That makes sense, I guess."

Milo flashed his infectious grin and turned away. I pulled him back around and looked into his eyes.

"Be careful and don't do anything careless. You know how David would feel if something happened to you during our rescue attempt."

Milo rolled his eyes again. "Yes, mother."

Playing along, I planted a kiss on Milo's forehead. "Be a good little boy in the big city. Look both ways when you cross the street and don't talk to any strangers."

The boy rolled his eyes a third time, but he laughed, too.

Two very long hours passed, each of them feeling more like a full day, before Milo returned. His information was worth the time we had spent waiting and I had spent worrying. David had been taken from the Envoy's airship and paraded straight to the lair of the rat king. It was such an unusual procession that it was still the main topic of conversation among those who saw him pass.

"He was walking on his own and nobody said anything about cuts or bruises or bandages. So the envoy must have treated David okay during the trip," Milo wrapped up his report.

"Did anyone notice you while you were out there, Milo? Or follow you back here?" Martin asked.

Milo crossed his arms and glared at Martin.

Martin crossed his arms and glared back. "I had to ask, lad."

"No you didn't."

I rolled *my* eyes. "Now that we've resolved the pressing issue of who had to ask and who didn't, can we get back to rescuing David?"

"Of course, Your Highness. And good job, Milo," Martin said. "Now, I want you to show me where the envoy took David to turn him over to King Rat's men. Along the way, I'll point out a few good bolt holes and some spots where you can land the *Pauline* if the airship has to cut and run while some of us aren't on board."

The man and the boy descended from our dock to the ground. They were quickly absorbed into the crowds teeming around the dock. That left Tristan, Nist, and me to wait and worry. Hiding my identity under the robes and veil of a desert tribeswoman, I paced around the *Pauline's* deck.

Inaction and worry drove my mind into dark places where it

delighted in summoning disturbing images. I envisioned tunnel rats killing David in unspeakable ways. Next, what I saw was David and Martin being fed to a tammar. Worst of all, from my mind's darkest corners came the image of Martin turning all of us over to the tunnel rats and keeping the crown jewels for himself. I didn't believe those last images for one second, positive Martin's turn of heart was genuine and his loyalty to David unquestionable. But minds can be insidious and my confidence in Martin didn't stop mine from conjuring those terrible images.

Driven to distraction by my dark thoughts, I wished for something —anything—to happen and grant me relief from the monotony. There is a reason the phrase 'Be careful what you wish for' became a cliché. As if on cue, I spotted Milo dodging through the crowded docks at a run. A gang of burly men pushed through the crowd behind him, losing ground as Milo slipped easily through the crowd.

"Nist! Tristan!" I called. "Milo is coming back here at a run and it looks like he's got an unwelcoming party behind him."

Milo burst from the mass of people and charged up the stairs to our dock. As he came close enough to be heard over the din of the crowd, he shouted, "Cast off! Cast off!"

Tristan and I ran to do as Milo instructed while Nist tossed a few more logs into the boiler. Nist had insisted on keeping the boiler pressure up—not that any of us had argued with him—and it proved to be a wise move. The gang of men had just reached the bottom of the stairs to our dock when Milo jumped onto the airship. The *Pauline* was fifteen feet above the dock and rising by the time the men reached the top of the stairs. I was relieved to see that they carried small clubs instead of crossbows. They could do nothing more than curse and shake their fists at us.

I fully expected our little drama to have attracted some attention— at home, the dock watch or the city guard would have come swarming in response to behavior like this—but no one gave us a second glance. Maybe foreign dockyards really were as rough and tumble as they were in the air pirate tales I'd read as a girl.

"Why were they chasing you, Milo?" I asked.

"They weren't chasing me, I was racing against them."

"What?"

"Word is out on the streets that Martin stole the Mordanian crown jewels. An awful lot of people know Martin went to visit the tunnel rats. Some of them are hoping to grab the jewels while he's down there. I overheard those thugs say something about 'Bane's airship' and knew that couldn't be good. Their boss must think Martin left the jewels here," Milo said. Pointing behind us, he added, "And that boss isn't going to give up easily."

Two large airships rose from the docks and swung into our wake.

12

YOU'RE SLIPPING, BANE

DAVID

I WATCHED FOR A SIGNAL FROM MARTIN, ANY KIND OF SIGNAL. I HAD NO idea what his plan was, but I had a pretty good guess what was going on. I hadn't been a guest of King Rat for long, meaning Callan went straight from seeing me off to talking Martin into coming to bring me back. Knowing Martin, she hadn't had to twist his arm.

King Rat waved his hand at me. "As you can see, he is unharmed. And he will stay that way until my preparations are complete."

The head rat spoke in the language of the city–states, which I was not supposed to understand. I cocked my head and adopted a puzzled expression.

"That last bit sounds rather ominous, King Rat. Dare I ask, preparations for what?" Martin also spoke in the local language.

"I have plans for the young man; big, bold, bloody plans. He will be the main attraction at an upcoming celebration, one that will prove fatal to *all* of the attractions, great and small," King Rat replied. "Now, Bane, why are you here and why do you believe I will profit greatly from your visit?"

"I would like to buy David from you," Martin said.

"I told you I have big plans for him," King Rat said. "Why do you think I would have any interest in selling him?"

"Because I'm offering the Mordanian crown jewels," Martin said. "They're yours in return for the lad. Less a small finder's fee, of course. Say, ten percent? It's a win all around, Your Majesty."

"Ah, so the rumors are true. You have reverted to your piratical ways," said King Rat. "That explains the Mordanian naval squadron patrolling a few miles outside of the city."

"Yes, it does. It's a good thing I had a fast airship or they'd have caught me before I reached the safety of Beloren," Martin said. "As for returning to my old profession, let's just say I could not bear to leave such valuable and poorly guarded jewels hidden away in an underground room—especially when those jewels could serve a higher purpose."

"Besides making you rich, you mean."

"That is but a happy side effect, King Rat."

"So, you stole the jewels and flew out of Mordan with the royal navy in your wake. I understand that. What I don't comprehend is why you came to me?"

"It was my plan to slip away unnoticed, unload the crown jewels at a cut rate, and then return to my new life with none the wiser. Alas, my theft was discovered while I was still within Morda's walls. I did only what any prudent thief does—I ran for it," Martin said. "Royalty tends to get more than a tad touchy when it comes to their crown jewels, so touchy that I doubt they'll ever stop hunting for me. On the other hand, I know Her Highness will happily trade the crown jewels to get David back. Since she has the king wrapped around her little finger, if I show up with her husband in tow I'll get a hero's welcome instead of a hangman's noose. You get rich. I get...less rich. And Morda gets their favorite son-in-law back. Have we an agreement?"

"I do believe you're slipping, Bane. Why should I accept *most* of the crown jewels when I can simply take *all* of them from you?" With a languid wave of his hand, a dozen armed men materialized out of the surrounding shadows. "An hour ago, I received a messenger bird from my spies in Morda. They sent word of your act of thievery and provided a quite accurate description of your airship. As we speak, my men are on their way to take the crown jewels from your ship. No one will dare oppose me after I feed an exiled prince, a princess's consort, and the king of the raiders to my new tammar."

King Rat's harsh laughter echoed through the tunnels as Martin and I were taken to the cell I shared with Raoul.

13

I TRUST HIS JUDGEMENT

CALLAN

EACH OF THE AIRSHIPS CHASING US WAS THREE TIMES THE SIZE OF THE *Pauline.* My gaze raked the deck of one of the pursuers. Men crowded the rails, all of them armed with some kind of club or blade. Worse, instead of dwindling behind us, I watched the hulking airships grow larger.

"Nist," I called, "our pursuers are gaining on us. I thought the *Pauline* was the fastest airship around."

"That she is, Your Highness. She is *much* faster than those behemoths. Alas, my girl cannot kick up her keel and really run until we build a bit more boiler pressure," Nist responded. "Milo, please go below and feed the fire."

Without a word, Milo scampered below. Nist scanned the air ahead of us, his eyes never still for more than a second. Without hesitation, Nist turned the *Pauline* toward the crowded space above the center of the dock. Airships of all shapes and sizes twisted and turned across our path, forming a living maze of rope and wood and gas envelopes

"What are you doing, Nist?" I cried. "All that traffic will do is slow us down."

"Indeed it will, Your Highness. But the *Pauline* is small and nimble. I can fly through it," Nist replied. "But those great tubs chasing us will have no chance of keeping up with us inside that tangle of airships. If they try to follow us, we'll be long gone before they can ever get clear. If they go around, it will give our boiler pressure time to rise."

Tearing my eyes off of the swirling mass of ships before us, I looked back at our pursuers. Nist was right. One airship swung ponderously to starboard, flying around the knot of traffic. The other ship went to port, giving the ships their best chance of catching us when we got clear of the other airships.

Nist's hands flew over the *Pauline's* controls, guiding our little ship in and out of the much larger ships around us. Shouts and curses rose in our wake as the *Pauline* skimmed so close to some ships that I could have reached out and touched them.

Tristan approached me. "Highness, Nist has bought us a little breathing space with this move. It would be wise to use that time to plan our course once we're free of these other airships."

"You're right, of course." Tristan should not have had to remind me. I had let myself get caught up in the excitement of the moment. "Do we even have a choice? Our safest course will be to head for the Mordanian naval squadron north of the city."

"That would be the safest course for *us*, Your Highness," Tristan said.

"But?"

"Is that the course a raider crew would choose? Tristan said. "Especially a crew who had, supposedly, been chased across the desert by that same squadron?"

I smacked myself on the forehead. "No, of course not. What was I thinking?"

I had been thinking like a princess, and that was a real problem. Mistakes like that would get my husband and Martin killed. With David at the forefront of my mind, I forced myself away from proper princess thinking. It was time to start thinking and acting like a criminal.

But what would a raider crew do in this situation? Approached from that point of view, the answer was simple—they'd do whatever it took to get away from the airships chasing them while also avoiding the Mordanian naval squadron.

"Tell Nist to set whatever course he thinks is best for both escaping our pursuers *and* steering clear of the naval squadron," I said. "I trust his judgement."

Tristan grinned. "An excellent idea, Highness. Do you have any idea what we'll do after we get away?"

"I haven't got a clue, Tristan," I replied. "But that doesn't concern me at all. If I haven't figured out what we're doing next, you can bet our enemies will be in deeper darkness than we will."

As Tristan relayed my command to Nist, I smiled to myself. Tristan had said exactly what I had needed to hear. By letting myself get so wrapped up making plans, I had abandoned my one real strength. It was time to stop planning and start reacting.

"Good instincts are nothing more than your brain working at top speed. Your subconscious mind analyzes situations faster than your conscious mind," Rob had told me. "Go with your gut, Your Highness. It will serve you well."

A minute later, we flew clear of the worst of the dockyard traffic. At the same time, our pursuers rounded the knot of airships and closed in on our path from both sides. Nist opened the throttle and the *Pauline* drove toward the narrowing gap between the airships.

14

A NEW CELLMATE

DAVID

SIX GUARDS ESCORTED MARTIN AND ME TO THE CELL I SHARED WITH Raoul. The guards took yet another circuitous route from the throne room to the dungeon. If nothing else, I had the beginnings of an excellent map of the inhabited part of the tunnels.

At any time during the walk, Martin and I could have taken the six tunnel rats with little trouble. The guards had never seen either of us Boost. They would be counting on their swords and superior numbers, neither of which would be anywhere near as useful against the two of us as they thought. But escape was not my plan—at least, not yet. And either Martin was waiting for me to make the first move or escape wasn't his immediate plan, either.

He did, however, play the part of a wronged visiting dignitary with convincing outrage.

"I demand to be taken back to King Rat this instant. Before entering this wretched warren of tunnels, I arranged for safe passage to meet with him. I insist he honor that safe passage."

One of the guards smacked Martin's back with the flat of his blade. "Watch your tongue, raider! King Rat always honors his deals. You wanted safe passage *to* His Majesty. You got to your meeting safe and sound. Your deal didn't say nothing about safe passage *away* from him."

"It most certainly *did* include safe passage out of these tunnels. I was not born yesterday."

"Like I said, raider, King Rat *mostly* honors his deals."

The guards all laughed at this display of tunnel rat humor.

"This is outrageous," Martin actually sputtered as he spoke. It was an impressive performance. "I am not some low–life beggar to be treated as King Rat pleases. I am-"

"Going to get in that cell and shut up," the guard said. For emphasis, he prodded Martin with the tip of his sword.

The guards chained Martin and me to the same wall. When the cell door swung shut, blocking the guards' torch, we were cast into absolute darkness again. Through the door, we heard the guards laughing and mimicking Martin's outrage as they walked away.

"Well, that was an unexpected development," Martin said. "Still, I suppose matters could be worse."

"Who's that?" Raoul's sleepy voice came from the darkness. "Rice? Are you back?"

"Yes, Raoul, I'm back."

"*Raoul*?" Martin asked.

"Bane? You came to save me, too?" Raoul's voice cracked with emotion.

"David, why does Raoul think I'm here to rescue him?"

"He thinks I'm here for the same reason. Raoul's been down here a long time, at least a couple of months." I shrugged, then realized no one could see it. "I think the darkness and isolation have affected his perception of reality. Knowing Raoul, he's probably got crazy voices in his head telling him we're here for him."

"Doesn't that just beat all?" Martin said. "Still, I suppose you could call his presence a good omen."

"Having Raoul inflicted on us is good? This must be some new and hitherto unknown definition of that word."

"David, surely you watched enough old adventure vids to know you can't have a dungeon escape without some crazy prisoner tagging along for comic relief."

"Ha. So you *are* here to rescue me!"

"Shut up, Raoul," Martin and I said in unison.

"I watched a lot of adventure vids, Martin. Isn't the crazy prisoner supposed to know some secret the hero can use to emerge triumphant?"

"Okay, our situation isn't an exact match with the vids. But that was the best spin I could put on Raoul's presence on such short notice." Chains clinked in the darkness as Martin changed positions. "Why didn't we jump the guards on the trip down here, David?"

"I want our escape to be more awe inspiring. I can't just clear out of here, I've got to make sure King Rat can never terrorize the city–states into doing his bidding again."

"Okay, I can see the sense in that idea. What's your plan?"

"Plan isn't really the word I'd use for it. It's more of a scheme..."

15

DARING PLANS

CALLAN

Traffic thinned around us and Nist angled the bow of the *Pauline* up. The two ships angled their bows up as well. Just as quickly, Nist dropped the bow of our ship, angling down toward the city below. The pursuer to port angled down while the ship to starboard didn't alter its course. They had our path covered regardless of what angle Nist took. But how were they communicating over such distances?

My gaze was caught by flashes of movement from the ships. Men waved flags on the decks of both of the airships. They must have signals to coordinate their actions. Now that they had our likely paths covered, I wondered what else they might be signaling. *Fly faster, me fine lads!* It sounded like a line from an air pirate story, so probably not. *Dibs on the girl in the veil!* That sounded like a line from an air pirate story, too, but it still sent a shiver down my spine. I decided it would be best to stop thinking about the signals.

"Nist," I called, "are we going to get past those airships before they can cut us off?"

Nist eyed the closing airships for a second or two then shook his head. "No, Your– um, I mean, no ma'am."

"Back in my room at the palace, I told you I needed a daring pilot, Nist." I tore my gaze from the converging airships and looked at Nist.

"So please tell me you've got a daring plan to elude those ships and get us out of the city."

"Of course he does, Callan." Tristan's voice boomed heartily, an adventurous twinkle lighting his eyes. "After all, I taught the lad everything he knows."

"We're all going to die!" cried Milo, emerging onto the deck after stoking the boiler.

Tristan struggled to keep a straight face. I laughed, amazed anew at the courage and wit of my companions.

"I do have a plan to get away from those ships and daring doesn't even begin to describe it," Nist said over my laughter. "You should all hold on to something."

I caught one of the stays with one hand and gave a mock salute with the other. "Aye aye, sir."

"You'll want to use two hands, ma'am." Nist never took his eyes from the other two airships.

A smile played across Nist's face as his hands flew over the *Pauline's* controls. My pilot's face had the faraway look I knew meant he was about to do something that bordered on foolhardy. I grabbed the stay with both hands and then wrapped one leg around it for good measure. A quick look aft showed that Milo and Tristan had done the same.

Our pursuers had changed their courses again, with one ship coming up from below us and the other coming down from above us. The flags no longer flashed and crewmen lined the rails of both ships. We were so close I could see individual crewmen clearly. One scratched his nose. Another leered at me with a toothless grin.

"Nist? Shouldn't you be doing something?" I tried to keep my voice level, but even I could hear the rising note at the end.

"Almost, ma'am." Nist adjusted the ailerons and braced himself. "*Now!*"

He spun the wheel hard to port with one hand and worked the ailerons with the other. The *Pauline* swung up so sharply our keel brushed the rigging of one of our pursuers. I heard cries as some of the other ship's airmen were knocked from their perches in that rigging. The remaining crews of the pursuing airships gaped as Nist leveled the *Pauline* and shoved the throttle wide open. With a roar, our ship surged away from the two ships. Too late, the captains of those ships remembered their courses. In a chorus of cries from the crews, the twang of taut rope snapping, and the crash of splintering wood, the two ships smashed into each other.

My heart raced, adrenaline surged through my veins, and the whole world seemed sharper and more alive. Was this what David felt when he Boosted? I struggled to hold onto the feeling, but it faded as quickly as it had begun.

Milo was the first to regain his voice. "That. Was. *Amazing*!"

Free of pursuit, we sped toward the edge of the city.

16

STORIES OF SPACEBABES

DAVID IS THIRTEEN

I PULLED MY PAD OUT OF MY POCKET AND ANSWERED THE VID CALL.

"Hi, Art. What's up?"

"A bunch of us are going over to Steve's to play some games. He got the new Virt Box for his birthday and he says it's fusing fantastic."

That sounded great, more than great, but I shook my head.

"I wish I could, but I'm going over to Mr. Hart's. I've got to help him with a few chores, stuff he can't do on his own any more."

Art rolled his eyes. "Is he going to tell you more of his stupid stories?"

"You didn't use to think Mr. Hart's stories were stupid."

"Yeah, when I was *seven*. Then I grew up and realized Mr. Hart just made all that stuff up."

"I think there's some real truth behind the stories. But even if he *did* make them up, we all loved listening to them." I paused for a second. "You know, he asks about all of you whenever I visit. It would make him real happy if you guys came with me."

Art held up his hands as if they were old fashioned measuring scales and looked back and forth between the hands.

"New Virt Box or old man's stories."

He repeated that several times, moving his hands up and down each time. Then he brought one hand up and left it there. "Virt Box. Sorry, David, stories lose."

"Yeah, whatever."

I thumbed the call off, pocketed my pad, and headed for the door.

"Where are you off to, David?" Mom called.

"I told Mr. Hart I'd come by and help him do some stuff around the house."

"You just want him to tell you more stories so you can dream about meeting a spacebabe of your own."

Why are little sisters so annoying?

"Shut up, brat."

"Sandra, don't tease your brother. David, don't talk to your sister like that." Mom glared for a second to drive home the point, then she smiled at me. "I'm proud of you for sticking by Mr. Hart, son. I know it means a lot to him, too. Dinner's at seven."

Walking across the street, I couldn't help but turn my gaze to the clear, blue sky. Two of the moons hung in the sky, visible reminders of all that lay out there, beyond the sky. Whether Mr. Hart's stories were true or not, he had been into space. He'd walked on other worlds. Even if he'd never met a spacebabe, he was living proof that the galaxy still had room for adventures.

That was the real reason I liked visiting with him. I still thought his stories were fun, but just knowing Mr. Hart had done all of that real stuff gave me hope that I could do something extraordinary with my life, too.

He answered the door before the bell had stopped chiming. He craned his neck a bit, looking to see if anyone else was with me.

"None of the other boys wanted to come along?"

His broad smile never wavered, but his eyes dimmed a bit.

"They're all studying for a big test in school tomorrow." The lie came easily, just like the other lies I told when he asked why no one else came to visit.

"Well, shouldn't you be studying, too, David?"

"Nah, I've got that stuff down cold, Mr. Hart."

"You always were a smart boy." He backed up a couple of steps.

"Well, come on in and let's get started on those chores. I don't want to keep you."

"There's no rush, sir. I'll stick around as long as you need me to help out." I gave Mr. Hart a smile. "And, as long as I live across the street, I always will."

17

THE SCHEME

DAVID

"*THAT* IS YOUR PLAN?" MARTIN ASKED.

I couldn't see him in the darkness but imagined him shaking his head in dismay.

"No, that's my *scheme*. There's a reason I told you I wouldn't go so far as to call it a plan."

"I like it," Raoul sounded chipper. We must have been more entertaining than the voices in his head. "I especially like the part where you kill the King Rat for mistreating me so badly."

"There, if Raoul likes the plan it can't possibly succeed," Martin said.

"If you've got a better plan, I'm all ears," I said.

Martin was silent for a while then asked, "What makes you think it'll work?"

"The tunnel rats don't know about Boost," I said.

"So we Boost, jump the guards, take their weapons, and disappear into the tunnels," Martin said. "Then we make a few hit–and–fade raids and watch for a chance to take out King Rat. But what do we do with Raoul?"

"We take him with us," I sighed. "Not even Raoul deserves to be eaten alive by a tammar. Besides, he'll warn the guards if we don't take him."

"And I can fight with you," Raoul added.

"Only if we're truly desperate," Martin said. "I guess we'd better get started. You want to go first or should I?"

"It's my idea, so I ought to be the one to try it first."

I stood up, wrapping links of the chain about my arm and wrist. In the light of the guards' lantern, the chain had looked old and badly rusted, as did the bolts holding the chain to the wall. I put my right foot against the wall next to the bolts.

Boost!

As adrenaline flooded my system, I threw my weight and all of my Boosted strength into pulling the chain from the wall. I thought I felt the chain give a bit and really wished I could see what effect I was having. Then I brought my left foot against the wall, as well, keeping myself up solely through the force I exerted against the wall.

With a shriek of tortured metal, the chain stretched and broke. I had just enough time to tuck into a ball before I hit the floor and rolled into the far wall. I dropped Boost.

"Ow."

"Good job, lad. I trust nothing is broken other than the chain?"

"Just a few scrapes and bruises. Your turn, old man."

A moment later, Martin crashed into the wall next to me.

"Ow, indeed. At least we're free."

"Which one of you is going to break my chain?"

"We're not breaking your chain, Raoul."

"But David said you were going to take me with you."

"Yes, I said that—and I meant it. But we're just going to unlock your chains with the key we take from the guards."

A sigh sounded in the darkness. "Oh."

Martin and I went back to our positions against the other wall, our chains balled up around one fist. Then we had nothing else to do but wait for the guards to return.

Scouts spend a lot of time traveling through space alone. A lot of our training centered around staving off boredom and remaining alert during long periods of inactivity. I'd never been very good at it and was even worse in the current situation. I was relieved beyond imagining when I finally heard the echo of approaching footsteps. A moment later, dim light shone along the bottom of the door. Metal scraped on metal as a key was inserted into the lock. We heard a click as the key turned.

Seven men—more than I was expecting—stepped into the room. One balanced three bowls on a tray. The other six held swords. In the dim light, I gave a nod to Martin.

Boost!

18

DIRECTIONS IN A DESERT

CALLAN

Our pursuers' ships spun around each other, each entangled in the other ship's rigging. Men who hungrily eyed our airship mere seconds ago reeled and tumbled across their decks. Some rolled over the railing, plunging to their death far below. Nearby ships climbed, dove, and turned to avoid being caught in the wreck. Those sudden maneuvers made ships farther from the gyrating wreck dodge and dive.

Like the ripple from a pebble dropped in a pool, chaos spread throughout the skies above the dock. Airships from the city watch, conspicuous by their absence a moment ago, finally put in an appearance, steaming into the maelstrom to investigate the situation. For the first time ever, the Beloren city watch proved helpful to me. Refusing to yield their path to other ships, the watch airships added to the confusion and further helped cover our escape.

"Nist, that was the most fun ever," Milo wore the widest grin I'd seen on his face since he'd kissed his first young lady-in-waiting at the palace. "Let's do it again!"

"I most strenuously insist we *not* do that again. Once was quite enough, young man," Tristan said. "I'm sure that little stunt shaved weeks off my remaining life."

"Her High- The lady did ask for a *daring* escape plan," Nist said, "not a staid old man escape plan."

"Never let it be said you don't give a girl what she asks for," I said. "I'll have to warn Kim about that when we get back home."

Even that mild jest caused scarlet blooms on Nist's cheeks. Daring pilot? Definitely yes. Clueless lover? Emphatically yes. Coaxing first moves out of Nist would require the help of an expert. I'd better talk to Mom when we got back. With her advising Kim, Nist would never know what hit him.

As we flew over what was left of the Beloren southern city wall, Nist asked, "What course should I set, ma'am?"

"Nist, please stop calling me *ma'am*," I said. "You're making me feel old. I'm younger than you are."

"I will try...Callan," Nist said.

"That's better. As for a course..." I turned to Tristan. "Tristan, how far is it to the nearest desert tribe camp?"

"The tribes are nomadic people, lass. They rarely stay in place for more than a few months." Tristan shrugged. "I know of four tribes who usually stay within a few hours flight of Beloren. They all leave signs so other tribes can find them. You just have to know what to look for."

"Please tell me you know the signs," I implored.

"Oh, aye. I'm not called the Desert Doctor for nothing, my dear," Tristan said. "Are you planning to hide out with a tribe for a day or two?"

"No," I said, "I'm going to ask them for directions."

"It's a desert, Callan," Nist said. "What are you going to ask directions *to*?"

With more confidence than I felt, I said, "The nearest trog settlement."

19

BREAKING OUT

DAVID

My implant flooded my system with adrenaline. The guards seemed to slow, their actions and reactions telegraphed far in advance. Our speed disrupted what little group cohesion the guards had, leaving them attacking empty air or even each other.

Only Martin moved at what was, to me, normal speed. We had no need to communicate or coordinate our actions. For decades, Scout Academy training covered tandem fighting under Boost. No cadet graduated without first mastering this skill. As long as each scout knew his role, coordination was assured.

It was my mission. It was my plan. It was my lead.

Surging past the man bringing our food, I grabbed his collar and flung him backward and into the guards gathered just inside the door. My chain-wrapped fist caught the closest guard with an uppercut, lifting him off his feet and loosening his grip on his sword. I snatched the loose sword in midair and used it to block an attack from another guard. I ducked a thrust from a third guard and then ran him through. Then the second guard was back. I batted his wild swing aside, catching the blade with the chain, then slashed him with the sword. Blood spurted from his shoulder as I cut it to the bone. His sword clattered to the floor and I smashed him on the head with my chain-wrapped fist.

As the second guard collapsed in a bloody heap, the first guard grabbed his fallen sword. Diving across the floor, he lunged for my legs. I skipped over the attack then stepped on the blade, pinning it to floor. As the guard tried to roll away, I kicked him in the head. He sprawled limp on the floor, down for the count.

I checked on Martin. He drew his sword from the belly of the last guard standing and the man sagged to the floor. In the sudden silence, I heard the receding footsteps of the man who'd carried the food tray.

We dropped Boost.

"Should we chase after the runner?" Martin asked.

"No. Better King Rat hears of the fight from an eye witness. The tale the servant babbles to the rat king will be incoherent and, most likely, exaggerated. King Rat won't believe half of it, but his people will."

I grabbed a ring of keys from one of the guards and removed the manacles from Martin's wrist and mine. Kneeling next to Raoul, I freed him as well.

"Get up, Spare Prince. It's time to get out of here."

"Let me grab a sword–" Raoul began.

"No," I said. "No sword until you prove we can trust you."

Grabbing the guards' lantern, I led our little band into the darkness.

20

CALLAN'S PLAN

CALLAN

A MOMENT OF SILENCE FOLLOWED MY ANNOUNCEMENT.

"Lass..." Tristan stretched the word out, as if searching for the best way to approach a delicate subject. "Why do you want to find a trog settlement? Except for attacks of retribution, I've never heard of humans searching for trog settlements."

"After our narrow escape from Beloren, I believe it's safe to say Martin's plan to buy David back didn't work."

Tristan nodded in agreement.

"We had no expectations it would, but we *did* expect Martin to come back to us. So we must assume Martin is also King Rat's prisoner, perhaps even sharing a cell with David."

"I suspect you're right on all accounts, my dear." Tristan spoke slowly, as if trying to calm down an emotional woman. Did he think I was about to get hysterical? "But that doesn't explain why you want to find trogs?"

"I doubt King Rat has a cell that can hold David against his will. That goes double if Martin is with him. But you know how David behaves when he's being noble. He won't even consider an escape from King Rat if he believes it will lead to the very war he stopped by surrendering to the envoy." I watched dawning comprehension in Tristan's eyes. "If I want to see my husband again, I need to go into those tunnels and fetch him. If I want to survive that trip, I'll need warriors."

"I see your point, Callan, but I don't believe you've thought this through." Tristan was still speaking slowly and it was getting on my nerves. "We have a Mordanian naval squadron only a few miles from here, one tasked by your mother to protect and aid you. Surely Mordanian marines would be a better choice than a bunch of trogs."

"My oh my, Tristan, why ever did I not think of that?" Tristan's eyebrows shot up at my tone. I guess he wasn't used to being on the receiving end of such deep sarcasm. "Yes, those marines would be just perfect for the job."

I got into Tristan's face, channeling Rob when he dressed down a young guardsman. "If the job was to start a war with Beloren and her allied city–states! Something David went to extreme measures to avoid."

"Well... Yes. Um, I see your point," Tristan fell back a step.

"Good. I'm not some love–crazed young woman risking everything just to save her man," I turned to Nist. "Swing around the city and fly past the squadron. Get close enough for them to identify us but not so close that they can hail us. Discreetly raise my flag during the fly–by so they'll know I'm on board. I expect they'll follow us."

I looked at Tristan. "If there are no other objections...?"

"No. None here, lass. None at all."

I flashed my best good–girl smile. "I didn't think so. Now, let's go find those trogs."

21

RAIDERS IN THE DARK

DAVID

THE LIGHT FROM THE GUARDS' LANTERN PROVIDED WEAK ILLUMINATION AS we forged into the dark tunnels of King Rat's domain. My implant recorded every twist and turn we took, expanding the map I began recording when the tunnel rats led me to the dungeon. Martin's implant recorded our progress, as well. We had to learn these tunnels so well we could navigate them in pitch darkness or if one of us was out on his own.

The beginnings of a plan took shape in my mind, but for it to succeed we had to know the tunnels better than the tunnel rats knew them. It was an impossible task made entirely possible by our implants. King Rat counted the maze of dark tunnels as his first line of defense. We would make it the front line of our offense.

For hours, we skirted the edges of tunnel rat territory. As the lantern oil burned down, we replenished our supply from wall lanterns just within the sections used by the tunnel rats. A picture of King Rat's underground empire emerged from our explorations. I expected to find squalor and filth, a sad existence for a pathetic band of ragged beggars and thieves, forced to eat rats and drink dirty water in order to survive. With the exception of an elite few, I expected disease–ridden savages barely scraping by under their king's iron rule.

Reality dashed my fantasy into little bits and then stomped all over the bits. We found a large and well organized food supply, complete with barrels of fresh water and freshly slaughtered meat. Tempting aromas wafted from a huge, bustling kitchen just down the tunnel from the food store. Just past the kitchen we found a vast communal dining area. We stole through the empty dining room to scout what lay beyond it. Room after room was furnished for sleeping, with separate quarters for women and men, as well as quarters for families.

The slave quarters were poorly furnished in comparison, but they far exceeded what I had expected to find. We even found a nursery where children stayed while their parents were out and about, doing King Rat's bidding. The children were the real surprise. Innocent childish laughter clashed with my original image of tunnel life. In retrospect, I realize I should not have been surprised. All human cultures reproduce, even the tunnel rats.

We retreated into unused tunnels, our map of King Rat's territory greatly expanded after the hours we spent exploring. The three of us retraced our path to an intersection of tunnels well outside of the populated areas. Torch and lantern light, which we would spot long before anyone came close to us, would offer ample warning if anyone came looking for us. The intersection also provided several lines of retreat, if King Rat sent a large force.

"There are a lot more people down here than I expected," Martin said. "How many do you think are down here?"

A voice whined from the darkness. "Why haven't you gotten me out of these tunnels?"

"Shut up, Raoul," Martin and I said in unison.

"I'd guess there are close to a thousand people, counting children and slaves." A thought occurred to me. "From the size of their quarters, there must be a lot of slaves. Do you think we can count on their support?"

"Maybe a few will support us. As for the rest, it depends on how long they've been down here. Raoul's only been here a couple of months and look at him. I expect most of the slaves have given up hope. When you get around to expanding your scheme into a plan, don't count on support from the slaves."

"You'll be happy to learn my plan doesn't involve the slaves."

"You have an actual plan?" Martin asked. "It's not David's Scheme Mark II?"

"It's an actual plan. I came up with it while we were exploring," I said. "I'd even go as far as to say it's tailor–made for you."

"Uh huh. Tell me the plan and then I'll let you know if I agree with your assessment."

I grinned. "We're going to be raiders."

Get Lost

Martin approved of my plan. Raoul, on the other hand, did not.

"As a prince of Tarteg, I will not sully my reputation by hoisting the raider flag."

"Yes, perish the thought, Spare Prince," Martin's tone dripped sarcasm. "Kidnapping princesses so a prince as pathetic as you can be reborn as a hero is just fine and dandy, though."

"You're forgetting a rather important part of that plan, raider Captain Bane. *You* are the one who kidnapped the princess." This was more like the Raoul I knew and loathed so well. "I knew nothing of that plan until after the deed was done."

"Yet you went along with the plan when you did learn of it, Raoul. A simple word from you and I'd have released the princess."

"And you could have released the princess at any time, with or without word from me."

"Both of you, *shut up!*"

"But Bane–"

"Shut. Up."

Raoul locked eyes with me and, in the lantern light, his eyes glowed red. Without another word, he jumped to his feet and charged down the tunnel and into the darkness. Martin and I watched him vanish from sight.

"Shouldn't we go after him, David?"

"Nah. Raoul has no idea where he's going. On the other hand, I know this tunnel turns right about a hundred feet from here." I listened to Raoul's fading footsteps. "He should hit the wall right about...now."

We heard a thud followed by the sound of a body hitting the floor.

"Okay, *now* we can go after him, Martin."

We rose and ambled down the tunnel.

"Does this mean I can finally slit the little jerk's throat?"

"I'm tempted to let you, Martin, but Callan would never approve."

"I just *knew* you were going to use Callan as a means of depriving me of my fun. Okay, if we're not going to rid the world of Raoul, what are we going to do with him?"

"Something worse than killing him, my friend. We're going to lock him back in the cell."

Raoul regained consciousness as I snapped the chain about his wrist. He screamed and cursed and pleaded and even cried like a baby. Martin and I smiled and waved as we locked the door.

Lighter of heart than we'd felt since ending up in the cell with Raoul, Martin and I planned our first strike.

Along with the implant-aided mental maps of the tunnels, we discovered King Rat kept the rat kingdom on a tight schedule. He had the place running like clockwork, and that made planning our raids all the easier.

We stuck with simple military tactics and raided the kitchen first. It doesn't matter how much people love or fear their leader, any leader who fails to feed his people is in for some serious control problems.

The kitchen staff appeared to have one job, watching the kitchen slaves and beating them if they didn't work hard enough to suit their masters. Martin and I waited until the kitchen staff arrived to start preparing breakfast then made our move.

"Get lost." The kitchen foreman's arm slashed the air, negating the request he expected to hear. "No food until morning."

I kept walking toward him. With a snarl, the foreman raised the wooden staff he used to beat the slaves and swung it at me. I stepped inside the swing, caught the foreman's wrist and twisted. He cried out in pain as bones snapped. I took the staff from the foreman's unresisting hand and broke it over his head. The foreman collapsed, moaning.

The kitchen staff and the slaves stared at Martin and me, too shocked to react. The shock wore off faster than I'd have hoped.

"Slaves, get them!"

With a smack, one of the staff hit a slave on the backside and the slaves shuffled toward us.

Boost!

Adrenaline poured into our veins. Time slowed for Martin and me. We brushed aside the half-hearted slave attacks, gently pushing them into a confused jumble. The kitchen staff backpedaled as we waded in among them. Each of them got the same treatment as the foreman. Seconds later, we dropped Boost.

The slaves retreated into a corner when I turned to face them.

"We're here to free you, not hurt you. Will you come with us?"

The slaves exchanged glances and a few shrugs before one spoke.

"We have little choice. They will kill us if we stay."

"Then gather as much cooked food and fresh water as you can carry. You are slaves no longer."

As the former slaves gathered supplies, Martin and I locked the staff in a cellar. Our next stop was the food store. We put the remaining food to the torch and then led our well-supplied band into the darkness.

We had struck our first blow against King Rat.

22

TWO HORSES, A HERD OF GOATS, AND A TENT

CALLAN

NIST SWUNG WIDE OF BELOREN, JUST AS WE'D DONE MONTHS BEFORE when the city was aflame. The afternoon sun shone from behind the squadron as we sped past it. Milo hoisted my flag at the closest point of our fly-by. With the early afternoon sunlight streaming in from behind the Mordanian ships, the glare kept us from watching for activity on those decks. Instead, I watched the green and gold colors of my country snapping in the breeze.

"Will their lookouts see the flag, Your Highness?" Milo asked.

"If they don't, my father will demote every last officer on board those ships. And I've told you many times that you may use my first name in private settings like this, Milo."

"Yes, I remember, Your Highness." Milo's infectious grin lit his face. "But, Your Highness, I couldn't do that while we're flying Your Highness's personal flag, Your Highness."

I crossed my arms and called forth what David calls princess mode. "Then take the flag down this instant, you wretched child. Yonder squadron is raising steam and getting under way."

"Your Highness's wish is my command, Your Highnessness!" Milo folded the flag and gave an innocent smile. "Will there be anything else, Callan?"

I pretended to swat at the boy, he pretended to be scared, and I had a much-needed laugh.

Over the next three hours, Tristan's gaze swept over the desert ahead of the airship, searching for signs of a desert tribe camp. I saw nothing but sand and dunes to the far horizon. Tristan's cries of "Ah ha!" followed by directions called to Nist had me wondering if my eyesight was failing.

"What does Tristan see down there, Callan? All I see is sand. And then I look more closely and I still just see sand. And then, look, more sand."

"You can search me, Milo."

Milo gave a sly smile. "Really? Don't you think David will object to me doing that?"

What happened to the innocent child I met in Faroon all those months ago?

My tone was drier than the desert below us as I asked, "What do you think? Besides, don't you have a girlfriend back at the palace?"

"Not really, no," Milo muttered.

Behind us, Nist gave a rather bitter laugh. "Milo hoped to have a girlfriend in the palace, Callan. Alas, young Lady Lucile's mother is wary of a street urchin with aspirations above his station."

"She did *not* say that about Milo, did she?"

"Yeah, she did, and right to Kim's face, too."

"Well, Milo, I will have quite a few choice words for *her* when I get back. The very idea of anyone treating a hero of Faroon like that boils my blood."

"Don't do it, Callan. I've got a reputation to maintain. Having my sort-of big sister rush to my defense won't help it one bit."

"Sort-of big sister? That's so sweet, Milo! But my mind is made up. The nerve of that woman." Then I caught sight of the pleading in Milo's eyes and reined in my temper. "Very well, Milo. I won't say anything to Lady Lucile's mother."

Then the answer came to me and I burst out laughing.

"Okay, Callan, what's so funny? You already promised you wouldn't talk to her."

"And I won't, Milo." I rarely get to use my evil princess smile very often, but this occasion called for it. "Instead, I will tell Mother about it."

Milo's evil smile was better than mine and he had a cackling laugh to go with it.

Tristan's voice rose over Milo's cackle. "If you three are finished dishing up court gossip, I require the aid of young eyes over here."

When Milo and I joined him, Tristan pointed off in the distance. "Is that smudge out there just another dune or is it something else?"

I looked past his pointing finger, gasped, and then planted a kiss on his cheek. "It's a camp, Tristan. You did it."

"It's easy if you know what to look for, my dear."

Ten minutes later, Nist brought the *Pauline* down just outside the camp. Per my orders—orders the squadron commander disliked in the extreme—the squadron stayed aloft and the rails of the airships were *not* teeming with marines.

The tribesmen were no more pleased to have the squadron hovering overhead than the commander was to be stuck up there. The tribal leaders only met with us out of respect for Tristan. In fact, the familiar sight of the *Pauline* was all that kept them from scattering into the desert. At least everyone was equally unhappy, right?

Tristan spoke to the tribal leaders with me standing decorously at his side. The leaders gestured wildly as they spoke and Tristan did the same when he replied. After a few minutes of this, an older tribesman pointed at me, his other arm pointing into the village. Tristan's eyebrows rose and then he responded far more energetically than before. The tribesman gestured to me again and then pointed some more. Tristan and the tribesman went back and forth several times before I got impatient.

"Tristan, this was supposed to be a simple introduction. Why is it taking so long?"

"I'm rather embarrassed to say, Your Highness."

"Get over your embarrassment and tell me what the hold up is."

"The elder wants to...buy you. He's been looking for a wife for his youngest son and you meet with his approval." To my amazement, Tristan blushed. "He believes you'll produce far more attractive children than his elder son's wife."

I faced the tribesman. "I am not for sale."

"I have told him that several times, Your Highness. He thinks I'm haggling and responds by raising his offer." Tristan grinned, his sense of humor returning. "He thinks quite highly of you, my dear. His offer is up to two horses, a herd of goats, *and* a tent."

I fought the urge to laugh, myself. "I'm flattered. Tell him I'm married to a mighty and jealous warrior. Then tell him about David's battles with the trogs. That ought to give the old guy pause."

Tristan chattered and gestured and even thrust an imaginary sword at an imaginary foe.

Excited chatter broke out among the tribesmen after Tristan finished speaking. The hard-bargaining tribesman faced me and bowed low. The rest of the tribal leaders followed his lead.

"Tristan, what's going on?"

Tristan turned a stunned face to me. "They've heard of David. Around here, he's known as the Hand of Death."

"What? Who could have possibly told the tribes about David?"

"That's the part that makes no sense, Your Highness. The desert tribes heard of David from the trogs."

A Translator

I stared at Tristan, my mouth hanging open in a most unprincess-like manner. I tried to wrap my mind around what Tristan had just told me and simply could not do so.

Seeing I was at a loss for words, Tristan nodded his head toward the tribal leaders. They all still held their bows.

"Oh. Thank you, Tristan. Please tell them to rise."

I regained some of my mental equilibrium as Tristan spoke to the leaders. They rose and faced me with expectant looks.

"Find out how the trogs could tell the tribes anything, much less stories about David. I thought the Great One was the only being—trog or human—who had ever been able to speak the other's language."

Tristan and the tribesmen spoke for several minutes, gesturing dramatically. It was fascinating, but also frustrating. I *hate* speaking through translators. Conversations take three times as long and even the best translator can make a mistake or miss a vital detail. What I wouldn't have given to have one of those implant things that David had in his head.

Finally, Tristan turned to me. "The story is long, as you no doubt guessed, but here is the short version. Many centuries ago, the growing city-states to the south and expanding kingdoms to the north pushed both the tribes and the trogs into the desert. Enemies of old, the tribes and trogs waged war against each other for many years. Declining populations on both sides led to the realization that their true battle was against the desert. Their shared enemy led the two groups to form a loose alliance of sorts. Your Highness, these people have been trading with the trogs for at least two centuries. Over that time, a fairly sophisticated sign language has evolved between the trogs and the tribes."

"So these tribesmen can ask the trogs where to find the Great One?"

Tristan shrugged. "So they say."

"Do you believe them?"

"Most definitely. I've treated all of these men and their families many times. I have never known them to be anything but honest in their dealings with me."

"Then ask them if we can borrow a translator."

Tristan relayed my request. The tribesman who had tried to buy me responded.

"What did he say?"

"First, he apologizes most profusely for attempting to purchase you."

"Tell him it is forgotten."

"There is no need. I took the liberty of accepting his apology on your behalf." A wicked grin creased Tristan's face, "Further more, as a token of their respect and admiration for the Hand of Death, he hopes Lady Death will accept the services of their best translator."

"Lady Death? You're making that up, Tristan!"

"I swear on all I hold sacred that I am not. What else should they call the wife of the Hand of Death?"

There was a phrase that described the grin Tristan gave me. When I was much younger, my mother had assured me it was not something proper princesses said.

"Could you at least *pretend* you're not enjoying this so much?" I asked. "Accept their generous offer and get this translator on board the *Pauline*. We leave in ten minutes."

Tristan swept into a bow. "As m'Lady Death commands!"

Ten minutes later, the translator came aboard and the *Pauline* rose to join the naval squadron. We were one step closer to the trogs and to rescuing David.

23

KING RAT'S THREAT

DAVID

EVERYTHING WENT AS PLANNED—BETTER, SINCE WE ONLY SAW RAOUL long enough to give him food and water and make certain he remained securely chained in the cell. The Spare Prince expressed his displeasure every time we visited, but even he was smart enough to keep his voice down. King Rat struck no one as an 'enemy of my enemy is my friend' type of person.

On our first visit, Raoul blustered and threatened. In a weird way, I was relieved to hear him rant like that. It meant Raoul was getting back to his usual, irritating self. Even that odious personality was better than the mewling shell of a man I'd originally found in the cell.

The next time we visited, he demanded his freedom a second time. Again, it was to no avail.

Meanwhile, our kitchen raid had achieved its purpose. King Rat's people were hungry and disorganized. The king tried to anticipate our next move and laid a trap for us at the armory. We hit his store of lantern oil and torches, instead. In the aftermath, the tunnel rats found piles of smoldering torches, smashed and crumpled lanterns, and flaming barrels of oil. The smoke and shortage of oil to light the underground kingdom forced the tunnel rats to move into a few large rooms far from the oil stores. Packed too closely together and with too few comforts, tempers frayed. In the beginning, the rats argued, voices echoing down the tunnels. Soon, fists replaced words. Then blades replaced fists.

King Rat's control slipped with each raid we made.

Hiding well away in unused tunnels, our little band of rescued slaves had all the light they needed and more food than they could eat. Martin and I also had free run through more and more of the tunnels making up King Rat's underground empire. Given our wandering, it was only a matter of time before we found an exit out of the tunnels and up to the surface. When we did find it, we released all of the former slaves. Even better, it finally gave us a chance to get rid of Raoul.

True to his nature, Raoul doubted our intentions. "Are you releasing or taking me away for slaughter?"

"Oh dear, Martin, I believe Raoul has been down here so long he's become delirious."

"How can you tell, David?"

"Isn't it obvious? The poor prince has confused us with his mother's minions in the Tartegian court."

Raoul sputtered, too angry to form words.

"See, Martin? The poor Spare Prince has even lost the capacity for human speech."

"It is sad, David. We should release him into the wild so he can live out his few remaining days frolicking in the meadows."

"What a fine and humane idea, Martin. Let's do that."

After Raoul ascended the ladder and exited the tunnels—at sword point—we closed and locked the grating behind him.. Neither Martin nor I thought Raoul could lay his hands on any armed men, nor was he likely to be able to find his way through the tunnels beneath Beloren, but we saw no reason to take chances.

Free of helpless people to watch over, Martin and I made our way back to King Rat's shrunken domain.

As we neared the inhabited parts of the tunnel system, we heard many voices echoing down the tunnels. They seemed to all be repeating the same message, but with all the overlapping echoes, I couldn't make out what they were saying. It took ten minutes to get close enough to concentrate on a single voice.

"David Rice, His Majesty King Rat orders you to surrender. If you refuse, all of the remaining slaves in the kingdom will be fed to His Majesty's new tammar."

A Native Guide

The heralds' shouts echoed throughout the tunnels as Martin and I withdrew to discuss our options. With a sigh, Martin threw himself onto the tunnel floor

"This is why it's so hard to be the good guy. You try to do what's right and the next thing you know, the bad guy threatens innocent people unless you surrender. I spent years raiding north and south of the desert and you know what? No one ever threatened innocent bystanders in the hope of forcing me to surrender."

"Spend a little more time as a noble hero and you'll get used to it. At least it tells us that we're hurting King Rat. This place would fall apart without the slaves to do the work."

"Yeah, the same thought crossed my mind. Considering that, do you think the old rat boy will carry through with his threat, David?"

"After this very loud, very public announcement, I can't see how he has any other choice. I only see three possible outcomes. We defeat King Rat. King Rat captures us and feeds us to the tammar. Or a miracle occurs."

"I notice you left out King Rat feeding the slaves to the tammar."

"That's because I'll surrender to him before I let that happen."

"It won't come to that, David. I promised Callan I'd help get you back and I am *not* facing your wife again unless you are standing safely at my side. So, what do we do now?"

"We gather more information on King Rat's situation. With what little we know right now, I don't see how we can make any real plans. Are you up for some more exploration of his kingdom?"

"Sure. Are we looking for anything in particular?"

"The last time I paid a visit to King Rat's tammar pit, things didn't go so well for him *or* his tunnel rats. Whatever else the man is, he's not stupid. There's no way he'll ever rely on a rope tether to restrain his tammar again. He has to have changed the setup in the pit. We must discover what he has changed."

"It could take hours to find the pit on our own, especially if we have to dodge a lot of tunnel rats." Martin eyes lit up and he grinned. "So why don't we get a native to guide us to it."

King Rat's heralds were positioned at the edges of his meager lighted territory, insuring their shouts reached our ears. Ever the thoughtful leader, he'd even sent a couple of guards to keep watch over each of his heralds. The heralds had been shouting their message so long that they and their guards had grown bored with the whole thing. They cried the message every few minutes, spending the rest of the time sitting around waiting.

"Hey, Jon, it's time to shout the message again.

"Let me skip this one, guys. My throat is raw." The herald's voice was getting raspy. "I've gotta rest it."

"Then this is your lucky day, Jon." I strode into the wavering circle of light cast by their torch. "I'm David Rice and I'm here to surrender."

All three men jumped to their feet in surprise. The guards raised their swords as the herald retreated behind them. My sword was sheathed at my side and I held my arms out wide, well away from the weapon.

They neither saw nor heard Martin dash up from behind them. He shoved the herald into the two guards. As the guards struggled for balance, Martin's sword pommel cracked against a guard's head. The first guard sagged to the floor, and Martin spun and delivered a similar blow to the second guard. The herald opened his mouth to cry for help. The cry froze in his throat as both of our swords pressed against his neck.

"Take your own advice and give your voice a rest," Martin said. "Unless David asks you a question, that is. Then you respond quickly and quietly. Do you understand?"

All too aware of the blades pricking his neck, the herald nodded his head very slowly.

"All right, David, you're up."

"King Rat says he wants to feed me to his tammar. I'll make it easy on him. Take me to King Rat's new tammar pit."

"I can't." The herald squeaked as Martin's sword drew a drop of blood. "I'm telling the truth. Nobody knows where it is except the king."

A Secret Pit

"Why would that be a secret?"

"Ask King Rat if you really want to know," the herald muttered.

"Mind your manners, herald," Martin punctuated his command by scratching the man's neck with his sword.

"I really don't know why it's a secret." The herald pointed to one of the unconscious guards, "He says the king has been...twitchy...since you released that tammar. Some people think the tammar almost got King Rat and he's terrified of another one getting loose."

"But you're just guessing."

The herald nodded at my statement.

"It doesn't matter why he's keeping it secret, just that he is." I shook my head. "A better question is how he's keeping a place the size of a tammar pit secret?"

"There are a lot of tunnels down here. No one knows them all. Each day the pit workers are blindfolded and the king personally leads them to the site," the herald replied. "He's threatened to execute anyone who tries to follow. Only the king and few of his guards know where the pit is."

"That's brutal, but I bet it's effective," Martin said.

"How long before the king leads another work party to the pit?"

"How should I know?" The herald sounded truly offended. "I am a herald of the court, not one of the lower classes."

"That means you're pretty useless to us, aren't you?" Martin smacked the herald with his sword's pommel. "What do you want to do now, David?"

"I don't quite know," I responded. "I do find the whole idea behind a hidden tammar pit really odd. If King Rat wants to draw us into the open, why not announce a time and place for the big event? He's got to know I'd try to stop him from feeding his slaves to the tammar."

"Maybe King Rat is trying to confront us without the rest of the tunnel rats knowing about it? If he fails to capture us, only a few people would know his trap failed," Martin mused. "I don't know. That kind of plan is way too convoluted for my tastes. Of course, even you must admit you are known to take a very direct approach to problem solving.

Maybe King Rat is counting on the shroud of secrecy to draw you into his trap?"

"If he's counting on that, let's give him exactly what he wants."

"I knew you were going to say that."

"Yes, you're very smart, Martin. So, if you were King Rat, where would you build the new tammar pit?"

"I would put it right where the old one was," Martin replied. "I'd make some changes—install a cage to keep the tammar from getting loose again—but otherwise, I wouldn't change much from the way it was before."

"I bow to your intimate knowledge of criminal affairs." I inclined slightly in Martin's direction. "Let's check it out."

"What about these guys?" Martin waved toward the unconscious guards and herald.

"Leave them. I don't want to stop and search for rope. Besides, as far as the herald knows, we believed his story and that's what he'll report to King Rat. That's assuming they even report this at all."

An hour later, we peeked down a dimly lit hallway toward the entrance to the old tammar pit. Six men guarded the doors. Martin had been right.

I'd Rather Be Flayed Alive

"David Rice, you've just found the tammar pit," Despite the whisper, Martin still managed to sound like some kind of advertising huckster. "What are you going to do now?"

"Feeding you to the tammar has a certain appeal, right about now."

"Tsk, tsk, my boy. Is that any way to whisper to your best friend in the whole galaxy?"

"I'm going to go with 'yes' to that question."

"Perhaps this attitude explains why you had to crash land on a lost human colony to find a wife and a best friend. I recall advising you to work on your people skills when we were back in Faroon. It grieves me that you chose to ignore it."

"Then perhaps it's best if I stop inflicting my presence on you, dear friend. You asked what I'm going to do now? *I* will wait for those guards to escort the blindfolded workmen home from the construction site, slip inside, and find a hiding place within. Meanwhile, *you* are going to slip out of the tunnels and report to Callan."

"Oh, that is *so* not going to happen, David. I would face King Rat, all his guards, and a tammar, while I was armed with nothing more than a soup spoon, rather than face Callan and tell her I left you alone down here."

"Coward."

"When it comes to your wife, damn right I'm a coward, If I bring you back in one piece, I might get a peck on the cheek as thanks. *Might*. But if I leave you down here to die alone in these tunnels—even free and armed, as you are now—searchers will never even find my body, When my name is spoken within the palace, it will be in hushed whispers, serving solely to remind others the peril of interfering with your wife's love life,"

"Don't be melodramatic. Callan would never do that,"

Martin heaved a dramatic sigh. "No, she wouldn't harm a hair on my head. Instead, her eyes would fill with unshed tears, she would put on a brave face, then she would tell me your death wasn't my fault. What's worse is that she would mean every word of it." Martin shuddered. "I'd rather be flayed alive than face that,"

"Okay, okay. You can stay with me."

Martin grinned. "I knew you'd see the sense in my position, lad,"

We hung around watching the doors to the tammar pit for hours before anything happened. At least no one else wandered the halls, this being King Rat's big secret location and all. Finally, blindfolded workmen came out of the pit.

Watching the guards form around the workmen, I said, "What I don't understand is why use the blindfolds at all? The first time the workmen see the location, they're bound to recognize it."

"I can think of two reasons. First, it serves as a reminder to the workmen to keep their mouths shut about this place. Second, if anyone sees the guards escorting the workmen, the blindfolds reinforce the secrecy surrounding the project. But don't ask me why King Rat is bothering with all this hoopla, unless he's just paranoid. You do seem to have that kind of effect on certain people." Martin shook his head as if disappointed in me, somehow. "It all comes back to people skills, David."

Martin and I faded into the shadows of a side passage and watched the guards and workmen walk right past us. We waited five minutes before slipping down the tunnel and into the tammar pit. Burning torches filled sconces around the walls, making it easy for us to see how busy the workmen had been.

A steel cage stood in the center of the pit. A long, caged passage led from the main cage over to the far wall. The caged passage ended at a large door, surely used to let the tammar into and out of the cage. A double-gated cage entrance—similar in idea to the airlock in a spaceship—allowed guards to put victims into the cage without letting the tammar get its claws on the guards. Always the considerate ruler, King Rat had even ordered bleachers built around the cage. What was next, souvenirs and popcorn?

Distant voices interrupted our inspection of the new construction. The voices came from outside the pit, but they were growing louder by the second.

"King Rat must be in a hurry to complete this place. It sounds like he's ordered a second shift of workmen," Martin observed

"We'd better hide,"

"Good idea, David. Where?"

I looked about the pit. There was no place to hide!

24

PRICKLY RULES STICKLERS

CALLAN

When I had a chance to talk to the translator, I discovered he was the son for whom the tribal elder sought to purchase a wife. Tristan took great relish in relating the tale of the haggling over my bride price to the two of us. I smiled at the translator to show I was not offended.

Despite my smile, the man immediately prostrated himself before me, his arms outstretched and his nose touching the *Pauline's* deck. "I humbly beg pardon for my father's foolish and insulting attempt to buy you, Lady Death,"

"No apology is necessary. Fathers excel at embarrassing their children. Rise and think no more about it," I said. "And please call me Princess Callan or Your Highness—not Lady Death."

The man rose to his feet. "As you command, Lady Death."

His face turned red and he threw himself to the deck again. "I humbly beg your pardon, Lady– um, Princess Callan,"

"It was a mere slip of the tongue. Think nothing of it. Rise." I began to see why this man was still single. "What is your name?"

"Treb, Your Highness Princess Callan." He bowed deeply from the waist. At least he didn't drop to the deck again.

As the *Pauline* rose into the air, the squadron commander brought his ship alongside.

"Have you concluded your business with this desert tribe, Your Highness?"

"I have, Captain Dorrin. Is there something you wish from me?"

"Most definitely. I *wish* Her Highness would finally see fit to share the particulars of her plan with her squadron commander. I *wish* those particulars would include any further destinations you have in mind. It's so much easier to give proper orders to the airmen when one knows where one is going."

Lovely. My mother had chosen a prickly rules stickler to command my escort squadron. No doubt, mother hoped he would keep me from doing something she would call 'unwise.' A pedantic captain selected to counterbalance my impulsive nature—yes, it had Mother's fingerprints all over it.

"Of course, Captain, Nothing would please me more." I gave him my most dazzling smile. The airship's junior officers and airmen perked up and smiled in return. The captain continued gazing stolidly at me. "I would have gladly told you earlier, had you asked,"

"And I would gladly have asked earlier, had my airship been fast enough to catch up with your little ship." The good captain ground his teeth beneath his grimace of a smile. "But I am asking now, Your Highness."

"I am going to send an armed force into the tunnels of Beloren with the express intent of retrieving my husband and forcibly removing King Rat from his throne."

A real smile broke across Captain Dorrin's face. "At last, someone is talking sense, My men are chomping at the bit to teach these tunnel rats a lesson, Princess Callan."

Behind Captain Dorrin, his men nodded enthusiastically.

"Why did you have us come all the way out here, Your Highness? Does this tribe know of hidden entrances to the tunnels?"

"I am afraid you have misinterpreted my intentions, Captain." My words summoned Dorrin's grimace back to prominence. "The force I will take into the tunnels must be one that cannot be traced to Mordan. David chose to surrender himself to King Rat to *avoid* drawing Mordan into a war with the city-states. I will not disregard the goal behind his sacrifice in order to rescue him."

"You wish to send a force of these desert tribesmen in place of my marines." Dorrin's tone was cold and formal in the extreme. "I see, Your Highness."

"Captain, were the consequences less dire, nothing would please me more than to have your marines storm the tunnels, slay the rats, and rescue David. I can think of no men I'd rather trust with David's life."

Dorrin's men straightened at the compliment, though their Captain appeared unconvinced.

"And yet you will send desert tribesmen instead."

"I did not negotiate for a raiding party, Captain. No tribesmen will attack the tunnels in place of your marines."

"Then who do you plan to send into the tunnels, Princess?"

"Correct me if I'm wrong, Captain, but I believe a battle is half won if the mere sight of your soldiers strikes fear into the hearts of your enemies."

"Of course, Your Highness. And there are no men on Aashla who inspire more fear than Mordanian marines."

"You are quite right, Captain. But I'm not going to send *men* into those tunnels."

The good captain blew out his breath in exasperation. "Please pardon an old navy man's ignorance, Your Highness, but who else *could* you send into the tunnels?"

"Trogs."

"Trogs? Absolutely not, Your Highness! I forbid it."

I'm a Fair Man

I gave Captain Dorrin the benefit of my most effective glare. It has everything; an arched eyebrow, folded arms, canted hips, a tapping foot, and smoldering eyes. Rob called it my Princess Glare and respected the effect it had on men. *Other* men, that is, as Rob was the one man completely unaffected by my glare.

The airmen crowding the rail shrank back from their captain, as if they expected him to burst into flames under the weight of the Princess Glare. I held my silence and waited for the captain to capitulate before my wrath. Captain Dorrin stood his ground, hands clasped behind his back, meeting the Princess Glare with a calm expression.

After nearly a minute, I admitted to myself that my glare was not working. What a horrible time to discover another man unaffected by it. Taking pity on Dorrin's men, I dropped the glare.

"You *forbid* me from pursuing my plan, Captain?" My tone implied my extreme disapproval of the captain's temerity.

"Even should it cost me my commission, I most assuredly do, Your Highness."

"My airship is faster than yours. We could simply outrun your squadron, Captain."

"Yes, but you could not pull away before I could order my men to attempt a boarding," Captain Dorrin responded. "Considering the risks of such a maneuver, I am confident you will not force me to endanger the lives of my men."

He was right, damn him. I relaxed my stance, nodding my head. "You are quite correct, Captain. Would you, at the very least, come aboard and allow me to explain my reasoning to you?"

"It will not sway my decision, Your Highness."

My arsenal of expressions was not limited to the Princess Glare. I reached into the arsenal and drew forth my Please Daddy look. That look had even worked on Rob—unless Mother was present. How fortunate she was far, far away.

"Please?"

My rising voice, subtly clasped hands, slightly canted head, and heavy-lidded eyes worked their magic. A paternalistic smile spread across the captain's face.

"Of course, Your Highness. Never let it be said I'm not a fair man."

As Nist brought the *Pauline* alongside Captain Dorrin's ship, Tristan murmured, "What is your plan, Princess?"

"Have you examined the good captain's left hand, Tristan?"

He did so. "All I see is a hand."

"Exactly!" Tristan still looked bewildered, so I added, "He wears no wedding band, nor is there any indication he has ever worn one. That means Captain Dorrin has no wife and, vastly more important, no daughters. I believe it is time to show the man just what he's been missing."

Tristan shuddered, backing away. "Try not to destroy the man, Princess."

Captain Dorrin hopped over the *Pauline's* rail. His body language screamed indulgence, making it that much easier for me to follow through with my plan.

I bowed my head but, through upraised eyes, met Captain Dorrin's gaze. Then I released all of the emotions I'd held in check ever since the envoy's ship carried David away from me. My voice trembled. My lips quivered. My breath caught with little hiccup sounds. My shoulders shook. My breast heaved. Tears streamed from my eyes.

Ten minutes later, we steamed off in search of a trog settlement.

25

INTO THE TAMMAR'S LAIR

DAVID

MARTIN AND I HAD A MINUTE, MAYBE TWO, TO GET OUT OF SIGHT BEFORE the work party and their guards entered the tammar pit. We cast about for someplace—anyplace—to hide. Work progressed in every corner of the pit—from the arena to the ascending rows of benches for spectators—but provided no place where we could conceal ourselves. Even the hole in the ceiling—the one through which a bound Callan had been shoved into the tammar pit—was sealed.

"I only see one place to go." Martin pointed to the center of the pit.

The steel cage stretched from the floor to the ceiling, with both doors to the cage standing ajar. A cage-tunnel, for want of a better word for it, stretched from the large cage to a door in the back wall of the pit. No great leaps of imagination were required to figure out the tammar would enter and leave the pit through the cage-tunnel. Neither of us wanted to open that door, but we saw no other options.

Martin and I jumped into the pit, ran through the two gates, then headed down the cage-tunnel toward the door.

"Do you think we'll find a tammar on the other side of the door?" I asked.

"I'd bet on it. Too many things have been going our way lately for there not to be."

"We're trying to hide in a tammar lair while plotting to kill King Rat so he won't force the city–states to invade Mordan, and *that's* your idea of things going our way?"

"We've had free run of the tunnels for several days and are seriously irritating King Rat. And we're not dead yet," Martin shot back.

"When I relate this tale to my yet–to–be–conceived children, I do hope they find humor in your optimistic summation of our situation," I replied. "Lord only knows, I do not."

"That's hurtful, David. I'd even go as far as to say your words cut me to the quick."

"Better my words than a tammar's claws, Martin. Or the swords and spears of a couple of dozen of King Rat's guards and workmen."

With workmen's voices drawing closer to the tammar pit entrance, Martin opened the door and we slipped through and into the lair. There wasn't one tammar to be found beyond the door—there were four!

Out of the Tammar's Lair

Martin and I froze as the torch light reflected from two pairs of large, alert eyes. The owners of the eyes regarded us with an unsettling intensity, heads up and ears pricked forward. Their bodies almost quivered with tension as the tammars sized us up. The other two tammars slept —a small blessing, since most predators wake in a flash, but a blessing none–the–less.

Tearing my eyes from the tammars' stare, I studied the lair. It was about forty feet across and maybe thirty feet wide, with a sloping ceiling that started just higher than our heads but was close to thirty feet high at the far wall. The only door in that wall was twenty feet off the floor and behind a barred catwalk. We definitely weren't getting out that way.

"Why am I so good at predicting bad news?" Martin whispered through unmoving lips. "Have you got any brilliant ideas?"

"Go back the way we came?"

"What about the workmen and the guards?" Martin sidled closer to the door we'd come through.

"Let's put a door between us and the tammars before we waste time worrying about a bunch of tunnel rats."

Never taking my eyes from the tammars, my hand found the door handle. Slowly, ever so slowly, I turned the handle.

One tammar rose to its feet, extended its forelegs and stretched. A casual observer might have believed the tammar hadn't a care in the world. As an active participant in this drama, I saw it never took its eyes off of us.

"*Now!*" We shoved the door open and ran through it.

The two alert tammars sprang at us, closing the gap with terrifying speed.

"*Boost!*" I cried to Martin while triggering my own Boost.

Time slowed as adrenaline flooded my body. The charging tammars seemed to slow, as well, but the huge predators still moved much faster than even a Boosted human could run. Martin and I threw our whole bodies into shutting the door, trying desperately to close it before the tammars reached it.

We were still a foot short of closing the door when the two beasts crashed into it. Our Boosted strength was nothing against the combined might of two tammars. Martin and I were thrown backward twenty feet as the door slammed open. The two tammars bounded into the pit, with the other two tammars close on their tails.

It's Rice and Bane

Flung from the door, Martin and I tucked and spun and landed on our feet. Had we landed on our backs—a certainty if we had not Boosted—the tammars would never have allowed us to regain our feet. As it was, we still had fifty feet of cage-tunnel to cover just to reach the full-sized cage. But if we could get to the cage, we had a fighting chance. The cage-tunnel was so narrow the tammars would be forced to come at us one at a time. With Boost, plus the freedom of movement afforded by the larger cage, maybe Martin and I could block the tammars from leaving the cage-tunnel. I had no idea what we would do after that, but decided to solve my problems one at a time.

The two lead tammars took a second to check their environment. I assume instinct drove them to look for threats, but anything that slowed them down was fine by me.

"Run!" Martin cried.

"No, swing!" I grabbed the bars above our heads, pulled my feet up, and began swinging along the bars of the cage–tunnel like some jungle lord from the adventure vids my father and I loved to watch.

Martin followed my lead just as the tammars decided it was safe to chase us. For most people, running *was* faster. With our Boost–enhanced strength and reflexes, Martin and I were much faster swinging.

The charging tammars snarled and snapped, getting in each other's way, each eager to be the first to make a kill. Despite their fighting, the closest tammar was only fifteen feet behind us as Martin and I swung into the full–sized cage. The first gate out of the cage hung open on the far side of the pit. It was no more than thirty feet away, but it might as well have been in Mordan for all the good it did. Martin and I knew the chase would be over for us if the tammars reached open space and could leap properly.

Beyond the cage, the pit echoed with the shouts of the workmen and the guards just entering the room. In seconds, the normal beginning–of–shift chatter gave way to cries of alarm.

"The tammars are free!"

"The gate is open!"

"It's Rice and Bane!"

"Let's get out of here!"

"Bar the doors!"

"Alert the king!"

"Ask for more reinforcements!"

The workmen were as scared of Martin and me as they were of the tammars. In other circumstances, I'd have enjoyed the notoriety we had earned among the tunnel rats. At the moment, I was happy they were running from us rather than firing crossbows at us.

At the end of the cage–tunnel, we drew our swords and prepared to fight the tammars.

Alone Against the Tammars

The first tammar leapt while it was still in the cage–tunnel. The bars rang from the impact of skull on steel and the tammar's charge slowed. I took advantage of its disorientation and slashed it across the cheek. Skin parted, blood flowed, and the tammar roared in pain. It swatted at my blade and, despite my Boost–enhanced speed, was quick enough to smack the blade tip. The tammar yowled as the tip of my sword plunged into its paw. The creature yanked its paw back, but the power of its blow almost knocked the sword from my hand.

I stepped back from my thrust, leaving the way clear for Martin. With a shout, he lunged at the angry predator. The tammar reared up on its hind legs, whacking its head on the low bars a second time. A line of blood welled behind Martin's blade as he scored a cut on the tammar's leg. He leapt back just ahead of a slashing claw from the second tammar, which we had thought blocked from the fight. When the first tammar reared, the second one saw an opening between the first tammar's legs and swiped through the legs. Its trickery almost caught Martin.

The first tammar dropped back to all fours and discovered the second tammar between its legs. With a yowl of protest, it raked its back claws in the other one's face, driving the second predator back behind it again.

"Martin, these things are too big and too fast for us. There's no way we can keep them bottled up long enough to kill one of the tammars, much less all four." I lunged for the tammar's right eye but ended up slicing through an ear.

"What do you suggest we do?" Martin tried for the other eye but his blade just scraped along the jawbone.

"One of us must attack from a safer direction. You run out of the cage and attack this beast through the bars of the cage–tunnel." I stabbed at a slashing paw and missed. The paw missed me, as well, but came within an inch of gutting me.

"Why me?" Martin asked.

"Because I've done a lot more Boosting than you have. I'm acclimated to it and can keep it going longer than you," I replied, slashing a leg. "Now go."

Someone else—such as my wife, to select an example purely at random—would have argued with me. Martin and I both had Scout training and, more, both knew I was the logical man to guard the tunnel. Martin made a wild swing to force the tammar back then bolted for the cage door.

I moved to block the center of the tunnel exit and stood alone against the tammars.

26

GET OUT OF THERE

DAVID

THE SECOND TAMMAR GOT TIRED OF WAITING FOR A CHANCE TO GET AT ME. It slashed the right flank of the tammar I had been fighting. A roar turned into a yowl as the wounded tammar's rear leg collapsed under the force of the blow. The impatient tammar started climbing over the lead tammar, pulling itself over that tammar with its claws.

As its flanks were ripped up, the tammar before me screamed in pain and fury. By instinct, it reared up on its hind legs to throw the enemy off of its back. As before, it banged its head on the bars over the cage–tunnel. As an added bonus, it whacked the second tammar's head against the bars, as well. Stunned, both tammars reeled as if drunk.

Seizing the opening their power struggle provided, I lunged at the wounded and distracted predator. My blade struck true, piercing the tammar's left eye and plunging into its brain. In a move my hoped–for children would probably find morbidly fascinating, I rotated my sword left to right, up and down, then back again. The blade cut up the tammar's eye but, more importantly, it also sliced the tammar's brain into many parts.

The tammar pulled away from me in reflex, almost jerking my sword from my hand. I'd been expecting that reaction, though. Using a two–handed grip, I held onto my sword and pulled it free. The tammar spasmed and convulsed in violent death throes as the last impulses from its destroyed brain went awry. The impatient tammar found itself flung left and right, unable to get past the dying predator.

That's when Martin dashed up to the side of the cage–tunnel. He thrust his sword into the throat of the impatient tammar and sawed through muscle and arteries. Blood fountained from the tammar, soaking it and its dying companion.

"The tunnel is blocked, David," Martin shouted over the screams of the dying and trapped tammars. "Get out of there before the other two start clawing their way over the two dead ones."

I sprinted for the cage door. Behind me, the two healthy tammars were already clawing at the dying ones, trying to get past them so they could get their paws on me. I reached the door before either of them could pull their way past the two corpses and out into the full-sized cage. With great satisfaction, I slammed the inner cage door shut. With a clang, the door rebounded and swung open again.

The first tammar was poking its head out of the cage–tunnel when I saw that the inner door had no latch. It took but a glance to see the same was true of the outer door. I had no way to lock the tammars into the cage.

No Latch

"There's no latch," I yelled.

"Lovely. I guess it's on backorder with the locksmith," Martin replied.

We both looked about for something to use to block one of the gates or fasten a gate to the cage bars. There were no spools of wire, no stacks of steel bars, and no handy padlock large enough to fit around the bars. Nor were there any wooden crates, large or small, we could push in front of the outer cage gate to slow down the tammar and buy us a few seconds to scramble for the door out of the pit. We would have to deal with the guards and the workmen, but right then two dozen men were much less intimidating than two tammars.

A boom echoed through the pit. The workmen and guards had slammed shut the only door out of the pit. A crash followed the boom; the guards barring the door, I guessed. Our only hope for escape was blocked. We no longer had any other choices open to us. Martin and I either found a way to deal with the tammars or the tammars would deal with us with gnashing teeth and slashing claws.

I glanced back at the cage–tunnel. One of the two remaining tammars clawed and wriggled its way past the two tammars Martin and I had already slain. We had mere seconds before that tammar came bounding across the pit floor and out of the cage. Even Boosted, there was no way I could get back inside the cage and slay the creature before it was free. Martin could kill it through the bars, except the tammar was on the other side of the cage–tunnel, far beyond Martin's reach.

Martin saw that, too. He crouched, then sprang up to the top of the cage–tunnel. Even Boosted, clearing the thing in a single bound was beyond his strength. Instead, Martin turned the leap into a vault. Grabbing a bar over the top, he swung his feet around toward the far side of the tunnel. It was a great move, just the kind of thing you'd see from the swashbuckling hero in an adventure vid. But, with his concentration on the nearly–free tammar, Martin's hand planted too near the fourth tammar.

I saw a tawny blur as the tammar's claw lashed at Martin's hand. Blood spurted over the bars. His hand ripped open, Martin lost his grip on the bar. With a cry of agony, Martin collapsed onto the bars at the top of the cage–tunnel. He lay within easy reach of the tammar below.

Another claw slashed at Martin and there was nothing I could do to help him.

Mauled

I charged around the cage toward Martin, hoping for a miracle. Maybe the tammar would strike a bar instead of flesh. Or maybe something even less probable would happen and save my friend.

Then Martin rolled over on the bars, bringing his unwounded sword arm down against the bars. Was he crazy, trapping his sword at his side like that? Then Martin shoved his upper body up and away from the bars with his sword arm. At the last second, he also snatched his good hand away from the bars. Martin's timing was perfect. The tammar's claw slashed beneath him, tearing his shirt sleeve but missing the hand and arm.

Dropping back toward the bars, Martin swung his sword between the bars of the cage–tunnel and slashed the tammar's eyes. With a yowl, the tammar rolled away, its paws batting at the sword, which Martin had already pulled back out of its reach.

Cradling his wounded hand, Martin jumped down next to the tammar attempting to pull itself past the two dead tammars. Martin stumbled on the landing, another cry of pain escaping his lips as he steadied himself with his wounded hand. Rising, he drove his sword again and again into the body of the tammar squirming to get past its dead companions. By the time I reached his side, the cage–tunnel was completely blocked by three dead tammars. The fourth, its eyes cut, slunk back toward the tammar lair at the end of the cage–tunnel.

"Sit down before you fall down," I said, catching his left arm at the elbow and helping him down.

"Does my hand look as bad as it feels?" Martin put on a brave smile to mask the pain. "I do hope not, because it feels terrible."

"There's too much blood for me to say. I'll let you know when I can stop the bleeding and get a good look. This is going to hurt, Martin."

I tore my shirt off and pressed it hard against the shredded palm. Martin hissed but held his hand steady.

"What a pity Callan isn't here to see you," Martin said through gritted teeth. "Here's her heroic husband, shirtless, stained with the blood of men and beasts, and glistening with sweat. I do believe we'd have a little heir in the making in no time."

"I had no idea my love life was of such interest to you, Martin."

"It's not, but I'll try anything to keep my mind off of my hand right now."

I worked fast, following my Scout training and drawing on the information fed to me from my implant. In the wider galaxy, medical nanites would repair the worst of the damage to Martin's hand in an hour or two. Here on Aashla...

The damage to the hand was extensive and blood kept oozing, making it difficult to get a clear look at the wound. Eventually, my implant built a clear image of the hand from the brief glimpses I got after wiping away blood. Three slashing cuts had opened the hand to the bones. None of those bones were broken, but I couldn't tell if tendons or ligaments were damaged. On top of all that, dirt from the tammar's claw and from the pit floor had worked into the wound. All in all, the hand was a medical mess.

"I'm no doctor, so take what I say with a grain or two of salt. But it's possible you're going to lose that hand, Martin."

Martin the Traditionalist

With the bleeding slowed down to a slow ooze, there was little more I could do for Martin's hand. Using strips torn from my shirt, I bound the wounded hand against his chest.

"This ought to help with the bleeding, Martin. According to my implant, immobilizing the hand should help with the pain, too."

Martin watched me work without really focusing on what I was doing. "So, I might lose the hand, huh?"

"Yeah. Maybe. I'm not a doctor, Martin. I mean, who knows what Tristan can do when he gets a chance to work on it? He saved me when I took that crossbow bolt through the chest. He might be able to save your hand, too."

Martin nodded absently. "Right... You know, if I do lose the hand, I'll be unconscious by the time the doctor finishes cutting it off. So, you have to promise to do something for me, David."

"You want me to give the hand a proper burial? Maybe have a carpenter construct a miniature coffin and hire a priest to say a few words over it?"

"Hm? Those are all good ideas, but they're not what I had in mind. Promise me you'll have the doctor give me a nice, shiny hook to replace the hand."

"A hook? Why would you want that? Have you got some strange desire to frighten little children or something?"

"You disappoint me, David. I thought you watched lots of old adventure vids when you were a kid. Raider? Pirate? Hook? How much more traditional can you get?"

"A hook. Right. Tell you what, Martin, let's worry about that *after* we get out of these tunnels with our lives."

"That's an excellent point, lad. And have you concocted any brilliant plans for doing that?"

"I've got an idea, though its brilliance is questionable. Last time I was down here, there was a big opening in the ceiling right above us. King Rat's pit master dropped victims through it to the tammar waiting below." I tied off the last of the bindings holding Martin's arm against his chest. "It's been sealed off, but I'll bet they left it till the end of the rebuilding. It would have been too useful for dropping construction supplies to the pit floor. If I'm lucky, they've only completed the first layer of plaster, meaning it will be fairly thin. Sit back and try to relax for a few minutes. I'm going to try to knock an escape hole in King Rat's new ceiling."

I scrabbled through the tools left by the workmen, selecting a hefty hammer I could swing with one arm. Climbing one of the cage bars, I leaned out from the bar as far as possible and started whacking the new plaster. The angle was awkward and my shoulder and arm ached within minutes, but I made fast progress. Then, over the sounds of breaking plaster, we heard shouted orders outside the door.

Reinforcements for King Rat's guard squad had arrived.

27

INHUMAN ALLIES

CALLAN

I rubbed my arms, feeling the goosebumps. The night air was cold five thousand feet above the ground. Below us, the moonlight did little to illuminate Beloren. I couldn't imagine how Nist saw well enough to spot the navel squadron, much less know when it was in position.

My heart hammered in my chest and my mind played over the events of the last few days. Convincing Captain Dorrin to follow my lead had been child's play compared to what had come afterwards.

Finding a trog tribe, which I'd expected to be difficult, was easy. Treb, the translator, led us directly to a tribe no more than an hour's flight from his own desert camp. Despite working through a translator using sign language, negotiations sped along nicely once the trogs discovered Lady Death was present. The ceremony in my honor, though, took hours. Worse, the next three trog tribes we visited also insisted on bestowing similar honors on me.

The trogs' veneration yielded one benefit—it impressed the heck out of Captain Dorrin and his men. The good captain offered no further arguments against my plan. That was a relief, as I doubted histrionics would work on him a second time.

When we finally found the Great One, he readily agreed to my plan. For centuries, the city-states waged a war of extermination against the trogs. He leapt at the chance to strike a blow against the largest and wealthiest among those city–states.

Then the true planning began. My plan had been simple—take a bunch of trogs into the tunnels, wipe out the tunnel rats and their odious king, then rescue David. Its simplicity horrified Captain Dorrin and his marine commander. After hearing the gist of the marine commander's plan, the Great One was convinced to turn away from my smash–and–grab approach, as well.

I readily admit the marine commander's plan was better than mine, but it was more complex. It required supplies and large–scale transportation and coordinated action. I came to hate the word 'logistics' long before the military leaders were satisfied with their plan.

David had been underground for days and days before we were ready to strike. At long last, though, it was almost time to act.

"What you see?" The Great One wouldn't come within five feet of the *Pauline's* railing. Who'd have thought the mighty leader of the trogs feared heights?

"I see a huge light spot where Beloren should be," I said. "And I see a big dark spot where everything else should be. Maybe Nist can tell us what he sees?"

"Of course, Lady Death."

Nist loved my new nickname and used it every chance he got. It did demonstrate a certain level of familiarity I'd wanted, so I strove for regal forbearance. I arched an eyebrow and waited for Nist to continue.

"The squadron is approaching the city from the north, as planned. The Beloren patrol ships haven't spotted them yet, but they will within the minute."

I leaned over the rail a bit, trying to see what Nist saw. Behind me, a soft moan slipped through the Great One's lips. It was a good thing the rest of his band of warriors were below deck, unable to see and hear his fear.

I pointed toward a darker than normal blob outside Beloren. "Is that the naval squadron?"

"Uh, no Lady Death. That's a herd of cattle. The squadron is over there."

I followed Nist's pointing finger. It was just more darkness to me.

"I'll take your word for it, Nist."

"Ah ha! The squadron has been spotted and the Beloren patrol ships are moving to intercept," Nist said. "Hang on, Lady Death. Our descent will be rapid."

I turned to the Great One. "You may want to go below to...prepare your warriors."

The Great One nodded and scrambled below.

Then the *Pauline* angled down and dove for the heart of Beloren.

I Won't Let You Fall

Milo sauntered to the bow of the *Pauline*. He was as comfortable on the sloping deck of the airship as he'd been in the palace and in the streets of Faroon. I meet people from all walks of life and with wide ranging abilities, but I've never met anyone quite like Milo. He truly is an amazing young man who impresses me more and more with each passing day. With the right training and education, I believe there is nothing Milo cannot do.

"What's bothering His Greatness? Looking at him, I finally understand what people mean when they say someone is green around the gills."

"As best I can tell, the smartest, mightiest, greatest trog warrior of all time is deathly afraid of heights."

"We've got a solid deck beneath us." The ship angled down some more and Milo grabbed a nearby stay. "Well, it's *mostly* beneath us. What is he scared of?"

I'd grown up around and on airships and always felt at home on board them. But I also remembered falling from Martin's airship at the trading post in the desert. Without David and a lot of luck, I'd have died that day.

"Have you ever been hurt in a long fall, Milo?"

"Nope. I'm too quick to have falls like that."

"How about falling dreams? I'm told everyone has those."

"Yeah, I've had those. They can be scary, but they're just dreams. They can't hurt you."

"No, they can't. But those dreams are so strong for some people that their minds recall them even when they are awake."

"So, it's like the Great One looks over the railing and can't help seeing himself falling?"

The memory of plunging from the airship returned, unbidden, and I shuddered. "That's the way it's been with me since..."

Milo linked his arm through mine. "I won't let you fall, Callan."

I wrapped my hand around his arm, holding on more tightly than I'd intended. "Thank you, Milo."

Rousing myself from my months–old memory, I changed the subject. "Can you see in this darkness? You're the one who has to guide Nist to the drop–off point."

"Oh, yeah– I mean, yes Your Highness. I found that sewer entrance David took when he rescued you from the tunnel rats and then scouted out the alley it's in. It was easy to find the building you guys ran to after getting away last time you were here."

"Are you sure you can find that building from the air and in the dark?"

"I've already found the building. It's right over there, Your Highness."

As usual, I saw nothing but varying depths of darkness.

"You called me Callan just a few seconds ago. Why have you suddenly gone all formal on me?"

Milo fidgeted for a second before answering. "I was giving comfort to you, then. And that's got to be personal, right?"

I leaned down and kissed Milo on the cheek. God, this boy was going to break a lot of hearts growing up. But the girl who captured *his* heart would be lucky, indeed.

"Yes, Milo, you're absolutely right. And thank you for the personal touch. But that doesn't explain your formal address."

"We're on the mission now. I'm using your title to show respect for you and your authority."

"Which guard told you that?"

"Captain Hunter. He's been training me some in his spare time."

It seems David and I weren't the only ones who recognized Milo's potential. I made a mental note to thank Captain Hunter when we got home.

"I've got to guide Nist the rest of the way into the city. Will you be okay up here alone, Your Highness?"

"I will now, Milo. Go on back to Nist."

Milo slipped off into the darkness. Murmured conversation rose from the pilot's controls and, a couple of minutes later, Nist leveled off the *Pauline*. Seconds later, he settled over a building. As the airship slowed, the Great One and two dozen of his best warriors came on deck.

"We aren't far from the entrance to the tunnels. With the exception of David—the Hand of Death, if you prefer—and Martin Bane, anyone you see down there is an enemy. If they run away, let them go. If they try to stop us, kill them."

I swung my legs over the railing. "Now let's go get my husband back."

28

GRADUATION

DAVID IS TWENTY-ONE

"David Eliot Rice, with highest honors."

The faculty applauded politely, my family with more vigor. Dad's piercing whistle rose over it all.

The light applause died down as I walked across the stage to accept my commission from the academy commander. And that's when my sister added her two credits to the proceeding.

"Woo hoo! Now he's off to find his spacebabe!"

I gave Sandra props for impeccable timing. Her voice carried to every corner of the amphitheater. Laughter rippled through the crowd, even though few of them understood the comment. My handful of friends in the academy roared, though. I'm sure Sandra swelled in pride at their laughter.

"Congratulations, Scout Second Class Rice." The commander shook my hand as he presented my commission.

"Thank you, Commander Gordon."

"I thought I had heard it all, Rice, but 'spacebabe' is a new one on me."

"It's a private joke, sir."

"And the young lady?"

"My little sister, sir."

"You may not believe it now, but you'll miss her once you're Out There."

"I am certain I will, sir, but please don't tell *her* that."

Commander Gordon laughed and released my hand. Back straight and eyes front, I left the stage.

Twenty minutes later, my family wrapped me in a big hug. Yes, even my little sister joined in.

Mom wiped away tears. "I'm so proud of you, honey."

"We all are," Dad added.

"Speak for yourself." Sandra socked me in the arm. "Okay, yeah, I'm proud of you, too, big brother. Hey, did you hear me holler when that old guy gave you your commission?"

"Yes, O Annoying One, you yelled loud enough that I bet they heard you on Terra."

"You think so?"

Sandra grinned so brightly I couldn't help but grin back.

Mom caught my arm. "I stopped by the nursing home to visit Mr. Hart a couple of days ago. He's just as proud of you as we are."

"Really? How's he doing?"

Mom bit her lip, telegraphing bad news. "Not well, son. The nurses think he's holding on until your graduation. Are you going to visit him before leaving for your training mission?"

"You know I am, Mom. I was planning to go tomorrow."

"As much as we want to celebrate with you, David, you should see him today. Tomorrow may be too late."

Three hours later, the head nurse at Mr. Hart's home smiled warmly as I entered her section.

"Hello, David. Don't you look handsome in your dress uniform?" She nodded her head down the hall. "He's waiting for you."

It had only been three months since I'd last been here to visit Mr. Hart, but his condition shocked me. He looked so frail, just skin and bones. But his eyes lit up when he saw me.

I snapped off my best academy salute. "Scout Second Class David Rice reporting, sir!"

He laughed and it turned into a cough.

"It's good to see you, David. Come over here and let me get a good look at you."

I sat on the edge of the bed and fought to keep a smile on my face and tears from my eyes. Mr. Hart took my hand in both of his, patting it absently.

"I'm glad I got a chance to see you before I go, David."

"I'm the one who's going, Mr. Hart. I leave on my training mission in two days. I can't wait to tell you all about it when I get back."

"You do that, lad. Your parents will know where to find me."

"Yeah, right here in this room."

"Don't kid yourself, David. I've had a good run, but now I'm run down. It's about time to scout out what comes next."

I blinked back the tears that suddenly filled my eyes. "At least you'll be with Princess Audrey and good ol' Roy."

"There is that, lad. There is that."

Mr. Hart's eyes fluttered and closed. It wasn't until the head nurse came that I realized my old friend had slipped away.

She left me alone with him for a few more minutes. When she returned, she handed a small box to me.

"Mr. Hart wanted you to have this after he passed. Your visits meant a lot to him, David. I wish all my patients had people like you."

The box held Mr. Hart's rank insignia and a short note.

David, I'd be honored if you wore my insignia during your service. Thank you for spending time with an old man and listening to my stories. Every man has a princess waiting for him somewhere. May you find yours out among the stars.

I had to get the nurse to pin Mr. Hart's insignia on my uniform. I couldn't see through my tears. I stayed with him until the men from the morgue came to take his body away. I snapped to attention and held my salute until his body was out of sight. My heart heavy, I headed back to the academy.

Two days later, I began searching for my spacebabe.

29

GOING UP

DAVID

THE SOUNDS OF SHOUTING AND BANGING GREW LOUDER OUTSIDE THE door to the tammar pit. The banging faded away as the shouting both grew louder and developed a cadence. The door made it impossible to understand what the men were shouting, but it sounded as if they were psyching themselves up to charge into the room and attack. Did they expect to fight tammars as well as a couple of scouts? I hoped so. In our current state—with Martin wounded and me tiring from swinging the hammer—the tunnel rats would definitely capture us or kill us unless we climbed out of the pit.

I made steady progress smashing through the new ceiling with the hammer, but would steady progress be enough? Should I Boost so soon after the last time or should I save it for the fight yet to come? Just as I concluded Boost was called for, the hammer broke through the new ceiling. Plaster rained to the floor below.

"Hey, give a guy some warning," Martin squawked, scurrying out from under the plaster drop zone.

The hole was far too small for us to fit through, but it wouldn't be for long. I smacked the ceiling from below, then hooked the hammer through the hole and pulled on the plaster from above. Alternating pounding and pulling created a network of cracks. Seconds later, a big chunk of ceiling crashed to the floor of the tammar pit.

Reaching through the hole, I grabbed the edge of the floor above and pulled myself up into the darkness.

"Bring the torch directly beneath the hole," I called.

Enough light shone through the hole to give dim illumination in the room above the pit. It was just as I remembered, including stout ropes dangling from half a dozen pulleys. Grabbing the closest rope, I tied a loop at the end of it and lowered it to Martin. Tossing the torch up to me, he secured one foot in the loop and held onto the rope with his good hand. With a nod from Martin, I hauled on the rope. It slithered through the pulleys and began reeling him up.

Martin hung midway between the pit floor and the ceiling when I heard the door to the tammar pit fly open.

King Rat commanded, "Crossbowmen! Shoot that man hanging on the rope."

Stop Dodging

So much for using the pulley to gently and easily lift Martin. King Rat's command dictated speed and brute strength. I hauled on the rope for all I was worth, but it seemed as if Martin barely moved. Working hand over hand was too slow, but what other option did I have? Then the first crossbow twanged and a quarrel flashed just beneath Martin's feet.

"Faster would be better, David."

Martin spoke too fast, his words sharp and clipped and seeming all the more urgent as a result. Martin must have Boosted, but I could not imagine what he hoped to gain.

Glancing through the hole, I watched Martin lean out from the rope as a quarrel flew through the space he'd just cleared. As quickly, he ducked under a second quarrel, which missed his head by inches. That answered my question. His Boost was buying me the extra couple of seconds I needed to pull Martin to safety.

Martin dodged two more quarrels and even kicked one aside with his free foot.

"Stop dodging or you won't be able to come through this hole," I called.

Putting the rope over my shoulder, I ran directly away from the hole. The pulleys squeaked and whined as the rope spun through them.

I heard Martin taunt the crossbowmen one last time, then he flew up through the jagged hole I'd created and stepped onto the floor.

Below, King Rat roared, "Imbeciles! How could all of you miss a man dangling right in front of you? If Rice and Bane escape, I'll feed each of you to my tammars!"

King Rat must have been really focused on us not to have noticed the three dead tammars in the pit. Martin, considerate man that he is, took time to enlighten King Rat.

"Hey rat boy," Martin yelled, "take a look at the pit floor. You should stop using the plural form of tammar."

Silence fell below us, then an inarticulate roar of rage echoed around the pit and through the hole.

"I'm afraid we broke three of your toys. But don't worry, you won't live long enough to miss them," Martin called. Flashing a grin my way, he said, "It's the simple pleasures that make life worth living, David. Never forget that."

Then we heard massed footsteps coming from the tunnel outside our room. King Rat had sent guards through the tunnels to block our escape.

30

MY HERO IS HERE

CALLAN IS TWENTY

HEAT WEIGHED DOWN UPON ME, SAPPING MY ENERGY. ROB LED EIGHT MEN, all who remained of my full guard contingent, and me deeper into the desert. He set a fast pace, putting as much distance between us and our raider pursuers as possible. Sand swirled around us, working into our clothing and scratching and chafing our skin.

"There's cover ahead, men," Rob's voice remained strong, calm, and clear, giving no indication of despair or fatigue.

I struggled to raise my head and look where Rob pointed. A jumble of rocks rose from the desert, the dark gray standing out in sharp contrast to the blinding white sand all around us.

I stumbled and would have sprawled into the sand had one of my guards not caught me. He wrapped an arm around my waist, keeping me on my feet.

"Lean on me, Your Highness."

"Th-thank you, Hoskins."

"It is my honor and my job, Your Highness."

Hoskins—Charlie to his friends—was close to my own age. A tall, strong man filled with good humor and dedication to his duty. In other circumstances, we could have been friends, perhaps more than friends. Instead, a vast gulf yawned between his station and mine. The gulf was not insurmountable, but a man like Charlie Hoskins could only bridge it with deeds of valor so great as to be beyond the abilities of most men.

Was it possible Hoskins could be the hero I'd searched for all these years? God only knew, we needed that hero right now. I could but hope that Hoskins, or one of my other guards, proved to be him.

With Hoskins' aid, I made it to the rocks. Hoskins and Rob saw me settled into shade cast by the rocks. Rob organized the camp with typical efficiency before returning to me.

"How are you, Little One?"

"Our situation must be truly desperate. You haven't called me Little One since I turned twelve."

A rueful smile spread across Rob's face. "As I recall, you nearly bit my head off for using a little girl's nickname."

I laughed without much humor. "I really was a brat, wasn't I?"

I expected Rob to offer a playful reply, make some attempt to cheer me up.

"No, Callan, you were never a brat. You have been difficult, willful, curious, and kind. But never a brat." Rob turned a serious face my way. "I hope you will forgive an old man's impertinence, but I am proud of the young woman you've become. You are a credit to your parents and your country."

"We aren't getting out of this one, are we, Rob?"

"And now I'm reminded that I left intelligent and observant off of my list of your qualities." Rob looked off into the distance. "We still live, Your Highness, and that is something."

"Call me Callan, Rob. Here at the end, I want no titles between us."

"I shall call you Callan only until such time as you are safe. And safe you may yet be. After all..."

Rob trailed off, leaving me to complete his oft–used saying.

"Where there is life, there is hope."

Rob turned his gaze back to me and this time his eyes held a true twinkle. "Besides, Callan, your hero could still arrive in time to save the day."

"Do you think he's just going to pop up out of the sand, Rob?"

"Or he could drop out of the sky. Honestly, I care not–"

"Trogs! To arms! Trogs are upon us!"

Blue-skinned terrors, creatures I'd seen only in illustrations, charged around the rocks not fifty yards from us and rushed toward our little camp. I counted ten and they still came. Then twenty. I stopped at thirty.

"Stay against the rocks, Callan. We will form a cordon and keep you safe for as long as possible. Take up a sword if you can and if you must."

Drawing his sword, Rob turned away.

"Rob?"

He looked over his shoulder.

"Thank you. For everything."

Rob sketched a salute and began organizing our defenses.

"I love you as I love my father."

Between the shouts and a strange, ear-shattering boom in the distance, he didn't hear me. He knew my feelings for him, but I wanted him to hear me say it.

Then the trogs were upon us and I could but watch as my guards, my brave defenders, fell one after the other before the trogs' superior numbers. Far too soon, only Rob and Hoskins still stood. I hefted a sword and waited to take my place in the fight. Seconds later, a spear plunged into Hoskins chest. With his dying breath, my youngest guard struck down the trog before him.

And so I took Hoskins place next to Rob, expecting nothing but a quick and painful death.

A loud, sharp crack sounded from above us and a small crater blew out in the ground beside the trogs. All eyes, trog and human alike, turned to see the cause. A man stood atop the rocks, some device clutched in one hand.

The man shouted in a language strange to me. The trogs shouted in return and most of them charged the man.

"This may be our chance to insure your survival, Callan. Be prepared to flee on my command."

Then the man on the rocks *moved*, and he was like nothing I had ever seen before. In a second he twisted, turned, dodged, and danced among the trogs. And where he went, death followed. He ripped through our enemies like a scythe through wheat.

Rob tore his gaze from the amazing spectacle, launching an attack against the closest trogs. Three minutes later, this amazing man rammed a spear through the last of the trogs and we were saved.

He met my eyes and a broad smile spread across what I now realized was a quite handsome face.

I smiled in return. “You have saved us. How can I thank you?”

He spoke in the strange language again and then collapsed.

Rob and I rushed to his side. We found no wounds and the man still lived.

“Considering how he moved and fought, I suspect the man is simply exhausted, Your Highness.”

I barely heard Rob as I drank in the sight of the man.

“He came, Rob.”

“Hm? I’m sorry, what did you say, Your Highness?”

“He came. When we least expected him and when we most needed him. I’d stopped believing in him. I’d stopped looking for him. And yet he still came, Rob. At long last, my hero is here.”

31

I CAN TAKE CARE OF MYSELF

CALLAN

I'D SPENT NO MORE THAN A MINUTE ON THIS ROOF, BUT THAT MINUTE WAS tied to the deepest of emotions. Fear, anger, and gut-wrenching loss rose unbidden when my feet touched the roof for a second time. Fear that those wretched tunnels would take another precious life from me. Anger at King Rat for all he had done to me, past and present. The gut-wrenching loss I still felt for Rob.

I stared off into the night, suppressing my emotions. When this night was over, I would give rein to them. But until David and I were free of this city, such emotions were distractions I could not afford.

Milo touched my shoulder. "We're ready, Your Highness."

"Thank you, Milo." I turned to face the Great One. "You know the plan. You know the stakes. Do you have any questions?"

"No."

"Then follow me."

I led the trogs down the stairs attached to the outside of the building, to the alley below. Once we were on the ground, Milo took the lead.

"You're sure this is the way?" I asked.

"Yes, Your Highness. After Martin showed me how to get into the tunnels, I memorized the alleys all around the entrance," he said. "If we have to run I won't lead us into any dead ends."

"That was clever thinking on your part. We'll make a guard out of you, yet."

"Nah, I'm going to be a spy. Captain Hunter says my um...skill set...is better suited for that sort of thing."

Did he, now? I edited my mental note of appreciation to Captain Hunter for training Milo. It's not that Hunter's assessment was wrong—Milo had the makings of an excellent spy—but I had bigger plans for my young friend. Those plans included a stability sorely lacking in his life thus far.

Moments later, Milo stopped at an opening in the ground. "This is it."

"Good job, Milo." I turned to the Great One. "Send your warriors below. I'll be right behind you." I turned back to Milo. "You stay here and wait for us."

"Oh no you don't. I'm coming with you, Callan!"

"Absolutely not. I promised Kim I'd keep you safe. She would kill me if something happened to you."

"Death is nothing compared to what *I'd* face from David if something happened to *you*."

"You know David would never hurt you, Milo."

"I know he wouldn't hurt me. But he would be *disappointed* in me if you got hurt. He'd try to hide it, but things would never be the same between us. Besides, I grew up on the streets." Knives appeared in Milo's hands and then vanished again. "I can take care of myself."

"You're just going to sneak in behind us if I order you to stay here, aren't you?

"Of course. If it makes you feel any better, I would feel guilty over ignoring a direct order."

"Really?"

"No."

"That's what I thought. Okay, you can come, but stay close to me."

Milo smirked, "Oh boy, I get to guard the royal body."

A genuine smile spread across my face. I turned and climbed down into King Rat's tunnels. The first thing I heard was the unmistakable sound of weapons echoing through the tunnels.

32

UNCLE MARTIN

DAVID

I TOOK A POSITION AT THE DOOR INTO THE TUNNELS DOWN WHICH WE heard running feet. We had two minutes, give or take, before the tunnel before us filled with tunnel rats.

"Keep an eye on the hole, Martin. I don't think anyone will try to climb up the cage bars like I did, but you never know. Even a one-handed man can guard that spot."

Martin joined me at the door. "Stand aside, Wonder Boy. I've got first dibs on door duty."

"Don't be ridiculous, Martin. You've lost a lot of blood *and* only have one good hand. By what tortured logic are you the right man to defend the door?"

Martin's lips twitched up in a tight smile. "By the logic of expendability. You, David, have too much to lose to even be considered for this job."

I waved the comment off. "I risk my life. You risk your life. The difference is both of my hands are intact and all of my blood is in my veins."

"You also have a beautiful wife who loves you. After everything you've each been through—and, yes, I realize I'm responsible for some of those things—I think the two of you deserve a long and wonderful life together. Besides, you've got the royal succession to think about, lad.

I have no doubt you find that an onerous duty, but I'm equally confident you and Callan spend most nights wrestling with this task. Nothing less than the future of the realm depends on you, my boy."

"Is there anyone in the kingdom who isn't discussing my private life with Callan?"

"It's distinctly possible, David. I feel sure there is a convent or monastery somewhere in Mordan where they restrict themselves to more heavenly matters. Everyone else in the kingdom is speculating whether your first child will be a beautiful little princess or a brave little prince." Martin grinned at me. "I'm hoping for one of each."

I decided it was past time to change the subject. "Okay, I have something to live for. Everyone does—even you."

"Me? I'm just a former raider whose passing would hardly be noticed. Besides, you've done a lot of Boosting today. Can't have you risking Boost burnout, can we? Safety first, youngster."

"Would you deprive my unborn children of the chance to meet their Uncle Martin?"

Martin raised a questioning eyebrow. "Uncle?"

"An honorary title, but one bestowed with sincerity."

"Uncle, huh? You make a compelling argument, young man. All right, what's your plan?"

"Thus far, surprise has worked wonders against these tunnel rats. Are you up for a bit more of that, old man?"

"I do believe I could manage that. What do you have in mind?"

"Since you insist on joining the fight, why wait for them to come to us? Let's take the fight to them. If we hit them hard and fast, we might be able to break through their lines and escape into the tunnels."

"It beats hanging around in doorways. Lead on, David."

We charged down the tunnel toward the approaching guards.

I'm Sorry, Callan

Ahead of us, the tunnel curved curved gently to the right. Echoes made it impossible to gauge how close our enemy was to us using sound, alone. Then I realized flickering light from their torches reflected off the outside wall of the bend in the tunnel. King Rat's men were almost upon us. Dropping our torch, I motioned Martin against the inside wall. Martin ground the torch out under his heel.

In a stage whisper, Martin said, "When the fight is joined, remember to yell 'For Callan and country!'"

There must have been just enough reflected light for him to see my raised eyebrow. "I thought you were raised on adventure vids, David. Don't you know that alliterative declarations of love and loyalty increase fighting prowess?"

I couldn't help but laugh. Through his own pain and exhaustion, Martin still worked to put me at ease. Then, two dozen or more of King Rat's men rounded the bend, charging headlong toward us. As planned, they had no idea we were there until Martin and I stepped into the small pool of torchlight.

I grinned and cried, "For Callan and country!"

Beside me, Martin yelled, "For Martin and Mordan!"

So much for my hopes of learning the name of some hitherto unknown lady love.

Boost!

The tunnel rats at the front saw us first. Expressions of alarm crossed their faces and they tried to stop their charge. The dozens behind them didn't see us and shoved the leaders toward us. One impaled himself on Martin's blade. Martin rammed the blade home and it went straight through the leader and into the chest of the man pushing him from behind. The two men shrieked in agony and terror. Finally aware something was amiss at the front, the men behind ground to a halt.

I spun past the two shrieking men and decapitated the third man. His head ricocheted off the wall and into the packed men behind. Cries of horror and disgust rose from them and several back-pedaled from the bouncing head. I grabbed the shirt of the headless man and, using the body as a shield and a psychological weapon, pressed it into the men before me. Hot blood spurted in their faces and they recoiled.

A quick slash to a sword arm and a sword clattered to the floor. A thrust to the leg and a man collapsed against his fellows, unable to stand. Then Martin was back at my side and our blades flashed too fast for King Rat's men to parry.

Our attack was too fast, too unexpected, and we pressed our advantage. The front rank wavered, putting up token resistance. The men at the back, only able to hear the cries from the front, edged away. We had them on the ropes, ready to flee before our onslaught.

Then a man in the middle, close enough to see us but too far away to fight us, regained his senses.

"There's only two of them and one is already wounded. Press forward and grind them under our feet."

Fear deepened on the faces of the men crossing swords with us, but the rest of their number took the instructions to heart. The mass of tunnel rats advanced. They even adopted one of my tactics, holding the bodies of their slain fellows as shields against our attacks.

Slowly, the inexorable tide of tunnel rats pushed Martin and me back. Martin stumbled from exhaustion and we lost several more steps as I steadied him. Neither of us could hold out much longer.

I blinked back tears of rage and frustration and cried out, "I'm sorry, Callan. I did my best."

33

DON'T YOU DARE DIE

CALLAN

DESPITE THEIR SQUAT BODIES, TROGS CAN MOVE FAST WHEN THEY WANT to. The Great One led the way down the tunnels at a run and I was hard pressed to keep up. He'd stop every now and then, listening and sniffing the air, giving me a chance to catch my breath. I don't know if he really could smell anything or if he was just trying to make us think he could, but I appreciated the brief stops. The problem was we didn't seem to be getting any closer to the fighting.

Sound echoed strangely in the tunnels, especially indistinct sounds such as clashing steel. If only someone would yell or call out, the sound might echo differently and help guide us to the fighting.

"For Callan and country!"

It was David's voice. He was alive!

"For Martin and Mordan!"

Martin was alive, too.

The echoes still made things difficult, but the sound seemed most clear from a tunnel to our right.

"Great One—this way."

The Great One shouldered his way back to us, sniffed once, then ran up the tunnel. Milo and I stood aside as the rest of the trogs charged off in his wake.

"Callan?"

"Yes, Milo?"

"May I please have permission to laugh at David and Martin for those battle cries?"

"Assuming we all survive the next few minutes, you most definitely have permission. But only if I get to listen in when you make fun of them," I replied. "Do you want to bet on who came up with the idea of the battle cries?"

"Only if I can bet on Martin."

"We can't both bet on Martin, so I guess we won't bet." Then, I fell in behind the last of the trogs and saved my breath for running.

The sounds of battle were growing louder. We were heading in the right direction.

"There's only two of them and one is already wounded. Press forward and grind them under our feet."

Their situation sounded dire. God help me, I couldn't come this close only to lose David in the end.

"Hurry, Great One!"

The Great One nodded and picked up the pace. It felt as if we charged on forever. I suspect it was mere seconds, but they seemed hours long to me. Then I heard a cry that froze my blood.

"I'm sorry, Callan. I did my best."

"David Rice, don't you dare die on me!" I yelled as loudly as I could.

A startled reply echoed down the tunnel. "Callan?"

"Damned right it's me, David! And I brought help."

The Great One rounded a bend in the tunnel and gave a ferocious cry of triumph. His trogs joined in as they raised their spears and charged into battle.

"Trogs!"

Even over the trog war cry, the terror in that cry was palpable. Screams sounded as the trogs pushed forward, Milo and me right on their heels.

"Tunnel rats, fight on and you will die. Surrender and your life will be spared. You have my word." David's voice rose above the din, calm and commanding.

Another scream sounded.

A sword clattered to the tunnel floor. "I surrender."

Another sword dropped. "Me, too."

Sword after sword fell, each followed by a cry of surrender. I had feared the trogs would keep killing, but the Great One kept them in check. Within seconds, the fight was over.

And then David pushed through the crowd of trogs and tunnel rats. He swept me into his arms and his lips met mine. I was whole again.

Business to Finish

David held me tightly, the feel of him and the scent of him overwhelming my senses. Then I realized part of that scent had the sharp, metallic tang of blood. I had been so overjoyed to see David, I hadn't noticed the blood splattering his clothes.

"Darling, how much of this blood is yours?" I asked.

"None of it," he said. "Or not much of it, anyway. I got a few scratches, nothing more."

"Yes, your Wonder Boy is hale and hearty and disgustingly unharmed," drawled Martin from behind David. "That's more than some of us can say. I'd wring my hands in distress, but it would hurt too much and my hand would probably start bleeding again."

I looked around my husband and gasped at the sight of Martin's mangled hand. "Oh my God, Martin! What happened?"

"I discovered that tammars are extremely quick, Your Highness. They also have big, sharp claws."

"We've got to take Martin to Tristan. The *Pauline* is not far from here and Tristan has a surgery setup to handle our wounded warriors." I glanced at the trogs, seeing nothing more than minor cuts and scrapes. "And it looks like Martin is the only one in need of a surgeon."

I took David's hand and started back down the tunnel. David did not come along with me.

"You and Milo take Martin back to the airship and let Tristan get started," David said. "The trogs and I have to finish business down here."

"What do you mean by that?" I asked. "I just got you back, David."

"Callan, David has sworn to kill King Rat," Martin said. "He's got some wild idea about freeing the city-states of the vile little rat boy's influence. You know, typical heroic and noble stuff about making the world a better place blah blah blah. What I find irksome is the lad thinks I'll let him take all the credit simply because a tammar scratched my hand."

"The right word is 'mauled,' Martin," David said.

"You say mauled, I say scratched. Whatever. I entered these tunnels to find you and take you back home," Martin said. "I am not leaving until you leave."

David massaged his forehead. "Why are you being so stubborn, Martin?"

"There's this princess, beautiful but possessed of a fiery temper who–"

"Don't you dare finish that sentence, Martin Bane." My smile and tone belied my words.

"You're all mad," David sighed. "Fine, Martin, come with me. But Callan, you and Milo–"

"Don't *you* dare finish that sentence, David Rice." I did not smile and my tone brooked no argument. "If you have got to kill this King Rat, then let's get it over with. The sooner the man is dead, the sooner we can go home."

David met my gaze for a few seconds then smiled. "As you wish, Your Highness. I'm too tired to argue, anyway."

Milo grinned and gave me a thumb's up. The Great One chuffed, a sound I'd come to recognize as trog laughter.

"Lady Death worthy mate for Hand of Death."

David looked at me. "Lady Death? Hand of Death?"

I patted David's arm. "I'll tell you after we're safely onboard the *Pauline*."

David had the trogs gather the swords dropped by King Rat's men and then ordered those men to lie face down on the floor. He left half a dozen trogs guarding the prisoners and, with a wave of his arm, led us back down the tunnel to find King Rat.

34

FACE ME

DAVID

I'D ONLY BEEN IN THESE TUNNELS FOR A FEW DAYS, BUT I'D OBVIOUSLY missed out on a lot up in the real world. From the way Milo snickered at the Great One's words of approval for Callan, quite a tale awaited me.

The map of the tunnels my implant had constructed didn't stretch into the area where we were. With a little guesswork on my part, I found my way into familiar territory in short order. Now certain of my course, I led the way toward the entrance to the tammar pit. King Rat had been there mere moments ago, so it was the best place to start. If he had wandered off, I felt certain I could find someone who would know where to find him. I was further certain that someone could be convinced to share the king's location with me.

Martin tried to hide it, but he was on the ragged edge of exhaustion. He'd lost a lot of blood and the fight we had just finished had worn him down even further. With every step he took, Martin's breath hissed quietly through clenched teeth. If I was the wounded one, my implant would have flooded my system with analgesics. But the pain killers weren't like adrenaline, which our bodies made and our implants stored. Martin had been on Aashla for fifteen years without access to implant resupply. By now, I doubted he had any analgesics remaining. I had to get Martin back to Tristan for proper medical care as soon as possible.

We swung into the tunnel leading up to the doors to the tammar pit. Two men stood guard. At sight of me, they raised their swords.

One shouted, "Rice is-"

Then the trogs padded into the tunnel behind me. The guards' eyes went wide and the talkative one screamed, "Trogs!"

The two guards bolted down a side tunnel. With the guards out of the way, I prepared to make one heck of an entrance.

"Great One, have two of your warriors slam those doors open as I approach."

The big trog spoke and two of his warriors slipped past me to the doors.

"Callan, please walk at my left side. Oh, and do that regal princess thing you do so well." Callan came to my side, her court posture and countenance settling over her like a favorite gown. I linked arms with her and wished I could match my wife's composure.

I looked over my shoulder. "Milo, please give Martin a steadying hand. It just wouldn't do for him to collapse and spoil our grand entrance."

With everything in place and everyone ready, we resumed walking. At my signal, the two trogs threw open the doors. They banged against the walls so hard one door cracked. The sound reverberated around the tammar pit. Silence fell and all eyes turned our way. The crossbowmen, my main worry, lounged near the door, their weapons propped against bench seats or lying on the floor.

"King Rat, you have threatened my country, imprisoned my friends, and kept me from my wife. I am tired of your dark, dank tunnels. I am tired of the scum you call subjects. I am tired of *you*."

I pointed my sword at King Rat, who stood rooted in place just outside the tammar cage. "Your kingdom is at an end and your power broken. Life as you have known it is over. Face me. Man to man. Blade to blade. Face me and die like a man."

Trogs Against Rats

The echoes of my challenge faded and still none of the tunnel rats moved or spoke. Then one of the crossbowmen shook himself free of his surprise. With an inarticulate cry of rage, he grabbed his crossbow and tugged on the cocking lever.

The Great One roared and charged past me. He rammed his spear straight through the man and out his back. He lifted his spear over his head, the dying man still impaled upon it, and roared again. With a heave, he flung the body at the feet of the other crossbowmen. He waved the crimson–coated spear before the eyes of the remaining crossbowmen, daring them to attack.

Eyes wide, the men stopped reaching for their weapons. One after another, they raised their hands and backed away from their crossbows.

"What are you doing, you cowards? He's just one trog. He can't kill all of you before some of you shoot him." King Rat waved his sword toward us. "Attack them! Defend your king!"

The crossbowmen obviously decided they were out of the fight and they showed no interest in getting back into it. They ignored the order and kept backing away. But half a dozen of the king's guards drew swords and charged up the stairs toward the Great One. With a blood–curdling yell, the Great One and his warriors leapt down the stairs to meet them.

The trogs outnumbered the guards three to one and didn't hesitate to take advantage of their superior numbers. The charging trogs encircled the overzealous guards. Lowering their spears, the circle of trogs closed in. Far too late to save themselves, the men came to their senses. Pleas and screams fell on deaf ears. On a command from the Great One, the trogs thrust their spears into the men packed before them. Again and again, the spears thrust until the men within the circle no longer cried or moved.

At my side, Callan paled but watched with resolution.

Seeing me eying her with concern, she said, "These men watched and cheered the slaughter in the tammar pit months ago. They watched and cheered as bound and helpless people were ripped to pieces by the tammar. At the very least, these men held weapons and had the choice to fight or surrender. That is far more than they granted the tammar's victims."

Callan was right. Perhaps this wasn't exactly her culture, but it was her planet. She knew its ways far better than I, who had been here but half a year. I kept my expression impassive and spoke only after the trogs stepped back from the bloody corpses.

"Does anyone else wish to die to defend a king who cowers from combat and watches the slaughter from a safe distance?" I waved my hand toward the trogs. "You all know the trogs' reputation. If you'd rather not face them across the tip of a spear, throw down your weapons *now*. Any who surrender will be spared. Any who still hold weapons ten seconds from now will die."

All around the tammar pit, weapons clattered to the floor.

"Smart move, rats," Martin called. "Now clear the pit floor. I really need a drink right now, but I can't go get one until my friend David kills your king in a fair fight."

35

YOU WANT SPECTACLE?

CALLAN

Tunnel rats backed away from King Rat while Martin's orders still echoed around the tammar pit. The king of the rats spun left and right, looking for support from someone. He called something, anger in his voice.

I turned to Martin. "Do you feel up to translating for me? I don't speak this language and would like to know what's going on."

"I would be honored, Your Highness."

With Martin speaking softly in my ear, I turned back to watch my husband and King Rat.

"Come back here and defend your king. We have a thousand rats in these tunnels. We can destroy them, but only if you defend *me*!"

Walking down the stairs to the pit floor, David shook his head. "You're wasting your breath, Vraal. No one in this room will waste their life defending a dead man."

"You will use my proper title and show proper respect when speaking to me, boy."

A laugh devoid of all humor escaped David's lips. "You truly are delusional, rat man. I show you more respect than you deserve simply by *speaking* to you. As for proper titles, I can think of many appropriate ones. I will not, however, use such language before my royal wife or my young friend, Milo."

King Rat's eyes blazed with fury and more than a little madness. "I could have killed you the moment you were dragged before me, you know. But I did not. You now owe me the same consideration, Rice."

"Apparently you *are* delusional." David spread his arms and spun in a circle. "You kept me alive for this. I bet you can see the spectacle in your mind. The seats packed with tunnel rats. Four hungry tammars circling the edge of the cage. The warmup victims littering the cage floor, nothing more than mangled corpses. Finally, I am dragged into the pit and thrust into the cage. A fitting end to the man who ruined your last great spectacle."

David stopped his slow spin and glared at King Rat.

"*That* is why you kept me alive. *That* is why I'm down here in the first place. You want revenge? Come and take it! You want spectacle? Congratulations, you get to be part of it!"

Regardless of how this duel ended, King Rat's rule was finished. David had shown the man had grown too weak to keep his throne. With my years in court, I could read the tunnel rats as if they wore signs proclaiming their feelings. Did David realize that?

"He's already lost everything, David," I called in Mordanian. "Don't expect rational behavior from him."

Giving me a tired smile and a nod, David turned toward King Rat and, with a flourish, drew his sword. The rest of us spread out around the wall of the pit, ringing the two combatants. The Great One spread his warriors around the circle, insuring none of the tunnel rats interfered in the coming duel.

"Let's get this over with, rat boy," David said, stalking to the center of the circle.

King Rat roared his fear and frustration and anger. Sword held high, he charged at David.

In the blink of an eye, David changed. Quick and graceful to begin with, he grew more graceful, and so much quicker my eye barely saw his sword. He straightened, his weariness washed away before my eyes. As I have done so many times since I first learned the possible dangers of Boost, I fervently prayed this Boost would not kill him.

David blocked King Rat's attack with contemptuous ease. He stepped aside, allowing the man to charge past him, and kicked King

Rat in the backside as he ran past. The king stumbled to a halt, his eyes blazing at the insult.

King Rat bent from the waist, clutching at his heart. As soon as David took a single step in the king's direction, the rat spun around, his sword swinging in a wide arc. David simply ducked under the swing. Then, with the flick of a wrist, he slashed open King Rat's sword arm. King Rat's sword dropped to the floor and he clutched his wounded arm. David swung the pommel of his sword across the king's jaw. King Rat collapsed in a heap, cringing and mewling at David's feet.

David shook his head in disgust. "I came down here to kill you so you'd never threaten me or mine again. But now I see you for what you truly are. And what you are is a man so pathetic I won't sully this fine blade with your foul blood. Crawl back to your tunnel rats, Vraal. They can dispose of you."

Weariness settled on him again as David dropped Boost. He turned his back on King Rat and walked toward me. Behind him, King Rat rose to his feet, a dagger raised to plunge into David's unprotected back.

36

FAMILY

DAVID

I WALKED AWAY FROM THE CRAVEN RAT KING, LONGING TO DO NOTHING BUT wrap Callan in my arms and hold her until this whole affair faded from my mind. Smiling, I reached for Callan. An answering smile spread across her lips and the fear in her eyes faded. Then the fear rushed back into her eyes. She pointed over my shoulder.

"David!"

Pushed to the limit by running battles, narrow escapes, and on-again, off-again Boosting, my body was slow to react. Sluggishly, I spun to face whatever threat Callan saw. Martin, standing at Callan's side and suffering from blood loss and exhaustion, was too far away and even slower than I was.

I saw the glint of polished steel.

I saw the white of King Rat's bared teeth.

I saw my death reflected in King Rat's eyes.

I saw the Great One and his trogs watching with great interest. As I understood their customs, this fight belonged to me. They would not dishonor me by interfering.

I saw King Rat lunge toward me. The dagger descending too fast for me to react. If I had a spare second more, I could dodge the blade. But it seemed I had used up my allotment of spare seconds.

In a blur, something small moved between my attacker and me.

King Rat screamed as a knife appeared and pierced his wrist. His hand spasmed and the dagger meant for my heart fell to the floor. Shock flooded King Rat's face. He stumbled away, hands clutching at a second knife protruding just below his rib cage. King Rat opened his mouth and blood flowed from it. He coughed once, spraying blood over the small figure between us.

"Leave my family alone!" Milo snarled, the sweet kid I knew so well replaced by the kid forced to fight for survival on the streets of Faroon.

King Rat's eyes rolled up into his head and he fell backward. The body convulsed once and lay still.

Milo spun to face me, concern written on his face. "Are you okay, David? Did I get him before he stabbed you?"

Callan swept past me and pulled Milo into a tight embrace. "Yes, you got him in time. The dagger never touched David. And I can never thank you enough, Milo!"

Then I reached out and joined the embrace.

"So, family, huh?" I asked.

"Um, it just came out wrong. I meant to say friends." Milo didn't meet my eyes.

Callan snorted. "You most certainly did *not* mean to say friends. And, as far as I'm concerned, you *are* family, Milo."

Milo looked up, tears glistening in his eyes. "Do you really mean that?"

"Of course, we really mean it," I said. "Now, what do you say we get out of these tunnels. I'm ready to see the sky again."

Any Other Stupid Questions?

I turned to the tunnel rats gathered around us. "King Rat is dead. There is nothing left for you down here. It's time to get out of the tunnels and give up this stupid excuse for a life."

Despite everything that had happened in the last few minutes, one of the tunnel rats still managed to dredge up some attitude. "And what if we don't want to leave? What if I want to be the new King Rat?"

"You see those blue guys over there?" I waved my arm toward the band of trogs. "If I hear anyone stayed in these tunnels—much less crowned himself the new king—I will personally lead a few hundred of them into these tunnels. If I have to do that, the only things we'll leave behind are the corpses of every tunnel rat we find."

The man opened his mouth again, but I kept speaking. "And don't think you can hide in the tunnels. I've got a better map of this place than any of you have. No one will escape my wrath."

The Great One spoke to his men, I assume translating my words for them. The trogs all chuffed. They leveled their spears at the man who had spoken and jabbed once. Though well out of range, the man jumped back and the trogs chuffed some more.

"Do you have any other stupid questions?" I asked.

The belligerent one shook his head, eyes wide.

"Then get out of my sight. Spread the word and clear the tunnels."

The tunnel rats backed from the room. Most ran the moment they cleared the door.

"Good threat. Much fun." The Great One jabbed the air with his spear. "Say before, say again. You make good trog."

"Thank you, I guess." I wrapped Martin's good arm over my shoulders, lending him my strength and support. "Come on, let's get out of here."

Ten minutes later, we climbed out of the tunnels. It took some work to get one-handed Martin up the ladder, but we made it without hurting him too badly.

I squinted into the gray light of predawn, thrilled to see the sky again. "Callan tells me you know the way to go, Milo. Please lead on."

Short minutes later, we climbed the stairs to the roof where the *Pauline*—and medical care for Martin—waited for us. Milo reached the rooftop and came to a stop.

"David," he said, "I don't think we're out of this yet."

"Then move so I can come up there and see what you see," I said.

Milo stepped aside, allowing Callan and me to reach the roof. The *Pauline* waited right where Callan said it would be. But ours wasn't the only airship in the area. Fifty feet beyond the roof's edge floated two Beloren warships. Both ships had all their weapons trained on us.

37

THE TROUBLEMAKER

CALLAN

David and I stared at the Beloren airships for a moment before he spoke. "I must admit this is an unexpected development."

"I had hoped this wouldn't happen, darling, but I knew it was possible."

"My dear, this is why smart women are so wonderful. As you knew it was possible, please tell me that you made plans for this?"

"Of course I did."

A voice rang out from one of the airships. "I speak Mordanian, so don't think you can just stand there and scheme in your own language."

I motioned for the trogs to stay on the stairs, out of sight from the Beloren airships, then led David to the edge of the roof.

"Who's in charge here?" I called to the airships.

The man who had spoken earlier said, "I am in charge. Now who are you?"

"David, you're so good at this. Would you mind terribly doing the honors?" I asked.

"Are you kidding? I love this bit." Raising his voice, David called, "You are addressing Her Royal Highness, Princess Callan, Heir to the throne of Mordan. I am her husband, Prince Consort David Rice."

"Ah yes, I've heard of you, Rice," the man replied. "You're the troublemaker."

David drew breath to retort, but I touched his arm. "You don't get to have all the fun, darling. It's my turn."

Drawing forth my royal voice, I said, "If, by troublemaker, you mean the only person within your little city–state who is man enough to fight the tunnel rats in their own territory, then you have the right of it."

Muttering and spluttering protests rose from both airships. It appeared more than a few of the crew understood Mordanian.

Their captain bristled and called, "I could take you and your friends prisoner right now, little princess."

"You certainly could try," I shot back. Looking over my shoulder, I called, "Great One, please bring your warriors onto the roof."

Silence fell when the trogs came to stand behind us.

"As you can see, we number rather more than four."

The captain swept his arm in an arc encompassing both airships. "And I *still* outnumber you five or six to one, little princess."

"Ah, I see you have failed to fully grasp just what these trogs standing before you represent. Indeed, your real problem stems from the trogs standing *behind* you." It was my turn to sweep my arm in a broad arc, one encompassing the southern and western edges of the city. "I suggest you have one of your men turn his spyglass that direction. Look out beyond those fallen walls, the ones you haven't gotten around to rebuilding since my previous visit to your ever–so–welcoming little city."

"Lieutenant?" asked the captain.

The man next to the captain brought the spyglass to his eye and gasped.

"She's not bluffing, sir." The man lowered the spyglass. "The desert is teeming with trogs, sir. There must be hundreds of them."

"Just over a thousand, actually. I don't have the exact number, but just imagine what that many trogs would do to your city–state, *little* captain."

"What do you want, Your Highness?"

"We want to leave, nothing more."

"And what of the trogs surrounding my city?"

"They will leave when we leave. Or they will come in and fetch us if we don't leave by full sunrise. I think that's in about fifteen minutes. Will you require more time than that to come to a decision?"

"No, Your Highness, I will not. You and your companions are free to leave."

I waved the trogs toward the *Pauline.* "Great One, we're leaving, now."

I turned back to the captain. "I suggest you point those weapons in another direction. You wouldn't want your men doing something stupid as we fly away."

Apparently, the captain agreed with me. He was busy issuing orders as David and I boarded the *Pauline*. Tristan, aided by Milo, guided Martin below to the surgery.

Standing in the bow of the little ship and watching the sun rise, I wrapped my arms around David and drew him into a kiss.

"Let's go home, darling.

SCOUT'S DUTY

1

LIGHTS IN THE SKY

THE NIGHTS IN MORDA HAD JUST STARTED TURNING COOL AND FALL WAS fast becoming my favorite season. Though the purple and gold leaves were glorious to behold, fall's status rose because Callan and I had taken to reclining out on the balcony and gazing at the stars.

And by recline, I mean we lay in each other's arms. Absolutely nothing drives away the night's chill like a beautiful woman sharing her warmth with you. Trust me on this.

"Have you figured out which star you came from, David?" Callan's soft, warm breath tickled my neck.

"It's slow going without the instruments I usually rely on. The astronomers at the Royal College get amazing results with their telescopes and, with their help, I'm narrowing it down." I pointed to a cluster of stars right above us, far away from the bright planetary ring. "I'm pretty sure it's one of those stars. The first thing a scout should do after exiting a wormhole is to take astronomical readings and determine exactly where he is. Of course, I was too busy dodging asteroids after popping out in the middle of the planetary ring to have time for that."

"You were just in a hurry to get down to the ground and rescue me from the trogs." Callan snuggled in even closer, though I would have sworn that was impossible. "And stop me from marrying Prince Rupor."

Remembering my frantic efforts to stay alive within the planetary ring, I said, "Plus saving you from having Raoul as a brother-in-law. So sure, let's go with that."

"Our children, when we have them, will hear my version of the story. It's much more romantic." Callan gave a contented sigh. "When I was a little girl, I'd have been beside myself with excitement if someone told me a story like ours. I can't wait to see the excitement shining in little eyes as they hear about their heroic father."

"Well *I* can't wait until they hear how their brave and brilliant mother concocted the plan to save the city of Faroon and defeat the trog army." I pulled back and looked into Callan's eyes. "You were going to include that part, weren't you?"

"When it comes time to tell the story, perhaps we should tell it together. That way we can make sure the whole story gets told."

"As always, your wish is my command, Your Highness."

We were silent for a few seconds, gazing into the heavens and lost in our own thoughts. Then Callan pointed toward the planetary ring. "Look at that, David!"

I looked where she pointed. Strange lights flared and vanished within the ring. Then bright trails blazed through the upper atmosphere as tiny asteroids fell from the heavens and burned up in the atmosphere.

"I thought I'd seen every sight the ring has to offer, but I've never seen anything like those flashing lights before," Callan said. "It's beautiful. Do you have any idea what it is?"

A knot of excitement and apprehension formed in my gut. I knew exactly what we were seeing.

"It's a spaceship blasting its way out of the ring!"

I whooped and pulled Callan into a kiss. "My emergency drone must have reached the wormhole and gotten through to the Federation Navy."

Callan propped her chin on one hand. "What is an emergency drone?"

"I never told you about launching the drone?" When Callan shook her head, I continued, "A drone is an unmanned spaceship that carries a message. In my case, the drone carried the coordinates of the wormhole to this system as well as the initial sensor readings when I exited the wormhole. The drone launched from my scout ship, but my sensors couldn't track it through all the asteroids. I hoped it flew into the wormhole safely, but had just about given up that hope."

"Then the drone flew out the other side of the wormhole and waited for someone to find it?" Callan puzzled through the idea. "So it's a lot like a message in a bottle?"

"That's sort of right, if the bottle could set sail for the nearest port. When the drone got through the wormhole, it would have flown back to the nearest Scout base."

"How does the drone know the way to the base if there's no one flying it?"

"It's complicated." How could I explain astrogation and autopilots to Callan? "Let me think a bit about the best way to explain it to you."

"Martin already understands, though." Callan waved her hand toward the flashes in the ring. "Whoever is on that ship already understands. And just about everyone in your part of the galaxy understands." Her next words were so soft I almost didn't hear them. "But *I* don't understand."

"That's not your fault, Callan. You just don't have the background for it and I'm not sure I can do a good job explaining it."

Callan laid her head on my chest and I felt a splash of warm liquid. Was that a tear?

Cupping her chin, I lifted Callan's head so I could look into her eyes. A second tear spilled from her eye and rolled down her cheek.

"Hey, why are you crying?" What had I said to make her suddenly sad?

"When that spaceship lands, the whole galaxy will be open to you again. Why would you stay on my backward planet when you could go back to exploring the stars?"

"Callan, why would I leave you just to explore a bunch of stars? I'll stay here *because* this is your planet. I'll stay here because *you* are here." I pulled her close and kissed her. "It's going to take a lot more than a sleek spaceship to lure me away from the life we've made together. And even if I am lured away, I'll miss you terribly and come home as soon as humanly possible."

Callan gazed into my eyes for a second. I willed the truth of my words to reflect in them. With a sigh, she snuggled even closer to me. "You do realize you're in serious hot water with me?"

I felt a jolt of alarm "You don't believe what I just told you?"

"I believe it." This time I could hear the smirk in her voice. "But if you think you're leaving me behind when you fly off to the stars, you've got another think coming."

"My deepest apologies, dearest. Of course I'll take you with me. If nothing else, I'd love to introduce you to my parents."

"And your little sister, Sandra?" Callan prompted. "From your stories about her, I'm certain she and I will become good friends."

"Yeah, sure, I'll introduce you to my little sister, too." I kept my tone light, but I hadn't seen my family in over two years. They must be worried about me and I missed them terribly.

"Now, shouldn't you be rushing off to tell Martin about the spaceship?" Callan asked.

"Not yet. We can't do anything until it breaks atmosphere, anyway." I stood up, pulled Callan up beside me, and looked toward our bedroom. "So, a while back you said something about children?"

Callan laughed, soft and sultry. "Well, if you insist..."

Bright light flared above us as an explosion lit the ring and the flashes stopped. An asteroid must have hit the spaceship!

2

WHERE'S MARTIN?

As the explosion faded away, a new red trail blazed to life in the upper atmosphere. I assumed it was wreckage or asteroid fragments and expected the trail to streak towards the ground. Instead, the angle of descent lessened and the red trail diminished as the object slowed. It was under intelligent control.

I jumped to my feet. "Some of the ship's crew must have survived that explosion. They're bound to have wounded among them—and there will probably be more when they hit the ground. We've got to gather a search and rescue team to find and help them."

Callan and I watched the red trail moving across the sky. "It looks like it's going to come down in the lands between Mordan and Tarteg. David, go alert Martin and Tristan and whoever else you want to have with us on this rescue mission. I'll speak to Mom and Daddy and make arrangements for a naval escort."

With a nod and a quick kiss for Callan, I ran off to find Milo. Milo didn't have any skills we'd need on the team—though he'd more than earned the right to join us if he wanted to do so—but Milo has a knack for knowing where everyone is at any given moment. When I found him, I was not surprised to find several young ladies-in-waiting vying for his attention. Not bad for an orphan who'd grown up on the streets of Faroon.

I bowed politely to the girls. "Please pardon my interruption, ladies, but I must speak with Milo for a moment."

The girls' eyes widened. They knew Milo had saved my life more than once, but apparently they never expected me to come to him. I guess it *is* more common for royalty to summon people, but I was in a hurry and still wasn't comfortable with the whole 'royal' thing.

Adopting a serious expression, Milo stood. "Of course, Prince Consort. Ladies, would you please excuse me?"

A chorus of yeses followed as Milo and I stepped just out of earshot. Once the girls could no longer see his face, Milo grinned broadly. "Thank you, David. You've given my reputation a bump upwards."

"What are friends for?" I asked. "And mentioning friends, do you know where I can find Martin?"

"Sure. At this hour on a Thursday you'll find him at the Drum and Fife on Waterford Street."

"For a former raider, Martin is awfully predictable." I shook my head in mock disapproval. "Is palace life making him soft?"

"Soft in the head, maybe. Or, more accurately, the heart," Milo replied.

"Martin has a girlfriend?"

"He usually has three." Milo grinned. "The pages are all in awe of his prowess with the fairer sex."

"Usually? That's not the case anymore?"

"Not since he met Megan, it isn't. She's very pretty."

"Does she work at the Drum and Fife?" I asked.

"Sort of. Megan's a very talented musician, too. She sings there every Thursday," Milo said. "She's at the Broken Barrel on Tuesdays, so that's where Martin goes every Tuesday."

"Well, I hope Martin will forgive me for pulling him away from his lady love."

"What's up, David?"

In a few short sentences, I brought Milo up-to-date on the crashing spaceship. "I hate to pull you away from your young ladies, too, but I need you to round up Tristan and Nist. Tristan should gather any medical supplies he thinks he'll need and Nist should start preparing the *Pauline* for flight."

Milo offered apologies to his female admirers as I struck out for the Drum and Fife. Two guards fell in behind me as I left the palace, something I was still getting used to. Waterford Street was but a few blocks away. The guards and I covered the distance in under ten minutes.

I opened the tavern door to find a sea of angry patrons blocking my way. Over their heads I saw the object of their rage. A defiant red-headed woman—Megan, I assumed—clasped a guitar to her chest and glared at the crowd. Sword drawn, Martin stood between the mob and the musician.

3

MEGAN

I WANTED TO CALL ON SOME OF THAT ROYAL AUTHORITY I DIDN'T LIKE using to calm things down, but I couldn't be heard over the crowd noise. I had to find a way to get to the stage and hope some of the crowd recognized me. I had no other hope for getting their attention. My guards were still nervously assessing the situation when I did the one thing I knew they didn't want me to do. I plunged into the crowd and began worming my way toward the stage.

I had gone but a few yards when someone in the crowd threw a bottle at the stage. Martin swept the bottle aside with his sword, otherwise it would have smashed into the woman's head. A crowd shouting and waving fists in the air could be calmed. A mob shoving and throwing bottles was a different matter.

Boost!

About to shove through the crowd, I suddenly remembered how, years ago, Martin had leapt over a line of Tartegian guards in the trading post cellar. I leapt into the air, hoping to fly over the crowd. It didn't work so well. With people packed around me, I couldn't jump as high as I needed, nor as far forward. Finding myself about to come down in the crowd, I tucked and pushed off from a couple of sturdy shoulders. I completed a flip and landed next to Martin.

Raising my arms, I yelled for quiet. The mob fell silent and I dropped Boost.

"What is the meaning of this?" I demanded. "How dare you attack this woman? You're acting like a lawless gang of Beloran tunnel rats."

A big man back in the crowd hollered, "Come down here and say that to my face, pretty boy! Ain't no way you'd say that to us if you knew anything 'bout tunnel rats."

I guess they didn't recognize me. "I know exactly what I'm saying, since I've been into the tunnels of Beloran and faced the tunnel rats."

The big man barked, "Ha! Only one Mordanian man has been into those tunnels and lived to tell about it."

I looked at the man, my eyebrows raised in inquiry. "And?"

The crowd looked at me, blank expressions on their faces.

"Take your time," Martin added helpfully. "It'll come to you."

My guards pushed their way to the front of the crowd, pained expressions directed my way. At sight of their green and gold uniforms, one man's face cleared.

"That man is David Rice, the Prince Consort."

Heads bobbed in agreement, even the big man who'd challenged me.

"Now that we've cleared that up, I'll return to my question." I glared out at the crowd. "What is the meaning of this demonstration?"

A voice from the crowd called, "She provoked us!" A chorus of voices added "Yeah!" and "Right!"

"One woman armed with nothing but a guitar provoked such a violent demonstration? How?" When no one answered, I looked to Martin. "Would you care to fill me in?"

"The crowd asked to hear new songs, ones they'd never heard before. She toured Tarteg before coming here, so Megan chose to sing some songs currently popular there," he said. "She led off with *Rupor's Lament*."

"Never heard of it."

"I'm not surprised, David. It's about Callan and Rupor and is strongly slanted to the Tartegian point of view. The song questions the prince consort's motives, his honor, and his off-world origins." Megan snorted at this, causing Martin to give me a half smile. "But the real trouble started when the song called Princess Callan a rather rude name. It...ah...rhymes with rich."

Even this cautious approach to the word brought mutters from the crowd. Megan chose to make it worse by saying, "From everything I've been told, the song doesn't go far enough."

I stepped between Megan and the crowd just in case another bottle was thrown. "Martin, can you please shut her up? We've got vastly more important matters to deal with than Megan's thoughtless song choices."

"No one shuts me-"

Martin clamped his left hand over Megan's mouth, wrapped his right arm around her waist, then picked her up. "What's going on?"

"Less than an hour ago, another spaceship came through the wormhole."

4

NO BARDS REQUIRED

UPON HEARING MY WORDS, MEGAN SNORTED AGAIN. EVEN WITH HER mouth muffled by Martin's hand, Megan had no trouble making her opinion quite clear. Her eyes spoke volumes as well and made me happy it was Martin's hand within range of her teeth rather than mine.

I glanced at Martin. "Does she know who you are and where you came from?"

Megan's flashing eyes turned to Martin and her eyebrows drew down. Was she giving him the evil eye for silencing her or trying to puzzle out where he was born?

"Our relationship hasn't really advanced to such personal revelations." Martin turned his winning smile on Megan and was rewarded with a steel-melting glare.

"That explains a lot. Meanwhile, we've got things to do." I turned to face the crowd. "Clear a path, please. We're leaving."

Most of the crowd moved aside, but one man planted himself in front of me. "Didn't you hear what that woman called our princess? We can't forgive an insult like that."

"Yes, my good man, I heard. And if I can forgive the singer, so can you," I said. "After all, I *am* married to the princess."

The man smacked his forehead and stepped aside. "Of course, sir. Please forgive me, sir!"

"There's nothing to forgive." I clapped him on the shoulder.

My guards took up position on either side of me as we exited the tavern. Outside, I filled Martin in on the spaceship's arrival. With Martin's hand no longer covering her mouth, Megan kept trying to interrupt with questions. I plowed ahead with my explanation, overriding her comments and ignoring her questions. I will say this for Megan, she didn't give up easily.

"So," Megan said when I stopped speaking, "you and Martin are heading off after one of these 'spaceships' you claim to have arrived in?"

"Martin, I'm tired of listening to this woman rant and rave about my origins and crashed spaceships." I shook my head in disgust. "Then again, there are none so certain as the truly ignorant."

Megan's head whipped up, her eyes widened, and her mouth opened and shut several times without a sound emerging. I found it a welcome change.

"Yes, Megan, we're heading off after a spaceship," Martin said. "I know you're well educated, so I truly don't understand why you're so determined to cast David as a liar or conman."

"He's part of the royal family and royals always lie." The fire in Megan's eyes and voice faded as she spoke, as if she spoke out of a long-ingrained habit.

Martin shook his head in mock sorrow. "I must say that you're quite cynical for one so young."

"Travel as much as I have and you'd be cynical, too," Megan replied.

"I've been on seven other inhabited worlds," I said, "and traveled extensively on this world, yet I'm not cynical in the least."

"No doubt due to the rapture of true love." Megan's voice was drier than the desert where I'd crashed.

"People say travel broadens the mind, Megan, but that only works if the mind is open." I stopped at the palace gate. "You're safe now, Megan. Run along home."

"And miss out on the great spaceship hunt and the chance to broaden my mind? Not on your life." Megan linked arms with Martin. "I'm coming with you."

"Whoa there, Megan," I said. "You most definitely are *not* coming with us."

"Why not? I'll stay out of the way." Megan widened her eyes and pouted, an effect designed to melt the heart of any man who faced it. From the look Martin turned on me, Megan's pout certainly worked on him. It might have worked on me, too, if I hadn't married the most beautiful woman on eight planets.

"That pout won't work on me." I made shooing motions. "Scat. We don't need in-flight entertainment for a rescue mission."

Megan dropped her wide-eyed pout and went back to glaring at me. "Are you afraid I'll find out the princess isn't nearly as sweet and beautiful in real life as *Rice's Rescue* claims she is?"

I turned to Martin. "What is *Rice's Rescue*?"

"It's the Mordanian counterpoint to *Rupor's Lament*. As you might guess, the crown prince of Tarteg isn't portrayed in the best light in the Mordanian version." Martin looked back and forth between Megan and me. "But I think you should reconsider your position concerning Megan. There are definite advantages to bringing her along."

I snorted. "Name just one and I'll let her join us."

"Songs will be written about this event. Everyone will benefit if those songs are more accurate than either *Rupor's Lament* or *Rice's Rescue*." Martin patted Megan's arm. "Who better to write some of those songs than an actual eye witness?"

He had a point—a minor point, but a point nonetheless. I sighed. "Fine, Megan can come along. But I'll warn you right now, if she insults Callan I'm throwing her overboard."

Megan smiled in triumph. "Well, if your princess is as sweet as you Mordanians say, that won't be a problem."

"Well, even if you can't stop yourself from throwing insults," Martin added, grinning, "rest assured David will land the airship before giving you the old heave ho."

"Wait—you're saying he's serious about that?"

I headed into the palace and didn't hear Martin's reply. Whatever he said didn't deter Megan. The two of them caught up with me just before I found Callan.

The palace swarmed in a controlled frenzy as pages, guards, and naval officers dashed about. The activity centered on Callan, who made quick decisions followed by crisp orders. The king and queen sat to one side, watching their daughter with proud smiles. They waved as I entered and approached Callan. She signed some order or requisition then turned to me. Rising up on her toes, Callan gave me a peck on the lips and one to Martin on his cheek.

Callan turned a welcoming smile on Megan. Eying Martin's and Megan's linked arms, Callan said, "Martin, is this lovely lady the reason you've declined my last two dinner invitations?"

"She most definitely is," Martin smiled. "Megan, this is Her Highness, Princess Callan."

Megan surprised me by dropping into a curtsey. "Your Highness."

Callan took Megan's hand and drew her up. "We don't stand on ceremony unless we're in formal court. At least, not among friends." Callan turned to Martin. "You know you could have brought her to dinner with you."

"Megan is a musician and was performing both nights," Martin replied.

I added, "Martin thinks she should accompany us and chronicle this mission in song."

"What a splendid idea," Callan smile grew wider. "It will be refreshing to have another woman on board the ship. Most of my trips with David are overwhelmingly masculine."

"Why thank you, Your Highness."

"Now Megan, I told you we don't stand on ceremony among friends. Call me Callan." Callan turned to me. "I've ordered four escort ships for the *Pauline.* The naval ships are already airborne. We can leave as soon as you're ready."

"I'm ready now." I waved my arm around us. "But what about all of this activity?"

"Oh, they're just working out logistics for the follow-on forces. I'm sure the admiralty will be quite happy to handle that without any guidance from me." Callan slipped her arm through mine. "Let's go."

Milo and Tristan were already aboard the airship. Seconds after we boarded, Nist piloted the *Pauline* into the air and the rescue mission was underway.

5

CRASH SITE SURPRISES

"WHY MUST ALL OF OUR ESCORT SHIPS BE SO...STATELY?" NIST GROUSED. 'Stately' was Nist's current euphemism for 'slow.'

"Seven hours and twenty-three minutes," called Martin. Several guards groaned and one cheered.

"What's that all about?" Megan asked him.

"Nist always chafes at the top speed of Callan's escort airships," Martin said. "The guards like to bet how long it will take before he voices his frustration aloud."

I tuned out their conversation as Callan came out of the airship's cabin and into the dawn light. She had retreated there with Megan shortly after lift-off. The two women passed the intervening hours chatting. I busied myself discussing rescue contingencies with Martin. Distracted as I was, I only realized I hadn't once heard shouting from the cabin when a quiet and thoughtful Megan returned to the deck. Considering how abrasive Megan was when I'd first met her, I'd expected Callan to adopt her icy, court-proper princess persona at least once during the trip. Yet Callan emerged all smiles from the cabin.

Seeing the direction I was looking, Callan said, "Megan is quite a talented and passionate woman."

"Lucky Martin," I murmured.

"Passionate about her *beliefs.*" Callan rolled her eyes before musing, "Though if their relationship ever becomes seriously romantic then yes, lucky Martin."

"You *like* her? I admit you've spent more time with Megan, but I found her rather irritating."

"You met her during her confrontation with an angry mob. One where people truly were ready to hurt her—and in my name, no less." Callan grimaced. "Fear rarely brings out the best in people, David."

"She was afraid?" I shook my head. "Megan hid it very well. I thought she was angry."

"She won't admit it, but Megan simply wasn't thinking when she started playing *Rupor's Lament.* She should have simply stopped playing when the tavern fell silent. An apology followed by a spritely tune probably would have settled the crowd. But she's a stubborn woman whose pride forced her to keep playing the song."

"Megan told you all of that?" I asked.

"Not directly, no, but any woman could have heard it in Megan's voice and seen it in her face." Callan looked up at my face. "So, did you and Martin figure out what you're going to do when we find this spaceship?"

Before I could answer, a shout rose from a lookout on one of the escort ships.

"Unknown object twenty-three degrees to starboard."

I looked in that direction and immediately spotted the line of broken trees and churned dirt. It extended over a mile. At its end, the crashed starship lay with its nose buried in the ground. It was a big ship, with at least a hundred and sixty yards of fuselage angling up above the tops of the trees.

A shout rang out from the lookout on board the lead escort. "Tartegian warships dead ahead."

I turned my gaze toward Tarteg and easily spotted the approaching warships.

"This is not good, David. They outnumber us seven to four." Martin, far more experienced with airships, assessed the situation before I'd finished counting Tartegian warships.

"Don't you mean seven to five?" Megan asked. "Did you forget to count the airship you're riding in?"

"I didn't forget the *Pauline*," Martin replied, "I left her out of the count on purpose."

"Why?" Megan asked. "This seems like a perfectly fine airship."

Nist beamed at the compliment to his pride and joy.

"She's a splendid airship—but she's not a warship. She has neither weapons nor a contingent of marines," Martin replied. "If it comes to a fight, Nist will drop David and me on the command ship then take Her Highness and you away from here at top speed."

Megan bristled. "Is that because we're women? Are you saying women can't-"

Callan interrupted the argument, "Nist, I wish to speak with the Tartegian commander. Please raise a white flag and then slowly fly forward."

Megan glanced at Martin and me, obviously expecting us to voice an objection. When we didn't say anything, she threw up her hands. "I don't get it. If you have to fight the Tartegians, you're going send us away. And it's all because we're women and this isn't a warship. But neither of you have any problems with this same non-warship—protected by nothing but a piece of white cloth—sailing in alone to parlay with those same Tartegians."

"While our two countries have their differences, Tarteg is a civilized country. Its navy will honor the flag of truce. I doubt their commander is any more anxious for battle than we are." As I finished speaking, a Tartegian airship raised a white flag and flew to meet us.

"Well, I must say that's quite a relief," Megan's incredulous expression said otherwise. "If it comes to a fight, I'm sure all of those who die will die a happier death knowing their killers followed the rules of war like proper gentlemen."

"Megan, the rules of war exist to protect the living by avoiding needless conflict and unnecessary loss of life." Suddenly, Callan turned her icy princess persona on the musician. "*Those rules succeed because they insure we can talk to each other safely and without fear.*"

"I realize this situation is outside of your experience," I said, "but you asked to come with us as an observer. Watch in silence or I'll have one of the guards take you below deck."

Megan's eyes blazed at me but she kept quiet.

"Ahoy, Mordanian vessel!" a familiar voice called from the Tartegian airship.

The Tartegian commander was Prince Rupor.

6

A VIABLE SOLUTION

"Awkward," Megan sang softly.

Ignoring Megan, Callan called, "Hello, Rupor. How have you been doing?"

"Callan?" Rupor couldn't keep the surprise from his voice. "What are you doing out here?"

"The same as you, Rupor. I'm investigating the crashed spaceship."

"I'm surprised your *consort* let you come to the unsettled lands," Rupor said. "Isn't he afraid you'll be kidnapped?"

"Point to Rupor," Megan said under her breath.

"With your step-mother and half-brother in exile," Callan shot back, "my *husband* doesn't believe he has to worry about Tartegian kidnapping plots."

"Ouch! Two points to Callan," Megan added.

Callan turned an irritated glare on Megan.

I took the hint, even if Megan appeared oblivious to it. "Guard, take Megan below deck and keep her there until further notice."

Megan's protests interrupted Callan's exchange with Rupor. By the time Megan was out of earshot, the airships were within a few yards of each other.

"You've come with an interesting pair of companions, Callan," Rupor said. "While I can understand traveling with your consort-"

"*Husband.*"

"-I must admit I'll be damned if I understand traveling with Bane." Rupor finished. "Don't you find it rather ironic that I was deemed unfit to wed you because my relatives contracted for your kidnapping but your *actual* kidnapper is deemed a fit companion for the very princess he kidnapped?"

"Isn't it odd how my kidnapper has atoned for his crimes—in rather spectacular fashion, I might add—while your relative, Raoul, remains an extremely irritating thorn in my side?"

The bickering was getting out of hand. I interrupted with a change of subject before the truce failed and fighting broke out. "May I humbly suggest the two of you save the verbal sparring for court, Your Highnesses? People may be injured within the spaceship."

Callan reddened. "Thank you for reminding me of my duty, darling. David is right, Rupor. We must put aside our differences and decide how our two nations can best respond to the situation at hand."

"Yes, I suppose he is correct." Rupor's gaze swept the entire scene. "May I suggest an approach by a combined party of Mordanians and Tartegians? I believe it is the only viable solution. Your... husband...should be among those selected. He speaks our language and, I assume, the language of those within the spaceship. I prefer not to rely on second-hand reports, so will represent Tarteg myself."

"I agree with your suggestions, Rupor, but wish to suggest one more member of the party." Callan placed a hand on Martin's shoulder. "If he's willing, I'd like Martin to go along, as well. He speaks both languages and, like David, can Boost should an emergency arise."

Rupor thought for a moment. "Our differences aside, Callan, I know you are a sensible woman. I agree to your suggestion. Bane may accompany us."

Callan turned to Martin. "I realize I've put you on the spot, Martin, but will you go with David and Rupor?"

"Try and keep me away," Martin grinned.

After another round of discussions, Rupor joined us on board the *Pauline* for the descent. Ten minutes later, the three of us hopped down to the ground.

"Take the ship back up, Nist," I said. "I don't know what to expect, but if anything happens, get out of here as quickly as possible."

"Is there anything I should watch for in particular?" Nist asked.

"Airships falling out of the sky would be a good indicator of trouble," Martin remarked dryly.

We set off at a slow jog toward the spaceship. Within minutes we were forced to reduce our pace as we scrambled over broken trees and mounds of dirt. It took ten more minutes to reach the crash site. When we came close enough to see details on the ship, Martin stiffened.

I barely avoided crashing into Martin's back when he stopped. "What's the problem, Martin?"

"We could be in for some serious trouble, David." Martin pointed to designs painted on the side of the spaceship. "Those look like pirate markings."

7

PIRATES AND LASERS

"Are you sure?" I asked. I'd been out in the wider galaxy far more recently than Martin had and the designs meant nothing to me.

"My Master Scout and I had a run-in with pirates prior to crashing onto Aashla," Martin said. "Those markings are similar to the ones used by those pirates."

"Well, I believe you, Bane," drawled Rupor. "Vermin always recognize their own kind."

"You're not helping, Rupor," I said. "If Martin is right, we truly are all in serious trouble."

"It's only one ship," Rupor scoffed.

"You wouldn't say that if you had any idea what a single spaceship like that is capable of doing," Martin growled.

"If it's a simple matter of education, then by all means do enlighten me," Rupor replied.

"Put simply, if that ship is fully crewed and functional, then whoever commands it rules this world," Martin said.

"You must be joking," Rupor looked back and forth between Martin and me. "He *can't* be serious?"

"Do I look as if I'm joking, Rupor?" Martin's gaze bored into the prince. "If this is a pirate ship, our only hope for stopping them is for at least one person to insinuate himself into their good graces, bide his time, and wait for the opportunity to strike."

"Oh ho! Now the plot comes clear," Rupor cried. "You wish this super ship for yourself. Well, I-"

I clapped a hand over Rupor's mouth and an arm around his throat. "I'm sorry for the rough treatment, Your Highness, but we don't have time for this bickering. For what it's worth, I believe Martin's suggestion has merit. Martin, what should our first move be?"

"Assuming there are survivors—and from your description of the partially controlled descent, I'm sure some of the crew is still alive—I'm going to try to make contact with them." Martin shrugged. "If they're not pirates, great. We help with their wounded and take it from there. If they *are* pirates, I'll try to trade on my old reputation as a raider to join them."

"Um, Martin, those on the ship are not going to know anything about your past activities on Aashla."

"I know that, David, but I *do* have that experience to draw on. I'm confident I can convince them of my bona fides."

"What about Rupor and me?" I asked.

"If these are pirates, they must *not* learn you're an off-worlder, too, David. A military hero who can also fly their ship will be too much of a threat. They'd kill you without a second thought."

"So I pretend to be a local?" I asked.

Martin nodded. "That includes pretending like you don't speak their language." At my nod, Martin turned to Rupor. "Prince, you *must* follow our plan or these men may kill us all."

Rupor stared at Martin for a moment, then nodded. Relieved, I released Rupor.

"You two stay hidden," Martin said, then picked his way to the ship's airlock. He fiddled with the airlock controls. A minute later, the airlock door slid open and Martin stepped inside.

Immediately after entering the airlock, Martin dove back out and rolled to the left. A bright beam of red light lanced behind him, tracking too slowly to hit him before he was out of the line of fire. The beam cut deep, smoking lines into the broken trees piled up beside the spaceship.

It sliced completely through smaller tree trunks, those only a few inches thick.

"By all that is holy, what was *that*?" Rupor stared, wide-eyed, at the damage left by the beam.

"It's called a laser." Since no language on Aashla had a word for 'laser,' I used the galactic basic word. "For simplicity, let's just say it's a highly focused beam of light."

"Light? Is that all?" Rupor asked. "Why didn't Bane just wear metal armor? Surely that would stop the light. Or he could have carried a mirror to reflect it."

"The laser would burn through metal armor in a heartbeat. It would do the same to a mirror. I realize this is all new and strange to you, but you have to believe me." I met the stare Rupor turned on me. "It gets worse, Your Highness. That is just a small laser, one a man could carry. The spaceship is armed with half a dozen much larger ones." I searched for a way to help him understand. "Think of the laser we just saw as a single-handed target crossbow. In comparison, the ship's lasers are ballistas."

"And Bane thinks these people may be pirates?" Rupor turned back toward the ship and stared with apprehension. "God protect us! No nation could stand against such power."

I placed a hand on Rupor's shoulder. "That is why you *must* follow our instructions in this matter. If these are pirates, our best—perhaps our only—hope is to infiltrate the pirate gang and bring them down from within. That means you're going to have to put aside your opinion of Martin and trust him to find a way to do just that."

Rupor wrinkled his nose as if smelling something foul. "And what of you, Rice? Are you certain they are pirates?"

"Certain? No. But I trust Martin and will follow his lead until we can learn more about our visitors," I said. "That means you *must* keep quiet about my background. If the pirates discover I am a crash-landed scout, they'll kill me out of hand."

"Why would pirates worry about a single scout? I've heard you're a formidable fighter, but it's obvious you can't defeat these pirates single-handedly."

"You're right, I can't. But the very nature of scouting brings us in contact with pirates far more often than any of the other military branches. We're trained to deal with them and, at the risk of bragging, succeed more often than we fail." I smiled grimly. "As you might guess, Your Highness, pirates tend to dislike us scouts."

Rupor nodded. "I'll do my best, Rice. And you might as well call me Rupor out here. It's quicker and quick communication may save lives."

Back at the airlock, Martin got to his feet and dusted himself off. The hiss of an opening airlock door came from the ship. Footsteps clanged in the airlock and a huge figure appeared at the outer door. Our situation had just gotten far worse. The figure wore military-grade powered armor.

8

TAKE ME TO YOUR LEADER

Ignoring Martin standing next to him, the armored figure scanned the area. I pulled Rupor down behind a mound of dirt and broken trees. If we were lucky, the heat from the crash would mask us from infrared scanning. The armor whined faintly—the armored head swiveling to complete an infrared sweep, I assumed. I put a finger to my lips and motioned for Rupor to stay down. Eyes wide and his face deathly pale, Rupor nodded.

"Hey, you in the powered armor," Martin spoke galactic basic. "Take me to your leader."

The man in the armor took two clumping footsteps.

"Put me down," Martin shouted. "I can walk on my own, you know. All you have to do is give me a chance."

Footsteps clanged from the air lock.

"This is no way to treat a guest, you know," Martin continued complaining until the airlock hissed closed and cut off his voice.

I risked a peek over our hiding place. As I'd expected, there was no sign of the armored figure or of Martin.

Ducking down again, I whispered, "Martin has been taken inside. I guess that counts as a successful start to Martin's plan."

"What was that thing?" The color still had not returned to Rupor's face.

"It was a man wearing...you don't really have a word for it." I tried to think of something within Rupor's experience. "The closest I can get is armor with an engine."

"An engine?" Color slowly seeped back into Rupor's face. "I know quite a bit about engineering and that armor gave off no smoke and had no place for a boiler."

"The engine is based on science and engineering you don't have on Aashla." I started crawling away from the spaceship. "I'll try to explain in more detail, but not until we're far away from this spaceship."

Staying low and keeping dirt mounds between us and the ship, Rupor and I scrambled through the debris from the crash. Ten minutes later, we broke free of the trees and picked up our pace, waving at the ships floating above us. Within seconds, the *Pauline* dropped down to meet us.

Milo was the first person to realize Martin wasn't with us. By the time we reached the *Pauline*, he had alerted everyone else on board. Megan was among those waiting on the deck. Callan must have ordered her released.

Impatient Megan spoke first. "Where's Martin? What have you done with him?"

"*We* haven't done anything with him," I said.

"He was captured," Rupor added.

I gave a quick account of the events. Megan's hand flew to her mouth when I described the powered armor and everyone else looked grim.

"I could say things have gone exactly according to Martin's plan," I said, "but not even someone as optimistic as I am can convince myself that's true."

"What are we going to do now?" Callan asked. "We can't just abandon Martin inside that spaceship."

"No, of course not, Callan. Fortunately, I know exactly what we're going do to."

Megan stared intently at me, then asked, "And what is that?"

"First, all of you are going to fly several miles away and wait for my signal," I said. "That includes you, Rupor."

"I can't say as I approve of this plan, Rice. A Prince of Tarteg doesn't run away from a fight."

"This is a tactical withdrawal, nothing more. Until we know more about that ship, there's no point putting you at risk." Rupor opened his mouth—to protest, I assume—so I added, "You don't send generals to scout enemy positions, do you Rupor?"

"Of course not."

"Then we're sure as hell not sending a crown prince to do the same job."

Rupor sighed and nodded.

"And what are you planning on doing, David?" Callan asked.

I gave her my most confident smile. "I'm going back for Martin, of course."

9

KNOCK KNOCK

Callan looked into my eyes for a few seconds. At last she said, "Don't get yourself killed, David."

"Have I ever?"

"Well don't start now." Then she wrapped her arms around me and kissed me long and hard. When she released me, she wore her princess mask once again. "That signal you promised—I suppose we'll know it when we see it?"

"You know me well, dear," I unbuckled my sword and handed it to Callan. "I doubt whoever is on that ship, whether they're pirates or not, will allow me to go armed on board. Keep this safe for me. Rob will come back to haunt me if I lose his sword."

As Callan took the sword, Megan began humming a haunting melody. Eyes closed and head tilted back, she swayed slightly and her hands moved as if plucking guitar strings. Perhaps realizing silence had fallen around her, Megan opened her eyes.

"Sorry." Megan's face reddened.

"I've never heard that music before. What is it?" Callan asked.

"A theme for the ballad I'm composing about all of this. It's the lovers parting." Growing more self-conscious as we watched, Megan crossed her arms and her eyes flashed defiance. "Well, that is why you brought me."

"It's beautiful," Callan said, disarming Megan's defensiveness with two words. "I don't know how you did it, but you captured my exact feelings in that theme. I can't wait to hear the theme you compose for the lovers' reunion." Callan turned her gaze back to me. "Now you have two women awaiting your return, darling. That *is* something men dream about, isn't it?"

"Only in their nightmares," Rupor muttered.

"I shall strive mightily to avoid disappointing either my lover or the lyricist," I proclaimed. I gave one last look at Callan then turned to leave.

"How will you get into that metal monstrosity?" Rupor asked, sucking all the romance out of the moment.

I shrugged. "I'll knock on the door."

Fifteen minutes later, I did just that. I knew the knock couldn't be heard inside the ship, but the local I pretended to be would not. After a few seconds, I knocked again and called, "Hello? Is anyone there?"

I was on my third round of knocking and calling when the airlock slid open, revealing the same armored figure. I let my mouth go slack as a massive metal hand dragged me into the spaceship.

"Hey, let me go!" I cried in Mordanian. "I don't want to be dragged like an animal."

The armored man kept his grip, pulling me into the spaceship. I flailed about, acting frightened and out of my element. Under the cover of my flailing, I examined the ship and the members of the crew we passed.

The ship's interior was impeccably maintained. The captain and crew took very good care of their ship. In the history vids we'd watched in high school, pirates were always depicted as slovenly and their ships in such a state of disrepair it was a wonder they didn't simply fall apart in space. Even taking into account the Federation bias behind the vids, if Martin's suspicions were correct and this was a pirate ship, it certainly was an atypical one.

None of the crewman I saw, including the man in the powered armor, did anything to dispel that notion. An unskilled or careless crewman wearing powered armor would crush my arm to pulp in his untrained grip. The armored man held my arm firmly, but did so without hurting me. That care didn't strike me as very piratical and I dared to hope that Martin's assessment was wrong.

The crewman dragged me to the bridge where I found Martin deep in conversation with another man. He was the captain. There was no doubt about that. The man stood almost as tall as Martin and me and had the look of a commander of men—confident, laser focused, missing little going on around him, and quite intimidating to those unused to dealing with such men. If it came to a fight, this captain would be a formidable enemy.

The captain turned my way and didn't see Martin scratch his head right over his implant. Then he extended his arms as if stretching. The hand he'd scratched with ended up pointing at the ship's computer. I nodded to Martin, as if in greeting, showing I understood. The captain obviously made Martin download his translation of local languages into the ship's computer. Somewhere, a crewman listened to a translation of our conversation. We had no secrets while on board the ship.

"Welcome aboard, young man," the captain said in galactic basic.

I shrugged, looked at Martin, and spoke Mordanian. "Captain Bane, what did he say?"

"This is Amaral Caudill, captain of this spaceship. He welcomes you aboard," Martin translated.

At the sound of the man's name, my blood ran cold. Mere feet from me stood one of the most vicious pirates ever to plague the Terran Federation.

10

CAPTAIN CAUDILL

MARTIN CRASHED ON AASHLA SEVENTEEN YEARS AGO. I COULDN'T remember when Caudill first appeared in news reports, but it was about the same time. Even if Martin had heard the name, he couldn't know of the death and destruction the pirate left in his wake. Caudill measured his legacy in thousands of butchered crew and passengers, vast fortunes in plundered riches, and a name that struck fear into the hearts of spacemen throughout Federation space and the frontier.

Struggling to block the horror Caudill's name conjured, I turned what I hoped was a pleasant smile on Caudill. "Captain Bane, would you tell Captain Caudill that I'm pleased to meet him and am most impressed by his ship of space."

As Martin relayed my greeting, I looked around the bridge. I kept my eyes wide and darting all around, as if I couldn't decide which instrument panel was the most wonderful. As my eyes flicked around the bridge, I had my implant record everything. The picture formed from the images indicated a bridge crew who all looked the worse for wear after their crash. Even Caudill favored his right arm and propped his right leg on a stool.

At a break in the conversation, I said, "The crew and the captain look banged up, Captain Bane. Should we summon our doctor?"

The ship would certainly have a nano-tech med bay, but if I were in

Caudill's position I'd save it for true emergencies. With no way of knowing how long he'd be stuck here, I had no doubt Caudill would ration high tech medicine with extreme care—probably saving most of it for himself.

"In my experience, medical care on primitive lost colonies such as this one is dicey at best. Is your doctor as likely to kill my men as heal them?" Caudill asked after Martin completed translating my question.

Martin held out one of his hands, pointing to the scars left from a tammar slash to the hand. "Our doctor saved my hand after a tammar —that's a damned big native predator—cut it to the bone in three places. The hand is a bit stiff, now, but otherwise as good as new. Tristan is good by most any standard—including what you'll find on rim and frontier worlds—and is superb for a primitive planet like this one."

Caudill peered at Martin's hand with interest then turned to one of the crew. "Have you got a final casualty count?"

"Yes, Captain. We have one hundred and twenty-six dead and thirty-six injured."

"Good God, you lost one hundred and twenty-six men in this crash?" Shock showed on Martin's face. I was shocked, too, but didn't dare show it since I wasn't supposed to understand gal base.

"One of the inertial dampeners failed during our exit from the wormhole. Everyone in the aft half of the ship disintegrated. At least it was a quick death." Caudill shook his head slowly. "The dampener shouldn't have failed like that. We keep them in good repair. And, yeah, send your man to get your doctor."

Martin, wincing at the thought of malfunctioning inertial dampeners, turned to me and switched languages. "That's an excellent suggestion, David. Please do go and fetch the doctor."

I nodded in acknowledgement, my mind already spinning through plans. Could Tristan find a way to drug or otherwise incapacitate most of Caudill's remaining crew? If we couldn't find some way to eliminate the pirate threat, everyone on the planet was in serious trouble.

11

A SURPRISE ADDITION

"CONSIDERING THE NUMBER OF WOUNDED, YOUR DOCTOR MAY NEED TO bring a lot of supplies." Caudill spoke to the armored figure. "Orrons, go with the lad. Help carry the supplies if necessary and make sure nothing...unfortunate...happens to Captain Bane's assistant."

"That's very...generous...of you, Captain Caudill," Martin said.

"It's nothing more than the courtesy due a fellow professional," Caudill replied.

Of course, both of them spoke in galactic basic, so I just kept walking. I did stop at the first clumping footfall from Orrons, though. Casting an inquiring glance back at Martin, I asked, "Am I to have company on the trip to get the doctor?"

Martin switched to Mordanian. "You are, David. This man will provide protection and, should you require help carrying Tristan's supplies, will assist with that as well."

I looked Orrons up and down. "The man looks to be very heavy, sir. He'll likely break through the deck of any airship he boards."

"Your lad is either a tad slow or is planning something," Caudill said.

"Ah, so you *do* have the translation files I provided up and running," Martin said, his tone neutral. In Mordanian, Martin added, "You're not to board the airship, David. Just have Tristan and his supplies brought to you. That should solve the problem of Orrons' weight."

I nodded, waved to Orrons, and left the ship. The walk back to the clearing went much faster than my trip to the ship. That's because Orrons simply picked me up and smashed through the debris and trees. I hoped both the Tartegian and Mordanian commanders had spyglasses trained on me. This display of power would do more to convince them of the threat posed by the pirates than anything Martin or I could say or do.

Orrons put me down once we reached the clearing. Happy to be back on my own feet, I looked up at Orrons and waved. "Hey in there. Can you hear me?"

Orrons nodded.

"And you can understand me—even better. I need to signal that airship." I pointed to the command vessel for the Mordanian squadron. "Can you help me with that?"

With a nod, Orrons picked up a flaming tree trunk and waved it like I would wave a stick.

A moment later, the command airship descended. Of far greater importance, the *Pauline* stayed aloft. The last thing I needed was Callan or Megan drawing Orron's attention.

The squadron commander was at the bow when the airship came within easy hailing distance. He snapped off a parade ground salute.

"What can we do for you, Captain Rice?"

The commander, unaware of the mild deception Martin and I had played on Caudill, had just revealed my actual rank to the pirates.

Orrons' armored head tilted down to look at me. Was he reporting this revelation to Caudill? Of course he was. The question was, what kind of reception awaited me when we got back to the spaceship?

I hid my consternation from the squadron commander. He could not know what Martin and I had done nor had he done anything wrong. The fault lay entirely with me. Had I explained the plan to Callan, she would have told her officers and told them how to address me. I could but hope lives were not lost because of my mistake.

"We have injured crewmen aboard the spaceship, Captain Subing,"

I said. “Please ask Tristan—Dr. Agrilla—if he would come with me to the ship so he may tend to them.”

Captain Subing saluted again and his ship returned to the squadron. As the airship pulled alongside the *Pauline*, a mechanical voice issued from the suit. “Explain your deception. Why did you pretend to be subordinate to Captain Bane?”

The voice spoke in Mordanian, meaning the suit’s translation system now included Martin’s translation files. No doubt, Caudill was asking Martin the very same question. If only I knew how Martin would answer.

“Captain Bane is fully capable of commanding this mission and accompanied us by royal request. He speaks your language and knows your culture and your habits. A wise man defers to those with superior knowledge. That’s why we had Martin make first contact with you,” I responded. “When he did not return, I knew we must send someone to investigate. I came because I had to see your ship first-hand. Martin has told us of the ship’s power, but seeing is believing. I treated him as a superior so your captain wouldn’t see me as a threat—which I’m not. Now that I’ve seen your ship and that armor you wear, I realize no one on Aashla could possibly threaten you.”

Orrons nodded but said nothing more. The two of us stood quietly, waiting for the doctor. Fifteen minutes later, Captain Subing’s ship descended again. The crew lowered Tristan’s medical kit, extra supplies, and then Tristan, himself, to the ground. As I worked to free Tristan from the harness, a commotion broke out on the deck above me. Amidst shouted commands from unseen officers, a lithe figure swung over the railing and slid to join us.

Wearing a wicked grin, Megan dropped the last few feet to the ground. Without a word, she helped me free Tristan from the harness.

“Captain Subing? Would you care to explain this woman’s presence?” I called.

“It’s nice to see you again, too, Captain Rice.” Megan’s voice simply dripped with honey.

“I do apologize, sir,” called Subing. “We had no idea she slipped onboard. She must have crossed to my ship while the men were occupied with Dr. Agrilla.”

"That's quite all right, Captain. I've been caught unawares by Megan, as well." I caught Megan by the arm. "Send some men down to fetch her."

"Don't you dare think you can have me manhandled back aboard that ship."

"Oh, I dare. I most certainly dare."

"No," The suit's mechanical voice startled everyone but me. "The woman will come with us."

12

HOSTAGE

Why did Megan have to do this? Caudill had enough leverage over us without having Martin's girlfriend as a hostage. There *had* to be a way to keep Megan out of the pirate spaceship. My mind raced, trying to find it. Leave it to Tristan to find the right approach.

"Do you have any medical experience, young lady? Training as a nurse or anything like that?" Tristan asked.

"I'm a musician, not a doctor." With no concept of the situation and the stakes, Megan got defensive. "How much experience have you got with the guitar?"

"I haven't played since my wife died." Tristan met Megan's challenging glare calmly. "So, definitely no more than forty years."

Megan's eyes widened and her mouth hung slack. I resisted the temptation to reach over and close her mouth.

"As you've no doubt heard, the woman won't be any help with your wounded crew mates," I said to Orrons. Looking up to the airship, I called, "Captain Subing, please send down a properly trained airman."

Orrons turned his attention on Megan and went still—conferring with Caudill, no doubt—then spoke in a booming voice. "Keep your airman aboard the airship. *I* want to bring this woman back to the ship and Captain Caudill has given me permission. He wishes to meet her, as well. Uninjured members of our crew will provide assistance for the doctor."

Megan flashed a triumphant smile and struck off toward the spaceship. I refrained from calling her an idiot, though God only knows how I managed to do it. Orrons lifted most of Tristan's supplies and the four of us trudged in silence toward the spaceship.

After we fought free of the debris and approached the airlock, I gave Tristan and Megan significant looks. "Please remember that none of the crew speak our language. Since Captain Bane comes from their civilization, we must ask Captain Bane to translate for us."

Megan gave me a puzzled glance. "But I thought you-"

Tristan pretended his foot caught on a root. Off balance, he stumbled into Megan and they both tumbled to the ground.

"Ouch!" Megan yelped, pushing at Tristan.

He flailed a bit, as you might expect from an old man, and used that as cover to whisper hastily in Megan's ear. Only then did he manage to push himself up and off of her.

"I am *most* sorry, my dear," he said, offering his hand to Megan to pull her back to her feet. "David, it will be rather awkward if I have to send for Captain Bane whenever I need a translator. Lives may be lost if I must wait for a translator to make my needs clear."

"That's an excellent point, Tristan. It is the first thing I will discuss with both captains when we get inside."

Orrons led us to the bridge. Once we stepped through the hatch, I noticed that Caudill's crew moved to block the hatch. Orrons stepped aside and I realized something had gone seriously wrong.

Caudill stood behind Martin holding a fully charged blaster to Martin's head.

Tristan glared at Caudill. "If this is some twisted form of coercion intended to force me to work on your wounded, I assure you it is unnecessary."

Caudill listened as the computer translated. "I do not threaten Captain Bane in the vain hope it will make you perform miracles. I trust pride will make you to do your best."

Tristan gave a start as the computer translated Caudill's words into Mordanian. "Then why do you hold a...I assume that's a weapon?"

"Yes, doctor, it is a weapon. It crossed my mind that you and your deceitful friend here," Caudill pointed at me with his free hand, "might take this opportunity to drug my crew and me. Unconscious men are *so* much easier to capture than conscious ones." Caudill turned a smile on Megan. "Wouldn't you agree, young lady?"

When the translation singled her out, Megan paled and squeaked, "Me? How should I know about these things?"

"Because it's one of the oldest tricks in the book. The bumbling but beautiful young assistant—that's you, my dear—provides a welcome distraction for a crew too long in space. While the crew concentrates on the obvious charms of his lovely assistant, the doctor administers incapacitating drugs to said crew. Didn't these fine gentlemen tell you the plan before asking you to accompany them?"

Megan looked back and forth between Tristan and me.

"Megan," I said, "not only did I *not* request your company on this mission, I quite specifically told you to stay on the airship."

Caudill shook his head as if in admiration. "Masterful manipulators always make you believe it was *your* idea, Megan."

"Remember who overruled me and insisted you accompany us?" I pointed at the armored figure. "Orrons did, with the added comment that Captain Caudill gave him permission to bring you."

"Captain Caudill, what is more important to you—arguing with Captain Rice or seeing your men receive medical care?" Tristan's stern doctor's voice cut off whatever Caudill was about to say.

Anger flashed in Caudill's eyes. "My crew matters most, of course."

Tristan stared down the angry pirate without expression. "Then perhaps you would be so good as to direct me toward your wounded men?"

"Morrison," Caudill pointed to a crewman, "will take you to them. Captain Rice will accompany you as an assistant. The lovely Megan will stay on the bridge. Captain Bane and I will be glad of such delightful company."

The look on Martin's face said no such thing, but there was nothing I could do. Megan fidgeted as Morrison helped Tristan and me gather the medical equipment. Her eyes darted around the bridge, perhaps searching for a place to hide. As irritating as her impetuosity was, I pitied her.

"Orrons told me that you're a musician, Megan." Caudill smiled, once again the charming and congenial host. "Perhaps you would grace us with a song?"

Megan nodded, the jerky movement of someone unsure of what to do. Then, her voice quavering but still beautiful, Megan began to sing. With horror, I realized the song she'd chosen was *Rupor's Lament*.

13

EMERGENCY DRONE

As she sang, Megan's posture straightened and her voice gained strength. Singing obviously calmed the woman. If only it would calm me, as well.

There once was a prince,
Handsome and gay,
Who loved a princess,
Lovely but fey.

I could not allow Megan to continue singing this song. The minute she sang the verse ridiculing the story of my arrival on Aashla would be my last. But I could think of no way to stop her without arousing Caudill's suspicions to the point he would kill me anyway.

"By all that's holy," Martin cried, "I beg you to kill me now so I don't have to listen to that insipid song one more time."

Startled, her face coloring red, Megan stopped singing.

Caudill looked at Martin, an eyebrow cocked. "From what little I heard, it was but a love song. Do you have a problem with love songs, Bane?"

"Oh no, not at all. Who wouldn't love such a song?" Martin sneered. "It's all about a handsome prince who falls in love with a beautiful princess. But the princess jilts the prince and marries a member of her royal guard. If you've got any lovestruck teenage girls in your crew, summon them forthwith! I have no doubt they will love every single sentimental verse."

"Fine," Megan snapped. "If you dislike it so much, I'll sing something else."

Megan's next song was a traditional ballad with no mention of crash-landed scouts anywhere.

With the brief dramatic outburst over, Morrison motioned for Tristan and me to follow him. He led us through the ship to a cargo bay that had been adapted to hold the wounded. Close to forty men lay within, some as still as death, others fidgeting and impatient to leave.

Tristan pointed to three men. "David, please have these men moved to those tables across the room. They're in the most danger."

The computer translated Tristan's words for Morrison, who frowned. "Four of the men are in worse shape than those three. Start with them."

When the computer finished with speaking the translation, Tristan turned a frosty look on Morrison. "Are you a doctor young man?"

"No, but it's obvious to anyone who isn't blind who's worse off, old man."

"Those four men are beyond my help. I will not waste time with them while there are those I can help." Tristan turned back to me. "Begin triage once you've moved those three men."

For the next hour, I worked my way through the room, rearranging the wounded as instructed, while Tristan did what he could for those who might be saved. When I finished, I stood and stretched my sore back—and spotted lights flickering against the back wall. Curious, I took a closer look.

A Space Forces decryption machine—stolen, no doubt—churned through a decryption routine. A metal tube—one I recognized immediately—was connected to it. The tube was the emergency drone I'd launched when my scout ship exited the wormhole.

Morrison, Caudill's representative in the cargo bay-cum-sickbay, saw me staring at the decryption machine and emergency drone. "Hey, you. We don't have any wounded crew over there. What do you think you're doing?"

I turned at Morrison's call but dutifully waited for the computer to finish translating his words before answering. "I just saw these things glowing and blinking and got curious. I've never seen anything like it before. What does it do?"

"That's none of your business. It's too advanced for a yokel like you and doesn't have anything to do with medicine." Morrison pointed toward Tristan's makeshift surgery. "Now get back to helping the old man with the surgery. I don't want any of my friends dying because you were too busy gawking at pretty lights to help."

"It looks like the doctor has everything under control, but if that's where you want me..." I shrugged and went over to Tristan.

"Our gracious host sounded irritated. What was that all about?" he asked.

"I have no idea, Tristan." I hooked a thumb over my shoulder toward the decryption machine. "They've got a machine over there that has some kind of lights that glow and blink. Morrison says it's beyond the understanding of a yokel like me. I'm sure he's right."

Tristan raised his eyebrows. "Is that so? Well, if they're so smart why do they need a yokel doctor to tend to their wounded?"

That was a very good question—one I hadn't given much thought to. Any ship this size should have at least one docbot—maybe even a human doctor—plus a plentiful supply of medical nanites. Caudill might want to conserve his supplies, but he'd already lost half of his crew to the inertial dampener failure. The pirate captain couldn't afford to lose any more crewmen if he ever hoped to fly this ship again. Most of their medical supplies must have been lost along with the men. The transition out of the wormhole would have pulverized those supplies along with the men. That thought got me wondering what other equipment and supplies might have been lost, as well. Maybe Caudill's position wasn't as strong as I had feared.

Later, when Tristan and I were tending to the last few wounded crewmen, Caudill came to inspect our work. Caudill worked his way through the room, speaking to every crewman who was conscious. When Tristan reported that five of the men probably wouldn't survive,

Caudill bowed his head in sorrow. If he was acting, he did a masterful job of it. Caudill knew how to inspire loyalty in his crew.

"My men will need food and better accommodations than this cargo bay," Caudill said to me. "I want to send a message to Prince Rupor and Princess Callan informing them that I wish to negotiate for the care of my men."

14

NOT STUPID

IT TOOK ALL THE CONTROL I HAD TO KEEP MY EXPRESSION NEUTRAL UNTIL the computerized translation ended. How had Caudill found out about Callan and Rupor? I trusted Martin to keep silent and, impetuous and thoughtless as she could be, I doubted Megan would talk, either. Not voluntarily, at least. Had Caudill forced one of them to talk by threatening the other? I'd find out soon enough.

I had to keep Callan and Rupor as far from Caudill as humanly possible. I played the only card I had. "Tell me what you need, Captain Caudill. I am authorized to negotiate on the behalf of their Highnesses."

I longed to speak in gal base. Waiting for translations I didn't need wore on my nerves.

Caudill turned an appraising look on me. "I suspect you really could negotiate for one of the countries. What's the one with the princess?"

"Mordan."

"Yes, Mordan. And the country with the prince?"

"Tarteg."

"Right. Them, not so much, I think."

"I'm sure the two kingdoms will work together to take care of you and your men," I said.

"I doubt that. You remember Orrons, of course. The man in the big suit of armor?"

"He's rather hard to forget. What of him?"

"You saw how easily Orrons waved that tree trunk? It's the armor that makes that possible."

"I assumed as much."

"You did?" Caudill looked closely at me. "For a man from a backward planet, you have a surprising grasp of modern technology, Captain Rice."

"No, I have a surprising grasp of common sense." I put a little irritation into my voice. "I may be ignorant of your worlds and your machines, but I'm not stupid."

"Stupid, no. Dangerous, yes."

"Was there a point to your comment about the armor, Captain?"

"There was. As you probably guessed, using the armor for brute strength is so easy even you could do it."

Of course I could. I'd received plenty of training in powered armor at the academy.

Caudill continued, "The real skill is handling fragile things without breaking them. Very few people can do that. Orrons is a master. No, it goes beyond that. He's a true artist." Caudill held his palms a foot apart. "Imagine a pretty musician's head between armored hands. Slowly—so slowly the human eye can't discern the movement—the hands press together. Inexorable pressure builds in the skull, causing exquisite pain. How much pressure can a human skull take before it cracks? For a former pirate, Captain Bane proved surprisingly uncurious about the answer. And he succumbs to persuasion rather easily." Caudill shook his head in mock disgust. "All it took was one scream.

"As a native of this planet, you know Tarteg and Mordan have warred for centuries. Now I know as well. And that's information a man like me can put to good use. You see, Rice, I'm not really negotiating with the prince or the princess. I'm selling my ship and services to the highest bidder."

Caudill's smile was as cold as his eyes. "With me backing one of those kingdoms, the next war between Tarteg and Mordan will also be the last war between them."

15

SUBTERFUGE

"Decades have passed since the last war between Mordan and Tarteg," I said. "You're counting on an enmity that doesn't run very deep anymore."

Caudill laughed when the computer completed translating my words. "How very optimistic of you, Rice. Old enmities can lay dormant for ages and then, when you least expect it, spring back with full vigor. And a peace that is desirable when neither country holds a military advantage becomes a burden when you can crush your enemy."

"Are you so certain your experiences on other planets apply here? I doubt you've ever been on a world like Aashla."

"Men are men wherever they live. And some men will always seek power over their fellows. It's our nature."

Caudill was right, something I knew from bitter experience. But I hoped he was wrong about Tarteg and Mordan. "I'll defer to your extensive experience in that matter. Meanwhile, are you sure you want to send someone as dangerous as me to deliver your message?"

Caudill turned an appraising eye on me. "Now that is an interesting question, Rice. You've piqued my curiosity—who would you send?"

"I'd send Megan. Her skills are of no use to you nor to the prince and princess. Your position is not weakened and theirs is not strengthened." It was a long shot, but worth trying.

"That's an interesting and accurate analysis." Caudill rubbed his chin. "Except you left out one vital point. Megan has great value as a hostage against Bane's good behavior. And, if I read you and the old doctor right, she'll insure your good behavior as well. While sending her doesn't strengthen the prince and princess, it does weaken me. No, you'll deliver my message."

"Fine. Give me the message then Orrons and I can leave."

"As long as I have your friends, I see no reason to waste Orrons' time. I'm sure a fine young officer such as yourself can deliver a message without supervision."

Five minutes later, I picked my way through the debris outside the spaceship, trying to figure out why Caudill hadn't sent Orrons with me. There were many possible reasons, but only one that fits our current situation so neatly. Caudill wanted to conserve the suit's power. Had his armor recharging unit been destroyed in the crash? It seemed likely.

Perhaps Caudill's position wasn't nearly as strong as he wanted us to believe.

As before, it took fifteen minutes to work my way clear of the debris from the pirate ship's crash landing. Once I reached clear terrain, I waved to the airships floating in the distance. Almost immediately, one of the Mordanian ships broke formation and descended.

When the airship was close enough, I called, "Captain Subing, drop a line so I can come aboard. I must speak with Their Highnesses."

The ascent seemed to take forever but lasted no more than ten minutes. Captain Subing smartly maneuvered his ship alongside the *Pauline.* Callan and Rupor leaned against the little airship's railing, all signs of the earlier tension gone. The two future monarchs chatted amicably and tried to hide their apprehension over the news I brought. Callan gave me a dazzling smile that did not wipe away the concern in her eyes. Rupor wore a neutral expression, but I saw tension lines in his brow.

"Callan, greet me as you would any other naval officer." I saluted as the sailors tied the airships together. "Holding Megan gives Caudill leverage over Martin and led to unfortunate, though understandable, revelations. Caudill is certain to watch this meeting. As I must return to him after our conference, I don't want him getting the idea he can use me to gain equal leverage over you."

I vaulted over to the *Pauline* and bowed respectfully to Callan and Rupor, just as any officer would do. Callan wore what I called her court face, which she adopted whenever she sat in royal court. It gave her that serene, knowledgable look subjects want to see in their monarch. The court face must be something royal family members learn in the nursery, as Rupor wore the male version of the expression.

I outlined what I saw inside the spaceship as well as the situation with Megan, Martin, and Tristan. I spent a lot of time explaining the destructive power of Caudill's weapons. But I spent the most time trying to explain what it meant if Caudill couldn't recharge the powered armor. Callan and Rupor concentrated hard on my explanation, asking several questions.

"If I follow what you're saying," Callan mused, "it's like tossing the last of your fuel into a boiler while your airship is flying in the middle of a desert. You can run the steam engine for a while, but once you're out of fuel the engine becomes nothing more than a useless hunk of metal."

"That's a fair description of the situation, Callan." I said. And Rupor nodded, his furrowed brow clearing after listening to Callan's analogy.

"In that case, our course is obvious." Rupor smiled, definitely happy to be back on more familiar ground. "As part of these negotiations, Callan and I must convince this pirate to burn what fuel he has left for his armor."

16

SIGNALS FLAGS AND RADIOS

"THAT'S A GREAT IDEA, RUPOR, BUT HAVE YOU GOT ANY IDEA HOW TO GET Caudill to do it?" I asked.

"No prince—or princess—worthy of the title would ever purchase someone's services without personally observing their capabilities," Rupor answered. "Waving a tree trunk around, while quite impressive, is hardly a sufficient demonstration to warrant the kind of money Caudill no doubt wants."

"That's an excellent point, Rupor," Callan responded. "David, tell Caudill we will only consider bidding after we've seen what his armored man can do."

"*I* know what that man can do and I don't want either of you getting anywhere close to him," I said. "For your own safety and the safety of your kingdoms, you two must watch Caudill's show from afar. You must also watch from different ships which hold positions far from each other."

"If you think that's best, David, Rupor and I will do as you suggest."

Rupor nodded his agreement. "But that still leaves us with a problem. Callan and I must have some way to communicate with this pirate. How else can we tell him what we wish to see?"

"Devices exist that allow people to talk across long distances. Captain Rice isn't supposed to know about them, so I'll have to make sure Caudill thinks to suggest them." I saluted and then hopped across to Captain Subing's ship. "Take me down, Captain."

Twenty minutes later, I presented Their Highness's demand for a demonstration to Caudill. It did not surprise me in the least that the idea had no appeal to him.

"How dare those spoiled, inbred barbarians make demands of me. They have *seen* the powered armor at work." Caudill stood inches from me, his shout filling the small bridge. "Can anyone on this backward planet wave a tree trunk around like it's a twig? No, they cannot!" Caudill pressed his thumb on the arm of is chair. "I could squash them and their pathetic kingdoms, if I so desired!"

I kept my face impassive and waited for the translation to complete. "If you are so powerful, Captain Caudill, why even bother offering your services to the highest bidder?"

Martin chuckled, "The lad has you there, Caudill. These people may be technologically primitive, but they are not stupid. The two kingdoms may *want* your services, but they do not *need* them. You, alas, are in the exact opposite situation."

"I hold the four of you hostage," Caudill shot back. "Those arrogant royals should pause and consider that."

"Sorry, old chap, but we're all Mordanian. I'm sure Her Highness will be quite put out if something happens to us, but I doubt Prince Rupor could care less. You're the one counting on old enmities returning in full force yet you expect a Tartegian to temper his demands to save the lives of Mordanian subjects?"

Caudill turned back to me. "Earlier, you said you could negotiate for both countries. I accept your offer. Let's negotiate."

I shook my head. "I could have negotiated before Their Highnesses got involved. I no longer have that authority. You negotiate with them or you don't negotiate at all."

"And if you don't negotiate," Martin added, "you don't get the food and medicine you need. That's quite a quandary you've landed yourself in, Caudill."

Caudill ranted and raged for another ten minutes, but my refusal to negotiate blocked his every suggestion. In the end, he agreed to the demonstration.

"Have the prince and princess land so we can get on with this circus." Caudill turned away, thinking our conversation was at an end.

I dutifully waited for the translation before speaking. "Their Highnesses will be viewing the demonstration from their airships."

Caudill whirled back to me, his face red. "After all of this, they aren't even going to come down and watch? No. Absolutely not."

"The royal heirs of the two most powerful kingdoms on Aashla do not endanger themselves needlessly." I put every bit of offense I could muster into my voice. After listening to this murderous pirate denigrate my wife, I found I had quite a lot of offense to draw upon.

"Then how will they communicate with me?"

"We'll use signal flags. The ships have skilled flagmen. Demands and comments will fly between their ships and us in a matter of minutes."

"Minutes? Tell me you're joking."

"Not at all Captain Caudill."

"Oh for God's sake, Caudill," Martin snapped, "give them a couple of handheld radios if you're too impatient for the flags."

Eyes blazing, Caudill called for radios. I could only hope the rest of the plan went as smoothly.

17

REMOVE HIS HELMET

THE LOGISTICS OF THE POWER SUIT DEMONSTRATION TOOK A WHILE TO setup. I took the radios to Callan and Rupor and explained how they worked. Then I offered a suggestion.

“After Caudill shows you a few basic things, Rupor should ask for a demonstration of weapons systems.”

“I agree we should see this man’s weapons at work, but what if Caudill asks how we know about... Drat, what was the red light called?”

“Stick with calling it a red light. Martin is the only one who knows the name and he never had a chance to tell you,” I said. “Since you’ve seen that in person, it’s easy to explain your curiosity. Seeing one weapon in action will pique your curiosity over other weapons.”

Callan nodded. “I’ll let Rupor ask about weapons first, but we’ll both demand to see more.”

“Good. One final thing—have your ships keep moving. They don’t have to move too fast, just fast enough to make targeting difficult.”

Rupor scratched his head. “Don’t they have some machine that makes aiming easier? It seems like they have a machine for everything else.”

“They do, but they’re designed to target other spaceships. I can’t go into the details now, but those machines aren’t designed to target steam-powered airships. In simple terms, the machine can't see the airship. That means aiming manually, which is a lot harder." I looked back and forth between Rupor and Callan. "Just promise me you'll turn and fly away if the pirates fire at you."

They both gave me their assurances, as did the captains of the ships they'd be aboard while observing. Then I was returned to the ground, where I contacted Caudill by radio.

"Everything is set for the demonstration, Captain Caudill," I radioed.

"Very well, Orrons and I are coming out."

That was unexpected. I hadn't expected Caudill to step foot outside the spaceship any time soon. Perhaps I could find some way to turn this to our advantage.

"Remember my crew holds your three friends," Caudill growled, as if reading my mind. "And, of course, Orrons can break you into little pieces. So don't get any ideas and don't try anything."

Moments later, Orrons tromped out to join me, Caudill riding on his shoulder. Orrons gently lowered Caudill to the ground and then awaited orders.

Caudill proved to be quite the showman, putting Orrons through a range of impressive maneuvers. And Orrons proved to be the powered-armor artist Caudill said he was. The longer I watched Orrons, the more I found myself praying the armor's charge would run out soon—*very* soon.

After ten minutes, Caudill spoke into his radio, "That's more than sufficient. Do either of you have any questions before the bidding begins?"

I expected Rupor to ask for the laser demonstration, but Callan got in first and with an unexpected request.

"Yes, have him remove his helmet. I'd like to see Orrons' face."

"Why would you care what he looks like, princess?" Irritation crept into Caudill's voice. "What's important is what he can *do*, not what he looks like."

"Martin has told us of mechanical men. How do we know this isn't some machine that will always do your bidding?"

"I find myself concurring with Callan," Rupor said. "I also wish assurances Orrons is not some form of construct."

Caudill pondered then sighed. "Fine... Take off the helmet, Orrons."

Callan's request created a crack in the powered armor. I only had to find a way to exploit it.

18

HE'S A SCOUT

ORRONS LIFTED HIS HANDS TOWARD THE NECK OF THE POWERED ARMOR and the metal fingers danced and tapped around the seam. Slide locks opened and button locks depressed. After a few seconds, the helmet popped up a fraction of an inch. Orrons grasped the helmet and lifted it off of his head.

I don't know what I expected to see—the scarred and hardened face of a pirate, I suppose. I did *not* expect to find a boy, no more than sixteen or seventeen, looking down at me. I wasn't the only one surprised by the sight.

"Why he's no more than a child!" Callan's voice exclaimed over the radio.

Teenage annoyance filled Orrons' face after hearing the translation.

"Boy he may be," Caudill said, "but Orrons is highly skilled with the powered armor and will follow my orders to the letter. Be it crushing your foes or crushing that musician's head, Orrons is man enough to handle the job."

Orrons smiled with pride and nodded to his captain. "Aye aye, Cap'n."

Rupor's voice crackled from the radio. "Unlike Her Highness, I'm not concerned over the lad's age. I *am* concerned that you speak of the lad obeying your orders. If I employ him, I expect him to follow my orders, as well."

"That's an entirely reasonable expectation, Prince Rupor." Caudill smiled broadly at this more traditional question. "All I need to do is order Orrons to obey your orders and he will do it. You do understand that he won't turn against me or any of my men."

"Of course." Rupor's tone said this was perfectly right and natural. "I wouldn't trust a turncoat, anyway."

"All right, I believe we've had more than enough talking," Caudill said. "It's time to get down to the bidding."

"I did have one more request-"

The radio crackled to life, interrupting Rupor. "Captain? You requested a call if a certain task was completed while you were outside. It's done."

"Excellent! There were times I feared it never would end." Caudill said. "What have you got for me?"

With Caudill distracted by the call and Orrons watching his captain, I studied Orrons, looking for a weakness. It didn't take long to determine the boy's head was his only weakness. If I kept him from donning the helmet again, I could knock him out.

"I've got something very interesting, indeed," came the reply. "I think you should return to the ship and hear my report in private."

"There is no need for me to go to all that trouble," Caudill said, impatience in his tone. "Just turn off the translator and spit it out. Whatever you have to say will be private enough."

"That's just it, Captain," the voice responded. "The report won't be private at all."

With a sinking feeling, I suddenly realized they'd broken the encryption on the emergency drone launched by my ship.

Caudill's bantering tone vanished. "What do you mean by that?"

The radio crackled. "That man with you isn't a native of this planet. He's Terran Scout First Class David Rice."

19

YOU'VE GOT HIM NOW

CAUDILL SPUN AROUND AND STARED AT ME, HIS EYES AS WARM AND FILLED with humanity as the eyes of a snake. His gaze flicked to Orrons. In a voice as devoid of emotion as his eyes, Caudill said, "Kill him."

Upon hearing the order, Orrons' face transformed. Pride in Caudill's compliment fell away as Orrons' lips spread in a feral grin. His eyes went cold as the flash of humanity faded. Looking into that face, it was no longer possible to think of Orrons as a normal teenager. Before me stood a sick and twisted human being—one who could crush me without even trying.

"And Orrons," Caudill added in a conversational tone, "we're trying to make an impression on an audience. So please do your best to make his death messy."

Now emotion flowed into Orrons' eyes, but it was not comforting in the least. No one could take solace from the anticipation shining in Orrons' eyes.

I only had one possible response to the threat Orrons represented.

Boost!

Time slowed as my implant poured adrenaline into my body. Orrons, already slowed by the cumbersome powered armor, moved in extreme slow motion as he lifted his arms to replace the helmet. If I was going to have any chance in this fight, I had to keep that helmet off of Orrons' head.

I charged Orrons, grabbing the helmet and swinging my feet up to plant on Orrons' chest plate. The armored boy shifted his grip, anticipating that I would pull the helmet from his hands. The suit's mechanical muscles made that impossible. Even Boosted, my strength couldn't match his. But I had a lot more experience than the young Orrons and went with something he never expected. I shoved the helmet at Orrons' head. With Orrons already pulling the helmet toward himself, the helmet slammed into Orrons' face. Blood spurted from his smashed nose and he instinctively released the helmet to hold his nose.

Helmet in hand, I shoved off the chest plate, flipping to land ten feet from the boy. Spinning, I flung the helmet as far from the three of us as possible.

Flowing blood and burning rage turned Orrons' face a mottled crimson. With a bellow, Orrons rushed toward me, his teeth bared, a guttural snarl on his lips. I held my ground, diving to the right just before the armored boy trampled me under his metal feet. Orrons thundered past but dug in his feet and, leaving twin furrows in the ground, slid to a stop far more quickly than I liked.

I had hoped to draw Orrons far out of position, giving me an opening to charge Caudill. If I got my hands on him, the fight was all but over. Orrons obviously worshipped Caudill and wouldn't do anything to risk his piratical father figure. But my hope was in vain. Caudill moved constantly, always keeping Orrons between us.

Orrons charged again. I dodged again. And, damn him, Caudill moved again. This fight reminded me of my fight with the trog leader in Faroon, back before Callan and I were married. I couldn't afford to let the trog get his hands on me then and I definitely couldn't let Orrons get hold of me now. The difference was Orrons had but one vulnerable spot—his head. And, because the pirates frowned on armed guests aboard their spaceship, I didn't even have a sword.

"Calm down, Orrons. You're just running around like a child. Slow down and take your time," Caudill called. "The scout can't use his Boost for much more than a minute. Be patient and wait him out."

And there was my one minor advantage. Caudill knew nothing of my extensive history with Boost. Could I draw Orrons in close by pretending to lose Boost? If I sold the act well enough, I'd have one chance to sucker punch Orrons. To have any hope of knocking him out with one blow, I had to hit him with something harder than my fist. I found that something the next time I dived and rolled away from Orrons. Pain lanced through my back as I landed on a rock twice the size of my fist. Ignoring the pain, I grabbed that rock and a smaller one close by.

Coming out of the roll, I flung the smaller rock at Orrons' head. He brought his arm up and the rock clanged off the armor. Then I staggered, held a hand to my head, and bent over.

"What did I tell you, lad?" Caudill crowed. "You've got him now. Remember to make his death messy."

Orrons grinned, stomping up to me. After chasing me all around the clearing, the teenager simply could not resist the temptation to gloat. A nasty smile on his face, Orrons leaned in close.

Grinning myself, I rose from my crouch and smashed the rock into Orrons' head.

20

SATISFACTION

DRIVEN BY MY BOOSTED STRENGTH, I EXPECTED TO HEAR THE SATISFYING thunk of stone on bone. That would be followed by Orrons toppling to the ground, unconscious. None of that happened. Instead, I heard the clunk of rock on metal.

Orrons yelled in pain and flailed his arms at me, knocking me away from him. An arm caught a glancing blow against my chest, knocking the wind out of me and sending me flying from him. I crashed to the ground a good thirty feet from the armored figure. Then I tumbled heels over head for another ten feet.

When I stopped rolling, everything hurt. I could do nothing but gasp to draw breath into my empty lungs. Dazed, I couldn't concentrate well enough to override my implant's safety protocols. Those protocols, incapable of judging anything but my physical condition, decided Boost was more harm than good and shut it off. Unable to move, I could do nothing but stare into the bright sky. Absently, I noticed several of the airships break from their holding patterns and descend under full power. To my dismay, I recognized the *Pauline* leading the way. No doubt Nist acted under orders from Callan. Why couldn't she understand how much I needed to keep her safe?

"That was quite a show you and Orrons put on, Rice. You should have seen the look on your face when you hit Orrons metal skull plate. It was priceless." Caudill laughed as the heavy tread of armored feet started toward me. "Do you want to know why Orrons is so skilled with the armor? I had his brain wired with a direct neural interface when he was five years old. That kind of interface gives a man astounding control over the armor. As an added bonus, Orrons got a metal skull. He's had a dozen years to practice since the operation, too. Add all that together and you get a true artist with powered armor."

I knew of many people with neural interfaces, but they got theirs as adults. No reputable doctor would even consider installing one in such a young, still-developing brain. The child was almost certain to die a hideously painful death.

"Are you insane? How many children died before you succeeded with Orrons?" I wheezed, finally starting to regain my breath.

"Let me think. Four boys, two girls. So, only six."

"Only? *Only*? How can you live with yourself?"

"Quite easily. After all, I did succeed with Orrons."

Then Orrons loomed over me, blocking the sun. He raised his foot, planning to stomp the life out of me, I assumed. Instead, Orrons rested his foot on my chest. The weight of the foot, alone and without any pressure from Orrons, sent pain shooting through my bruised ribs. Meanwhile, I scrambled to discover some way to escape from this with my life.

"I'm going to take my time killing you." Orrons' smile twisted in a sick imitation of joy. "This will be like squeezing that woman's head between my hands. I'll build the pressure so slowly you won't feel it at first. Second by second, the pain will build until your bones begin to crack. Then it will continue building until your organs pop. And all the time, I'll be right here, looking you in the eye as you die."

"You are one truly sick and twisted boy, Orrons." I looked at Caudill. "You must be so proud of him."

"Indeed I am, Rice." Caudill regarded the armored boy with something akin to paternal pride. "Orrons is absolutely loyal and he never questions my orders. In many ways, Orrons is the son I never had."

"Like any sane woman would ever have a child with you," I spat through teeth gritted against the pain. "How much do you have to pay them to be with you, Caudill? Or are you the type who prefers a woman in a drugged stupor?"

All emotion fled Caudill's face. Dead eyes met mine and, in a flat tone, he said, "You'd be surprised just how many women want a man exactly like me, Rice. They may deny it, but I can see the desire in their eyes. But enough of this chit chat. This game grows tiresome. My time is valuable and yours, alas, is short. I believe it's past time to finish you. Orrons-"

The radio crackled to life and Callan's voice burst forth. "Spare David's life and I'll give you everything you're asking for!"

Caudill's eyebrows rose and he gave me an appraising look. "David? Not Captain Rice? Well, Your Highness, that *is* an interesting development—one I find very intriguing. Princess Callan, would you care to elaborate on the true nature of your relationship with the nearly deceased captain?"

Silence stretched for several seconds.

"No? Then perhaps you would allow me to make a guess. Forced to marry against her wishes and now trapped in a political marriage—to the prince of a troublesome neighboring kingdom, perhaps—the young princess found true love in the arms of the dashing and mysterious Captain Rice." Caudill's smirk returned in full force. "How am I doing, princess? Please do let me know if I've gotten the wrong idea."

Once again, Callan held her silence.

"I'm sure your story would have quite a romantic ending if you didn't already have a husband." Caudill shook his head in mock dismay. "That's quite an unfortunate detail—unless you and Captain Rice have plans to do away with the unfortunate fellow. Am I on the right trail?"

Callan's continued silence kept Caudill heading down the wrong path.

"And what of poor, betrayed Prince Rupor. I wonder if he will reward me better for killing Rice than you will for sparing him?"

"I most certainly will not reward you for killing that man!" Rupor's voice burst from the radio. "But if you grant me the satisfaction of killing him myself, I'll give you everything you're asking for and more."

Caudill's smirk broadened into a smile of true pleasure. "That,

Prince Rupor, is an offer I simply cannot refuse. Captain Rice is yours to kill."

21

A FAIR FIGHT

Orrons sulked at Caudill's order to remove his foot from my chest, but he did as he was told. Obeying a second order from Caudill, Orrons stood straddling me, insuring I stayed put.

"Prince Rupor," Caudill said, "I suggest you have Her Highness attend this event along with you."

"I see no reason for that," Rupor replied.

"You don't? Then perhaps you have earned the disrespect she shows to you." Caudill's voice took on an edge, "If you coddle Princess Callan and shield her from witnessing the end result of her infidelity, you will simply encourage her to stray again."

"There is no need to order me to attend. I *insist* on witnessing this duel, Rupor!" Callan replied. "I will take great pleasure in watching David slice you to pieces."

"Foolish woman, where did you get the idea that Rice would be armed?" Caudill snarled. "I promised Prince Rupor he could kill Rice. I did not promise Rupor could duel with him."

"That is unacceptable, Captain Caudill." Rupor struck a perfect tone of effrontery. "Rice *must* be armed and I must slay him in a fair fight. It is the only way I can restore my tattered honor."

Caudill stared at the radio in disbelief, but he desperately needed

Rupor's aid and good will. "If you say the fight must be fair, then fair it shall be. Her Highness may bring a sword for Rice."

With an annoyed shake of the head, Caudill turned off his radio and turned to me. "Don't think you've earned a reprieve, Rice. Should you manage to win this duel, I will have Orrons kill Princess Callan. After you've seen your lady love ripped apart by Orrons, I'll have him do the same to you. So, if you truly love Princess Callan, I very strongly suggest you let Rupor slay you. Orrons will do the same thing if you make any attempt to warn her. Are we clear on this matter?"

I nodded.

"Oh, and I hope I don't need to remind you to make this look convincing."

I shook my head.

"Good. Enjoy the next few minutes. They're all you have left."

With that cheery comment, Caudill fell silent as we waited for Their Highnesses to arrive. The *Pauline*, bearing Callan, began descending when Caudill discovered my real identity. The fast little ship was minutes ahead of the others and was the first to arrive.

Nist brought the *Pauline* to within three feet of the ground and flew toward us. The airship moved slowly compared to an aircar—so slowly that I doubt Caudill ever realized just how fast the airship was flying. As the ship came adjacent to Orrons and me, Nist twisted the controls and spun the *Pauline* sideways. The stern swung around and smacked into Orrons back.

Small for an airship, the *Pauline* still greatly out-massed the armored boy. Orrons flew ten feet away, landing in a sprawl. Like an angel from heaven, Callan dropped my sword into my hand.

22

NO OTHER CHOICE

I DREW MY SWORD AND SPRANG TO MY FEET AS NIST THREW THE *PAULINE'S* throttle wide open and twisted the ailerons up. The airship nosed up but it would be long seconds before it was too high for Orrons to jump to it.

Servos whined as Orrons shoved off the ground with mechanically enhanced strength. Popping up and onto his feet, the boy's eyes smoldered and his face went white with rage.

"I'm going to pull off your arms and legs and then laugh while you die, Rice!" Orrons' voice cracked as he screamed my name.

"Hey, at long last you've hit puberty." I could only hope goading worked as well on the boy as it had on Raoul.

Orrons roared wordlessly and lumbered toward me. Good, better me than the airship.

"Rice has already Boosted, Orrons. He's just a normal man, now. I can handle him," Caudill yelled over the roar of the *Pauline's* steam engine. "You go teach the crew of that airship what it means to mess with a man wearing powered armor. I want the princess alive but you can do what you wish with the rest."

Orrons turned toward the rising *Pauline*, flexed his knees, and jumped. He caught hold of a piece of the airship's ornate trimming. I hoped the trim would break off in Orrons hand, but the airship was too well made. It held and Orrons climbed toward the deck. I didn't even pause to consider my next action.

Boost!

Orrons and Caudill were in for quite a surprise. I leapt after Orrons, catching hold of a foot. Then I used Orrons like a ladder and climbed over him to the deck. As Orrons pulled himself over the railing, I bounded to his shoulders and jumped to the deck ahead of him.

Sword drawn, one of Callan's guards rushed at the armored figure. With a bellow, Orrons backhanded the guard, sending him crashing against the cabin. Knowing there was no reasoning with the boy, I charged. As expected, Orrons' swung his fist at me. I ducked under the punch, grabbed Orrons' elbow, and swung around the arm and onto his back.

My sword flashed in the sunlight as I swung at the only unprotected part of Orrons' body—his neck. The blade sliced through flesh and bone with ease. In terrible slow motion, Orrons' head spun through the air before dropping over the railing.

The powered armor stumbled forward a few steps, following the residual impulses left after Orrons' death. The headless figure hit the far railing and tottered off balance. Before the internal stabilizers could restore the balance, two of Callan's guards slammed into it from behind. The armor tumbled over the side of the airship and fell from sight.

I dropped Boost as I collapsed to my knees and buried my head in my hands. Tears stung my eyes as the full impact of my actions hit me. Orrons was barely older than Milo—a child with his whole life ahead of him. My mind replayed the scene, searching for anything I could have done to save Orrons. In a grotesque mockery of reality, in my mind the severed head spinning away belonged to Milo rather than Orrons.

Then a pair of arms wrapped around me and rocked me in a tight embrace. I felt warm breath on my cheek and soft lips kiss away my tears. Callan.

In ragged gasps, I said, "He was just a boy, Callan. But I didn't hesitate to kill him."

"You had no other choice, David," Callan whispered fiercely.

"How can you be so sure?" I asked.

"I looked into his eyes and recognized what I saw in them," Callan said. "I saw the same thing in the eyes of King Rat when he tried to kill you. And I saw it in Raoul's eyes when he thought Gort had killed you. I'm sure I'd have seen it had I ever looked Windslow in the eyes, too. You cannot reason with madness, David."

My reply died in my throat as a red beam of light blazed overhead. The laser punctured the *Pauline's* gas envelope and then the beam tracked along the taut fabric. The beam easily burned a long cut in the envelope. The envelope collapsed and the *Pauline* dropped out of the sky.

23

MY UNDIVIDED ATTENTION

I WRAPPED A PROTECTIVE ARM AROUND CALLAN AND GRABBED A LINE WITH my free hand. Next to me, Nist worked the ailerons furiously. Surely he realized the airship was falling from the sky. What did he hope to accomplish? We weren't more than thirty feet above the ground. The fall probably wouldn't be fatal but it was far enough to cause serious injuries.

"Everybody, slide when we hit the ground!" Nist shouted.

I had just enough time to wonder what he meant by that when the *Pauline* tilted sharply to starboard. I suddenly understood Nist's plan and my respect for the man's skill as a pilot—already considerable—rose several more notches. The tilt would allow the airship to land on its hull rather than the much stronger keel. Then the collapsing hull could absorb much of the force from the impact. The angled deck allowed us to slide to the ground, dissipating even more of the force in the slide.

The *Pauline* struck the ground and my ears were filled with the sounds of breaking timber and shouting men. I released the line and wrapped my other arm around Callan. Then I lifted her off the deck, protecting her from splinters, scrapes, and cuts as best I could. My feet slammed into the starboard railing and my knees flexed to absorb the impact. Pain shot up my legs and agony burst anew from my bruised and battered chest. Then all was quiet except for the groans of the *Pauline* and her crew. With a soft rustle of fabric, the gas envelope settled over us and blocked everything from view.

"Callan, are you all right?"

"I'm a little shaken up, but fine. What about you?" she said.

"Never better." I eased my grip on Callan. "Nist?"

"Over here."

"That was brilliant flying."

"But I broke the *Pauline*."

"Callan and I will see that she is rebuilt as good as new. You have my word," I assured him.

Fighting our way clear of the collapsed envelope, Callan and I emerged into the sunlight. Before us stood Caudill, his laser pistol trained on me. Knowing the pirate could burn a hole through my head before I could do anything to stop him, I went very still. Then Callan wriggled out next to me.

"I found your sword, darling. You-" She broke off as she noticed Caudill.

"Have her slide the sword to me," Caudill said.

"You're trusting me to translate accurately?" I said. "Why don't you turn on your radio and let the ship's translator handle that for you?"

"You've already Boosted twice today, something I'd thought impossible until now. If I split my attention between you and the radio for even a second, you might Boost a third time and take my laser."

Yeah, my plan was exactly that.

Caudill continued, "Instead, I'll just give you my undivided attention and let you translate. Oh, and tell your guards to stay where they are or I'll burn both of you down."

"What about the pilot?" I asked.

"That was quite a clever job he did landing this tub. I'd say he's much too clever to leave where I can't see him. He will come out as well. Hands empty and where I can see them, of course."

"Callan, slide my sword to Caudill." I raised my voice. "Everyone besides Nist, stay under the envelope. Nist, show empty hands first, then you can crawl out into the open."

Caudill's eyes flicked to Callan as she slid the sword to him but were back on me in an instant. Leering, he said, "She's quite the lovely paramour, Rice. I can certainly see why you risked your neck to be with her. Once my ship is repaired, I do believe I'll take her with me. Her sale price will almost cover the cost of replacing Orrons."

Nist's empty hands poked out a few feet away. He pulled himself halfway out and sat up. Pulling his knees up, Nist pivoted on his backside. As his feet swung free, I realized something was clamped between his feet. Nist's legs kicked out and sent Orrons' head crashing into Caudill's chest.

The hardened pirate recoiled from the severed head of his young crewmen. Caudill uttered a cry of mingled horror and disgust as he stumbled back a step. The head splattered blood over Caudill's chest and the pirate wiped at it out of reflex. In that split second, the laser pistol swung down to point at the ground. Finally, his attention wasn't on any of us.

Boost!

And nothing happened. Time did not slow and adrenaline did not flood my body. There was no time to wonder why Boost failed. I still had to act while Caudill was distracted.

I launched myself into a somersault toward Caudill, grabbing my sword as I came out of the roll. Surprise and horror made Caudill continue backing away, but I saw his laser pistol already tracking back toward me. Lunging as far as I could, I struck the pistol with the flat of my sword. The force of the blow sent the gun flying from Caudill's hand.

Grinning in triumph, I pulled my sword back for another thrust and stepped toward Caudill. "Surrender or die."

Caudill's shoulders slumped and his hands raised. Then he leapt forward, a vibroblade humming to life in his left hand. I jumped back. The vibroblade missed, but I heard the buzz of the blade as it passed.

I thrust wildly with my sword, but my backpedal gave Caudill the same opening I'd needed from him. Dropping the vibroblade, he dove for his fallen laser pistol. Rolling up onto his knees, Caudill raised the gun and trained it on me.

I tensed for a dive of my own—and then a crossbow bolt ripped through Caudill's throat while another buried itself in his back. Two of

Callan's guards lay just under the collapsed envelope, spent crossbows in hand.

Caudill dropped the laser pistol as both hands flew to his throat in a useless attempt to staunch the spurting blood. As Caudill thrashed and gurgled, I picked up the laser pistol and turned toward my wife and men.

With no one to see his death throes, the most feared pirate in the galaxy breathed his last.

24

A ROYAL SECOND-IN-COMMAND

CALLAN, NIST, AND THE GUARDS ROSE TO THEIR FEET AS I APPROACHED. I had nothing more in my mind than sweeping Callan into my arms. As I reached toward her, she turned to her guards and Nist.

"Thank you for your quick thinking and quicker actions, gentlemen." She kissed each of them ceremonially on the cheek. "Without the three of you, I'd be a widow now."

The younger of the two guards actually blushed. "We were just doing our job, Your Highness."

Callan crossed her arms in mock disapproval. "David, can you believe what Voss just said?"

"Never, ever say you're 'just' doing your job—especially when your job may mean sacrificing your life to save ours." I took Voss's hand and shook it. "Callan and I are honored to have men such as you guard us."

While smiling and making similar comments to Nist and the other guard, I queried my implant to discover why Boost failed me for the first time. I found the answer and my concentration returned to the real world—where I found Callan watching me.

"Well, what does your implant have to say for itself?" Callan asked when I looked up. I must have looked surprised, because she added, "You get an introspective look when you're talking to that machine in your head, darling. I assume you asked it why Boost didn't work?"

"You knew I tried to Boost?" I asked.

"Of course I did, David."

"Is that another look of mine?" Callan nodded and I continued, "It turns out the implant has a safety override I didn't know about. Apparently, Boosting several times close together—even if the Boost only lasts for a few seconds—is as dangerous as one long Boost. I'd already Boosted twice within just a few minutes, so the implant blocked my third attempt. But don't worry, I'm pretty sure I can find a way to turn the override off."

"Don't you *dare* think about doing that, David Rice!" Callan's green eyes flashed with anger and...fear? "Boosting is dangerous. Those overrides exist for a very good reason and you are not to fiddle with them. Consider that a royal decree, if you must."

"But, Callan, Boosting has saved our lives many times."

"No, David, *you* have saved our lives. Boosting is a tool, just like your sword is a tool. What matters is the man who uses the tool, not the tool itself." Callan wrapped her arms tightly around herself. "David, Tristan can heal many wounds, but we both know Boost burnout is beyond anything he can heal." Loosening her arms, Callan flashed her sweetest, most dangerous, husband-pay-attention-to-me smile. "So leave those safety overrides alone or you'll spend the next month sleeping in the guardhouse."

"You had but to ask, my dear. You know I can refuse you nothing." I lifted her hand to my lips. "But now we've got to figure out how to rescue our friends from the surviving pirates."

"Do you think a rescue is possible?" Callan asked. "Won't the pirates on the spaceship know their captain is dead and be preparing for an attack or a siege?"

"I don't think they know anything that just happened. Caudill turned his radio off so he could threaten me without you and Rupor hearing. He didn't turn it on again after you and Rupor played on his suspicions. And the wreck of the *Pauline* blocked their line of sight from the spaceship. Caudill's men don't know he's dead yet, but they will get suspicious if they don't hear from him soon."

"Could you wear the powered armor? With the helmet on, couldn't you just march right onto the spaceship and smash anyone who refused to surrender?" Callan asked.

"I'm afraid not," I replied. "Only Orrons could control the armor. It's another machine-in-your-head thing, but it's a different one than I have."

At that moment, Rupor's airship glided into position above us and began venting gas. Rupor, I realized, was onboard a Tartegian warship rather than a personal craft like the *Pauline*.

Looking at the descending ship, I asked, "Callan, do you think your ex-betrothed would lend me a few of his marines to lead against the pirate ship?"

Callan sighed. "You're the only one of us who's been inside the spaceship. And you're the only one of us who knows how to open the doors. I don't like the idea of you going back in there, but you're the only person who can lead. Rupor won't like it, either, but he'll agree."

Callan was right about Rupor on both counts.

After reluctantly agreeing, Rupor added, "Of course, I'll be there as your second-in-command."

I opened my mouth to talk him out of it, then looked at his determined face. "I will be honored to have you at my side, Your Highness."

Callan gave me a smile and a nod. Apparently, I'd given the correct response. Shortly, the marines from Rupor's ship gathered around me.

"We have too many unknowns to consider anything but a simple plan." I gave a feral grin to the marines. "And this one is as simple as it can get. Once inside the ship, you capture or kill everyone who doesn't speak your language."

"Direct and to the point, Rice." Rupor nodded his approval. "I like it."

"Am I safe in assuming there are no questions?" At the marines' laughter, I gave them a tight smile. "Now, let's go capture a pirate ship."

25

A PRINCESS-STEALING NE'ER-DO-WELL

OF COURSE THE PLAN HAD MORE DETAIL THAN I'D SAID, BUT NOT A LOT more. Nist rounded up a canvas sack from the wreckage of the *Pauline* and I put Orrons' head in it. Next, I pulled on Caudill's bloody shirt and donned his hat, which was blessedly free of blood stains. Mixed in among Rupor's men, I hoped to pass myself off as Caudill. The deception only had to last long enough for us to get inside the spaceship.

"How do I look?" I asked Callan, spreading my arms wide and striking a pose.

Callan studied me with a critical eye. "Quite a lot like a dead man walking."

"With Rupor's marines packed around me, none of the pirates will see the blood stains. How does the hat look?"

"Is that hat fashionable out in the wider galaxy?"

"I've been away from galactic civilization for a few years," I answered, "but it was all the rage before I left."

"Then let us desperately hope that galactic fashion has come to its senses."

"You don't think it gives me a rakish look?"

"I love you, David, but no." Callan smiled, shaking her head. "If you pull the brim low and keep your head down, it will hide your face. That is your primary reason for wearing that monstrosity, isn't it, darling?"

"Of course."

Perhaps my face displayed disappointment, because Callan rose on her toes and kissed me lightly. "You don't need a hat to look rakish to me, David."

I heard laughter behind me. Turning, I found Rupor and his marines watching Callan and me with amusement.

Callan crossed her arms and glared at Rupor. "Shall I tell your men what *you* wore when we met for the first time, Rupor?"

Rupor's men laughed all the more as their prince's face reddened.

"All right, men, you've had a good laugh," I called. "Now it's time to get serious. Let's form up."

Rupor's men gathered around me. Rupor assumed a prideful look and, the bloody sack held before him, struck out toward the spaceship. I prayed the flash of laser fire would not be the last thing we saw.

The men marched with quiet purpose appropriate to the true situation. My plan hinged on the marines' ability to convince those aboard the spaceship that they were celebrating, not attacking.

"You're supposed to be happy, men. Laugh and joke," I said quietly. "Keep your hands away from your weapons and act as if your prince has won a great victory over that princess-stealing ne'er-do-well, David Rice."

As I'd hoped, that brought a laugh from the men and even Rupor chuckled.

"That's the spirit, lads," I said. "Rupor, try swinging that sack in a jaunty manner, as if it held a treasured trophy. These pirates think you're all a bunch of savage barbarians, anyway. Have some fun and live down to their expectations."

That did the trick. The marines strutted and capered, laughing all the while. One man moved ahead of the group with an exaggerated march more appropriate for the stage than the battlefield. He bowed low to Rupor and requested the honor of carrying the sack. Rupor presented the sack to him as if awarding him a medal for valor. Each man stepped forward for his turn; some hoisting the sack like a trophy, others swinging it in time to a few dance steps, and one peeked inside and cackled. Through it all, we drew closer to the spaceship.

Grinning, one of the marines spun past me and asked, "Won't these pirates just cut us down with weapons like the one their captain used on your airship?"

"You'd think so, but no. Every bulkhead in a spaceship is crammed with vital machinery or conduits for vital machinery. No spaceman uses a laser inside the ship if it can be avoided."

"What weapons will the pirates use?" he asked.

"They'll use swords. That's one of the few things adventures stories get right about combat aboard a spaceship." We climbed over the last pile of debris and the pirate ship loomed above us. "When we get to the hatch, keep up your chatter and pack tightly in front of me. The noise will help cover the difference between my voice and Caudill's. Packing tightly will also give me an excuse to ask for someone to open the hatch."

Seconds later, we entered the airlock. The ruse had gotten us this far. Would it get us inside the spaceship?

26

SURPRISE ATTACK

RUPOR LED THE WAY INTO THE PIRATE SHIP'S AIRLOCK, HIS MEN CROWDING in behind him. It was tight in the airlock and I couldn't step forward to give the crew a clear look at my face. The men continued their boisterous celebration, with the close confines of the airlock amplifying their noise. Rupor ignored the comm next to the door and, with a flourish, knocked on the airlock. Several long seconds crawled by before the knock drew a response.

"Yeah, what is it?" The voice spoke galactic basic and was barely audible over the din caused by the marines. After a short delay, the computerized translation repeated the question in the language of Tarteg and Mordan.

"Your captain has brought us to your ship to celebrate my victory and cement our alliance with you," Rupor yelled over the ruckus, holding up the sack. "Open this door and let us begin the celebration in earnest."

We endured a pause as the computer translated back to galactic basic before we received a reply. "If the captain wants you in the ship, he can open the door when he gets there."

It was time to see if the noise would help mask the differences between my voice and Caudill's. Without waiting for the translation, I deepened my voice and rasped, “Did you even bother to look at your view screen? If I could reach the blasted airlock, I would open it.”

The next few seconds felt like hours. At last the voice replied, “My apologies, Captain. I didn’t see you back there. I’ve sent someone to open the airlock.” There was another brief pause, then the voice added, “Uh, Captain, the bottom of that bag is red and looks wet. What’s in it?”

“The bag holds that scout’s head. Turn off the translation for a minute, would you?” I said, sticking to the deep, rasping voice.

“It’s off.”

“Taking the head is some kind of local ritual. We need these barbarians right now. Order the crew to just smile and nod when the savages show it off.”

“Will do, sir.”

Machinery hummed to life and the airlock door slowly slid open. I thought our ruse had worked, right up until I saw a squad of armed pirates waiting for us.

I feared the entire squad would be armed with laser pistols. We were in serious trouble if they had modern weapons. Fortunately, old shipboard habits die hard. Either the pirates never considered arming everyone with lasers or too many of the laser pistols were destroyed when the inertial dampeners failed. Whatever the reason, only the leader held a laser. The rest of the pirates held drawn swords. The leader could still burn us all down with the laser. We needed a distraction and needed one quickly.

Gambling that the translator was still turned off, I said, “Rupor, give the pirates a stern and disapproving look, then shrug and pull the head out of the bag. Men, when their leader is distracted, all of you must duck. Stay down until I give the word.”

Rupor straightened, his stance radiating royal disapproval of this breach of protocol. The squad leader, irritated that he couldn’t understand what I was saying, called out to the intercom, “Turn the translator back on.”

Then Rupor pulled Orrons’ head from the bag and thrust it toward the leader. Every one of the pirates recoiled at the sight of Orrons’ head dangling before them. Then Rupor added to their horror by tossing the head to their leader. All pirate eyes followed as the head arced toward their leader.

He instinctively fended off the head with his hands. "Yaaaah!"

The man's laser pistol swung away from the airlock and I called, "Duck!"

The marines before me dropped into a squat and I raised Caudill's laser pistol and fired. The bright beam flashed over the marines' heads and burned the leader's gun hand off at the wrist. Gun and hand fell to the floor as the leader screamed in pain. Clutching his wrist, the man stumbled backward into his squad.

"Now!" I cried.

Scooping up the fallen laser pistol, Rupor shouted, "Up and at them, men."

With a roar, the Tartegian marines charged from the airlock and into the squad of pirates.

Stuck toward the back of the pack of marines, I could only watch as Rupor and his men slammed into the squad of space pirates. Disorganized by the flailing of their one-handed leader, the pirates tried to regroup in the face of the onslaught. But Rupor picked his boarding party well. The men in front blocked the pirates' desperate attacks and slammed them into bulkheads or down onto the deck. The marines behind them stabbed, hacked, and trampled the pirates as they passed. Lastly, those bringing up the rear finished off the wounded before rushing to rejoin the boarding party.

The attack was brutal and deadly. The pirates, used to fighting poorly trained merchant spacers and terrorizing space liner passengers, had no response for the efficient, organized violence dealt by Rupor's boarding party.

Bloody sword held high, Rupor voiced a savage cry of triumph. His men joined in and the metal bulkheads reverberated with the din. Rupor charged down the nearest passageway, he and his men deaf to my shouted instructions to take the next corridor, the one leading to the bridge.

The Tartegian's tactics, skill, and enthusiasm would only carry them so far. The pirates still outnumbered us four or five to one and knew the ship's layout intimately. Eventually, superior numbers and superior knowledge would carry the day. Our sole hope lay in controlling the bridge, the heart of the spaceship and from where the crew would direct the defense of the ship.

With a sigh I could just barely hear over the fading cries and footfalls of the boarding party, I jogged in the opposite direction. After all, someone had to take control of the bridge.

I had no allies. I had no Boost. I had no plan. But I had a laser pistol and, more importantly, I had the sword Rob had given me as he lay dying. It was enough to win the day. It *had* to be.

27

SHHH!

THE CLASH OF WEAPONS ECHOED UP THE CORRIDOR AS RUPOR'S BOARDING party found more pirates to fight. As a distraction, the Tartegians had the full attention of the pirates aft of the airlock. But would the fighting behind me distract the pirates in front of me?

I reached the ship's main corridor, running from stem to stern right through the middle of the spaceship. Aft held crew quarters, ship's stores, and the cargo bays. Forward lay officer's territory and the bridge. At least, that's the layout found on a military or merchant spaceship. Since pirates tended to steal their ships rather than have them built under contract, chances were this ship didn't break from that mold. I was gambling my life—and the lives of Martin and Megan—that Caudill was a traditionalist.

The Scout Academy requires courses on space piracy for all cadets. Scouts travel far from the space lanes, it's pretty much our job description. Even though the Scout Corps is much smaller than any of the other military branches, scouts are far more likely to encounter pirates. A scout's survival could depend on knowing pirate tactics and recognizing the signs of a pirate lair. In other words, I knew more about pirates than most people. Martin did, too, but added personal experience to the mix.

Shipboard discipline among pirates is vastly different than among law-abiding crews. There is usually one punishment for breaking the pirate compact—spacing. That means a smart pirate captain finds ways to keep his crew entertained during the long, boring hunt for prey. Pirate ships are known to have well stocked bars, full emersion gaming consoles, and top of the line video rigs. Some even have live entertainment, usually provided by captives taken from space liners or from rim settlements.

All of this came back to me as I started up the main corridor toward the bridge. I moved in short dashes, slipping from one side passage to another, staying out of sight as much as possible. I had just ducked into an aft slanting passage when I heard the hiss of the bridge hatch sliding open. A second after that came the sound of footsteps pounding down the corridor toward me.

I pressed up against a recessed hatch but it provided little concealment. With the aft slant of the passage, I stood well within the peripheral vision of the approaching pirates. One of them was bound to see me.

The pounding of pirate footsteps grew louder and louder. I raised the laser pistol I'd taken from Caudill's body and readied my sword. If luck was with me, I could cut them down before they reached me. But I'd also warn the pirates on the bridge they had an enemy close by. So much for having the element of surprise when I reached the bridge.

With a soft sigh, the hatch behind me slid open and hands dragged me into the compartment. I spun, sword raised to strike, as the hatch sighed shut again. A single finger pressed against my lips.

"Shhh!"

A pretty, petite blonde stood before me. To her right stood a lovely brunette with startling blue eyes. To her left was a stunning redhead. Beyond those three, close to two dozen more women eyed me warily. All of them held makeshift knives and appeared prepared to use them.

One woman, her eyes locked on a vid screen, called, "All clear."

"Are you the scout who's got Caudill's men so scared?" the blonde asked.

"They're scared of me? That's good. Scared men make mistakes." I looked around the chamber the blonde had pulled me into. The women were quite pretty and every single one of them was dressed like a lingerie model, though ones with worse fashion sense than even I possess. Milo would almost certainly like their look, being a teenage boy, but Callan had long since taught me the difference between mere revealing clothing and alluring attire.

"We didn't choose the clothes," the blonde said, reading my expression.

"Of course not." I turned my attention to the blonde, making sure my eyes met hers. "I assume you're all Caudill's captives, no doubt brought on board to entertain his crew?"

She nodded, her eyes suddenly shining with unshed tears. My already considerable loathing for Caudill increased five-fold. "I'd kill Caudill over this outrage if he wasn't already dead."

Every woman in the room pinned me with a laser-like gaze as the blonde asked, "You killed Caudill?"

"No, my men killed Caudill before he could kill me. I found myself forced to kill Orrons."

The redhead threw her arms around me and kissed my cheek. "Oh, thank you so much!"

"We know *why* Orrons was a basket case, but he still had some sick interests—and a...thing...for redheads," the blonde explained. Then she blinked away her tears and was all business. "I assume you're trying to rescue your friends on the bridge?"

I nodded. "And take control of the bridge, so I can help the boarding party heading aft."

"We can help you with that, but in return you've got to agree to help us rescue our husbands."

"Of course I'll help you. It's what scouts do, you know. Are they being held forward or aft?"

The blonde shook her head. "I'm afraid they aren't on board the ship. They're three wormhole jumps away, in Caudill's pirate base."

I shook my head. "I'm sorry, I can't help you. You're sitting in the only intact spaceship on the planet and I'm told it can't fly any more. I wish there was something I could do to help your husbands, but I can't." I looked around the room, locking eyes with several of the women. "Are you still willing to help me rescue my friends?"

"You know, all you had to do was tell us you'd do it," the blonde said. "We wouldn't have known the difference until it was too late."

My face must have given away my opinion of that course of action.

"Please excuse us. We've spent far too much time around pirates lately." The blonde met my gaze, a smile tugging at her lips. "Are there any more men like you at home?"

"That depends on which home you mean," I responded. "I don't know about my birth planet, but on this planet there are whole armies of honorable men who I struggle to emulate."

"I doubt you struggle over anything concerned with honor," the blonde said. "But your answer is just what we wanted to hear. We're going to need men like that to rescue our husbands."

"But I just told you I don't have a working spaceship."

The blonde reached up and patted my cheek. "Don't worry your handsome head over that. If you can take this spaceship, we'll make her fly again."

I could tell there was more to their story, but I could get the rest later—after we were finished dealing with the pirates. "You've got a deal. What I need most right now is to get to the bridge unseen. Can you help with that?"

"I've already got that covered," called the woman at the vid station. "I've got an override on the cameras in that passageway. Ever since you came aboard, all they've seen outside the bridge is an empty passageway."

"That's perfect." I thought furiously for a second. "Can you open the hatch to the bridge from here?"

Fingers danced over the makeshift control panel. "I can now."

"Good. Open it just before I reach it."

The blonde opened the hatch out of their chamber and I slipped into the passage. Sword and laser at the ready, I charged full speed toward the bridge.

28

FREE MARTIN

THE BRIDGE HATCH LOOMED LARGE AS I SPRINTED DOWN THE PASSAGEWAY. Ten feet from the hatch, my brain yelled for me to stop before I slammed into the hatch. Then the hatch slid open and I charged onto the bridge.

From various bridge stations, half a dozen pirates directed the ship's defense against Rupor and his boarding party. On the far side of the compartment, a seventh pirate stood guard over Martin and Megan. Martin's arms twisted behind his back, no doubt with his hands bound. But Megan's hands were free and clasped together in her lap. Obviously, the pirates did not consider a musician from a primitive world any kind of threat. If all went according to plan, they'd regret that decision.

The closest pirate looked up at the sound of the hatch sliding open. I swung my sword, slashing his throat as I charged past. He collapsed to the deck, gurgling, as blood sprayed across his console. The remaining pirates stared at me, shocked disbelief written on their faces. Their hesitation only lasted for a second, but that was all I needed to bound across the compartment.

I barreled into the pirate guarding Martin, driving my sword up into his chest and out his back. Yanking the sword free, I dropped the laser pistol in Megan's lap.

"Free Martin. I'm going to need his help real soon."

Shouts of rage echoed around the bridge as the pirates drew their swords and converged on me. At least one of my gambles had paid off. The bridge was so packed with vital instruments that the pirates weren't willing to use their lasers. I knew I could take any of them in a straight fight, but the pirates outnumbered me five to one. With Boost available, there would be no doubt of the outcome. But you can't have everything and, in this fight, I couldn't have Boost.

I leapt toward one of the pirates and away from Martin and Megan, drawing the attention of all of the pirates along with me. Two of them came at me together, one from the right and one from ahead of me. My sword flashed as I parried their thrusts. I tried every feint and trick I knew, but without the added speed of Boost I couldn't mount an attack against either man. Then a third pirate joined the fight and their combined attacks overwhelmed my defense. Within seconds, I felt cold steel plunge into my left shoulder.

Pain exploded as the pirate's sword grated against my shoulder blade and my left arm dropped to my side, useless. My balance thrown off, I swung my sword wildly across the attacks of the other two pirates. As much by luck as skill, I beat aside both attacks with the single parry. But my wild swing also left me open to attacks from all three of the pirates.

The man who had stabbed me grinned and leaned into his blade, still sticking into my shoulder. Then, when the pirate had me pinned and vulnerable to attacks from his fellows, the pirate pulled his sword from my shoulder. A second later I realized the pirate was no less surprised than me. He rose off the deck and flew across the bridge, crashing into the two pirates not yet in the fight.

Moving almost too fast to see clearly, Martin Bane flowed past me, his mouth stretched in a feral grin. "Megan, David is hurt worse than he knows. Help him sit down before he falls down."

The other two pirates fighting with me brought their swords to bear on me, each looking for a killing blow. In an instant, they forgot all about me as this new, deadly threat came at them. They attempted a defense but Martin moved too fast for them. Sliding in between the two men, he slammed their heads together. With a dull crack, both men collapsed to the floor, senseless.

Scooping up their two swords, Martin advanced on the remaining pirates. The three of them struggled to their feet as Martin's swords flashed in a dizzying pattern. The swords moved so fast you could actually hear them cutting through the air.

The pirates' eyes widened and Martin said, "I can kill or capture. It matters not to me, but maybe it does to you three."

Their swords clattered to the deck.

In the sudden silence that followed, I heard lots of feet pounding down the corridor toward the bridge.

The just-surrendered pirates grinned at the sound of what they knew could only be reinforcements. Believing the approaching men had diverted Martin's attention, one of the three reached for his sword. One of Martin's swords changed direction. With a howl of pain, the pirate pulled his hand back—minus the tip of its middle finger.

"Help me get back up," I said to Megan, who had just helped me sit down. "I need to be ready to fight."

"You can't fight with that wound, David. But maybe we could shut the door. Do you know how to do that?"

"No. I've got some allies who have taken over the door controls. They'd have to-" I stopped speaking as a thought struck me.

"They'd have to what?"

"They can see the passageway and control the door," I mused. "Why haven't they already shut the door?"

"You're asking the wrong person," Megan said.

Megan was absolutely right. Raising my voice, I shouted in Mordanian, "This is Captain Rice. Who approaches?"

The reply came clear and strong and, most importantly, in Mordanian. "We're marines from Her Highness's flagship, sir."

The pirates' grins vanished at the sound of the unfamiliar language. Seconds later, a dozen Mordanian marines crowded into the bridge while several dozen more stood in the passage. Beside the marine commander, looking woefully out of place among the heavily armed men, stood the petite blonde woman from the room down the passageway.

The commander saluted. "We couldn't understand a word this young woman said, but she was most adamant we follow her."

"I'm glad you did. And your timing is most excellent. Now that you're here, I've got to go aft. Rupor and his men charged off in that direction and may require our help."

"Oh hell no, David! You are in no shape to lead these men anywhere," Martin said. "You have to see a medic. I will go with the marines."

"I'd not have chosen those exact words, sir," the marine commander said, "but I must agree with Captain Bane. Your wound must receive attention."

The commander detached four marines to help me out to the medic station, then he and Martin led the Marines aft in search of Rupor. I could do nothing more but wait for news.

29

INCORRECT CONCLUSIONS

"LET'S GET YOU OUTSIDE TO THE MEDIC, SIR," ONE OF THE MARINES SAID, pointing at my shoulder.

"Of course, private," I said. "Sorry I'm keeping you from all the fun."

"Your health is more important than another notch on my blade, sir."

"Callan will appreciate your concern." I pushed off from the bulkhead I'd been leaning against. To my surprise, I pitched right past 'upright' and fell toward a face-first landing on the deck. Megan and the blonde reacted quickly, catching and steadying me. I'd lost more blood than I'd thought.

"Thank you, Megan." I turned to the blonde and switched to gal base, "And thank you, um-?"

"Laura."

"Thank you, Laura. Are the rest of the women still in your compartment?" At Laura's nod, I continued, "If you don't mind, I'm going to assign a squad of marines to guard your compartment until we finish dealing with the pirates. Can you turn on the translator so my people can talk to you?"

"Thank you for the marines." Laura motioned for one of the marines to help her. "They're the kind of men you told us abounded on this world?"

"Each one is honorable to a fault. My oath on it."

"There's no need for an oath. I trust you." Laura handed me off to the marine she summoned. Then she stepped over to the communications station and flipped some switches. "That should do it."

A second later, a translation came from the ship's intercom.

I switched to Mordanian. "Megan, this is Laura. Are you willing to act as a liaison between my men and Laura's women?"

"She and her friends are the allies who helped you?" When I nodded, she continued, "That ought to make an interesting verse in my song. What will Her Highness think?"

Laura smiled at the translation. "You can assure the princess that her... Oh, what's the word they used? Ah, yes, assure the princess that her paramour has been a perfect gentleman."

Megan frowned. "David is Princess Callan's husband, not her paramour."

Laura's eyebrows shot up. "Husband? But Caudill-"

"Jumped to an incorrect conclusion," I interrupted. "One Rupor and Callan played along with so they could get Orrons off my chest. And I mean that quite literally."

We reached the hatch to the ladies' compartment. I assigned one of the marines with me to guard the hatch. "I'll send more men and more...appropriate...clothing as soon as possible."

When we neared the airlock, we met more Mordanian marines boarding the ship. I selected a squad to help guard the women's hatch and directed the rest toward the fighting. Exiting into dazzling late afternoon sunlight had all of us squinting and blinking.

Apparently, it's a medical emergency when the prince consort is bleeding. Rather than wait for the marines to carry me to him, the medic rushed toward me. Right on his heels ran a very concerned Callan.

I gritted my teeth as the medic poked and prodded around my wound. After a moment, he said, "He needs a surgeon, Your Highness, not a medic. I'm afraid the sword nicked an artery."

Callan's face paled at the medic's pronouncement, but she kept her composure. "David, can that thing in your head do anything to fix the wound?"

"My implant? Nothing it hasn't already done. If we had medical nanites, it could direct repairs, but we don't have any of those."

Ignoring the confused look the medic gave us, Callan asked, "Could there be some of those nan-whatevers on this spaceship? I'd think pirates would want a whole lot of them."

"I'm sure you're right about the pirates, but I think the nanites were destroyed in the crash. I can't think of any other reason why Caudill needed Tristan to tend to his wounded," I said. "But maybe the women who helped me hid some nanites. You should send someone to ask Laura."

"Who is Laura? No, tell me later." She turned to one of the marines who had brought me out. "Private, do you know who Laura is and where to find her?"

"Yes, Your Highness, I do."

"Good. I want you to take Milo and go find her."

I'd almost forgotten Milo was with us before he stepped up to Callan's side.

"Milo," she said to him, "ask this Laura it they have..." Callan got a faraway look in her eyes as she searched for the right phrasing. "Any tiny medical machines. Tell her about David's wound, if it it helps."

Milo looked as pale as Callan and twice as serious. I hated to see his spirit weighed down worrying about me. Fortunately, sixteen year old boys are easily distracted.

"And Milo," I added. "Look Laura in the eyes when you talk to her."

"What?" he and Callan both asked.

"The pirates chose the clothes the ladies are wearing. Their attire leaves a lot to be desired, starting with sufficient fabric to cover them decently. Strive to be a gentleman, Milo. Don't let your eyes wander too much."

A hint of Milo's impish smile returned. "I'll try, David."

The private and Milo bounded into the spaceship and disappeared from view. While they were gone, I told Callan everything that happened after Rupor, the marines, and I set off for the ship. Just as I got to Martin's heroics on the bridge, Laura and Milo dashed through the airlock.

Ignoring all the marines ogling at her, Laura came straight to

Callan, "I hate to say it, but we don't have any medical nanites. But that's not the worst of it. I'm afraid the pirates overwhelmed Prince Rupor's marines and captured the prince. They're holding both the prince and the doctor hostage."

30

PROMOTE SOMEONE ELSE

CALLAN FROWNED IN CONCENTRATION AS SHE LISTENED TO THE computerized translation of Laura's words. As the computer finished speaking, she assumed her court face. "Private, give this woman your shirt."

Laura's eyebrows climbed as the private removed his shirt.

Callan allowed a smile to light her face briefly. "Laura, you have traveled with these pirates and know them better than anyone else I know. I will need your advice during my negotiations with them. At the same time, I can't have my marines distracted by the pretty, half-naked woman I've brought into their midst."

Obviously relieved to have the shirt to wear, Laura replied, "You realize there's no chance your marines will pay any attention to me with you standing right beside me."

I said, "Sure they will, Laura. After all, Callan isn't half-naked."

Callan and Laura glared at me.

I wilted under their gazes. "Um, blood loss makes me say stupid things?" The glares didn't break. "So, why don't I just lay here and listen to you over the radio?"

"I think that's a good idea," Laura said.

Turning toward the airlock, Callan added, "And make sure you don't die."

Callan, Laura, and an escort of marines vanished into the pirate ship. I listened as Laura told Callan about the remaining pirate officers and answered Callan's incisive questions. Otherwise, I concentrated hard on not dying. Callan had better appreciate how seriously I was taking her last order to me.

At the end of Laura's briefing, I heard Callan call out, "I am Princess Callan of Mordan. I wish to speak to the pirate commander."

After translation lag, one of the pirates yelled, "Captain Caudill is our commander. You can talk to him."

"No, I can't. Caudill is dead." Callan let that sink in for a few seconds. "It appears someone just got a promotion."

The pirates were silent for several seconds before the same pirate spoke. "My name is Artin. If you're telling the truth, I guess I'm in command."

"I most assuredly am telling the truth. Now, Captain Artin, I've been told you are holding my doctor and the crown prince from our neighboring kingdom."

"That's right, lady," Artin sounded more confident of himself on the topic of hostages. "Here's a list of our demands. We-"

"I am here to accept your peaceful surrender, Captain Artin. I will not listen to, much less accede to, any demands."

Callan's response caught Artin off guard. "Well, um...Maybe we'll start cutting up that prince. Yeah, if you don't start satisfying our demands, that's exactly what we'll do."

"Captain Artin, sometime in the near future you and your crew *will* end up as my prisoners. Any atrocity visited upon your hostages will, in turn, be visited on each one of you tenfold."

"You can't do that!" Artin sounded like he was trying to convince himself more than he was Callan. "Torture and mistreatment of prisoners is against Terran Federation law."

"You do not seem to grasp the situation, Captain Artin. My country is not a member of this Terran Federation, nor are we bound by its laws. Furthermore, in Mordan my word *is* law." Callan blew out her breath in irritation. "I grow tired of this, Captain Artin. The choice is yours. Surrender peacefully or I swear that you and every single one of your men will die slowly and in unspeakable agony, begging for the merciful release of death."

Silence stretched for several seconds. I could only imagine the looks of disbelief plastered over the pirates' faces at Callan's response to their demands. Artin's next words confirmed the accuracy of my mental image.

"Look, princess, is there a king or another prince I can talk to, because I don't think you get the picture. We have your prince and your doctor. *We* hold all the cards."

"No, Captain Artin. You hold nothing more than a single compartment in a crashed spaceship. *I* hold everything else. That includes all the food, all the medical care, and hundreds of men-at-arms who want nothing more than my permission to come in there and carve you scum into little pieces." Callan spoke slowly, as if explaining this to a child. Alas, the sarcasm in her voice was lost in the mechanical translation.

"Can you believe this, men?" From the tone of his voice, Artin obviously couldn't believe it. "You don't even care what happens to our hostages, do you princess?"

"I care more deeply than a vile and violent man such as you could ever hope to understand. That is why I am giving you one last chance to surrender peacefully." She paused for several seconds but Artin didn't take the hint. "The rest of you pirates, is there someone I can speak with in that room who *isn't* stupid?"

"The captain speaks for the crew, lady. Seeing as you're the one who promoted me by killing Caudill, you're just going to have to deal with me."

Callan sighed then spoke quietly. "Sergeant, who is your best marksman?"

"That would be Corporal Dobbs, Your Highness."

"Corporal, I am tired of speaking to this idiot. Would you please promote someone else."

"Hey!" Artin called. "What are you muttering-"

There was the snap of a crossbow firing and Artin's voice cut off with a gurgle. Pirate voices rose in shocked surprise.

"I do hope your new captain is more intelligent than your previous one," Callan called over the hubbub. "Whom do I congratulate on their promotion?"

More muttering among the pirates was followed by a tentative voice. "Um, this is Captain Rondle?"

"Are you asking me or telling me, captain?"

"I... Uh..."

Martin's voice cut in. "May I speak to the pirates, Your Highness?"

"Oh God yes, Martin. Please be my guest."

Switching to galactic basic, Martin said, "Princess Callan represents the most enlightened monarchy on this planet. If you surrender peacefully, she will take that into consideration when dealing with the rest of you. Unfortunately, her tolerance for fools was sorely tried by Artin. She won't be as patient with you, Rondle. If you want to come out of this alive, *don't* be another Artin."

Rondle responded with remarkable alacrity. "I see your point. We surrender!"

Minutes later, Callan and her escort of marines swept out of the airlock and came my way. My wife was in full princess mode. She assumed this bearing as easily as she put on a new dress—easier, when I considered how many ladies-in-waiting were required to help her change clothes. Most of the time, Callan only went into princess mode while presiding in court or during official royal appearances. Today, she used it as armor to hold her worry for me at bay.

"Private?" Callan smiled at the private who gave his shirt to Laura. "I'm afraid we have twenty-two more women in need of proper clothing. On my authority, please gather a shirt for each of them. My page, Milo, will be along shortly to guide you to them."

She turned to the medic. "Corporal, please prepare to move my husband. Tristan will be operating in a surgery on board the pirate ship."

Callan's princess armor cracked a bit when she knelt beside me. I wiped a single tear from her cheek as she said, "I see you're still alive. Thank you for following my orders."

"I strive to please, Your Wifeness."

Callan gave a bark of laughter, quickly smothering it into a quiet fit of giggles.

"I've been saving that one for just the right moment," I said.

Through her giggles, Callan replied, "How very thoughtful of you."

"Your Highness, we're ready," the medic said.

Once again, the princess armor snapped shut around Callan as she rose to her feet. "Follow me."

She led the way to the surgery. Inside, we found Tristan staring goggle-eyed at what I considered a somewhat outdated ship's surgery. Once I arrived, Tristan's attention focused entirely on me. His face grew serious as he examined my wound.

"He's lost a lot of blood and is losing more by the second. Let's get started while there's still a chance to save him."

31

SABOTEURS

TRISTAN'S PRONOUNCEMENT HUNG IN THE AIR FOR A SECOND, THEN PEOPLE bustled all around me. One of Laura's women—a med tech, I assumed—hooked me up to one of the machines in the surgery.

"Are you ready for me to put him under, Doctor?" she asked.

"Yes, Pamela."

As Pamela fiddled with her machine, Callan lifted my right hand to her lips. "I'll be here waiting for you when you wake up, darling."

I squeezed her hand. "That's good, because I can't think of anyone else I'd rather see."

Then Pamela's machine did its job and everything faded to black.

Despite the anesthesia, some small part of me remained aware of what happened around me. Or maybe what I think I remember is simply sounds my implant picked up and then leaked into my dreams.

"There's the cut in the artery. Now, let's see if- Damn! Clamp the artery! Now!"

"His blood pressure is dropping, Doctor."

"Pamela, we need to try that blood transfusion thing you told me about."

"Tristan, what's happening to David?"

"Martin, get her out of here and find me some blood donors. At least three, preferably more."

"Martin, don't you dare try to take me away from David!"

"Callan, you're distracting Tristan and neither he nor David can afford the distraction. You've got to leave."

"Hang on just a little longer, lad!"

I woke up. Callan, dry eyed and calm, sat next to me, holding my hand. Tristan stood on the other side of me, watching Pamela take readings from her machines. Laura was at the foot of the bed, along with four other women. All of them wore marine shirts and, to a woman, looked quite fetching in them.

I grinned at my wife. "We have *got* to get you one of those shirts, Callan."

Callan rolled her eyes. "You nearly died and *that's* the first thing you think of? Maybe you should try thanking those women for donating their blood instead of ogling at them."

"Or, even better," Laura said, "you could thank us by keeping your promise."

"David has my full support, but don't you need a working spaceship before David could hope to lead a mission to rescue your husbands?" Callan asked. "As I understand it, this one is rather badly broken."

"Oh, it's not broken, Your Highness," Laura said. "Merely sabotaged."

"Who sabotaged the ship?" I asked.

Laura grinned. "We did."

"You women committed sabotage without Caudill or his men discovering it?" I asked.

Laura nodded. Her grin grew wider, as did the matching grins of my blood donors.

"Is that why the pirates didn't simply threaten to blast our airships out of the sky with their lasers?"

"Yep. The external lasers were the second system on our list."

I considered Laura's comment for a moment. "Let me guess, the aft inertial dampener was the first system on the list?"

"Got it in one," Laura said. "A bunch of Caudill's men, including most of his best officers, manned the aft laser banks during wormhole exits. We knew killing the inertial dampener would also kill half the crew."

"You and David have talked about inertial dampeners a lot lately. Could you please explain what one is?" Callan asked.

"Sure..." Laura's brow furrowed as she thought through something. "You know how you sway back when an airship speeds up and sway forward-" Laura began.

"I know what inertia is, Laura," Callan interrupted with a smile. "I don't know why you need to dampen it for space travel."

Laura reddened. "Oh, right, sorry. So anyway, inertia is the big problem entering and exiting wormholes because a spaceship instantly accelerates to well over the speed of light going in and does just the opposite coming out."

"Ah, that explains a lot," Callan nodded. "So these dampeners keep everything inside the ship from being crushed against the ship's walls when it accelerates or decelerates."

"Such strong forces generally just cause everything to disintegrate, but you've got the gist of it," I said, then turned to Laura. "From what you're telling me, I'd guess you and your husbands weren't just a random bunch of tourists on a space liner?"

"Right. We were supposed to be part of a second colonist wave." At Callan's quizzical expression, Laura added, "The first wave is mostly agronomists and farmers. They get the farms working so future colonists don't starve. The second wave is mostly engineers and technicians to build the infrastructure for future waves of colonists."

"So, you're all engineers and technicians? And, what, Caudill kept your husbands at the base to repair ships? So, you women were..." I trailed off, unwilling to bring up such a painful subject.

Laura was less squeamish than I was. "My friends and I repaired Caudill's ship, served as hostages against our husbands' good behavior, and served as...entertainment...for the crew in our spare time."

Staying well away from that last 'duty,' I said, "So you had plenty of opportunity to insert backup controls into ship's systems and then bided your time. But why did you choose this wormhole for your sabotage?"

Laura smiled. "Because we knew we'd find you at the other end."

Callan turned to me. "Are you famous in the star-spanning civilization you've told me about, darling? Some kind of galactic hero?"

"No, I'm just a Scout."

"Just a Scout?" Laura interjected. "Your Highness, the Scout Corps are a rare breed among a complacent and unadventurous people. They blaze trails, discover new planets, and find lost civilizations. Scouts are the last heroes in a civilization desperately in need of them.

"When we discovered the pirates were following a Scout's emergency drone," Laura continued, "we knew the Scout would find a way to help us."

"That's a lot of faith based on an emergency drone," I said.

"You're here. The pirates are dead or captured. We're free," Laura said, ticking each item off on her fingers. "I'd call that faith well placed."

"Don't laud me too much, Laura. I had a lot of help capturing this ship and freeing you. Beyond that, all I did was my duty. It's nothing more than any man would have done."

Laura and Callan exchanged glances. "He believes that to his core, Laura."

"You married a remarkable man, Your Highness. A most remarkable man, indeed."

Callan leaned over and kissed me. "I know."

"And if I have anything to say about it, David *will* be a famous galactic hero," Laura said. "Milo told us tales of your adventures. Even discounting his exaggerations, it's an amazing story."

"What exaggerations?" Callan asked. "Milo is usually quite truthful."

"Let's see, the most unbelievable one had David Boosting for over ten minutes while single-handedly defending a trapdoor from creatures Milo called trogs."

"Milo first heard that story from me, Laura." Callan leaned her head on my shoulder. "I was in that cellar and saw it all. It really happened."

Laura's eyes went wide and her jaw went slack. Finding this whole conversation embarrassing, I took advantage of the brief silence to change the subject.

"Now that you're free, how long will it take you to repair the ship and train a crew?"

Laura closed her mouth and pondered for a moment. "I'd say it'll take three weeks to repair the ship. Training a crew is an iffier proposition. Considering the tech level we've seen here, I *think* we can train a crew to handle the less technical jobs in six months."

"Then I think you'd better get started," I said. "We've got a pirate base to take and your husbands to rescue."

32

AASHLA'S HOPE

SIX MONTHS TO TRAIN A CREW SOUNDED OPTIMISTIC IN THE EXTREME TO me, but Laura's approach didn't occur to me. Training astrogators and engineers was impossible to do in six years, much less six months. The educational foundation just didn't exist to support teaching such advanced skills. But Martin and I already knew astrogation and the women's combined knowledge formed the foundation for a good engineering crew. A true emergency would run our small technical crew ragged, but we could handle the load long enough to reach the pirate base and, assuming a successful rescue and escape, the nearest naval base.

We'd train Aashlanders in laser gunnery and missile control. And, if we found anyone with the right mindset, we'd train one or two helmsmen as backups for Martin and me. Our training was well short of what you would find on a naval vessel—or a pirate ship, for that matter—but if we found ourselves fighting a ship-to-ship battle with the pirates we were in deep trouble anyway.

My bigger concern centered around training helmsmen, a misplaced concern as it turned out. Once he learned the control layout, Nist proved himself just as talented flying a spaceship as he was flying an airship. The real surprise was our second best helmsman. Perhaps it was youthful reflexes or his absolute dedication to making sure he got to come with us, but Milo was almost as good as Nist.

Rupor worked with Tartegian and Mordanian marines, forming a shipboard force split equally between the two services. The marines chosen to accompany us split their training time between shipboard tactics and unit cohesion drills, which Rupor insisted Martin and I perform, also.

Every crew member and marine received intensive language lessons from Heidi, Laura's communication specialist. Our crew would hold a huge advantage over the pirates if they understood the pirates' language. Fortunately, a designed language such as galactic basic is easy to learn. All the crew were fluent weeks before launch. Megan, of course, disapproved of the language. She declared gal base a soulless language bereft of poetry and emotion and claimed she'd never compose a song in the language. Despite her displeasure with gal base, she spoke it better than anyone else on the crew.

Preparing a crew for a single voyage was easy compared to what Callan and Rupor went through. Every country and city-state on the planet clamored to be included. Alliances formed and dissolved daily as politicians maneuvered to secure a spot for their representatives. Callan squashed three attempts to make us renege on my promise to rescue the women's husbands. Her father, King Edwar, fought against nobles intent on traveling with huge retinues. Laura's team repaired the ship and trained the crew weeks before the diplomatic wrangling ended.

Six and a half months after it crashed, the newly christened spaceship *Aashla's Hope* rose into the sky. After nearly three planet-bound years, I finally returned to space.

33

WHO ARE YOU?

AS THE *AASHLA'S HOPE* CLEARED THE ATMOSPHERE, EVERYONE NOT BUSY AT a work station rushed to the view ports. Gasps rose as the crew got their first look at their planet from space. Fortunately, Martin and I had seen this coming and had a work schedule setup that allowed everyone to get a look at the planet within the first hour.

We had plenty of time to enjoy the sights while the nav computer scanned the area of the planetary ring close to the wormhole entrance. The computer began plotting the movement of every rock large enough to threaten our spaceship. Martin and I watched the process for a while, verifying everything was proceeding as expected.

Martin turned to me. "I'll take the first bridge watch. Why don't you go find Callan and relax for an hour or two."

"You don't want to spend some time with Megan doing the same? It's been a lot longer since you saw the view from space."

"She'll be busy staring out the view port and strumming on her guitar. I will just be a hinderance until she finds the right melody. And I can live without a space view for a couple of hours." Martin waved me toward the hatch. "Now, get out of here. Go kiss your wife or something."

I found Callan sitting next to Megan, who *was* experimenting with melodies as she gazed out a view port.

"You know, our cabin has a view port, too," I said, wrapping my arms around Callan.

Callan smiled and, without a word, took my hand and led me back to our cabin. Taking Martin's advice a step further, I kissed my wife *and* something.

Eight hours later, the nav computer displayed a winding course to the wormhole entrance. Martin and I took one look at the twists and turns required and summoned Nist.

"Do you think you can follow this?" I asked, showing him the course projection.

Nist nodded. "Sure. It doesn't look that complicated."

"Well, it looks like a hopeless tangle of spaghetti to me." Martin waved Nist toward the helm. "Take us in, Nist."

Seventeen nerve wracking minutes crawled past. The bridge crew gasped at close brushes and even ducked instinctively when one asteroid barely slipped over the ship. Only one person on the bridge remained calm. In truth, Nist looked like he was having the time of his life. Finally, the *Aashla's Hope* slipped past the last asteroid and plunged into the wormhole.

In the early days of space exploration, wormhole travel proved deadly. The invention of the inertial dampener fifteen hundred years ago changed all that. Now travel through a wormhole is deadly dull. To combat boredom, Martin and I kept the crew on their toes with simulations and exercises. Rupor kept the marines busy with shipboard drills. Laura and the women with her kept an eye on the spaceship's systems and struggled to quell their rising anticipation. No one aboard begrudged them their excitement since they'd be seeing their husbands for the first time in over a year.

Everyone had some job to do except for the diplomats, Callan, and Megan. The two young women—already fast friends before we lifted off—spent many more hours together. Megan asked for Callan's opinion on various songs she was working on, including one that was shaping up to be an epic ballad about Callan and me. Megan's lyrics did not exaggerate our adventures, but listening to it embarrassed me all the same. Callan loved it, though, and requested it often. In fairness to Megan, the song was exciting and moving. The verse where Rob died always brought a lump to my throat and Callan openly cried. The verse where Martin and his fleet arrived over Faroon just in time to save me always had my heart hammering.

Between wormhole jumps, Martin and I plotted courses past small asteroid fields. The gunnery crews gained hours of invaluable live-fire experience during those passes. Sometimes Milo and I went out in the pinnace, as well, allowing the gunners to practice firing—simulated, of course—against an evasive, human-controlled target. It had the added benefit of giving Milo hours of piloting experience. By the time the ship entered the wormhole to the pirate base, the crew's rate of fire and accuracy had tripled and Milo's skill flying the pinnace rivaled Nist's.

The final wormhole jump seemed interminable, as was the slow crawl through real space from the wormhole exit to the asteroid field concealing the pirate base. We approached to within five light seconds of the field before we received the pirate's recognition challenge. Martin keyed the response code Rupor's interrogators had...coaxed...from the pirates and we waited.

"We're being hailed," called Heidi from the communications console.

Martin rose from the command chair. "It's about time. Put it on screen."

A lean, hard face filled the view screen. "Ya took yer sweet time returning, Cau-"

The pirate's eyes locked on Martin. "Who are you and where is Captain Caudill?"

34

NOT INTERESTED?

"I REGRET TO INFORM YOU THAT CAPTAIN CAUDILL WAS KILLED AFTER HIS spaceship crashed onto a lost colony world. Most of his crew were also killed in the crash." Martin inclined his head. "I am Martin Bane, new captain of this ship."

On the view screen, the pirate's lips compressed. "Caudill had himself an experienced crew and a top o' the line ship—something you look to have figgered out fer yerself. Would ya care to be explainin' to me how that ship and that crew managed ta crash?"

"They crashed the same way *I* crashed on the planet eighteen years ago." Martin took a couple of steps toward the view screen. "The wormhole exits into the middle of a planetary ring. The collection of great big rocks flying all around that exit tend to take care of the rest. It didn't help that Caudill's aft inertial dampener failed on exit."

The face on the view screen winced, the first sign of actual emotion from the pirate. "Ya got logs that back up yer story?"

"Of course. Only a fool would approach this location without them. Name a comm channel and I'll send them to you."

"Channel four three one." The head tilted to one side. "Now lad, you say Caudill was killed *after* his ship crashed. I sure would like a mite more details than that."

Martin shrugged. "Caudill was under the impression a few laser pistols and a crashed spaceship made him king of the world. I showed him just how wrong he was."

"Yer saying ya killed Caudill and then had the gall ta come to this here base and stake a claim on his spot?" A mirthless grin split the face. "You sure you ain't a big ol' idiot?"

"No, I am a pirate. Based on Caudill's logs, I've been a member of the brotherhood longer than he was. The difference is I was stuck flying airships in an atmosphere while Caudill had this spaceship." Martin smiled. "*Had* is the operative word."

"Ain't you jest a laugh riot." The compressed lips were back. "Gimme one good reason not ta blast you into little bitty pieces and maybe I'll let ya live."

"I come bearing gifts, ones you won't get if you blast me out of space," Martin replied.

"Well don't that beat all. And what gifts could a backward, lost colony have that we'd give a tinker's damn about?" sneered the pirate.

"My gift doesn't come from the planet." Martin leaned toward the screen as if sharing a secret. "My gift comes from Caudill's personal files."

The sneer vanished from the face. "I be listening."

"As you might guess, it took me a long time to break the encryption, but I had plenty of time while my crew repaired the ship." Martin returned to the command chair and lounged in it. "I know where Caudill hid his treasure."

I struggled to keep my face impassive. Was Martin out of his mind? We found no heavily encrypted files on Caudill's computer. We found no treasure maps, either. Besides, the myth of buried pirate treasure is millennia old, dating back to the days of wind-powered ships plying the oceans of Terra. Did Martin expect an actual pirate to fall for such a silly story?

Given my train of thought, I almost missed it when the glow of avarice lit the pirate's eyes. The pirate blinked it away a second later, but I knew what I had seen.

"If Caudill had a hidden treasure trove, *I* never heard of it," the pirate spat.

"Yes, no doubt you and Caudill were like brothers," Martin drawled.

"I'm sure you and he shared all your deepest secrets. Why, I bet you can tell me all about Caudill's childhood, his parents, the object of his first schoolboy crush, and what drew him into this piratical life. We pirates are such trusting folk. Yep, we're just one big happy family."

Martin and pirate on the view screen stared at each other for several seconds.

"Not interested? Very well." Martin looked at Nist. "Helmsman, plot a course for-"

"What's yer offer, Bane?" the pirate growled.

"Equal shares of Caudill's treasure, split between me and all the captains who use this base. In return, you allow me to join your brotherhood on an equal footing with the other captains. I won't accept status as a junior captain or some such."

"I'll go tell the other captains o' yer petition. You jest hold yer position. We'll holler when we's made a decision."

The view screen cleared.

"Signal terminated," Heidi announced.

"What were you thinking, Martin?" I didn't yell, but it was close. "Buried pirate treasure is one of the oldest stories in the book."

"It's old because people believe it, David." Martin maintained his calm in the face of my fury. "Even pirates believe it. They're sure the big, famous raiders hold far more wealth than they display. Raiders being an untrustworthy lot, they assume men like me have all of that excess hidden away somewhere remote. I know of three groups currently searching the desert for *my* buried treasure. All three of the expeditions are led by men who served under me." Martin dazzled me with a smile. "I know how pirates think. Trust me."

Thirty-eight minutes later, the pirate was back on the view screen.

"We be grantin' ye docking permission. Will ye be takin' a piratical name?"

"I've gone by Martin Bane for eighteen years and see no reason to change that now."

"Very well. Welcome ta the brotherhood, Capt'n Bane."

"I'm looking forward to a profitable relationship," Martin replied. "Now that I'm one of you, perhaps you'd care to introduce yourself?"

"Where be me manners? You can call me Captain Quint."

Martin's eyebrows rose and he sketched a half bow. "I am most honored to meet a living legend such as yourself."

"Scorch the honor, Bane. I be plenty satisfied if'n you git us to Caudill's treasure and then do yer part ta support the Brotherhood."

Martin smiled. "I foresee exciting and profitable times ahead for us, Quint."

"Buoy channel eight one three be today's safe course ta the base. T'other captains an' me will meet ya in the docking bay."

"I look forward to it," Martin said. "Oh, I do have one other request. In order to repair the ship, I required the cooperation of the women Caudill had on board. I offered them time with their husbands in return for their help."

"Ya done got their help or ya'd still be stuck on that there planet. Ya be a pirate, Bane. Ya ain't got ta keep yer end o' the bargain."

"And you'll happily accept that explanation if I choose to keep Caudill's treasure to myself?"

Quint's eyes narrowed. "Tain't the same thing, Bane. We be yer partners. Them women be jest useful playthings."

"I've been a pirate for a long time, Quint, and having a reputation for keeping my word has been very profitable." Martin's face hardened, transforming from my genial friend into a ruthless pirate in the blink of an eye. "Do not presume to tell me how to run my ship. We will work within your current repair schedules, but my women *will* have time with their husbands."

Quint glared at Martin before giving an abrupt nod. "All right, Bane, ya gets yer way this time. I'll give the repair bay manager the word."

Martin's face relaxed and my friend was back. "It's been a pleasure negotiating with you, Captain Quint."

"Transmission terminated," Heidi said. "And thank you for standing up to him. I haven't seen my husband in over a year."

"Soon you'll be able to spend all the time you want with him," Martin smiled. "Nist, we have families to reunite. Take us in."

35

DOCKING BAY

As Nist wove the ship through the asteroids, following the course laid out by the buoys, Martin and I called a final meeting of our command staff. Callan and Rupor, along with their respective marine commanders, represented the Aashlanders. Laura and Heidi represented the women whose husbands were held in the base.

Tristan invited himself. "Someone has to be around to speak common sense and rein in you impetuous young people."

"In a few minutes, we'll be docking at the pirate base," Martin said. "We've had to work around a lot of unknowns formulating our plan. We don't know how many pirate ships are docked at the base nor the crew complement carried by the ships."

"One of those unknowns turned out to be your story of buried treasure," Rupor said.

"An inspired bit of improvisation, don't you think?" Martin grinned.

"Perhaps you could explain why that is so, Martin?" Tristan asked.

"First, it got us access to the base. Quint looked more like he was ready to have the base defenses open fire rather than allow us to dock," Martin said. "But the story will also sow discord among the captains. They'll debate and argue and discuss who will come with me to fetch the treasure. In the end, all of the captains will come with me. That will create a power vacuum at the top, hampering the pirates' response when you make your move."

"What if they return in time to lead their men?" Laura asked.

"I'm not planning on bringing any of them back with me," Martin replied.

Laura gasped and Heidi's hand flew to her mouth. In contrast, the Aashlanders just nodded.

The intercom buzzed and Nist reported, "We're on our final approach to the base."

I looked around the table. "Everything we've done for the last six months has led to this point. Our success will not only free those held by the pirates, it will save countless thousands of lives that would have been lost to these pirates in the future. Today, Aashla emerges from galactic obscurity. Today, we write her name into galactic history!"

Heading back to the bridge, Martin spoke quietly. "That was a very inspiring little speech you gave at the end of the meeting, but you know it's complete bunk. It's a big galaxy and news of our raid against the pirates—no matter how daring—won't hold the public's attention for more than a few hours."

"I don't know, Martin, you're the one talking about the pervasive mythology surrounding pirates. There's something about piracy that sparks our imagination and it includes those who fight it." Martin still looked skeptical, so I said, "Let's test it. How many pirates can you name from Earth's ancient days of salt water sailing ships?"

Without thinking, Martin replied, "Blackbeard, Long John Silver, and Captain Jack Sparrow. I could name a few more if I gave it some thought."

"I'm pretty sure Blackbeard wasn't real—the stories have his headless body swimming around his ship, you know—but you've still proven my point. It's been thousands of years since any of those men hoisted the black flag, but you know their names because humans find piracy fascinating. A thousand years from now, someone will probably still tell stories of the infamous pirate Captains Caudill and Quint and how they were brought low by a bunch of Lost Colonists flying a captured pirate ship and led by a reformed air pirate."

"Well, when you put it *that* way, there is something rather mythical about this whole venture," Martin mused. "If you want to take it even deeper into mythology, our tale even has overtones of the Trojan Horse."

I clapped Martin on the back. "Now you're getting into the spirit of the adventure."

The hatch opened before us and we strode onto the bridge, Martin taking the command chair with me taking a computer station.

"Nist, report."

"We are just about to round the last buoy, Martin."

"Good." Martin turned toward me. "David, has the course through the asteroid field been uploaded into your old messenger drone?"

I began verifying the upload right after we entered the bridge. Heidi suggested using the old drone I'd fired off when I first exited the wormhole over Aashla as our insurance policy. The idea met with universal support. The drone led Caudill right to our planet and caused me some problems when Caudill's crew cracked the encryption and figured out who I was, but now it might save our lives.

"Yes, this course is recorded, another course is set for the nearest naval base, and our cry for help is intact. The thruster burn timer is set to thirty minutes," I said.

"Good. Release the drone."

The drone drifted free, then we rounded the last buoy and a huge opening yawned in the large asteroid before us. Beyond the opening, we saw a well-lit, well-equipped docking bay. Within, I counted six ships with space marked for one more.

"Oh joy. It looks like all the pirates are at home right now," I said.

"Of course," Martin sighed. "The rescue would be too easy if half the ships were out prowling."

"Oh mighty pirate captain?" Nist sang out. "The big hole in the bigger rock is glowing."

"Hm? Oh, that. Don't worry about it, Nist. That's an atmospheric energy shield. It keeps the air in the docking bay from leaking out. We'll pass right through it."

I went to the communications console. "Heidi, can you give me a ship-wide channel?"

Her fingers flew across the console. "You're on, fearless leader."

"All hands, this is David Rice. We are entering the pirate base as I speak. Everyone knows the plan and their part in it, but I want to remind you all of a few things. All of you now speak galactic basic well enough to understand what the pirates are saying. I cannot stress how important it is for us to hide that knowledge for as long as possible. There's no telling what we can learn if the pirates believe we can't understand them.

"With that said, don't wander far from the ship, do not go out alone, and check your honor at the airlock. Reacting to an insult will give away our language advantage and put the pirates on alert.

"Finally, all of the pirate ships using this base are docked. The bad news is we're more heavily outnumbered than anticipated. The good news is we can take out half a dozen of the galaxy's worst criminals all at once. Keep a clear head and stick to the plan. Failure is not an option. Rice out."

"David?" Martin said. "We may have to modify that plan a bit."

"What do you mean?"

Martin pointed at a dozen locations in the docking bay. "Those are military-grade automated defense lasers. If we take off without sending the proper pass code, the lasers will cut this ship to pieces."

36

YOU DON'T TRUST US?

MARTIN AND I STARED THROUGH THE VIEW SCREEN AT THE AUTOMATED defense lasers.

"We can't leave the docking bay with those in place and the navy will get sliced to ribbons if the lasers are active when they come to our rescue." Martin turned to me. "Have you got any bright ideas?"

I shrugged. "We'll have to find a way to disable them, obviously."

Laura, who had been on the bridge observing, stepped up to Martin and me. "Let me guess, you're scrapping the carefully laid plan."

"*Bad* plans are scrapped at the last minute, my good woman," Martin said. "*Good* plans simply require a few revisions."

"Well, my good man, when you put it that way I feel so much better," Laura replied.

I couldn't tell if this was stress-relieving banter or if nerves were stretched to the breaking point. Before I could think of something to say to defuse the situation, Callan stepped in.

"Laura, to protect their wives, your husbands are forced to perform maintenance for the base, right?" When Laura nodded, Callan continued. "You and the other ladies on this ship were in the same position with Caudill. You used your positions to sabotage his ship."

Martin and Laura flashed grins at each other.

"I told you we had a good plan, Laura."

"And the simple revision is our husbands disabling the lasers."

"While David and I are leading the captains on the wild treasure chase, yes."

"And when the two of you get back, we can just power up and leave."

Callan frowned. "You hadn't mentioned David going with you, Martin."

"We'll need a pilot and I can't trust anyone the captains choose. And six against one is much worse odds than six against two." Martin gave her a smile. "Consider it one last adventure for David. Something he can tell your grandchildren about when he's a doddering old man."

Callan sighed and slipped her arm around my waist. Anything she might have said was cut off when Nist spoke.

"We've docked, Cap'n. All engines stopped."

Through the view screen, we saw men entering the docking bay.

"Time to go meet the Brotherhood," Martin said.

A moment later, the airlock cycled and we stepped off the ship. Arrayed before us were the six pirate captains.

Footsteps rang on the ramp behind us as Rupor ran out to join Martin, Laura, Callan, and me. The pirates didn't so much as glance at the prince. They were much too busy leering at Callan. It appeared women were as rare among pirates as the stories said, because the six pirates acted like they hadn't seen a woman in ages.

Speaking his native language, Rupor said, "I have half a dozen men armed with lasers stationed just inside the airlock. I doubt we'll need them, but I prefer to err on the side of caution."

It was a good idea, one I wish I had considered. Rupor's military training proved useful months ago when we captured the ship and it was proving useful again.

Quint grimaced at Rupor and growled, "What's the elsie sayin'?"

"Elsie?" Martin asked.

"El Cee. Lost Colonist," Quint said. "How long you been on that planet, Bane?"

"Eighteen years."

The pirates all nodded as if that explained everything. "There been a spate o' lost colonies being found in the last few years. Newsies called 'em Lost Colonists but most folks just shortened it to elsie," Quint said. "So, what's the elsie sayin'?"

"He said he stationed six men with lasers inside our airlock as a precaution against treachery."

The pirates muttered and exchanged glances before Quint scowled and said, "You don't trust us, Bane?"

"Ah, how utterly foolish of me," Martin replied. "I thought I had joined a *pirate* Brotherhood, not the Fractured Feelings Fraternity of Fragile Flowers."

Quint's scowl deepened and the other five pirates cast hard glares at Martin. Martin folded his arms and met the glares with the mocking smile he does so well. Quint barked a laugh, quickly followed by the other five captains.

"I believe you'll do right fine, Bane," he said.

The light patter of feet on the ramp sounded behind me. I didn't even need to hear her speak to know who it was.

"What did I miss?" Megan asked.

Megan's arrival did draw some open stares away from Callan, at least.

"Well now, seems t' me you found yourself a secret source o' fine lookin' women, Bane." Quint was back to growling. "The rules of the Brotherhood say share and share alike."

The other five captains muttered "Yeah" and "Tha's right" while their eyes darted back and forth between Callan and Megan. They were almost drooling after Quint's pronouncement. I wanted to step between the pirates and Callan in the worst way. Callan laid a hand lightly on my arm, so I stayed put.

Martin's voice cut through the building tension. "You don't have any kind of stupid 'sharing' rule, Quint."

"I been part o' this Brotherhood fer nigh on thirty years, Bane. You been part o' it fer ten minutes. Who do you think knows more 'bout the Brotherhood?"

"Caudill's files had a copy of the captain's agreement for the Brotherhood. If I'd found anything so idiotic as a sharing agreement in the articles, I'd never have contacted you."

One of the other captains piped up, "It's an unwritten rule."

The other four captains nodded. Quint kept his gaze steady on Martin, watching and, I expect, evaluating him.

"Is that so?" Martin asked. Martin pointed at Laura. "Then perhaps one of you gentlemen could explain why Caudill had all of the wives on his ship?"

More muttering from the five, then one said, "Caudill was different. And you ain't Caudill."

"No, I'm not. Caudill is *dead*. His ship is *my* ship now." The captains stopped nodding. "One of your *written* rules provides very detailed rules for settling disagreements between captains. Quint, the next time you or your little Greek Chorus make another ridiculous claim, I will follow those rules to the letter and deprive one of these six ships of its captain."

Martin's glare swept across the six captains. "Are we clear, gentlemen?"

For the second time since we exited the ship, Quint burst out laughing. "Caudill was a good captain, but I think we be trading up with you." Quint pretended to wipe tears of laughter from ice cold eyes. "Now, 'bout Caudill's treasure-"

"We'll talk treasure after Laura and her friends see their husbands."

"I told you we'd work that out, Bane."

"And I'm telling you we'll work it out first, Quint."

"You puttin' pleasure slaves ahead o' treasure?"

"No, I'm putting my crew ahead of a treasure that isn't going anywhere."

"Yer crew?" one of the Greek Chorus said. "But Caudill-"

"For the last time, I. Am. Not. Caudill." Martin turned back to Quint. "Well?"

Quint raised a wrist comm to his mouth. "Send 'em in."

The docking bay hatch slid open and a crowd of men hesitated before walking forward. Laura gave a small gasp and went flying across the bay. Behind us, dozens of feet rang on the boarding ramp as the rest of the women followed her.

Martin watched for a few seconds then said, "Now we can talk about treasure."

37

THEIR INSIDE MAN

Martin turned to me and spoke in Mordanian. "I'm off to discuss treasure with these lovely gentlemen. You're in charge until I return."

Martin's lines were for the recordings the pirates were bound to be making. In the short time we expected to be with the pirates, we doubted they would record a large enough sampling of Mordanian for their computers to complete a translation. Even so, we saw no reason to take chances.

"Yes, sir, Cap'n," I replied.

Martin turned back to Quint, switching back to galactic basic. "Lead on, Captain Quint."

Quint cocked an eyebrow as Laura and the man I assumed was her husband strolled, arm-in-arm, toward the boarding ramp to our ship. "And where do you think you be goin', Mister Barrages?"

Laura's husband stiffened and I heard a tremor in his voice when he replied. "I'm going to spend time with my wife, Captain Quint, as you promised I could."

Other couples trailing along behind Laura and her husband stopped to watch. I saw fear written on the faces of the men and uncertainty on the faces of their wives.

"I know what be promised and what ain't promised," Quint growled. "You got a big ol' room where all of y'all sleep. Git on along back there."

Martin stepped between Quint and the couple. "I told you, Quint, I take care of my crew. That includes a little privacy for family reunions." Martin turned to the couple. "You may carry on, Laura."

Laura started toward the boarding ramp, pulling on her husband's arm.

Martin looked at the other couples. "That applies to the rest of you, as well. Enjoy yourselves."

Quint and the other captains scowled but said nothing as the couples streamed past them.

"You made a bunch o' pleasure girls part o' your crew, Bane?" Quint asked after the last couple had entered our ship.

"No, I made skilled techs my engineering staff," Martin replied. "If I hadn't done that, I'd still be on that lost colony and you wouldn't be about to discuss the division of Caudill's treasure." Martin motioned toward the docking bay doors. "Shall we have that discussion, gentlemen?"

Watching Martin and the captains walk away, Megan said, "Those men are *not* happy with Martin."

"Tell me something I don't know," I replied.

Typical of Megan, she took it as a challenge.

"Those husbands are all terrified of their captors," she said. "All of them except Heidi's husband."

As Megan's words sank in, I nodded my head toward our ship. "Let's go inside and discuss this further."

Switching from observant to obstinate, Megan asked, "Why? It's not like any of the pirates can understand us."

"Is 'because I asked politely' sufficient?"

"Oh, wait," she said, comprehension dawning. "It's because of those 'recording' things you've told us about, right?"

A few pirates looked up at Megan's words. Well, at one of her words. There is no Mordanian word for 'recording,' so we'd simply used the gal base word. Hearing a familiar word from people who aren't supposed to speak his language might make a pirate suspicious.

I looked at the men around us and didn't see any narrowing of the eyes or anyone hurrying off to report the verbal slip to a superior. Callan was already speaking before I turned back to Megan.

"That's exactly right, Megan." Turning toward the boarding ramp, my wife added, "Come on."

I entered the ship in time to catch the tail end of Callan's admonishment to Megan. All I can say is that Callan took a more gentle tone than I'd have done—*far* more gentle. Nodding and biting her lower lip, Megan listened attentively to my wife. I left her to it, since Callan's approach was working.

"Your impetuous nature is one of your most endearing qualities," Callan wrapped up, "but for the next few hours you must keep a tight rein on it."

I put a smile on my face and carefully kept my tone neutral as I asked, "Could you tell us what you observed concerning Heidi's husband?"

"When that old, scary pirate spoke, all of the men reacted like whipped dogs," Megan said. "They looked down and scrubbed all expression from their faces. Heidi's husband kept his head up, looking at the other men and smirking. It's like he thinks he's above them or something."

I thoroughly disliked the sound of that. "Do you think he's working for the pirates—like he's acting as their inside man among their hostage tech crew?"

Megan gave my question careful thought before nodding. "It's possible there's something else behind his expression, an indomitable will or something heroic like that, but I don't think so. He's nothing like you."

"Thank you for that assessment, Megan. And for the compliment." I turned to one of the guards Rupor had stationed inside the airlock. "Please bring Heidi and her husband to me."

Moments later the guard returned—alone.

He snapped off a salute and reported, "Sir, they're gone."

38

A CHALLENGE

"Check with the guards at the forward airlock," I said. "Have them seal the exit if Heidi and her husband haven't gone out that way."

The guard saluted and ran off. I strode off toward the bridge. Callan, Megan, and Rupor fell in behind me.

"Does anyone know why Heidi's husband would even bother boarding the ship if he only planned to stay for a few minutes?" Callan asked.

"There could be any number of reasons," Rupor said. "Once aboard, it's likely Heidi told her husband of our plan to sabotage the lasers—that is an integral part of the plan, after all. If he's working for the pirates, he'll want to report our plan as soon as possible. It's also possible he just wants to show off his beautiful wife. After all, the pirates have quite a severe shortage of women here. It's a petty and foolish thing for a prisoner to do, but men do foolish things when women are involved."

As we approached the bridge, the guard I'd sent to the forward airlock returned.

"The woman and her husband left the ship no more than a minute before I reached the airlock," he reported. "The guards say the woman appeared reluctant but left voluntarily."

Nodding to the guard, I strode onto the bridge. “Give me a video sweep of the docking bay. Stop and zoom in if you see Heidi out there.”

Seconds later, Heidi and her husband filled our view screen. The pair stood less than a hundred yards from our ship. A gang of grinning pirates had them surrounded and one of their number laughed and talked with Heidi’s husband. Heidi pressed close beside her husband, fear written on her face. Her husband, fear building on his face, argued vehemently with the pirate.

“The man may be working with the pirates, but they sure don’t seem to like him much,” I said. “I’ve got to get out there and defuse this situation.”

“I’ll come with you,” Rupor said.

“You’re our military commander, Rupor. You need to stay here with your command,” Callan said. “Megan, do you mind going with David? You can be his translator.”

“Why would she speak gal base and not the ship’s second in command?” I asked.

“Captain Bane taught me,” Megan answered. “He would want his woman to speak his language, wouldn’t he?”

“It sounds reasonable to me,” I said. “Let’s go.”

A moment later, Megan and I approached the outer edge of the pirates gathered around Heidi and her husband.

“I’m getting tired of arguing with you, Chapman,” the pirate said. “If you won’t share your woman with us, there’s only one thing I can do. Erwin Chapman, I challenge you to a duel. If you win, you get my rights within the Brotherhood. If I win, I get your woman.”

As if our situation weren’t complicated enough, Heidi’s husband had managed to find a way to make things more precarious. If Chapman was the only one involved, I’d have left him to his own devices. But I couldn’t just stand by and let Heidi suffer through this.

I turned an expectant look on Megan and tilted my head toward Heidi and her husband. Catching on, Megan gave a Mordanian translation of what had just transpired.

Over the excited talk from the pirates, I called out in Mordanian, “Megan, tell them Heidi is a member of our crew and not a prize to be fought over.”

The chatter around the two men died down at the sound of my voice. Curious, the pirates turned their attention our way. Megan took advantage of the lull in conversation and spoke in exaggeratedly careful gal base. "Commander Rice says you can do what you want with the spy but the woman is ours!"

In Mordanian, I said, "Um, Megan, that's not exactly what I said."

"I know, David, but if I repeat what you say exactly won't that make it easier for the machines to translate our language?"

She made a very good point. "That's a very smart move, but that means you're in charge of these negotiations. I'll try to offer advice if it's needed, but that's the best I can do."

"Words and reading crowds are my business, David. You have to trust me."

"I do. Carry on as you see fit. If the situation really goes downhill, we can always switch to you directly translating my words."

By now the pirate arguing with Chapman had gotten over his surprise. "How did an elsie woman learn gal base?"

"I speak five languages native to my planet. Learning your soulless language didn't pose much of a challenge," Megan replied. "Now, Heidi is coming with us."

The pirate suddenly remembered the original discussion. "Wait just a minute. What do you mean the woman is yours?"

Maintaining the act, I said to Megan, "Just nod your head as if I guessed the gist of the pirate's question."

Megan nodded, then I muttered a bunch of unassociated Mordanian strung together.

Megan turned back to the pirates and switched to gal base. "Heidi is a full member of our crew. Our captain is a member of this Brotherhood. That means you can *challenge* her to a duel but you cannot *win* her in a duel—especially not a duel with a hostage who's wormed his way into Quint's good graces by spying on his fellow hostages."

The pirates exchanged glances. "What are you talking about? Who said he's a spy for the captains?"

Megan looked my way and switched to Mordanian. "Blah blah blather pretend to translate."

I suppressed the urge to laugh. "Don't do that! It would ruin the scene if I started laughing in the middle of the negotiation."

Megan turned back to the pirate. "All of the men other than Chapman were terrified when Quint ordered them away. Chapman just smirked. It wasn't hard to figure out the rest."

"Erwin, that's not true, is it?" Heidi asked, her eyes wide and pleading.

"It's...complicated," Chapman said.

The pirate laughed. "Yeah, it's complicated. But I'm going to uncomplicate it for you, honey. Chapman, the challenge still stands, only now I'm going to kill you just for the fun of it."

Chapman paled at the pirate's words. "B-but I'm useful to you. Captain Quint said so!"

"You *were* useful, Chapman," his challenger said, "but we got those other men toeing the line right nice like. Your tech skills aren't real good. And your other skills are—what was the word the captain used, boys? Oh yeah—redundant."

Another pirate got into Chapman's face. "Do you know what that means? It means we can live without you, Chapman."

As raucous laughter rose from the other pirates, Heidi turned an imploring look on me. I sighed and nodded to her. Relief spread across her face.

Megan eyed me with an appraising look. "You're going to save Chapman's sorry hide, aren't you?"

"I'm doing it for Heidi, not Chapman. But yes, unless we can find a way out of this duel, I'm going to try to save his sorry hide. See if you can find an angle that will let us buy these guys off or something."

Megan raised her voice and switched back to gal base. "You can't kill Chapman."

"Yeah I can, lady. And you can watch me," the challenger called back.

"Chapman is married to a member of our crew. That means he belongs to her. You may only challenge him if she grants him permission to duel."

Hope flared in Chapman's face.

"Nice try, woman, but Chapman is just *married* to her." The pirate jerked a thumb at Heidi. "That don't mean he *belongs* to her."

"Tell that to my ex-wife!" one of the other pirates quipped, drawing more laughter from the pirates.

As the light of hope faded from Chapman's eyes, the challenger continued, "I'll grant you had a point about the woman, but not about her husband. Chapman is ours."

"It was a valiant try, Megan," I said, "but these pirates want blood. It's time to get me involved in the duel."

"You know Callan won't approve of this," she replied in Mordanian. Switching back to gal base, she said, "Commander Rice says he is disappointed in his fellows in the Brotherhood."

The challenger turned mocking, wide eyes my way. "Gosh, I don't want to disappoint *Commander Rice* none. Please tell me how we disappointed him so we can fix it right up."

"He and I are both displeased to learn what cowards you lot are."

The mocking expression vanished, replaced by a hot glare. "Who you calling a coward, lady?"

"You, obviously. Who but a coward would challenge a man wholly incapable of defending himself?" Megan's voice dripped with disdain. "Your cowardice disgusts him so much that Commander Rice issues challenge to you. Should you defeat our commander in a fair fight, Chapman is yours to do with as you wish. Should you lose, well, you won't care about anything ever again, will you?"

One of the other pirates spoke quietly to the challenger. A grin spread across the challenger's face as he listened.

"Well now, this is more like it. We got us a new challenge, boys!" he called. Putting a hand on the other pirate's shoulder, the challenger said, "Simmons and me are going to meet Chapman and Rice together. A two-on-two challenge to the death."

A cheer rose from the pirates, Chapman's face went white, and Heidi buried her face in her hands.

Megan hung her head. "I'm sorry, David. All I've done is make things worse."

"Don't blame yourself. You did a lot better than I could have, Megan. Like I said, the pirates want blood."

A gruff voice cut through the commotion. “What be the meanin’ o’ all this, then?”

Martin and the other pirate captains were already back. The negotiations must have gone smoothly. Seeing the captains, hope returned to Chapman’s face.

“Captain Quint! These men challenged me to a duel,” he cried. “Me! Your inside man.”

“An’ why should that matter to me?” Quint asked.

The response shook Chapman, but he tried another appeal to Quint. “But what if I’ve learned something important?”

“I s’pose there be a first time fer everything,” Quint spat.

Chapman tried one more time. “But Captain Quint-”

Quint spun around, a blaster materializing in his hand. “Shut up, Chapman, or I’ll kill you m’self.”

Chapman backpedaled, his hands held out in supplication.

Turning away and holstering his blaster, Quint added, “Have a good time killin’ him, boys.”

39

HE'S RUNNING

MARTIN STAYED BEHIND AS QUINT AND THE OTHER FIVE CAPTAINS WALKED away. Taking in the scene around me, he spoke to me in Mordanian. "You're involved in this fight, aren't you David?"

"He's doing it for Heidi. After all she went through to get back to her husband, David couldn't just let the pirates kill her man in front of her. It's all quite gallant on David's part." Megan turned a level stare on me. "I prefer heroic songs with happy endings, so don't get yourself killed."

"At long last, I have a good reason to survive a fight," I grinned just in case Megan didn't figure out I was kidding.

Megan grinned in return. "I'll make sure to tell Callan of your good fortune."

"Bane!" Quint and his pirate chorus stopped about fifty feet away. "Come on. We got us a treasure to find."

"I'd love to join you, Quint," Martin replied, switching back to gal base. "Unfortunately, your men dragged my pilot into this fight. We'll have to wait until the duel is finished."

"I gots plenty o' pilots. I'll have one git out here," Quint said.

"I am not getting into a pinnace outnumbered seven to one," Bane said.

"We be headin' out for the treasure now. If'n my pilot ain't ta yer likin' you can get another one o' yours. You do got another pilot, don't you?"

"Of course I have another pilot, Quint." Martin looked at me and shrugged. "I'll go get him."

"Are you taking Nist?" I asked in Mordanian

"No, I'll take Milo." Martin switched back to Mordanian. "His size and age won't alarm them and, as much as I like Nist, Milo will be more useful if it comes to a fight." Turning toward the pirate captains, he added, "Try not to get yourself killed, David."

As he walked away, I turned to Megan. "Find out the details of this challenge. What weapons we can use, where we fight, who can watch, that sort of thing."

Moments later, we were back on our ship as the pirates made preparations for the duel. Laura and some of the other women consoled Heidi. Chapman sat alone, ostracized and avoided. Rupor watched Chapman with unconcealed disgust.

"How could a woman as courageous and intelligent as Heidi marry a cur such as him?" Rupor hissed in a low voice.

"In normal circumstances, he may be a fine, upstanding man," I said.

"You're excusing him?" Rupor asked.

"No, I was answering your question, Rupor. Adversity doesn't always bring out the best in a man, but the man only finds that out when adversity strikes." I eyed Chapman. "I suspect life on a colony would have broken Chapman, but it would have taken longer."

Callan slid in beside me. "Everyone's here, David."

I switched to gal base so everyone could understand me. "You all know that Chapman and I are fighting a couple of pirates. The duel is held in a zero gravity room surrounded by viewing platforms. Most of the other pirates will be there to watch, so that's when you and your men," I pointed to Laura's husband, "will disable all of the defense lasers in the docking bay. We'll draw the fight out as long as we can, but don't waste any time. Come back to the ship as soon as you're done. We'll leave once Chapman and I get back. Questions?"

There were none.

"Keep your composure, do your job, and we'll be safe on a naval base this time tomorrow." I turned to Chapman. "Let's get this over with."

Chapman and I stepped out of the ship and then red lights began flashing all around the docking bay. The pirates took note of the flashing lights but simply returned to their tasks. Was this some kind of test or a minor warning? I wanted to stop one of the nearby pirates and ask what was going on, but I wasn't supposed to understand gal base. I couldn't ask Chapman for the same reason.

Looking back to the airlock, I called, "Could someone please send Megan out here?"

As the marine guard in the airlock headed into the ship, I turned back to the docking bay. Chapman was thirty feet away, running for the hatch out of the docking bay and into the main base. Cursing, I took off after him. If Chapman got into the base proper, he might be as good as gone.

The pirates watched him dash past, laughing. One or two tried to trip him, but most just settled in to watch the fun.

"Twenty credits says the elsie catches him," one pirate called.

"Done," called another. "But the bet is off if someone trips Chapman."

More bets were called and accepted and, within seconds, all attention in the docking bay focused on Chapman and me.

Behind me, I heard Megan call, "David, what are you doing?"

"Chapman's running away."

Megan used language quite fitting for a pirate base and, based on the catcalls from the pirates, joined the chase.

"Go back to the ship, Megan," I yelled without turning.

"I won't," she yelled back. "You can't run around the base without having a translator."

There were good reasons behind the decision to pretend ignorance of gal base, but I really regretted that decision now. If I caught Chapman before he got out of the airlock, though, it wouldn't matter. And that looked to be the likely result before Megan cried out behind me.

"Get your hands off me!"

One of the pirates cried out in pain and more harsh laughter erupted from the other pirates.

"That ain't no way for a pretty plaything to act," a pirate said.

"Let me go!" Megan shouted.

I risked a look over my shoulder. A handful of pirates clutched at Megan, trying to pull her into a rough embrace. I found myself torn between my desire to help Megan and the absolute necessity of catching Chapman.

"Unhand that woman, you miserable pirates," demanded a strong voice.

The pirates didn't understand the command as it was in Mordanian—or Tartegian, from the speaker's point of view—but the meaning was clear. The pirates backed away as Rupor charged across the bay, two squads of marines backing him up.

Relieved of a difficult decision, I turned back to the chase—just in time to see a cargo boom swinging toward my head. I dropped and slid under the boom, losing precious time as a result. As I rolled to my feet, Chapman ducked through the hatch and disappeared into the main base.

40

CHASING CHAPMAN

I RUSHED TO THE HATCH OUT OF THE DOCKING BAY. THE DOCKING BAY wasn't in vacuum nor was there any imminent threat of decompression, so I should have just been able to yank the hatch open and move on. Instead, the hatch held firm. Two blinking lights caught my eye—a green light showing the airlock was cycling and a red one showing someone had manually switched the airlock to operate under vacuum conditions. Chapman had plenty of time to get lost in the base while I waited for the airlock to recycle.

I looked back toward Megan. Rupor and the marines had safely removed her from the clutching pirates. Rupor's face contorted in righteous rage while Megan's displayed offended anger. The pirates muttered among themselves and eyed the marines arrayed between them and Megan. The situation looked volatile, to say the least, but it would become explosive if Chapman found anyone to listen to him.

That's why, when the airlock finished recycling, I switched off the vacuum conditions override and left Rupor and Megan to handle the situation. With a last glance back to the docking bay, I saw Callan descending from our ship. Perhaps she would ensure cooler heads prevailed.

Beyond the airlock, I found corridors leading left, right, and straight ahead. I didn't see Chapman anywhere. A couple of pirates lounged against the wall, grinning at me.

"I bet you wish you could speak civilized, elsie," one said.

I looked at him and shrugged then peered down the corridor straight ahead as if looking for something.

"Chapman didn't go that way, moron," the other pirate said.

I whipped my head back to the pirate. Maybe I could get them to tell where he went. Speaking slowly, I said, "Chapman?"

"Send him the wrong way," the first pirate said.

The other pirate pointed down the corridor to my right. Could he be telling the truth? It wasn't likely.

Swinging my head to the left, I pretended to spot something and yelled, "Chapman!" Then I dashed down the corridor to my left.

I dodged around pirates who mostly ignored me. A few tried to trip me up or get in my way. After I 'accidentally' knocked a couple of pirates down, the rest stayed out of my way. Seconds later, I rounded a bend in the passage and saw Chapman. He sauntered along fifty or sixty feet ahead of me, acting as if he hadn't a care. I hid behind a pirate just as Chapman looked over his shoulder. Somehow, he didn't see me. I trailed behind him for close to a minute, managing to avoid being spotted. The pirates just went about their business, ignoring both of us.

Chapman turned a corner and I took the chance to sprint closer. I peeked around the corner and spied Chapman just twenty feet ahead. A chill settled over me as I spotted his destination.

Chapman's path led straight to the base's communications center.

What could Chapman do from the base's communications facility that he couldn't already do? He didn't need a radio to reveal our identities and our plans. Then it dawned on me that Chapman's plan went beyond getting out of the duel. He hoped to gain prestige at the same time. That was far less likely to happen if he spilled everything to just any pirate in the base. No, he'd need to get the attention of people with rank. Everyone of sufficient rank was aboard our pinnace and not due back until after the duel.

Twenty feet ahead of me, Chapman entered the communications room. When I followed, he stood before the pirate officer on watch, an earnest expression on his face..

"Go away, Chapman. I ain't callin' the captains fer ya," the officer said.

"Why not? It's extremely important," Chapman whined.

The officer gave Chapman a nasty grin. "I got a hundred credits bet on you dyin' in the first minute o' that duel. You ain't gonna talk yer way out of fightin' them two fine lads o' the Brotherhood."

"But I won't even mention the duel. I swear. Please, just thirty seconds!"

"Even if'n I wanted to let ya speak to the captains, ya know we gotta go silent right after one of the wormholes opens up."

So, the pirates had detected the wormhole opening for the messenger drone we launched before docking. That explained why the flashing lights didn't seem to alarm anyone. I saw the sense in the pirates' approach, too. They shut down communications until they discovered what triggered the wormhole. No doubt they extended communication blackout if they detected ships traversing the system. Barring naval patrols, those ships were likely easy pickings. But the one place where the pirates did *not* want ships disappearing was the system where their base was hidden.

The pirate officer crossed his arms. "You gots somethin' to say, you say it to me."

Chapman's shoulders sagged. "Yeah, okay, I'll tell-"

I grabbed Chapman's shoulder and spun him around to face me. Alarm registered on his face as I drove my fist into Chapman's gut with all my strength. He doubled over, the wind whooshing out of him. I stepped into my next blow, putting all of my weight and strength into an uppercut to Chapman's chin. He rose a foot off the floor and flew back four or five feet before sprawling, unconscious, at the feet of one of the other pirates.

The officer of the watch stared at me, his mouth hanging open. I grinned and made a show of dusting my hands off. The pirate officer laughed at my little act. Still grinning, he drew his laser pistol and leveled it at me.

41

EXCELLENT TIMING

STARING DOWN THE MUZZLE OF A LASER PISTOL, I HALF RAISED MY HANDS. Once the pirate understood I had no plans to do anything stupid, I mimed pointing the gun at Chapman.

The pirate shook his head. "I got no idea what Chapman wanted ta tell me, but I figger you clobbered him to shut him up. Suddenly, I'm right curious what he aimed to say."

I shrugged as if I didn't understand what the pirate had said. Inspiration struck and I continued with my pantomime. I pointed to Chapman then wove my hands in the curving motion that has meant 'woman' to every man since before recorded history.

The pirate leered. "Yeah, Chapman's got himself a hot wife. Wish I knew how that gutless wonder hooked a babe like her."

Keeping a hand held out, as if on the shoulder of the woman, I threw a fist at what would have been the woman's head.

"Chapman punched the babe, huh?" the pirate said. "That ain't against the rules 'round here."

"And to think you call *us* uncivilized," Megan's voice sounded behind me. She strode up beside me, five marines trailing in her wake. The marines carried lasers but kept them pointed at the floor.

"I heard one of ya spoke gal base," the pirate said. "That'll make this easier. We're gonna hold yer boy here till Captain Quint gets back."

"No, I'm taking David and Chapman back to our ship. You're going to stand aside and not interfere."

"And why would I do that?"

"Because David didn't break any of *your* rules, but Chapman broke one of *our* rules."

"Okay, we don't got rules against a bit of fightin' as long as the work gets done. So you can take yer boy, but yer rules don't count on the base. Chapman stays here."

"Chapman hit Heidi while aboard our ship," Megan countered. "Our ship, our rules, our punishment."

The pirate shrugged. "Seems like a lotta trouble just 'cause he punched his wife."

"Oh, it does? Let me tell you something about our planet." Megan's voice dropped an octave and she leaned forward. "One of our greatest heroes is a man who spent his life challenging abusive men to duels. When he left a town, he left behind fresh graves, new widows, and a far more polite population. So you see, we uncivilized lost colonists take this kind of behavior very seriously."

Megan ordered one of the marines to carry Chapman, spun on her heel, and led us out of the room. The pirates in the hallway gave us a wide berth as we marched back toward the ship.

Keeping my voice low, I said, "You have excellent timing, Megan. How did you come up with that story about the duelist so quickly?"

Megan gave me a meaningful look.

"Wait, do you mean you didn't make that up?" I asked.

"If you like, I'll sing the song for you sometime. Make sure you've got a couple of hours to spare," she smiled. "The full version has eighty-six verses."

Moments later, we returned to the docking bay—just in time to see Milo landing our pinnace next to the ship.

"Why is the pinnace back so soon?" Megan asked.

"It's probably because one of the system's wormholes opened," I replied. "It's the same reason the base is operating under radio silence. The pirates don't want to risk giving away their position to passing spaceships."

I turned to the marine carrying Chapman. "Sergeant, we're going to delay the pirates long enough for you to get Chapman into the ship. Stuff him in a room with only one door and keep a guard on that door at all times. If he causes any problems, just hit him until he stops."

"Yes, sir," the marine replied. Speaking to his second-in-command, he added, "Corporal, you and the men stay with the Prince Consort and the young lady."

As the corporal acknowledged the order, I spoke to Megan. "Make a big show of kissing Martin when we get to him."

A devilish smile lit Megan's face. "With all these people watching? How scandalous! Of course, it does sound like fun, but please explain why I am doing it?"

"You're the only one of us known to speak gal base. You may have to wander the base a lot more than I'd prefer and you're an extremely attractive woman."

Megan batted her eyes. "Why, David, I do believe you've been letting your gaze linger on women other than your wife. What would Callan say about that?"

"She'd say that I'm married, not blind. The point is, you've got to show these pirates that you're Martin's woman. They *must* believe that messing with you will draw the ire of a pirate captain. That belief may be your only protection away from the ship."

Megan heaved a theatrical sigh. "Very well, David, I shall do my best to display some modicum of attraction to Martin."

When Martin exited the pinnace a few seconds later, Megan's eyes lit up, she flashed a dazzling smile, ran lightly forward, and threw herself upon him. Arms wrapped around Martin's neck, she locked her lips on his and gave him quite the hero's welcome. After a startled second, Martin returned her greeting with obvious enthusiasm. Either he was a better actor than I believed possible or he held deeper feelings for Megan than I'd ever realized.

When the two finally came up for air, Megan asked, "Did you bring me something from the treasure? You promised me a pretty jewel."

Martin played his part to the hilt, playfully tapping Megan on the nose with a finger. "We didn't get to the treasure, my dear. The wormhole opened up and the other captains insisted we return to base."

Rolling his eyes, Quint turned to me. "I saw Chapman's body being carried aboard your ship. I guess the duel be over?"

Megan slipped from Martin's arms. "Excuse me, Martin, I've got to go translate for your lunkhead first officer."

As I stood there with a look of incomprehension, she told Quint, "Chapman is unconscious, not dead. We've taken him on board our ship to face punishment for striking a woman. The duel will have to wait."

"Wrong, woman. The duel be first. The challenge be given and accepted afore Chapman hit his wife." Quint turned to the other captains. "I don't rightly see why hittin' yer wife is a crime, no how."

Megan's voice chilled considerably. "What makes you think Chapman didn't hit his wife before the challenge was made?"

"Ain't no way yer 'lunkhead' here woulda stepped in ta help Chapman if'n he'd already done smacked the woman. So the fight be on—and there ain't no time like the present, I say," Quint raised his voice until it echoed through the docking bay. "Stop workin' boys. It be time fer the duel!"

42

YOUR BEST IS EXCEEDINGLY GOOD

Quint gave us five minutes to gather Chapman and report to the dueling arena. That left us little time to modify our plans to fit this ever-changing situation.

"Our top priority is still disabling those sentry lasers in the docking bay," I told our hastily gathered command staff. "Laura, has your husband briefed all the other men? Are they ready to go?"

She nodded. "They know what to do and one of the men had a suggestion for speeding up the process. Instead of spending ten minutes disabling each laser, they're going to disable the four control clusters for the docking bay. Each one will take about fifteen minutes, but they'll be able to work on all four simultaneously."

"Good. Wait until the docking bay clears for the fight before sending them out. The fewer pirates they run into, the better." I turned to Rupor. "Have you got squads of marines assigned to guard each of the sabotage teams?"

"Yes, Rice," Rupor replied. "But I strongly disagree with your plan to simply 'run for the docking bay' after this duel. That might have been acceptable when none of the pirate captains were here, but it will not work now."

"Rupor's right," Callan said. "The captains will expect Martin and

Megan to sit with them. As Martin's royal benefactors, Rupor and I will be expected to be there, too."

I hadn't considered that. "None of you will be able to just slip away from the captains. Okay, Rupor, what did you have in mind?"

Rupor outlined a plan for a fighting withdrawal, with the marines bearing the brunt of the fighting. "The plan is short on details and will require considerable initiative from the officers, but they're well-trained men. They can handle it."

"How will we get away from the captains?" Megan asked.

Martin answered, "For the most part, we'll make it up as we go. We don't know enough about the arena setup to do any real planning." He looked at Rupor. "I suggest we wait for the first serious wound and then make our move while the pirates are distracted by the blood."

Rupor nodded agreement and I added, "That just leaves one question. What do we do about Chapman? He's proven we can't trust him. If he has the chance, he's sure to try to alert the pirates from inside the arena."

Rupor said what was on everyone's mind. "Get him killed early in the fight or, if you have to, find a way to kill him yourself."

"I'm afraid you're probably right. We can't risk the lives of hundreds of people over the life of a man who is actively trying to get us killed." I looked around the room. "Do we all agree?"

One by one, everyone nodded.

"Then let's get this over."

Tristan gave me smelling salts to revive Chapman. "Remember, he'll be groggy for a minute or two after he wakes up."

"I'll keep that in mind," I said.

Throwing Chapman over my shoulder, I joined Martin, Megan, Rupor, and Callan at the airlock. One of Quint's pirates waited for us at the foot of the ramp.

"Cap'n Quint sent me to lead the way."

Together, we set off for the arena.

As the pirate led us away, Heidi dashed up. Her eyes were red and swollen, though any tear tracks had been scrubbed from her face.

"I'm coming with you," she declared in accented Mordanian. "Erwin is my husband and I should be there."

Laura ran out of the airlock, her face creased with concern, as we turned to face Heidi. I expected Callan would be the first to speak, but Rupor surprised me.

Stepping in front of Heidi, he gently took her hands in his and looked her in the eye. "No good can come of this, m'lady. Regardless of Chapman's current deeds, he is a man you have held in your heart for many years. The anguish you feel now will be as nothing to that which you would feel watching him fight in the arena. I implore you to stay on the ship and draw strength from the love of your friends. Leave this harsh business to those of us who have less gentle souls than you."

"But the princess will be watching her husband fight."

"She accompanies us as the royal benefactor to Captain Bane. Were she not required to play that role, she would remain with the ship, as well."

Laura placed an arm around Heidi and steered her back toward the ship. "Prince Rupor is right, Heidi. Come back to the ship with me."

The lovely redhead allowed herself to be guided back to the ship. Everyone turned to follow the pirate so only I noticed Rupor's gaze linger on Heidi for a second. He realized I was watching and gave a parade ground about-face.

Quietly, so only I could hear, he said, "If you can find some way to save her husband's worthless life, you will have my support. She must have the opportunity to break her marriage voluntarily or I fear she will carry guilt for the rest of her life."

I regarded Rupor for a few seconds, realizing for the first time just how deeply his feelings ran for Heidi. Considering his behavior over the previous six months from this light, I wondered that I hadn't figured it out much earlier. I'm sure Callan and Megan would shake their heads and mutter about clueless men. On the other hand, I expect comprehension was just dawning on Martin, too.

"I'll do my best, Rupor."

"That's all I can ask, Ri- David." A friendly grin crossed Rupor's face. "And in all honesty, your best is exceedingly good. If any man can find a way to bring Chapman out of this alive *and* keep him from alerting the pirates to our intentions, it's you."

A busy couple of hours loomed ahead of me. I had to find a way to draw out the duel so the control systems could be sabotaged, kill two pirates without giving away my identity as a scout, join the fighting withdrawal to our ship, and somehow keep Chapman alive in the bargain. No pressure. Just another typical day at the office.

I spent the next ten minutes making and rejecting plans and then the time for planning was at an end. Our guide pirate showed me into a room, telling me to come out the other side when the bell sounded. As soon as we were alone, I waved the smelling salts under Chapman's nose. He awoke, looking about wildly. He moaned as he recognized the room.

"Chapman-"

I was interrupted before I could say more.

Ding.

43

KILL 'EM

Cheering swelled from the arena, making Chapman even more frantic than the ringing of the bell had done. As Tristan warned, the man was also groggy after returning to consciousness. I had to grab him by the shoulders and hold him still.

"There's no time to explain my plan." Because I didn't *have* a plan, not that he needed to know that. "Do as I tell you to do and you will get out of this alive. Do you understand?"

Chapman nodded and I reached for the handle to open the door. Catching Chapman's eye, I let my true opinion of him shine through. He quailed at my expression.

"But if you even *think* about warning the pirates of our plans, I will cheerfully kill you myself."

I felt the brief disorientation that comes from stepping through a gravity field then pulled Chapman along behind me. We hung, weightless, in a big cube of a room measuring about a hundred feet on a side. Half a dozen spheres moved lazily within the arena, serving as cover and objects to use for changes of direction.

All but the two walls opposite each other—I chose to call them the floor and ceiling—held seats. Wide-spaced bars gave the combatants something to push off from, but the pirates filling the seats were also free to reach into the arena and interfere with anyone who got too close to them. With the exception of the pirates who had bet on Chapman and me, I knew we had no friends in the stands.

To my left, in the center of the wall, was the captains' chamber. Rank had its privilege, as walls separated the officers from the common pirates. Quint and the other five captains sat with Martin, Megan, Rupor, and Callan. The six captains leaned forward in their seats, faces lit with the same anticipation shown by their men.

The door swung shut behind us—no retreat for those in the arena, obviously—revealing a small weapons locker bolted to the back of the door. I found two big, wicked knives inside the locker. Taking one for myself, I handed the other to Chapman.

A cheer rose from the pirates as our two opponents pushed off from their side of the room, each heading for a different sphere within the arena. Grabbing Chapman's collar, I pushed off toward a different sphere, one closer to the pirate on my right.

"What are you doing?" wailed Chapman.

"They're planning to come at us from two sides, probably so one can keep me busy while the other deals with you. If we're in position and closer to one than the other, I'll have an easier time disrupting their plan. All you have to do is stay with me and cover my back if one of the pirates gets close. I'll handle the rest."

I brought us to a stop against my chosen sphere. Seconds later, the pirates worked their way around their spheres to face us. The pirate farther away prepared to push off from his sphere toward us, but held his position. I turned back to the other pirate and crouched, ready to take the attack to him if he moved first. He suddenly grinned and shoved off hard toward the door Chapman and I had come through. Looking back, I realized why the man was so happy.

Chapman had panicked and fled back the way we had come. He floated slowly toward the door, a sitting duck for the grinning pirate. The pirate, obviously experienced in zero G, flew as straight as a well-aimed crossbow bolt toward Chapman. Their paths would cross in a few seconds and I held no illusions as to the end result. I could already picture crimson spheres of Chapman's blood floating around the arena. Would Chapman's body become some sort of macabre version of the beach ball sports crowds bat around for fun?

Shaking off that gruesome image, I glanced at the other pirate. The look dashed my hope that he would launch himself at me or Chapman. The man hung onto his sphere, watching me like a hawk. Once I committed myself, he'd be free to choose the best counter to my move. I fought a strong temptation to leave Chapman to his fate, but I also believed Rupor was right. If Chapman died in this duel, Heidi might spend her life wondering what she could have done to save her husband. Painful as it would be for her, she needed to see him for the low-life he was and then make a break from him on her own terms and of her own accord.

Without another thought, I launched myself toward the grinning pirate. I pushed off *hard* from the sphere, planning to overtake the pirate before he reached the panic-stricken Chapman. The other pirate shouted a warning to his friend. A quick glance backward showed the second pirate following me. He moved more slowly than me, though, having put less muscle into his launch. Was that because he felt a twinge of cowardice or simply a tinge of caution? Whatever the reason, it meant I'd have a few seconds to deal with the grinning pirate before his partner reached us.

Warned by the shout, the grinning pirate spun around to face me. Then he opened himself into a knife-fighter's stance. In full gravity, it would have been a good move. In zero gravity, not so much. The grinning pirate held his knife low, ready for a thrust to my gut, with his other arm held high to block my knife. Holding my arrow-straight posture, I raised my knife above my head as if preparing for an overhand slash. The pirate's grin widened as he waited for my unprotected chest to get within knife range.

At the last second, I tucked and spun one hundred and eighty degrees. Then I kicked out at the pirate with my feet. The pirate's knife slashed the bottom of my boot just before my kick connected with his chest. The pirate's knife spun away and the man tumbled backward toward the seats. I, on the other hand, now flew straight back toward the second pirate.

Caught unprepared, the trailing pirate did the same thing his fellow had done. Had no one ever bothered to teach zero gravity martial arts to these pirates? Everything I'd done so far had been covered in the first few weeks of basic training at the academy. I went for a backward spin this time, planting my feet in the pirate's groin and shoving hard away from him. The pirate howled in pain as I shot away from him and toward Chapman.

Catching Chapman, I spun us about and prepared to use the bars in front of the crowd to propel us back toward the center of the arena. With howls of glee, the watching pirates reached through the bars and grabbed our feet.

"We got 'em, boys," a voice called from the crowd. "Now git over here and kill 'em!"

44

SURRENDER OR DIE

Before the pirates grabbed our feet, I thought Chapman was as panicked as a man could possibly be. It turns out I was wrong about that. His breath coming in short gasps and pants, Chapman gyrated and flailed and kicked, struggling to free himself. The only thing he accomplished was to make the pirates laugh all the harder.

Straining to break myself free, I only looked Chapman's way when his left arm smacked me on the side of my head. I saw his right hand, knuckles white as they gripped the knife, swinging my way. Training and instinct took over. I blocked his swing with my right arm, grabbed his wrist with my left hand, and twisted the knife free. Being disarmed by his 'partner' so surprised Chapman that he went still.

Around us, the pirates went still, too. Arms still reached through the bars to hold onto us, but they directed all of their attention toward the center of the arena. Looking over my shoulder, I saw our two opponents twenty feet away and gliding slowly toward us. Both of them played up to the crowd, making flashy slashes and jabs to show how they planned to deal with us.

Through the comparative silence, Quint's voice rang out. "Looks like yer boy be done fer, Bane."

"Ten thousand credits says my second-in-command gets away safely *and* takes Chapman with him."

Quint barked a laugh. "Done!"

Well, that settled it. I couldn't let Martin lose a small fortune betting on me. Bending over, a knife gripped in each hand, I slashed hard and fast at the arms stretching through the bars to grasp Chapman and me. Cries of pain and anger broke out from the pirates below me. They snatched their arms back from my blades and backed away from the bars.

With our feet free, I wrapped an arm around Chapman and launched us away from the bars and just out of reach of the two pirates floating toward us. By the time the two pirates finished their slow drift to the side of the arena, I had the two of us safely hanging onto one of the spheres in the middle of the arena.

The crowd of pirates went deadly quiet. They'd gotten the bloodshed they wanted, but the wrong bodies had shed the blood.

"My oh my," Martin said. "It seems my 'boy' left quite a mess in his wake. And, I might add, you owe me ten thousand credits, Quint."

"Yer boy were clever, Bane, I'll grant ya that," Quint growled. "But them what's watchin' ain't part of the duel."

"The second those men reached through the bars, they made themselves part of the duel. But I think your real worry is the money you just lost. I'm feeling rather generous at the moment, Quint, so how about another bet? Double or nothing."

"Name it."

"I bet my lad can stay alive in the arena for another five minutes without killing his opponents."

"*And* he's gotta keep Chapman alive fer the same five minutes."

"I'll agree to that, Quint."

"Then the bet be on, Bane."

If everything was going according to plan, the docking bay lasers would be disabled in five more minutes. Bane's bet gave me free rein to lead the two pirates on a merry chase without drawing suspicion from the captains. It was a good idea, but we'd barely been in the arena for a minute and it was nothing short of a miracle Chapman was still alive.

Of course, Chapman heard everything Bane and Quint said. His reaction was entirely predictable. Chapman panicked. Eyes wide with terror, Chapman flung himself toward Quint and the other pirate captains.

I lunged for Chapman, trying to catch his feet and keep him with me. My hands hit the bottom of his boots but had nothing to grab onto. My near miss sent Chapman tumbling, but he was still heading straight for the captains' box. Meanwhile, I lost contact with the sphere and drifted just out of reach of it. I found myself stranded in midair and an easy target for the pirates.

Our two opponents grinned at our predicament while the watching pirates roared in laughter. The two pirates exchanged a glance and then they both launched themselves at me. I'd have done the same thing in their situation. Unarmed and panicking, Chapman posed no threat. They could kill him at their leisure once they didn't have to worry about me. And here I was, just hanging around and inviting them to attack me.

Spinning back toward the sphere, I tried swimming in its direction. Given time, I could stop my slow drift away from the sphere and begin drifting toward it. But that was time I didn't have. The pirates arrowed in on me, each with one arm in front to block any attacks and one arm ready to slash or stab with the knife. My strokes grew more frantic as I tried to get back to the safety of a solid surface.

At least, that's what I *hoped* it looked like. I had very little going for me. The illusion of panic might yield a split second of advantage just as the pirates reached me. I also prepared for the one thing I hadn't expected would be of any use to me in this duel—Boost. Working and fighting in zero gravity is all about finesse and control. Boost is just the opposite, being all about strength and speed. In almost every zero G situation, Boost hinders far more than it helps. With a bit of luck, I could create that rare situation where it helped far more than it hurt.

With the pirates almost upon me, I stopped thrashing and pulled my knees up. Just before they were close enough for me to reach, I kicked at them. The two pirates laughed aloud at what they took to be mistimed kicks. Reaching out with their free hand, each pirate grabbed onto one of my legs. I flung my legs wide as if trying to throw them off. In response, each pirate wrapped his arm tightly around the leg he held. And *that* was what I'd been waiting for.

Boost!

Adrenaline flooded my bloodstream and time slowed. I had just enough time to see the pirates' grins begin to fade as I brought my legs back together with all of my Boosted strength.

Crack! The pirates' heads slammed together. Stunned, the two men lost their grips on my legs and one of them lost his grip on his knife. I pulled my knees up and kicked them again. This time they tumbled away toward the far wall and I floated back to my sphere.

Dropping Boost, I looked for Chapman. He was still tumbling, but had begun shouting something as he neared the captains' box. The crowd noise remained too loud for anyone to hear what he was saying, but I could read his lips.

He was shouting, "Captain Quint! They're not pirates. It's a trap!"

I wanted to grab the knife floating close by—it would have given me three of the four in the arena—but shutting Chapman up was far more important. Tensing my legs beneath me, I shoved off hard toward Chapman. I was tired of dealing with this loathsome excuse for a man and his cowardly attempts to ingratiate himself with the pirates.

With anger written on my face and a knife clutched in each hand, I must have looked like death incarnate falling toward Chapman. His voice rose to such a shrill tone that it pierced the roar of the crowd. But he no longer cried his warning to Quint. Instead, he squealed, "He's going to kill me! Help!"

The pirate captains heard his cries, as did most of the pirates watching. To a man, they all roared with laughter at this unexpected addition to the drama of the arena.

I glanced at the others in the captains' box. Megan, remembering our script, was shouting in Mordanian about Martin's most recent bet. Callan stepped to the back wall of the box, out of the way if a fight broke out, and pulled Megan along with her. Hand lightly resting on his sword hilt, Martin moved close to Quint. Rupor met my gaze and slowly shook his head; tacit agreement that Chapman could not be saved from himself. Then Rupor stepped as far from Martin as the box would allow.

Turning my attention back to Chapman, I was surprised to see he'd managed to stop tumbling and was now mere feet from the captains' box. He still screeched in a higher pitch than a man his size should ever be able to reach, but he had changed his tune yet again.

"Captain Quint! They're not pirates. They're Scouts. It's a trap!"

This time, Chapman was too close and his voice was too piercing to be ignored. As the words got through to Quint, his laughter faded. Concentration sharpened his features and Quint's eyes shot about the box, noting everyone's position. The other captains were just starting to take notice of Chapman's words when I caught up with the coward.

Putting a knife-wielding hand on the back of Chapman's head, I smashed it hard into one of the bars in front of the captains' box. Chapman went limp as his head bounced off the bar.

I swung my arms up and caught a cross bar with bent wrists. Tucking, I swung around the cross bar and between the two side bars. Gravity returned as I landed inside the captains' box.

Knives held ready, I straightened before the startled captains. The watching pirates fell silent at yet another unexpected development in their entertainment. When I spoke, my voice carried throughout the arena.

"I am David Rice, Scout First Class of the Terran Exploration Corps. Surrender or die."

45

THE BLOOD SINGS

From Chapman's warning, Quint already knew something was amiss and the other captains were starting to figure it out. Once we attacked the captains, the pirates around the arena would come to the same conclusion. So, my ultimatum gave away nothing the pirates weren't going to discover in the next second or two. It did achieve the effect I hoped for—it gave the captains pause. It lasted only a second, but when you're outnumbered every little bit helps.

Steel rasped against leather as Martin and Rupor drew their swords. At the same time, Quint broke for the zero gravity arena. With a bound, he dove between the bars, kicking off from them to launch himself toward one of the spheres.

Once he was clear of us, Quint bellowed, "Take 'em afore they git away, lads."

That broke the spell. With a roar, pirates surged through the bars and into the arena. In the box with us, the pirate captains went for their swords.

With a flick of my wrist, one of my knives flew across the box and buried itself in the throat of a pirate captain. Gurgling, blood fountaining from his neck, the man stumbled into another pirate. Off balance, that pirate made an easy target for Rupor's flashing blade.

I wish the remaining three pirate captains got unnerved by the sudden violence and the rapidly shifting situation, but it didn't happen. Violence and chaos are part and parcel of the life of a pirate. Drawing their swords, the pirates advanced to meet us. The box rang as steel met steel.

No one rose to the position of pirate captain without being skilled with a blade. These men were no exceptions. They knew hundreds of pirates were swarming their way. If they fought defensively, they could hold us off until their men arrived and overwhelmed us.

Martin and Rupor pushed their pirates' defenses to the limit, but I only had a knife. Fighting at such a disadvantage, there was no chance I could finish off my opponent quickly without Boosting. I hated the idea of using Boost so early in what could become a running fight, but I saw no other option. Then I saw six inches of bloody steel push out of my opponent's chest.

The pirate fell forward, revealing Callan holding my blood-coated sword.

"The pirates don't allow lasers within the base, darling, only blades," she said, reversing the sword and handing it to me. "So I brought yours."

"Remind me to kiss you when we have the time," I said, slashing the back of the pirate fighting Martin.

As Martin thrust his sword through the wounded pirate, I spun and ran my blade through the pirate facing Rupor. The prince sketched a salute with his sword.

Megan opened the door out of the captains' box and ran through. The rest of us followed. The first pirate had just reached the bars of the captains' box as I slipped through the door. In the corridor, Mordanian and Tartegian marines fought shoulder to shoulder against more pirates. Our escape route was blocked.

"Martin, find us a way out of here," I called, spinning to guard the door I'd just stepped through.

"Already on it," Martin replied over the clash of weapons.

"Marines, withdraw from your position slowly until the door Captain Rice is guarding is in front of you," Rupor ordered. "We'll be surrounded, otherwise."

Sword at the ready, Rupor joined me at the door into the captains' box. He lunged as the door swung open and was rewarded by a cry of pain from inside.

"Takes you back to when we stormed the pirate spaceship a few months ago, eh what?" he grinned.

I slashed an extending sword arm and the blade dropped to the floor. "What, being heavily outnumbered and too close to the dark edge of death?"

"Exactly, my friend," Rupor enthused, parrying a hastily jabbed pirate sword. "A man is never more alive than when he's defying death. It makes the blood sing!"

"Last time my blood sang, it also leaked in large quantities. And I recall that you were captured." I lunged at a face inside the door. The face disappeared as the pirate jumped back and tripped over someone behind him.

"True, but we have your friend Captain Bane with us this time," Rupor said, pulling his sword from the belly of a pirate.

As if on cue, Martin called, "I've found something. Keep up the fighting withdrawal while I get the ladies into the air duct."

Air ducts? Not bad, and they might even get us quickly and safely behind our own lines—assuming we didn't get hopelessly lost in them, instead. But I could see one problem with that escape route.

"How are we all going to get into the ducts without leaving some marines behind to die?"

The sergeant leading the marines replied, "That's our job, sir, and we're damned good at it. The pirates will pay heavily before they get past us."

The marines' fighting withdrawal reached Rupor and me. I fell in beside a young private who couldn't be more than a couple of years older than Milo.

"Martin, there's got to be something we can do to give all of us a fighting chance."

Rupor fell in beside me as we backed down the corridor and away from the door. Overeager, the pirates inside the captains' box rushed into the corridor and smashed into the other pirates' front line. It was a golden opportunity and the marines took full advantage of the confusion. Swords flashed and men screamed. Seconds later, nine pirates lay dead or dying and the pirates paused to regroup.

In the comparative silence, Martin didn't have to shout. "I've got an idea for getting all of us away from here."

Martin's tone was as casual as possible under the circumstances, but there must have been something in his look that gave Callan pause.

"What kind of idea?" she demanded.

"It's simple. We take advantage of the confusion and everyone retreats into the duct."

Before us, the pirates were already regrouping. Their confusion hadn't lasted nearly long enough for Martin's plan to succeed.

"And what, exactly, is going to cause this confusion?" Megan asked.

"David and I will," he replied. "When we attack the pirates while Boosted."

46

THE CRIMSON BALL

THE ADVANCE OF THE PIRATES SLOWED AS THE PIRATES ARGUED OVER WHO would be on the front line. It appeared everyone wanted the first crack at us. That gave Callan and Megan time to express their opinions of Martin's plan.

"Isn't that *always* the plan?" Callan asked. "Danger looms, David Boosts, and his life gets shortened because Boost abuses his body. I didn't marry the man just to watch him Boost himself into an early grave."

"And, speaking as the expedition's bard, do you have any idea how hard it is to find rhymes for Boost?" Megan added.

"There's always loosed," Martin said. "As in 'The men did Boost, and death was loosed.'"

"Dearest, I'd have starved years ago if I had your way with words," Megan replied.

"That's it!" Callan exclaimed. "Megan, words and images are your livelihood. Why not tell the pirates exactly what will happen to them if they attack us again. Be as colorful and graphic as you like."

Megan grinned, grabbed Martin and me by the arm, and stepped toward what would soon be the line of battle. "Come on, boys, let's put on a show."

Facing the pirates across ten feet of corridor, she began singing in gal base. Seriously, Megan sang to a blood-thirsty gang of pirates.

Come one, come all
To the crimson ball!
I've a Scout to my left,
And a Scout to my right,
And Boosted they'll be,
When they join in the fight!
With a wink and a glance
They'll ask you to dance.
Then their blades will flash,
They will cut and slash!
Then your heads will fly,
And you each will die,
As we paint the hall red
With the blood of your dead!
So come one, come all
To the crimson ball!

I found the grisly song all the more jarring for the spritely tone Megan used. But she abandoned that tune for the last two lines. Those were delivered in a tone so menacing I felt a shiver run up my spine.

"All fun aside, boys," Megan said into the silence, "you will end up looking just like a girl's dolls after her spiteful little brother finishes playing with them—heads and arms scattered everywhere. Look at the bodies you just dragged aside. Hacked and slashed as they are, those are *pretty* corpses compared to what David and Martin will leave behind if they Boost."

Turning toward the air duct, Megan looked back over her shoulder. "Or you could just say we slipped away when you eager lads from the arena crashed out into the stalwart fellows in the corridor. It's such an easy story to remember and who could say otherwise?"

With a parting smile, Megan began walking away.

"Let's go, everyone," she hissed. "They're non-plussed right now, but I don't know how long that can last."

While Megan sang, two marines had pulled the grating up from the air duct. One by one, we jumped into the duct. Dropping down last, I yanked the grating back in place. Bending double, we hurried through the duct, unsure where it would lead.

The hubbub surrounding the arena faded as we rushed away from it. Martin slipped around everyone to take the lead while I stayed at the back to guard against pursuers.

"That was nicely done back there, my love," he said to Megan. "When did you have time to come up with that song?"

"I just made it up as I sang it."

"Callan," Martin said, "could I suggest you have Megan appointed as the official bard of the Mordanian Court when we get home?"

"Please ignore Martin," Megan said to Callan. "My songs are meant to be sung in taverns, on trails, and on street corners, not cooped up in a stuffy palace filled with stuffy nobles."

Megan suddenly remembered she was talking to a noble who lived in the palace. "Um, no offense, Your Highness."

Callan laughed. "None taken, Megan. I hope you'll agree to perform at the palace someday, but you have too much wanderlust to be happy stuck in one place. How fortunate for you that Martin shares your love of the itinerant lifestyle. You'll give us enough advance notice to catch up with the two of you for the big day, won't you?"

"What big day?" Megan asked.

"Your Highness, has anyone told you that you are much too observant?" Martin said.

"I *am* sorry, Martin," Callan said, contrition creeping into her voice. "You've always been one to act once you made up your mind, I just assumed..."

"Would someone mind letting me in on this big secret?" Megan said, her voice rising.

"I'd hoped to be on one knee rather than bent double running through an air duct, but it seems the universe had other plans." Martin looked over his shoulder. "Megan, will you marry me?"

"Oh, is that what this is all about?" Megan asked. "Sure, I'll marry you."

"Until we have more time, please consider yourself thoroughly kissed, my dear."

"Consider my heart to be all aflutter and me near to swooning, dear heart."

"You've made me the happiest man in the air duct."

"My congratulations to the both of you," I called. "But can you see a way out of this duct, Martin? My back is killing me."

"David, you'll be my best man, of course," Martin called back. "And I see a grating about fifty feet ahead."

"I'd be honored," I said. "Do you hear any sounds from ahead?"

"Excellent," Martin called. "I don't hear anything. We can assume there isn't any fighting above the grate, at least."

"We might as well complete the wedding party while we're down here," Megan said. "Callan, would you be my matron of honor?"

"Matron makes me sound so old. I'm only twenty-three, you know."

It was Megan's turn to laugh. "There is a specific connotation to the term 'maid.' Unless you're saying David and you have not-"

"Matron it is," Callan interrupted. "And, like David, I'd be honored."

"My compliments to the happy couple," growled the marine sergeant, "but could I suggest you hold off setting a wedding date until we're back aboard the ship?"

"Good idea, Sergeant," Martin said. "The corridor above sounds empty. This is as good an opportunity to get out of this duct as any."

At a nod from me, Martin lifted the grate and climbed out. Two marines followed him before Chapman's voice rang out.

"There they are, Captain Quint. Just like I told you."

47

I DON'T KNOW WHAT I WAS THINKING

RUPOR, WHO WAS ABOUT TO ASCEND INTO THE CORRIDOR, SIGHED. "MY apologies, David. I shouldn't have suggested you try to save that snake Chapman. I don't know what I was thinking."

"You were thinking about the woman you love, Rupor," I said.

Rupor's eyebrows shot up. "Is it so obvious?"

Moving up next to Rupor, I pulled myself up into the corridor. "I'd wager all of the women on the ship have probably figured it out. The men are probably as clueless as I was before you sent Heidi back to the ship."

Rupor rose from the air duct to join us in the corridor. "Then, if the chance presents itself, you know why I must be the one to kill Chapman."

"He knows nothing of the sort, Rupor," Callan called from below. "David, don't let Rupor kill that slime unless there is absolutely no other choice."

"Martin, I expect you to help David with that," Megan sang out.

"But I-" Rupor began.

"Your Highness," growled the sergeant, "a wise man listens to what women have to say concerning affairs of the heart."

Rupor stared at the marine for a second.

"I've been married nearly as long as you've been alive, Prince

Rupor," the sergeant said. "After that many years, a man either learns a few things about women or spends a lot of cold nights on the couch. I've never slept on the couch. Now, gentlemen, could I suggest we turn our attention to these pirates?"

Our section of the corridor got quite crowded as two more marines climbed up to join us. One more marine, the young private I'd fought next to only a few minutes ago, prepared to join us.

"Stay down there, Harris," the sergeant ordered. "If we can't break through the pirate lines, it's your responsibility to get the women back to our ship."

"Yes, sir!" Harris replied.

We turned our attention back to the pirates. Two groups stood to either side of us, blocking all exits except the air duct. Despite having the numerical advantage, the pirates just milled about. Quint, arms folded, glared at us from behind one group. Chapman, eyes bright and looking all the world like a weasel, stood next to Quint.

"Why aren't they attacking?" one of the marines asked.

"Quint's probably waiting for even more men to arrive so he can overwhelm us," Martin said.

"Then let's not wait for them to attack us," I said. "Marines, stand aside and give Martin and me clear paths to the pirates."

Stepping forward, I looked in the eye of each pirate on the front line. Switching to gal base, I said, "There's a warlike indigenous race living on my adopted planet. Do you know what their name for me is?"

The pirates exchanged confused glances before one responded, "Um, no?"

"Pay him no never mind, boys," Quint called. "We got 'em outnumbered."

"Then why aren't you attacking, Quint?" I said. I turned my attention back to the front line. "They call me the Hand of Death. If you don't stand down, my hand will deal your death."

The four on the front line exchanged nervous glances.

"Ignore his yammerin'," Quint commanded. "He be outnumbered. Ain't no way he attacks."

Sword raised, I charged.

The eyes of every pirate watched me. None of them saw Quint's face go slack and his eyes go wide when I attacked. Slowly, he backed away from his men, opening his mouth twice before finding his voice.

"Ha!" It sounded more like a cough than a laugh. "I goaded him right good. Twenty thousand credits to the man what deals the death blow."

The gleam of greed replaced fear in many of the pirates' eyes. They stopped backing away and readied their blades. Over their heads, I saw Quint and Chapman turn and run back down the corridor. I wanted to Boost, jump over the men, and chase Quint. But there were too many men to leap and the ceiling was much too low. I'd have to settle for Boosting and taking my frustration out on the pirates standing before me.

"Boarding party discipline, sir," called the sergeant from close behind me.

That made me pull up short of the pirates' line. A second later, Rupor, the sergeant, and a private stood beside me.

"Hold to the drill, gentlemen," Rupor said, "and we'll set this rabble on their heels."

The sudden change in tactics sent the pirates edging back again. With Rupor calling the cadence, the four of us stepped forward in unison and engaged the pirates.

The popular image of pirates is one of vicious bands of cutthroats swarming throughout a ship, cutting down all who dare to stand in their way. For once, the popular image matched reality. But 'vicious' is nothing more than an attitude and 'swarm' is a tactic long abandoned by military-minded men. Pirates never fight trained military units unless they're cornered or can overwhelm them through sheer numbers.

The pirates outnumbered us five or six to one, but the confines of the corridor kept the number of men actually fighting us to four. We advanced, slashing and stabbing with coordination and an economy of motion strange to the pirates. Unsure how to react, the pirates fell back on their preferred fighting styles. They hacked and slashed with big, strong strokes that were as likely to get in each other's way as they were to force one of us to block the blow.

Within seconds of the first clash of steel, blood dripped from our swords and four new pirates stood before us. Rupor blocked a pirate's attack and immobilized the blade.

"Bind!" he snapped.

The private's blade stabbed into Rupor's pirate as the sergeant and I shifted into defensive mode, covering the two men dealing with the immobilized pirate.

"Clear!" Rupor called as the pirate fell away from him.

Five more pirates fell before the rest of them realized they didn't have the skill or tactics to win against four blades working as one. Our opponents turned and ran, abandoning the three men still engaged with us.

"Your fellows have left you," Rupor said. "Be smart chaps and drop your swords. If you do, I give you my word we won't kill you."

Three swords clattered to the deck.

"That's the first smart move I've seen all day," I said. "When you see your fellow pirates, tell them we simply want to get back to our ship, nothing more. If they don't get in our way, we won't kill them. Now, scram."

Pirate footfalls faded quickly and we headed back to the air duct. Martin and his marines finished routing their pirates as the sergeant called to his man.

"Harris? It's safe to come up now."

Harris didn't answer. Heart leaping to my throat, I rushed to the opening. A dead pirate lay below in the air duct. There was no sign of Harris, Megan, or Callan.

48

INTO THE AIRLOCK

Afraid of what I'd see, I leapt into the air duct. Martin was right behind me. A quick look around told the story well enough.

Up toward the arena, a new opening yawned in the side of the duct. If I looked through the opening, I was certain I'd find a metal plate and a maintenance tunnel. I assumed Chapman told Quint about the tunnel and Quint sent men through it to either cut us off or attack us from behind. The plan would have worked, too, except the pirates found easier, more tempting prey waiting for them in the air duct.

"Looks like Harris killed one of the pirates and then took off with Megan and Callan," Martin said.

"And the pirates chased after them instead of attacking us," I added.

Bent double, I set off down the duct as fast as the cramped conditions would allow. Martin was right behind me.

"Keep up with them, lads," the sergeant ordered. "Our captains won't be thinking clearly 'till their women are safe."

Part of my brain—a very small, very remote part—knew the sergeant was right. The animal part of my brain and the husband part of my brain already pictured me hacking every last pirate into very small pieces for what I feared they'd done to my wife.

"Harris is a smart lad, sir," the sergeant called, perhaps trying to convince Martin and me to show more caution. "He'll run if he can and fight if he has to. He'll keep the ladies safe."

It was a good try and might have worked if we hadn't come across the blood stain. It wasn't much, a smear of blood on the side of the duct. It might not even have been Harris's blood. Even if it wasn't, it was evidence of more fighting.

Rounding a bend, we saw the duct end in the side wall of a hallway. As we drew closer, I saw the grating leaning crookedly against the far wall of the corridor, red blood shining from a spot in the middle of the grate. Harris must have barreled into it without slowing down, clearing an exit for Callan and Megan. It also told us Harris was wounded.

Exiting the duct, Martin and I rose to our full height and looked both ways down the corridor.

"There!" I shouted and set off running to the right.

A knot of pirates hacked and slashed at Harris, who stood resolutely between the pirates and the two women. With every stroke he exchanged with a pirate, Harris and the women retreated a step. The marine bled from half a dozen minor cuts and a wound to his left shoulder.

We were fifty yards away, shouting to draw the pirates' attention and running as fast as our feet could carry us. The sounds of their own battle must have drowned out our voices, because none of the pirates turned our way. Then Callan and Megan ran out of room to retreat and Harris was forced to stand and fight. The pirates pressed the attack for a couple of seconds then suddenly pulled back. One of the pirates hit a control on the wall and a heavy door slid between the pirates and the trio.

The pirates had driven the three of them into an airlock!

Harris obviously realized it, too. Through the window in the airlock door, I saw him spring forward. He was too late. Steel hit steel as the door finished closing. Without taking his eyes from the airlock window, a pirate slapped the control to open the airlock to the void of space.

49

A RED HAZE

THROUGH THE SMALL WINDOW IN THE SLIDING AIRLOCK DOOR, CALLAN caught sight of me racing down the corridor. For a second, hope flared in her lovely face. But as Harris lunged toward the closing door, she realized there was no way I could reach her in time. Hope gave way to despair before my view of her was blocked by pirates crowding around the window to watch the three meet their doom.

I felt as if my heart had burst inside my chest. A red haze fell across everything before me and my vision narrowed until I could see nothing but the closest pirate. From far away, I heard myself vent a howl of inarticulate rage and remorse. Beside me, Martin did the same.

Boost!

The pirate at the end of my tunnel vision was just turning around when my sword cut him in two.

As the pieces of the pirate fell away, another pirate appeared at the end of my red tunnel. His sword came up in slow motion then fell away as I severed his arm at the elbow. Terror etched itself on the man's face as I drove my sword into his chest, stopping only when the hilt hit his breast bone. With a heave, I flung the body over my head, yanking my sword free as the dying man fell to the corridor behind me.

On the edge of my narrowed vision, I saw a pirate trying to sidle around me. My left fist shot out and crushed the man's throat. The gurgling, gagging man slid down the wall, doomed to a slow death by asphyxiation.

The next pirate tried to back away, both hands held before him imploring me to spare him. Pirates behind him shoved him back toward me. I swung and my sword sliced his throat wide open.

With no hope of escape, two pirates charged at me. I stepped forward to meet them. With a broad sweep of my sword, their heads bounced off the corridor wall.

Finally, I came to the man who had closed the airlock door. The man who had pressed the button and consigned my wife, my reason for life, to the cold void of space. He huddled against the wall, hands raised in supplication. Tears streamed down his face and his mouth moved frantically as he begged for his life.

I was not in a forgiving mood.

Sword raised to give the man a faster death than he deserved, I stepped toward him.

"David! No!"

Oh, God, I could almost hear Callan's voice calling to me.

"Darling, stop! For me, for us, stop!"

Green eyes appeared at the end of my red tunnel. Soft, loving hands wrapped around my neck and pulled me toward the eyes. I dropped my sword and, not daring to hope, reached toward the vision before me. My hands met warm, live flesh and I pulled Callan into my embrace.

My vision cleared. Hearing returned. I was vaguely aware Martin and Megan were similarly entwined. Covering my wife's face with kisses, I rejoiced.

Callan was alive!

50

IT'S THE LAW

At last convinced that this wasn't a dream from which I would awaken, that Callan truly was alive, I stopped smothering her with kisses and simply held her close.

"How?" I asked. "I saw the airlock door close. I saw the pirate cycle the airlock. How did you survive?"

"Ask Private Harris," Callan said. "He's the one who saved us."

Martin and I both turned to the private, who looked uncomfortable under our gazes.

"Go on, Harris," the sergeant encouraged. "Tell them what you were telling me."

"Well, sir, I realized we were in an airlock as soon as Her Highness and Miss Megan," and here Harris turned to Megan, "I'm sorry ma'am, I don't know your family name."

"It's Tuttle, but you're more than welcome to call me Megan."

"Like I was saying, I figured out it was an airlock when we ran out of room to retreat. I mean, it would be stupid to make a corridor that didn't go anywhere. Then when those bast- uh, pirates jumped back, I figured out their plan. I remembered all that spaceship safety training we got from those ladies who used to be prisoners of the pirates, especially how airlock doors won't open if the other door isn't fully shut and sealed."

Harris held up a mangled sword. "I jumped forward and stuck my sword between the door and the wall. The door looked like it shut and it sounded like it shut, but it didn't shut. Of course, we'd have been in real trouble if you and Captain Bane hadn't shown up, sir."

"That was quick thinking, lad," the sergeant said. Turning to me, he added, "Like I told you, he's a smart one."

I grasped Harris's hand. "Thank you. Those words are inadequate, but they're all I have."

Martin followed suit. Then Callan and Megan surrounded Harris. He blushed a deep scarlet when they both hugged him and kissed him on the cheek. Finally, Rupor pumped the private's hand, offering a hearty, "Good show, lad."

"I hate to interrupt, sir," the sergeant said. Pointing at the lone surviving pirate, the one who had tried to cycle the airlock, he added, "But we need to decide what we're going to do with him and then get out of this corridor before some other pirates trap us down here."

The pirate sat huddled on the deck, staring at me with wide, wild eyes.

"He's guilty of the attempted murder of a member of the royal family of Mordan," I said.

The pirate started shaking his head violently. "I can't be guilty unless I have a trial! It's the law! I've got to have a trial!"

"What a staunch defender of law and order you are all of a sudden," I sneered. "What due process did you follow before attempting to murder my wife?"

"I didn't know who she was!"

"Well, ignorance won't be a problem for you much longer. There is only one penalty for your crime—death by beheading."

"You can't do that! You're a sworn officer of the Terran Federation. You have to follow the law."

"Damn me, but the man is right," I said. "Neither Martin nor I can carry out the sentence."

"My planet is not a member of this federation," Rupor said. "Perhaps you would allow me the honor?"

"By all means," I replied. "Does anyone have anything to say in this pirate's defense?"

My companions all shook their heads. The marines dragged the pirate to his feet and down the hallway a dozen yards. The man blubbered and pleaded for his life, something I felt certain would draw harsh laughter from the pirate if our positions were reversed. Then Rupor's sword flashed and pleading stopped.

"They- they just executed him! Chopped off his head." The voice came from down the corridor.

Pirates crowded into the corridor from the same air duct we'd come through moments earlier.

Just as the sergeant feared, we were trapped.

51

OUT THE AIRLOCK

THE PIRATES CONTINUED TO PILE INTO THE CORRIDOR FIFTY YARDS AWAY. Silence fell over them as each pirate took in the scene before the airlock. Bodies and pieces of bodies lay scattered around us, with splashes of crimson breaking the monotonous gray of the rock from which the pirate base had been carved. One of the pirates said something to his fellows. The distance reduced his words to an indistinct murmur, but his fellow pirates heard him clearly enough—including the one in charge.

"Shut yer trap, Benson," Quint ordered. "This ain't no ball, crimson or t'otherwise. Now git down there and take 'em, men."

"Martin," I asked, "any bright ideas?"

"Actually, yes. See if you can delay them for a minute or two."

Turning my attention back to the pirates, who started a slow shuffle in our direction, I called, "Hey, Quint, if you want someone to 'git' us, why don't you step to the front and lead by example. Bring my old pal Chapman with you." I held up my blood-stained sword. "I've got a few pointed remarks to make to him."

Some of the pirates laughed.

"Stop yer laughin' and git moving," Quint bellowed.

Once again, a few pirates took a few steps in my direction.

"I've got to say, Quint, you do seem to have a way with commanding men," I yelled. "How do you manage to get them to go to their deaths while you stay in the rear, ready to run if the battle goes against you?"

The pirates who had shuffled forward stopped and looked behind them.

"Did Quint tell you what he did just a few minutes ago, when we met in a different corridor?"

"Pay him no never mind and charge," Quint commanded.

"Maybe you could ask Chapman about it. He was right by Quint's side throughout the fight." All the pirates looked back at the pirate captain, uncertainty written on their faces. "Quint, they all know Chapman for the coward he is. What does it say about you that you've been shoulder to shoulder with him every time we've met in battle?"

Quint's face went so brightly red I thought he might pop an artery. Grabbing Chapman by the arm, he dragged the hapless turncoat through the crowd to the front.

"Ain't nobody gonna git away with callin' me no coward, Rice," he yelled. Turning back to his men, he shouted, "Like I said, let's git 'em!"

Sword in one hand and dragging Chapman with the other, Quint led the charge. Their faith in Captain Quint restored, the pirates roared and charged after him.

"Martin, how's that idea coming?"

"Surprisingly well, David," he said. "You did such a good job distracting them, I don't think any of the pirates noticed me rummaging around in the storage locker at the end of the corridor. It held more vacuum harnesses than we need. Once you put on your harness, we can get out of here."

I sprinted back to the airlock. Martin tossed a harness to me and started closing the airlock door to the corridor. I slipped into the harness quickly and was ready by the time the door closed. As the door cut off the pirates' shouts, I grabbed the safety strap looped along the wall and wrapped an arm around Callan.

"Ready."

Martin pressed the emergency release. There was a brief rush of air escaping as the outer door opened. Then I led the way out onto the airless surface of the pirate's asteroid base.

52

ON THE SURFACE

CALLAN GLOWED IN THE NIMBUS OF THE AIR-PRESERVING FORCEFIELD HER vacuum harness projected around her body. I would have loved nothing more than to admire her heavenly form, but we had to get away from the horde of pirates bearing down on our position. Martin finished showing the others how to activate their comm units, so I stepped through the base's gravity field and into the almost-nonexistent gravity on the surface of the asteroid.

"Keep your movements controlled and gentle after coming through the gravity field," I warned. "One wrong step could send you spinning off into the asteroid field. In fact, it's best if we all clasp hands. It will slow our progress but we will all be anchored to each other."

Taking my hand, Callan grinned with excitement and stepped through the gravity field. Her grin faded and she turned a slight green.

"Oh, I feel like I'm going to hurl," she moaned. "What's wrong with me?"

"It's just a touch of space sickness," I explained. "Most people suffer from it the first time they experience low or no gravity."

And, indeed, the rest of the Aashlanders also suffered from it, though none quite so badly as my wife.

"You usually look lovely in green, my dear," I said, trying for a light tone, "but that shade just doesn't suit you."

"Ha, ha. Maybe I'll throw up on you and see if green suits *you*."

"Perhaps a change of subject is in order."

"Good idea, husband." Callan still looked sick, but at least there was a bit of humor reflected in her eyes.

"Martin, how many harnesses are left in the locker outside the airlock?" I asked. "We need to prepare for pursuit."

"No pursuit is coming from that airlock, David," Martin replied.

"Our good Captain Bane had each of us grab extra harnesses," Rupor said. "We piled then next to the airlock exit and they blew into space when the air rushed out."

I gave Martin a thumbs up. "Very clever."

"I think 'very obvious' is the more appropriate phrase—at least to anyone familiar with vacuum and pirates," Martin said.

"Okay, since you insist we'll go with 'very obviously clever,'" I said. "The upshot is the pirates have to find another airlock before they can come out here after us. With luck, we'll reach another airlock or the docking bay before they find us."

"Sir?" Harris asked. "How do you know where to go without a sun to guide your direction?"

"My implant has a fairly accurate idea of where we are in relation to the docking bay. I'm just following the map it has constructed of the asteroid—both inside and out."

"So our lives are in the hands—figuratively speaking—of that tiny machine you tell us is in your head?" Rupor asked.

"Welcome to my world, Rupor," Callan said.

I recognized Rupor's and Callan's words for what they were—banter meant to keep everyone's minds off their roiling stomachs. I was about to answer in kind when a bright light flashed across my vision. Looking to my left, I spied a squad of pirates about a hundred yard away. They moved with easy familiarity on the surface of the asteroid. Far worse, they all carried laser pistols.

53

DON'T GET YOURSELF KILLED

"WE'VE GOT TO GET UNDER COVER BEFORE THEIR AIM IMPROVES," I shouted.

"David, let's split into two groups," Martin called. "Once everyone else is under cover, we can figure out what to do."

Doubling the potential targets while making those targets half the size struck me as a very good idea. "Sergeant, Rupor, let go of each other."

Our low gravity conga line broke in two, leaving me with Callan, Harris, Megan, and Rupor. Fortunately, the asteroid was pockmarked with craters and rubble from countless collisions with smaller asteroids. It should only take a few seconds to get under cover.

Bright light flashed at my feet and another light blazed past Harris's head, reminding me that we might not have a few seconds. The pirates were getting the range and it was only a matter of time—a very short time—before they scored a hit. I had to put rock between us and the pirates *now*.

I was leading my group toward a very low ridge only a few feet away. Our slow pace meant it would take too long to get us all behind the ridge. Then I had an idea.

Wedging my foot under a tiny outcropping, I said, "All of you, hold onto each other as tight as possible. Those of you at the end of the line brace yourselves."

Wrapping both hands around Callan's wrist, I pulled her up and over my head. In the light gravity, five full grown adults had a combined weight less than a child's weight in normal gravity. Callan arched up and over me with the other three trailing like a whip cord. My foot pressed against the underside of the outcropping as the line of men and women pivoted about that one spot. My wife came down on the uncovered side of the ridge, but the rest came down just over the crest.

Slipping my foot free, I said, "Harris, pull us over to you."

The young guard's hard yank brought Callan and me barreling into him. The three of us flew past Rupor and Megan. I feared we might spin off the surface of the asteroid and out into space when, with a hard jerk, we came to a stop and slammed down onto the rocky surface. Glancing to the other end of our line, I saw Rupor hugging a small spire like a lover.

Next to me, Callan's weak stomach gave way and she retched miserably. Megan reeled Callan in, wrapped my poor wife in a sisterly hug, and tried to comfort her. I longed to do the same but our lives were at stake.

"Martin?" I called over the comm.

"That was quite a show you put on over there," he replied. "Is everyone okay?"

"Scrapes and scratches, but we'll live. Do you think we have piratical eavesdroppers?"

"There's no doubt about it. All the harnesses were set to the same channel." Martin was silent for a couple of seconds. "Were the seniors still playing the search and rescue prank on plebes when you were at the academy?"

"Of course they were. Traditions die hard at the academy. Switch now."

Every plebe in the Scout academy spent one night in a two man ship, monitoring channel five sixteen for orders to move in on a pirate ring. It was the space-based equivalent of a snipe hunt. I changed my channel, showing the others how to do it at the same time.

"Do you read me, Martin?"

"Loud and clear. Now that we can have a private conversation, have you had any bright ideas?"

"Yes. I think you and I ought to go for a swim."

Megan asked the question that was on the mind of every Aashlander. "How are you going swimming when there's no water? Is this some kind of Scout thing?"

"Asteroid miners developed it and named it, but they do teach it in the Scout Academy," I answered. "It's a fast way of moving across uneven surfaces in very low gravity. You lay down and pull yourself along with your hands and feet, pushing off the surface just enough to stay a few inches above it. The miners called it swimming because it looks more like someone swimming underwater."

"So we're all going for a swim?" Callan asked.

"More or less. Martin and I are going to use it to get close enough to attack the pirates," I said. "The rest of you will use it as best you can to get closer to the docking bay."

"David, what makes you think your fellow fighting men would not follow you into battle?" Rupor asked, bristling just a bit. "Leave a man or two to guard the women, of course, but do not presume that we are unworthy to join you."

"Rupor, would you take an untrained soldier into battle? One who had listened to a very brief description of the principles of swordsmanship but had never held a sword?"

"Of course not, but swordsmanship is a complex science while this swimming you describe sounds quite simple."

I pointed to a high outcropping about twenty yards away. "Tell you what, Rupor, if any of you reach that rock before Martin and I reach the pirates, I'll withdraw my objections and you're welcome to join us fighting the pirates."

Rupor nodded, both satisfied and more thoughtful.

Callan kissed my lips. "Don't get yourself killed."

Megan scooted up next to me and kissed my cheek. "Don't let Martin get himself killed."

Rupor pulled himself past me. "I'm not going to kiss you, but would appreciate it if the two of you came back alive. Your deaths would put quite the damper on my courtship of Heidi."

"I wouldn't want my death to inconvenience you, Rupor. You have my solemn vow that I will endeavor to stay alive," I replied. Turning to Harris, I said, "You've got good instincts, Harris. Pay attention to them and I know you'll get the women safely back to the ship."

"If you're quite finished kissing your wife and being kissed by my wife-to-be," Martin said, "perhaps we could get on with this?"

"Yes, O Jealous One. You go northwest and I'll go northeast."

"Got it. Last one to the fight buys the drinks when we get back to civilization."

With that, I swam quickly away from my group. Swimming across the surface of an asteroid looks easy and sounds easier, but it takes a lot of practice to achieve a balance of upward push and forward pull. I hadn't gone asteroid swimming in close to four years, but I was quite accomplished at it before crashing on Aashla. The rhythm came back to me within seconds and I flowed across the asteroid's surface faster than I could have run in full gravity.

A couple of laser shots flashed around me, but neither one was close. I was too low to present a good target and too fast for accurate aiming with a hand weapon. Meanwhile, the shots told me where to find the pirates. I slithered and swam around rocks and craters and ridges until I got behind the pirates' position. Then I headed straight in, hoping to catch them by surprise.

I came upon a band of four pirates moving and shooting toward the ridge we had hidden behind. With a grin, I pulled myself forward at top speed. Then luck turned against me. One of the pirates looked down at his belt to get a fresh energy pack for his pistol and saw me out of the corner of his eye. We were on different comm channels, so I didn't hear his shout, His friends most definitely did.

I was twenty feet from the pirates when they spun about, pistols raised to burn me to a crisp.

54

ARE EITHER OF YOU DEAD?

THREE PIRATES BROUGHT THEIR LASERS TO BEAR ON ME WHILE THE FOURTH pirate fumbled to replace his discharged energy pack. I had no cover available and the pirates could easily burn me before I covered the twenty feet separating us. That left only one option.

Instead of reaching forward for my next swimming stroke, I planted my right hand at my side then pushed hard to the left. Laser blasts flashed where I had been a split second before, but I was five feet to the left now. As the pirates swung their aim in my direction, I pushed off a lump of rock with my left hand and passed just under the pirates' aim before they realized what was happening.

After missing me twice, I doubted the pirates would overreact to my movement again. But I thought they would expect more of the same from me. Rather than zigging back to my left, I pulled my knees in tight and then kicked out and down. Pushing off that hard and at any kind of upward angle should have sent me flying off the asteroid and into empty space. But I'd closed in on the pirates, so crashed into three of the pirates instead.

Two of the men tumbled backward with arms windmilling and legs kicking. Both lost hold of their lasers, which went spinning off to who knows where. The third staggered back and tripped over the fourth pirate, who still crouched trying to reload his pistol. The tripping pirate smacked his head against the rock the pirates had been using for cover and dropped his laser.

That left me standing over the fourth man. Made clumsy by his haste to replace his laser's energy pack, the man dropped both of them. I grabbed the straps of his vacuum harness and heaved him straight up. The pirate's mouth opened in a scream I could not hear as he flew off into the void.

The pirate who had hit his head was groggy and unresisting as I stripped off his spare energy packs and sent him up to join his fellow. I picked up both lasers, reloading the empty one.

"Martin?" I called on the comm. "I've got a couple of lasers. Two of the pirates are out of the fight and two more have been disarmed. Where are you?"

"Having less success than you, it appears," Martin replied. "Assuming you're responsible for the two pirates heading into space, I'm about forty feet west of you, pinned down by laser fire."

Now that I knew what to look for, I spotted laser flashes to the west.

"I'll be there in a few seconds. In the meantime, do as Megan instructed and don't get yourself killed."

"Thank you for that advice, David. It would never have occurred to me."

I was already swimming in the direction of the laser flashes when I replied. "Don't thank me. I'm just relaying Megan's orders. But if you like *that* advice, just wait till you're married."

"I heard that," Megan said over the comm.

"So did I," Callan added dryly.

"Um, the stress of combat makes men say things they don't really mean?" I offered as I came up behind the two pirates firing at Martin.

"Yeah, what he said," Martin added.

My first shot burned a hole right through the pirate on the left. The pirate on the right reacted as if he was in normal gravity, spinning and jumping so fast he lost his footing and rose off the ground. Martin swam up, grappled the laser from the floating pirate, then shoved him up to join the other two in orbit.

"Are either of you dead?" Megan asked.

"No, sweetheart," Martin replied. "And thank you for the invaluable advice on dying, which I shall always endeavor to follow to the letter."

"You'd better, dearest," Megan growled.

Martin looked at me. "As a reformed pirate, it pains me to admit that I don't really like pirates any more. Let's finish this."

Without another word, Martin and I slithered off toward the remaining pirates.

"Far be it from me to interfere with such bold battlefield heroics," Rupor said, "but this might not be the best time to engage in a full assault on the rest of the pirates."

Martin and I exchanged glances and slowed our advance on the pirate's position. It was hardly the sort of comment either of us expected from Rupor, so it caught our attention.

"We're listening," I said.

"You've rather suddenly and spectacularly shot or scattered half a dozen of the pirates. We may not have heard the cries of those six men, but the other pirates will be sharing the same comm channel. They heard everything."

"And why does that mean we shouldn't continue attacking?"

"You attacked their superior numbers, overcame their superior weaponry, and took six of their number out of the fight. Now is the time for us to make a tactical retreat while the pirates are still back on their heels and reluctant to engage us."

The sergeant added, "His Highness has a point, sirs."

"In case there is any doubt, I fully support Rupor's suggestion, also," Callan said.

"Do I need to add my vote to the tally?" Megan asked.

"I believe we're outvoted, David," Martin said. "The rest of you keep moving toward the docking bay. We'll catch you up."

Without another word, we changed directions and swam back toward our family and friends. A couple of minutes later, we caught up with them. They had gotten beyond the large rock I'd pointed out to Rupor before Martin and I went on the offensive, but not by much.

"Yes, David, you were right," Rupor said. "Swimming on an asteroid is far more difficult than I imagined."

"I didn't say anything about your progress."

"No, but you were thinking it."

What can I say, he was right. Were my thoughts really that plainly written on my face?

"Yes, love, anyone who knows you well can see your thoughts clearly written on your face," Callan said.

"To your credit, your words and actions always match your thoughts," Megan added.

"Enough with the fawning over Honest David," Martin growled. "I've been thinking how best to get us moving faster. David's game of crack the whip, when he flung four of you behind the ridge, gave me an idea. We'll split into two groups again, line up head-to-foot, and David and I will each tow a group behind us. The rest of you just have to use your free hand and foot to keep yourself a few inches off the ground."

"Just like a train," I exclaimed. I got blank stares from everyone but Martin. "But I guess most of you have never heard of trains..."

It was the work of but a moment to create the two line ups. For simplicity, we went with the two groups we'd split into earlier. That left me towing Callan, Megan, Rupor, and Harris. Rupor suggested Martin and the marines serve as our rearguard, just in case the pirates went on the offensive sooner rather than later. With that decided, I towed my four passengers in the direction of the docking bay. It took a few minutes for everyone to get into a rhythm, but once they did we made good time across the asteroid.

"How long will it take to reach the docking bay?" Callan asked.

"At the rate we're going, we should reach the entrance in another five minutes," I replied. "In fact, the ship should be within range of our comms about now. Heidi is monitoring channel ten seventeen. Switch to that channel after your next push off from the ground."

Since I didn't have to hold onto anyone's foot, I went ahead and changed channels with one hand while keeping us moving with the other. The signal had some static, but I had no trouble hearing Heidi's voice.

"*Aashla's Hope* to the captain. Do you copy?"

"Loud and clear, Heidi."

"Oh, thank God. We've been worried sick, David. Where are you and who's with you?"

"I've got their Highnesses, Martin, Megan, and a squad of marines. We're swimming across the surface of the asteroid toward you. We should be there in-"

"Get under cover, now!" Heidi cried. "Quint just sent an armed pinnace out to find and destroy you."

55

FLYING BODIES

We were surrounded by all sorts of good cover against an attack from the ground, none of which would do any good against an attack from above. I scanned all around us hoping to spot something close by, but came up empty.

"David, look to your right and back a bit," Rupor called.

I immediately swung to my right, trusting Rupor to know what he was talking about. A jumble of boulders lay scattered across the surface, just thirty yards away from us. The rocks were far enough apart for us to wriggle in between them but close enough to give cover from every direction except directly overhead. In truth, it was better cover than I'd hoped to find.

"Martin, do you see the cover Rupor found?"

"It looks great," Martin said. "Get the ladies and His Highness wedged in there as fast as you can."

"What about you? Aren't you coming?" Megan asked.

"No ma'am," the sergeant answered. "We're going to keep heading straight."

"What?" Megan cried. "You'll be an easy target out there."

"Yes, they will, miss," Harris said. "It's a marine's duty to protect civilians from the enemy, even at the cost of his life."

Megan stifled a cry but, to my relief, she didn't break our train.

"Don't worry, Megan," Martin added, "we won't be quite the sitting ducks you imagine. The pinnace will come upon us suddenly and probably be past us before they even realize we're here. I think we can reach that overhang ahead of us before they can get back to us."

"*Aashla's Hope*," I called, "how long before you can come after us?"

"We began the startup procedure as soon as the marines retreated back to the docking bay," Heidi said, "but the reactor won't be online for another seven minutes."

"Do *not* cut any corners to get to us sooner," Martin ordered. "A reactor containment breach would be far worse than the eleven of us being forced to hide for a few minutes."

"Heidi is piping your conversation throughout the ship," Laura said. "As chief engineer of this ship, I acknowledge and accept your order, sir."

I reached the edge of the boulder field and pulled up. Catching Callan's hand, I guided her in between two of the larger ones.

"Keep moving, Callan. Megan is coming in right behind you."

As Callan slipped from my sight, I sent Megan in after her.

"You're next, Harris," I said. "Whatever happens, stay with the women and guard them with your life. The prince and I will be just inside the edge of the field, keeping an eye out for pirates."

It was a tighter fit for Harris, but he managed to pull himself in after Megan. Before Rupor and I could get under cover, the pirate pinnace swept up from the direction of the docking bay.

As Martin predicted, the little ship overflew our positions, but the pilot really knew his business. Braking thrusters fired and the pilot threw the ship into a flat spin. The pinnace was still moving away from Martin and the marines, but the gunner got off one shot before the pinnace passed beyond the horizon. The bright beam cast the bleak landscape into sharp relief for a fraction of a second. And, in terrible silence, the laser struck the ground and bodies went flying.

56

THEY COULD BE DEAD

Blasted bits of rock spun off into space as I struggled to see through the afterimage of the bright laser beam. I saw two bodies tumbling across the surface of the asteroid and out of sight. A third body pin wheeled into space. I had no idea what had happened to the remaining two men.

"Martin?" I called. "Sergeant?"

Over the comm I heard a gasp and the sound of someone trying to stifle crying. I received no reply to my call.

"David?" Callan's voice was quiet, calm, and controlled. "What happened?"

"The pirate gunner took a shot at Martin's group before the pinnace passed over the horizon. It appears to have been a hit or a very close miss."

"What of Martin and the marines?" she asked.

"I...don't know. They aren't answering their comms, but they could be unconscious or the comm could be damaged."

"Or they could be dead," a small, shaking voice added.

"We don't know that yet, Megan," Callan said, her voice stronger and more commanding than before. In that voice, I recognized her switch to princess mode. The situation demanded decisiveness, not emotions. If Martin was dead, she'd cry later.

"David, swim over there and find out what happened to the men. Go as fast as you can, but also be careful. That pinnace will be back soon."

"What will the rest of you do?" I asked.

"Stay here where we have some cover. Now go."

I swam off as fast as I could go, terrified of what I might find but even more terrified of the uncertainty I felt.

"Heidi," Callan called, "how many casualties do we have under Tristan's care right now?"

"My latest report shows fourteen dead, six in critical condition, and dozens of wounds ranging from serious to minor," Heidi replied. "According to Tristan, none of the injuries in the last group are life-threatening."

I zipped over the ground, swimming faster than I'd done since academy relay races. The laser had scorched a three-foot line in the asteroid. Even if the shot was a direct hit, no more than two of the men could have been struck by the beam.

"Those casualties are lighter than I'd feared, but heavier than I'd hoped," Callan said.

"According to reports, as long as our men were withdrawing, the pirates only fought hard enough to keep them moving backward," Heidi replied.

"Odd," Callan said. "Why wouldn't the pirates fight harder? If they *wanted* us to escape, they could have just let us go."

"Callan, the pinnace is returning," Rupor interrupted.

"They could have transmission scanners," Heidi said. "Maintain comm silence for your own safety."

At the scorch mark, I'd turned toward the docking bay. Martin was towing the marines in that direction. If the blast struck behind him, it was likely he'd be thrown in the direction he was already going.

I risked a quick look over my shoulder, hoping to spot the pinnace. It was easy to find. The pilot flew back to us slowly, the canopy of the little ship facing down toward the asteroid.

"Maintain comm silence," I said. "The crew is trying to spot us visually."

I heard an exhalation of breath. Callan did that when she was exasperated with me.

"Yes, dear, I know I'm not maintaining comm silence," I said. "If the crew of the pinnace is going to find anyone, I'm going to make sure it's me."

I got my wish. The pinnace rolled over to bring its belly gun to bear on my position. I zigged to the right then zagged to the left. A hurried laser blast struck a good ten yards from my position. All I needed was another couple of seconds and I could reach some form of cover.

I put my hand into a dark depression, planning to push off the side of it. Instead of rock, my hand touched clothing. Instinctively, I grabbed a fistful of fabric. My momentum pulled the man out of the shadows. He was covered in burns and blood, but a scar stood out on his cheek.

I'd found Martin.

57

I'M COMING TO HELP

I COULDN'T TELL IF MARTIN WAS DEAD OR ALIVE AND WOULDN'T BE ABLE to find out until I could put some cover between the pinnace and me. As if to drive that home, the landscape was lit by the flash of another laser shot. The ground boiled not more than three yards from where I would have been if grabbing Martin hadn't checked my speed.

"I found Martin."

The pirates already knew where I was, so there was no reason not to give Megan some hopeful news. I slung Martin over my back in a miner's carry, another thing included in the low-gravity vacuum training at the academy. I wouldn't be as fast or maneuverable as before—something that might get me killed—but at least I knew how to carry a wounded man.

"Is he alive?" Megan asked.

I wished she hadn't made even a short broadcast over the comm, but I understood why she did it. Meanwhile, I was swimming again, trying my best to move fast and change directions even faster.

"You know Martin," I said. "He's hard to kill."

Another laser blast flashed. That one hit so close the heat conducted by the rocky surface burned my hand. Bits of blasted rock pelted Martin and me, giving both of us new cuts and bruises.

"Heidi, please tell me you're about to pull out of the docking bay and blow this pinnace out of the sky," I called.

"I'm sorry, David, but the startup sequence still has-"

"Hang on, David! I'm coming to help."

"Milo? What do you mean?"

Instead of zigging or zagging, I came to a complete halt. The next laser blast hit even closer than the one before it. This time, I lifted my hand off the ground before it could burn, but my toes got uncomfortably warm through my boots.

"He took the pinnace," Heidi replied. "We assume he's coming to pick you up."

"You were all just sitting around in the ship hoping David and Callan weren't going to get killed," Milo said. "When I lived on the street, hoping never got me anything. And it's not going to save my friends now."

With each shot, the pirate gunner got closer and closer to burning Martin and me. No matter how random I tried to make my movements, some pattern must be emerging. Maybe I was too slow. Or maybe it was time for a complete change in evasion tactics. I pushed my upper body off the ground with my hand and pulled my legs up tight against my chest. When I was pointing a bit above the distant ridge I'd been trying to reach, I kicked hard off the surface of the asteroid. Martin and I arrowed toward the ridge, moving faster than I could swim across the ground. But now I was going in a straight line course—one I could not change for several seconds.

The move took the gunner by surprise. His next shot hit well to the left of where I had stopped, as if he had guessed I would head off in that direction. I would have gone that way, too.

"Milo," Heidi called, "what are you planning to do?"

"I'm going to save the only people besides my sister who have ever cared about me."

"We're going to be fine, Milo," I said.

"No, you're not," Milo said. "Not without help. I can see you and the pirate pinnace. The laser is already tracking your path."

It looked like my gamble had only bought me a few more seconds of life.

"Callan, Megan," I called. "I'm sorry."

"No! You're not dying if I can help it!" Milo shouted, drowning out the cries from Callan and Megan.

Milo's pinnace sped past me, mere meters above my head. The pirate laser flashed but the pinnace blocked the shot.

"Take care of Kim for me," Milo said.

The pirate pilot didn't realize what Milo was doing until it was too late. Milo crashed his pinnace into the pirate ship and they both disintegrated in a ball of flame.

58

HE'S ALIVE

In the vacuum of space, the fiery explosion lasted less than a second, but it seemed as if it went on for years to me. The image seared into my brain as I passed over the ridge I'd hoped to hide behind. The image consumed my attention as I landed, instinctively cradling Martin to protect him from further injury. The image remained clear and horrible even as my vision blurred from the tears filling my eyes.

"No, Milo!" Callan wailed, far too late for Milo to hear her or heed her.

Megan's quiet crying for Martin gave way to sobs as the loss of Milo and her dread for Martin overwhelmed her.

In a quiet, controlled voice, Rupor recited a prayer for the dead.

And the mild jolt of our landing caused Martin to moan in pain. *He was alive!*

"What's going on?" Heidi called. "What happened to Milo?"

"Martin is alive, Megan. Concentrate on that. He's *alive*!" I forced as much hope and joy as I could muster into my voice. I didn't feel any of it —I didn't feel anything, at the moment—but Megan and Callan needed *something* hopeful to cling to.

Megan's sobs eased a bit. "A-alive? Are you sure?"

"Yes, Megan, I'm sure. I told you Martin was hard to kill."

Rupor flowed straight from the prayer for the dead to a prayer for Martin to remain among the living.

"Is someone going to tell us what's going on out there?" It was Laura this time. I'd forgotten Heidi was broadcasting to the whole ship.

"Milo is dead." Callan was back in princess mode, using it as armor to protect herself from the pain. "He rammed the pirate pinnace, sacrificing himself so the rest of us could live."

Gasps and cries sounded over the comm as Callan's words hit home.

"We will have time for our grief later, after we're away from this God-forsaken rock." Callan's voice grew stronger as she spoke. "But I will *not* allow Milo's death to be in vain. We *will* leave this place. We *will* bring these pirates to justice. And we *will* make Quint and Chapman pay for all they have done!"

"This is all my fault," Heidi's cry was full of anger and sorrow. "If I hadn't married-"

"There's no time for that, Heidi," Callan cut in. "I understand why you blame yourself. I blame myself for Milo's death, as well. But none of us can afford the luxury of guilt or self-pity. Can you put those feelings aside and handle communications for me?"

"Yes." There was a sniffle after the word, but Heidi's voice was firm again.

"Good. David, do you think it's safe to move Martin?"

I gave Martin a very fast check over. His worst injuries appeared to be burns. If we got him to a modern medical bay—like the one on the *Aashla's Hope*—his wounds weren't life threatening. "Yes, he can be moved."

"Good. You're closer to the docking bay, so we'll come to you. We won't be as fast as you, but we'll get there."

"As you wish, Callan. Permission to search for the rest of Martin's team?"

"Of course, David. We'll call when we reach Martin."

Ten minutes later, we were all together behind the ridge. There was no sign of the pirates who'd been on the surface chasing us. Maybe they were scared off after the loss of their pinnace. They left us alone, which was all I cared about. I'd found the bodies of the sergeant and one of the other marines. A third marine still lived, though with worse burns than Martin. I remembered the fourth man flying off into space and resigned myself to never finding his body.

With Harris carrying the wounded marine, we swam to the docking bay entrance. I slid carefully up to the spaceship entrance to the bay and peered inside. Hundreds of pirates milled about under the watchful eye of Quint. Chapman stood just behind Quint. But I spotted something else that made my blood run cold.

Without the crew of the *Aashla's Hope* realizing it, the pirates had fastened docking clamps to the landing gear. The ship and all aboard her were trapped in the docking bay.

59

BLOW THE CLAMPS

"*Aashla's Hope*, the pirates have locked you in place with docking clamps," I said.

"Oh." Laura's single-word exhalation carried more feeling, more frustration, and more defeat than the loudest, most profane rant imaginable.

"David, most of us were raised with airships rather than starships," Callan said. "Please explain what you're talking about."

"Docking clamps are a safety device designed to hold a ship in place during repairs. They're like the ones holding the pinnace-" My voice broke, my vision blurred, and once again I saw the awful explosion that had taken the life of a young man I loved like the little brother I never had. Knowing this was not the time to mourn Milo, I took control of my voice. "In a large, immobile bay like this one, docking clamps allow engineers to perform engine test burns at high thrust without worrying about balancing thrust vectors."

There was silence for a few seconds before Megan said, "So, the clamps keep the ship from moving no matter how hard you run the engines?"

"Right. That's what I said."

"No, darling, that's what you *meant*," Callan said. "Megan, thank you for the translation."

"Now that we all understand the situation," Laura said, "what are we going to do about it?"

"Once the ship is fully...online? Is that the right word?" Rupor asked.

"Yes, Rupor."

"Good. Once the ship is online, why not use the ship's laser batteries to burn all the pirates in the docking bay? Then we can release the clamps and be on our way."

It was a reasonable question from someone unfamiliar with ship-mounted laser batteries, but I could imagine Laura's mouth working as her brain tried to find just the right words to convey her horror at the thought. I jumped in to answer before she found her voice.

"Rupor, firing the lasers in such a confined space would be deadly to all of us. The reflected heat, alone, would melt the ship's skin. And rock blasted from the docking bay walls would only have one place to go—back on the ship."

"What he said," Laura confirmed.

"Ah," Rupor mused. "Remind me to study up on these modern weapons after we're done dealing with this pirate rabble."

"I wish I had his confidence," someone murmured over the comm.

"Come now, people," Rupor said. "This is a puzzler, certainly, but we have as fine a collection of people as I have ever had the pleasure to serve with. There *is* a solution. We *will* find it."

"At the very worst, we can just sit tight until the navy sends a task force," someone said. "They're bound to have gotten that messenger drone by now."

"No, I'm afraid we can't just wait," Laura's husband spoke up. "These pirates hit planetary settlements as well as shipping. They've got mobile laser batteries that *can* be fired in the docking bay. Quint has probably already sent for them."

The comm was silent again as everyone digested this latest news.

"Use shaped explosive charges to blow the ship free." The voice was weak and rasping.

"Martin!" Megan cried. "You're awake."

"Indeed, dear heart," Martin gasped. "I've been awake for a minute or so, but couldn't quite find my voice until just now."

"I'm glad you're speaking again, my friend," I said, "but your suggestion won't work. Anyone leaving the ship to place explosives on the docking clamps would be an easy target for the pirates."

"I'm disappointed in you, David. Don't you claim to have watched every adventure vid in existence?" Martin replied. "Haven't you seen *Star Ranger and the Space Pirates*?"

"I said I watched the *good* vids, Martin."

"You're insulting a classic, Wonder Boy."

"Would you boys quit arguing about vids and enlighten the rest of us?" Callan demanded.

"Star Ranger faced just this situation in that vid. His solution can be our solution." Martin paused, perhaps to gather strength or perhaps for dramatic effect. "We don't blow the docking clamps. We blow the landing gear it's clamped to."

60

THE MADNESS OF MEN

THERE WAS ANOTHER SILENCE AS EVERYONE CONSIDERED MARTIN'S IDEA. The crew had access to the landing gear without getting out of the ship. And flying without landing gear was a lot better than not flying with landing gear. I couldn't find any obvious flaws.

"Laura, you're our engineer. What do you think?" I asked.

"Well, we're going to be in for one heck of a jolt when the ship drops two meters to the deck after we blow the landing gear," she said, "but the ship can take it. Give me a minute to check the specs for the landing struts."

"I might be able to keep the ship from dropping to the floor," Nist offered. "We can bring the repulsers online just before the explosives go off. If we time it right, the repulser's hum won't alert the pirates and the ship won't hit the floor."

"Good idea, Nist. Figure out what you'll need to do to pull it off," I said. "And Martin? Not a bad suggestion for an old man."

"I attribute my brilliance to a misspent youth and a weakness for Star Ranger adventures. So, did I miss anything while I was out?"

"I'll tell him," Megan said.

I watched her turn off both of their comms and lean in close so their atmosphere shields overlapped. Seconds later, Martin's face screwed up in pain that had nothing to do with the burns covering his body.

Despite those burns, he pulled Megan into a hug with one arm and reached the other out to clasp Callan's hand. A moment later, he thumbed on his comm.

"I'm sorry, David." Martin's voice was quiet, the emotion he felt over Milo's death evident.

"I know, Martin. We all are."

Laura chose that moment to check back in.

"David, I've checked the specs for the landing gear and Martin's idea will work. We'll need a shaped charge attached to the right spot on each of the six struts."

"I sense a 'but' in that explanation, Laura," I said.

"You're right. The weak spot in the landing struts is about a foot below the well the gear retracts into after liftoff."

"Will you have to leave the ship to place the charges?" I asked.

"No, we can get into the well and place the charges without leaving the ship," Laura replied, "but if any of the pirates notice what we're doing, it won't be hard for them to stop us."

"It sounds like we need to make sure the pirates aren't paying any attention to the ship while you're placing the charges," I said.

"Well, yes, a distraction would help." Weary sarcasm tinged Laura's voice. "I suppose I could open the ship's airlock, point to the other side of the docking bay, and shout 'Oh my God, what is that?' But I don't really think that will work, David."

"It might work if she was naked," Martin said.

"It's going to take my teams at least a minute to place the charges," Laura said. "Maybe Callan could hold their attention that long. I know I couldn't."

"No one is getting naked in front of the pirates, least of all my wife," I said. "How long will it take to prepare the charges?"

"They're ready now. Pirates keep plenty of explosives on hand to blow the airlocks of ships they're attacking."

"Good enough. Arm a squad of marines with laser rifles and get them to the ship's airlock," I said. "I expect I'm going to need some covering fire."

"You're planning something dangerous, David," Callan said. "What is it?"

"I'm going to walk into the docking bay and arrest Quint and Chapman."

"That's not dangerous, David," Martin said, "that's suicidal."

"Listen to Martin and don't do this," Callan pleaded. "It's bad enough that Milo is gone. Don't make it worse by sacrificing yourself, too."

"My soon-to-be ex-husband isn't worth it," Heidi added, her voice quiet but forceful. "Cowards like him and snakes like Quint aren't worth your life, David."

"I am not planning on dying, people," I said. "But I am also not planning on letting those responsible for so much death—Milo's and countless others across the galaxy—escape justice. I owe this to all the dead whose souls cry out for a reckoning. By God, I am David Rice, Scout First Class of the Terran Exploration Corps. It is my *duty* to follow this through."

"Aw hell, you had to go and drag duty into it, didn't you?" Martin muttered. "Could someone loan me a sword?"

"*What?*" Megan cried. "Don't be stupid, Martin, you're half covered in burns! You can't be thinking of joining in this madness."

"He can and he is, Megan," Callan said. "There is no talking to David once he starts going on about a Scout's duty. I can only assume the Scout Academy inflicted the same madness on Martin."

"You are quite correct, Your Highness," Martin said. "I managed to forget that madness for a long time—until your husband reminded me of who I had been and who I could be again. Where David leads, I *will* follow."

"As will I," Rupor said.

"You're all mad!" Heidi cried.

"Mad we may be, Heidi," Rupor replied, "but ours is the glorious madness of honor, of oath, and of duty. It is the madness of men. It is this madness that draws the love of the best and brightest women the galaxy has to offer. And it is this madness that will bring down that most loathsome pirate, Captain Quint."

"If only..." Heidi whispered. I doubt she meant it to be heard, but it fell into the silence that followed Rupor's speech.

In the most gentle voice I'd ever heard Rupor use, he said, "You do yourself a disservice, Heidi. You are not responsible for your husband's actions."

"But I'm the one who fell in love with a coward instead of one of you mad warriors. How can that not be my fault? How can I ever show my face around any of you again?"

"Perhaps you had to marry Chapman so you could meet your rightful madman," Rupor said. In a lighter tone, he added, "Have you ever considered just how beautiful you would look in Tartegian black and gold?"

A collective gasp sounded over the comm before Laura's husband asked, "Am I imagining things, or did Rupor just propose to Heidi?"

"Rupor of Tarteg," Heidi said, her voice more full of life than it had been since we reached the pirate base, "you had better survive this mad scheme of David's and make your intentions clear in person. *Do you understand me?*"

"Of course, my dear," Rupor said. His voice was even, but he wore the biggest grin I'd ever seen on his face. "It should be easy enough. After all, there are three of us."

"Begging the prince's pardon, but he has miscounted," the marine commander said, "There are *one hundred and sixty-three* of us. The men are already gathering at the airlocks, ready to sally forth on Captain Rice's command."

"One hundred and sixty-four," Harris said.

"I appreciate your fervor, Harris," I said, "but you will stay here and guard the women."

"That's what I'll be doing, sir," Harris replied. "I believe I can best protect Her Highness and Megan by keeping you and Captain Bane alive. I realize I risk court martial for disobeying your order, but I am coming with you."

"I like this one, David," Callan said. "He reminds me of you."

I sighed. "Martin, have you got a sword?"

"Yes. The wounded guard's sword was still buckled about his waist."

"Very well, gentlemen, it's time to let madness reign."

61

BAD AT MATH

I pulled Callan to me and kissed her. "I'll be back for you soon."

Her cheek tight against mine, she whispered fiercely, "You'd better be."

Martin and Megan broke apart at the same time Callan and I did. Then the four of us swam off toward the lip of the docking bay.

"Laura," I called over the comm, "are your teams ready to go?"

"It took some persuasion on my part to keep them from taking up swords and joining you in your glorious charge into the docking bay," Laura replied, "but they've got the charges and are in their positions now."

"Good. Blow the charges as soon as all your teams have gotten to safety. Pick up Callan, Megan, and the wounded marine before you do anything else. After that, you're in command until Martin or I get back on board. You've got good instincts. Follow them."

"Aye aye, Captain Rice!" Laura said.

There was something in the way she snapped off her response that made me ask, "Are you saluting, Laura?"

Laughter erupted over the comm. "Um, yes, sir."

"At ease, Chief Engineer."

We reached our position just below the lip of the docking bay. I pulled myself up enough to see over the lip of the bay floor. There were at least four hundred pirates gathered in various places throughout the docking bay. Half of the pirates were formed up around the *Aashla's Hope.* Their swords were sheathed but close at hand. All but a handful of the rest manned various positions close to vital controls. That left a dozen formed up around Quint as his personal guard. Chapman stood just behind Quint, subservient but readily available in case Quint needed to speak to him.

I looked at my companions. Rupor wore a grin of suppressed excitement. Martin wore a grimace of suppressed pain. Harris wore a smile of suppressed nervousness. I could only imagine the faces of the marines on board the *Aashla's Hope*. I felt as if I should say something before we charged out against such superior numbers—something to settle the men's nerves and channel their excitement. I drew a blank until I remembered something from ancient Terran history. Without a hint of shame, I stole it.

"Gentlemen, Tarteg and Mordan expect all men to do their duty."

Next to me, Martin spoke but his voice was drowned out by a roar from the men echoing over the comm. Martin stopped trying to speak and just gave me a thumbs up. Then we pulled ourselves up and into the docking bay.

The pirates glanced about, nerves set on edge by the roar they'd heard from inside our ship. Heads turned toward Quint, looking for guidance. Irritation crossed Quint's face and he prepared to speak. That was just what I'd been waiting for.

"Heidi, broadcast my comm outside the ship so everyone can hear me," I said. "And crank the volume."

"You're on, David."

"Git yerselves under-" Quint began before I drowned him out.

"To all pirates within this base—in the name of the Terran Federation, I order you to lay down your arms and surrender!" I stalked forward, flipping my sword in the casual manner of one who has had to live by the blade. Martin, Rupor, and Harris matched me stride for stride, all three flipping their blades in unison with mine.

A few pirates spotted us and pointed. Within seconds, every pair of eyes in the docking bay turned upon us.

"Yer an idiot, Rice," Quint shouted, but his voice was still weak compared to my amplified one. "We got you outnumbered four hunnert to four."

Rupor chose that moment to bark, "Marines, form up!"

With a whoosh, every airlock in the *Aashla's Hope* opened and the marines poured out of the ship. As our marines took up their positions around the ship, the pirates surrounding the ship stirred nervously.

"Were you always this bad at math, Quint, or is it a recent thing?" I raised a hand in salute to the marines. "Either way, you've seriously miscalculated the odds."

"Maybe so, but we still got more than twice yer numbers," he shouted back.

"That you do. And if your men faced their typical prey—a bunch of merchant spacers or the crew of a space liner—your numbers would make a difference." I waved my arm toward the marines. "Take a long, hard look at our marines. Do those men look like they're afraid of you? You pirates are used to being the foxes rampaging through the hen house. But today your fox den has been invaded by wolves—and one wolf is worth five of you little foxes."

I pointed my sword at Quint. "You can stop the slaughter, Quint. Surrender or we'll destroy you, just like we destroyed Caudill and his crew."

Quint glared across the docking bay at me. "I'd rather die first."

"So be it." I raised my sword above my head and cried, "For Milo!"

With a roar, I charged into battle.

62

QUINT'S GETTING AWAY

Charging with me, my three companions joined in my battle cry. "For Milo!"

At a barked command from their commander, one hundred and sixty marines raised their voices as one. "For Mordan! For Tarteg! For Milo!"

The marines charged the encircling pirates. Unnerved by the marines' precision, both in maneuvers and in voice, the pirates fell back before the onslaught. I must remember to congratulate the marine commander's choice of battle cry later.

"Heidi?" My voice boomed out across the docking bay. "Route me back to the ship's channel and cancel the broadcast."

"Done, sir."

The four of us engaged half a dozen pirates, steel clashing against steel. We pushed the pirates back a couple of steps before they found a rhythm of their own. Precious seconds ticked away as we traded blows. They were seconds Laura's teams would use to place the charges on the landing struts. They were seconds Quint or Chapman might use to disappear into the base. They were seconds I could not afford to waste on these men.

"I'm going to Boost in ten seconds. Be smart and get out of my way." The pirate in front of me looked at me in disbelief. "Yes, I'm talking to you and your friends. I don't care about you but if you don't surrender now I will cut you down where you stand."

"Believe him lads." Martin's voice still sounded rough, but the pain from his burns was driven away by the excitement of combat. "David takes duty very seriously and you're standing between him and Quint."

Comprehension dawned on the pirates' faces. They dropped their swords and moved aside. As pirates rushed to join those fighting the marines, hardly any pirates stood between me and Quint. The opportunity was too good to waste.

Boost!

Adrenaline poured into my system. Time slowed. Fatigue faded. Vision sharpened. Muscles surged. I flew across the docking bay, an arrow aimed at Quint and Chapman. My focus was so tight on Quint that I was halfway across the bay before I realized I was not alone. I looked to my left. Martin ran with me, stride for stride, lips stretched wide in a savage grin. Footsteps pounded behind me and I risked a look over my shoulder. Rupor and Harris sprinted for all they were worth, almost keeping up with us.

At Quint's shouted command, a squad of his pirate guards blocked our path. They held their swords raised, ready to defend their captain. I lowered my shoulder and Martin did the same.

I switched from gal base to Mordanian. "I'm going to tuck and roll low past the first row and come up in the middle of them."

"Good idea. Make sure to swing your sword to the right. I'll be on your left."

As one, Martin and I dropped and rolled between startled defenders. We rose to face pirates unprepared for immediate combat. I swung my blade in a wide arc, cutting three pirates and driving all of them back a step. Behind me, Rupor and Harris engaged the pirates Martin and I had bypassed.

Confusion reigned among the pirates as a result of our surprise arrival in their midst. Martin and I took advantage of it and laid about us indiscriminately. I thrust my sword into the side of a pirate. He screamed as I ripped it free and slashed the man next to him. I blocked a swing from a third pirate and kicked him in the groin. Grabbing his collar as he doubled over in pain, I threw him into the back of a pirate battling with Rupor.

I looked for Quint and spotted him, Chapman, and his remaining guards heading for the airlock.

"Quint's getting away!" I hacked off a pirate's sword arm.

"Not if I can help it," Martin pulled his sword from the shoulder of another pirate.

One man stood between us and Quint's retreat.

I pointed my sword at him. "I want Quint, not you. Move."

The pirate's eyes widened in panic and indecision. Martin's sword flashed and the pirate crumpled to the deck.

"He took too long to make up his mind."

Clear of the pirates, Martin and I raced on as Quint and his men reached the airlock. The captain looked back at us and punched buttons on the airlock control with frantic haste. I had to reach him before he could disappear into the base.

Then a thunder clap drowned out all sounds of battle. Fighting paused as the docking bay reverberated with the sound of the explosions. Though I was looking in the wrong direction, the airlock door reflected the scene behind me.

Aashla's Hope floated free and was already moving ponderously toward the docking bay exit.

63

A BIG PITY PARTY

A cheer rose from the marines as our spaceship majestically glided out of the docking bay. Over the comm, I could hear the ship's crew preparing to pick up Callan, Megan, and the wounded marine. Around the docking bay, the fight went out of the pirates and they began dropping their swords to the floor in surrender.

"Cap'n David, sir," Heidi's voice held more life than I'd heard since her husband had dragged her off the *Aashla's Hope* many hours before. "A rescue team is assembling in the airlock. We'll have Her Highness and her companions back on the ship in two minutes."

Tightness I hadn't even realized was gripping my chest loosened. I released a long sigh and dropped Boost.

"It's over, Quint. My ship is free and your pirates are defeated. Do the smart thing and surrender."

Quint punched one more key on the airlock controls and the door hissed open. To my surprise, Quint didn't dash into the airlock. Instead, one of his men walked through the door.

"I don't think so, scout."

"You can't win, Quint. Do you remember the wormhole alarm a few hours ago? That was our messenger drone, launched just before entering your docking bay. The drone carries the location of this base, the approach path through the asteroids, and the identity of the senior captain. Honestly, I'm surprised a Federation Navy task force hasn't already popped out of that wormhole."

"I figgered out 'bout the drone when you done told us who you was, boy."

"If you knew we had alerted the navy, why did you bother fighting us? Why didn't you just let us go and get away while the getting was good?"

"Yer askin' me why, boy?" Rage filled Quint's eyes. "Take a gander 'round you. You think a place like this jest pops up all set and ready ta use? I remember when ol' Caudill and me stumbled 'cross this place. It was jest a big rock chock full o' caves. Me 'n Caudill got us some lads and worked our tails off ta build this place. My blood 'n sweat be in every nook and cranny o' this place. You think I's gonna let the man who be takin' it from me just fly away?"

The man in the airlock began handing something out to each of the pirates around Quint. I couldn't see what they were passing around, but all of my mental alarms began ringing.

"So this resistance of yours is just a big pity party because you're going to miss your old pirate base?" I sniffed and pretended to wipe away tears. "I feel your pain, Quint. Really, I do. I feel it so much, I wish all the victims of your decades of piracy could be here to shed a tear over your loss. But they can't because you or your men killed them. If losing this rock causes you pain, I say hurrah." I waved my sword toward Quint and his men. "Escape is impossible, so stop whatever it is you and your men think you're doing and surrender."

Quint's fingers danced across the keypad again.

"Yer right 'bout one thing, Rice. Escape be impossible fer most o' me men. But it ain't fer me and these lads with me."

"Martin, I'm tired of talking to this old man. Time to take him down."

We strode toward Quint. Quint's fingers touched two last keys then hovered over a button.

"Take another step, boy, and I'll drop the atmo shield and flush ya all out inta space."

We stopped. Four of us still wore vacuum harnesses, but none of the marines had them.

"You know you'll kill more than my men. You'll kill your men and yourself, too."

The pirate handing out stuff from the airlock came back wearing a vacuum harness. He carried another. As that pirate slipped the vacuum harness around Quint, the rest of Quint's guards donned harnesses, too.

Chapman looked wildly around him. "H-hey, where's my harness?"

Quint shook his head. "Now why would I be wantin' ta save you, Chapman?"

"But I've helped you! I told you who these men were. I've been *useful* to you."

"Yep, but there be plenty o' other useful idiots in the galaxy. I 'spect I's gonna find you right easy to replace."

Quint looked around the docking bay. "Sorry, lads. Wish I could save ya all, but that jest ain't in the cards today."

Quint looked me in the eyes. "An' now I got ta git busy makin' that impossible escape."

Then Quint's finger stabbed toward the button.

64

SPACE HIM

Time slowed to a crawl as I watched Quint's finger stab toward the button. Once pressed, the button would drop the atmosphere shield protecting the docking bay from the vacuum of space. The old pirate was too far away for me to reach him in the second he needed to press the button. Unbidden, my mind conjured the image of hundreds of men swept into the void, still living but beyond any power in the universe to save. And I would be swept into space with them, safe in my vacuum harness, mute witness to the last seconds of their lives.

"Nooooooooooooooo!"

Chapman barreled into the pirate captain. Quint's finger missed the button and the two tumbled to the ground.

There come times in every man's life when inaction is more dangerous than action. In that moment, even the coward can act decisively. Quint had pushed his useful idiot too far and Chapman had snapped.

Every man in the docking bay stood frozen, transfixed by the drama playing out beneath the keypad. The keypad with the still-active button that would drop the atmosphere shield.

"Now's your chance, lads. Get 'em!"

My cry still echoing around the docking bay, I charged to Chapman's aid. With a roar, pirates and marines alike charged with me.

Quint's pirate guards saw the tidal wave of humanity sweeping their way. Abandoning their leader, they scrambled to escape into the airlock. A band of their fellow pirates piled in behind them. From the cries of rage and the screams of pain and fear, I was happy I couldn't see what happened inside that airlock.

Quint and Chapman flailed at each other, rolling around on the floor of the docking bay. Quint was a wily fighter and the stronger of the two men, but Chapman had gone berserk. The fight was too close to call.

"Martin, can you disable the button on that keypad?"

"Already on it, O Fearless Leader."

Pirates and marines joined me around the struggling pair, cutting them off from everything else. None of us interrupted the fight. None of us liked Chapman and we all agreed the man was nothing more than a useful idiot. But in this moment, he was *our* idiot. Even if he had acted in his own self-interest, Chapman's attack saved hundreds of lives. His actions hadn't earned him much, but they had earned him the chance to pound on Quint.

A moment later, it was over. Bloodied and battered, Chapman rose from the moaning pirate captain, Quint's vacuum harness gripped in one hand. With an animal roar of triumph, Chapman thrust the vacuum harness into the air. Hundreds of voices roared with him.

Chapman looked around him, his eyes bright with the fervor of battle.

"Let's give Quint a taste of his own medicine. Let's space him!"

I was elbowed aside as men pushed to reach Quint. A dozen hands hoisted the pirate captain over our heads. Marines and pirates alike passed Quint from hand to hand toward the entrance to the docking bay.

A chant broke out from the men. "Space him! Space him!"

The chant rose in volume and drowned out my calls to stop. Hemmed in by the crowd, I could do nothing but watch the mob—for they were no longer pirates and marines—pass Quint, now struggling and flailing, toward his doom.

Martin's hand fell on my shoulder. "There's nothing you can do, David."

"I wanted Quint to face justice for all he's done, Martin."

"He *is* facing justice, lad. It's rough justice, I'll grant you, but so was beheading the pirate who tried to space Callan and Megan. Quint has earned this death a thousand times over."

Martin was right. It's not what I would have chosen, but I couldn't claim the earlier execution was right yet claim this was wrong.

I made myself watch as Quint, finally facing the terror he had inflicted on countless others in his long career, was heaved through the atmosphere barrier.

I made myself watch Quint's futile struggle for life as he drifted in the void.

I made myself watch Quint die.

65

HE'S AT PEACE

Quint's still and lifeless body tumbled away from the pirate base, shrinking until it was too small to see. I gave myself a mental shake and pulled my gaze away from the airless abyss beyond the atmosphere shield.

Chapman, a smug smile pasted on his face, stepped in front of me.

"Well, Rice, I guess you're pretty happy I was around to save everyone."

I punched him, flattening Chapman's nose.

"Ow! What the hell-?"

"Don't you *dare* proclaim yourself the hero."

"But I stopped Quint!" Chapman's voice rose with each word.

I punched him in the stomach and heard the breath whoosh out of him. Good. Maybe that would shut him up for a few minutes.

"This whole situation is *your* fault, Chapman."

I hit him with a left cross and he stumbled back a step.

"If you had simply kept your big mouth shut and stayed on our ship, *none* of this would have happened."

My right fist cracked into his eye and Chapman reeled back against the wall of the docking bay.

"If you had simply kept your big mouth shut, you wouldn't have been challenged to a duel."

I grabbed Chapman's shirt in both fists and pounded him against the wall.

"If you had simply kept your big mouth shut, I wouldn't have had to join the duel just to keep you quiet."

I smashed Chapman against the wall, again.

"If you had simply kept your big mouth shut, my wife and friends wouldn't have had to put themselves in danger just to keep our story intact. The story *you* were determined to reveal."

Chapman sagged as I thumped him into the wall a third time.

"If you had simply kept your big mouth shut, dozens, maybe hundreds, of men—marines and pirates, alike—would still be alive."

Thump.

"If you had simply kept your big mouth shut, *Milo* would still be alive."

Thump.

"He."

Thump.

"Was."

Thump.

"Only."

Thump.

"Sixteen!"

Thump.

I heard a voice from far away. "You're on a private channel, Your Highness."

"David? Talk to me."

I released Chapman and he slid down the wall to the floor.

"Callan? Are you safe?"

"Yes, darling, we're all on board the ship. We're all safe."

"Milo's not safe. He'll never be safe again."

"You're wrong, David. He'll never be in danger again. He's at peace."

"Do you truly believe that, Callan?"

"After all we've been through, how could I not?"

I paused to consider her words. Callan couldn't see it, but I nodded slowly and pushed my emotions down. Having mastered myself, I turned to survey the scene in the docking bay.

"All right, men, it's time to get back to work."

Rupor stepped forward and placed a hand on my shoulder. "We can handle this, David. When the fighting ends, a man must take the time to properly mourn the dead."

The marines did appear to have everything under control. Squads of marines herded the pirates into small, manageable groups and disarmed them. Others directed the collection of the dead and wounded from both sides. Medics moved among the wounded performing triage. And beyond the atmosphere shield, our ship's remaining pinnace detached and maneuvered into the docking bay. Tristan bounded out as soon as the hatch opened, rushing to tend the wounded.

And then Callan emerged and ran across the docking bay to me. She flew into my arms and kissed me. It was long and tender and I felt my emotions rising again. This time I did not try to hold them back and the tears flowed.

Tears of rage and relief.

Tears of loss and love.

Tears for Milo.

Tears for the marines.

Tears for Martin and Megan.

Tears for the woman who held me.

I sank to the deck and Callan held me while I cried.

Sometime later, I became aware a marine stood silently ten feet away. Callan and I rose from the deck and looked around the docking bay. The *Aashla's Hope* was inside again, floating on repulsers but tethered in position. Tristan still moved among the wounded, barking orders and tending patients. The pirates sat, hands upon heads, in small groups scattered around the bay.

"Yes, private? What can I do for you?" I said to the marine.

He snapped off a salute. "I'm sorry to interrupt, sir, but you're wanted aboard the ship."

"Do you have any idea why?"

"Yes, sir. They said to tell you the wormhole has opened."

66

WELL DONE, GENTLEMEN

"Your Highness?" a marine asked as we turned toward the ship. "Should we space Chapman, too?"

Callan glared at the man slumped against the wall. "No, corporal. I'm not kind enough to give him the easy way out."

Without another word, she led the way to the ship.

"Please excuse my ignorance, dear, but this must be some new definition of 'kind' I'm not familiar with."

"That's because you haven't spent enough time among the sycophants in court, David." With a smile Callan took my arm. "There are people for whom status is everything. They must belong to the 'right' groups and be seen with the 'right' people. Such people would rather die than lose status."

"You're saying Chapman is one of those people?"

"Absolutely. If we dig into his past, I'm sure we'll find a high status education and a high status job. All you have to do is look at Heidi to realize she's his high status wife."

"Okay, but that doesn't explain why he sucked up to the pirates like he did."

"Of course it does, darling. Different societies have different definitions of high status. Whatever gave Chapman his status before his capture did nothing for him in a society of pirates. He had to change who and what he was or face being a low status outsider. That's the one thing he couldn't accept."

That did explain a lot about Chapman's behavior. "And spacing him would spare him being dragged back into galactic society as a traitor against his fellow prisoners and a spy for the pirates. God above, even the other prisoners will despise him."

A grim smile played across Callan's lips as she nodded. "I have no sympathy for the wretched man. He brought it on himself."

We climbed the ramp into the *Aashla's Hope* and headed for the bridge. Crewmen hunched over each of the ship's sensor displays. Laura stood next to Heidi as the comm officer scanned subspace bands for any activity.

"Have you found anything, Heidi?" I asked.

She shook her head. "All of the bands are clear, David."

"Try broadcasting an SOS on all bands. And put the comm on speaker."

Heidi's fingers flew across the keyboard. The sound of the automated SOS signal filled the bridge. We received a reply within seconds.

"Unidentified ship, what is the nature of your emergency?"

The response was fast and professional. It had to be a naval ship.

"This is David Rice commanding the *Aashla's Hope*. We are currently moored in a pirate base docking bay-"

A new voice broke in. It held the no-nonsense, take-charge tone you find in experienced officers.

"How dire is your situation? We're on a hard burn toward the coordinates you provided in your drone. Can you hold out for another twenty minutes?"

"We don't need to hold out, sir. We've taken the base. The pirate captains are all dead and the surviving pirates are our prisoners."

There was a pause. "Well done, of course, but why did you broadcast an SOS?"

"We've taken the base, but have many wounded from both sides. We are woefully short of supplies and personnel to attend to them all."

"Understood. I have a fully equipped medical ship as part of my command. We will make all haste to the base."

"Thank you, sir. Rice out."

While waiting for naval aid to arrive, Callan and I went out to the makeshift hospital. My wife's eyes welled as she gazed upon the row of neatly laid out dead, each draped in the flag of his native country.

The marine commander approached and sketched a bow. "Your Highness? Perhaps you could say a few words? I believe it will mean a lot to the men."

"Of course, Commander." Callan touched her comm. "Heidi, please broadcast my comm throughout the docking bay."

"You're on, Princess Callan."

Callan walked in among the wounded, looking each in the eye and flashing her dazzling smile. She raised her head and her gaze took in the unwounded marines around the docking bay.

"My brave warriors, Tartegian and Mordanian alike, your world owes you a debt of thanks. You have fought well." She looked back to the rows of dead. "And too many of you have died well."

Callan turned back to the living. "Today, we have lost friends, brothers-in-arms. Back home, though they do not yet know it, families have lost fathers and sons and brothers. Yet these sacrifices will save lives untold. The lives of fathers and sons, of mothers and daughters, of brothers and sisters.

"We shall never know how many lives have been saved by your actions here today. More importantly, those you have saved will never know you saved them. They will sail peacefully through space and arrive safely at their destination, all because men of honor and courage dared to venture beyond the sky of their home world. Those saved will never know—but *I* know.

"And I swell with pride knowing our countries—our world—produce men such as you. Well done, gentlemen. Well done, indeed."

The docking bay rocked with cheers as Callan knelt to speak with one of the wounded. She was still comforting the wounded when the navy arrived.

67

A ROYAL PROCLAMATION

THE NAVY'S MEDICAL SHIP CAME FULLY STAFFED AND SUPPLIED. THE SHIP'S med team rushed to our wounded, injecting swarms of medical nanites into those with the worst wounds. Tristan could only watch in awe as wounds beyond his ability to heal closed as if by magic. Once those on the brink of death were safe, the doctor in charge of the medical team sought out our doctor.

"Sir, are you Doctor Agrilla?"

"I am, though after watching you at work, I'm not so sure I should call myself 'doctor' anymore." Tristan's gaze swept the organized chaos in his makeshift hospital. "From the bottom of my heart, thank you for saving those I am too unskilled to save."

"It's not our skill, sir, it's our technology. Without the nanites, my team would not have saved anywhere near as many men as they did."

Tristan's eyebrows rose. "Really?"

"It's God's own truth, sir." The doctor smiled at Tristan. "I sought you out because I want to ask you about some of the procedures you used."

Gesturing to some of the wounded men, Tristan and the naval doctor fell into a technical discussion well beyond my capability to follow.

Once the initial rush to help the wounded and establish naval control of the docking bay was over, the navy reverted to its thorough, though tedious, routine. Armored marines swept the rest of the base section by section, rounding up the last of the pirates. The records of the pirate captains were secured and unsold plunder recovered. Naval repair crews even fixed the landing struts on the *Aashla's Hope*.

A long and busy thirty-five hours after they arrived, naval demolitions crews rigged the base with explosives and we finally set a course for the wormhole. All who were onboard our ship watched the vid display as the explosives detonated and blasted the pirate base into thousands of tiny asteroids.

The only thing worth noting during the trip to the navy base occurred shortly after we exited the wormhole. The trio of Rupor, Heidi, and Megan approached Callan in the recreation room.

"Your Highness?"

Something in Heidi's tone sent Callan right into princess mode. She stood straighter. Her shoulders drew back. Her gaze sharpened.

"Yes, Heidi?"

"I have a problem I hope you can solve, Princess Callan," Heidi continued with the formal tone. "In the Federation, divorces can be complicated, even if both parties agree to the divorce. I rather doubt Erwin will cooperate."

Heidi stopped and met Callan's eyes for a moment. Callan nodded for her to continue.

"Megan told me that you can issue a royal proclamation of divorce."

"I can, Heidi, but only for Mordanian citizens."

"Megan also told me you can grant Mordanian citizenship by royal proclamation."

"I can do that, also, but Rupor can do likewise for Tartegian citizens."

Rupor cleared his throat. "As I have a vested interest in this outcome, I feel it will be more seemly if the proclamations came from someone other than me." A bright smile crossed Rupor's face. "Besides, Callan, at one time my subjects expected me to marry a beautiful Mordanian citizen. I believe many of them are still rather partial to the idea."

Callan smiled in return. "Heidi, I don't have the oath of citizenship memorized, but I've accepted nontraditional oaths in the past. Do you swear to uphold the laws of Mordan, obey the monarch, and support Mordan in peace and in war?"

"I so swear."

"Then by the powers granted to me as a princess of the realm and heir to the throne, I accept your pledge and welcome you as a subject of the kingdom of Mordan."

Applause broke out around the bridge and Callan raised a hand to request quiet.

"Furthermore, it has come to my attention that you are unhappy in your marriage to one Erwin Chapman and wish to terminate the bond of matrimony between the two of you. Is that correct?"

"Damn right it is!" Heidi blushed when she realized what she had said. "I beg your pardon, Your Highness. Yes, that is correct."

"Again, by the powers granted to me as a princess of the realm and heir to the throne, I hereby grant your request for divorce and order your marriage to Erwin Chapman dissolved."

Applause broke out again, louder than before.

Callan looked at Rupor, who wore the widest grin I'd ever seen on his face. "For God's sake, Rupor, stop grinning like an idiot and kiss Heidi."

He did and we all cheered.

Thirty minutes later, we docked and emerged into a madhouse.

68

UNDER SIEGE

We docked at Velron Station, orbiting the border world of Darthan. Planets on the edge of Federation territory could rarely afford multiple space stations and Darthan was no exception. The single space station served both military and civilian ships and personnel. As seems to be typical in these situations, space for military ships was severely limited. Station control ordered the *Aashla's Hope* to dock in the civilian section.

The first hint of trouble came when some of our crew—all men and women formerly held by the pirates—ran out to help the station crew attach magnetic grapples and seal the airlocks. Thirty seconds later, they all ran back into the ship, sweat beaded on their faces and short of breath.

Martin and I exchanged glances before I spoke to one of the crew. "Is there a problem, Natalie?"

Her wide eyes focused on me and her breathing slowed. "It's crazy out there, sir."

"What do you mean by crazy?"

"It's wall-to-wall newsies out there, sir. Half a dozen of them surrounded me when I tried to help the station crew, all of them pushing and shoving to get my attention, shouting questions the whole time. I- I'm not used to crowds like that after all the time I spent with the pirates and then you Aashlanders. I panicked." Natalie looked around at the others who went out with her. "We all did."

I patted her on the shoulder. "Why don't you and the others go to the med bay. Ask Tristan to give you something to calm you down."

Thumbing my comm unit, I said, "Heidi, please have the senior staff meet Martin and me in the Captain's office. Also, can you tap into the station's vid feeds and find a view of our docking bay?"

"I'm on it, David. Do you want me to scan the news channels, too?"

"Good idea. Be ready to route what you find to the screens in the office."

A moment later, we stared at the images Heidi sent to the office. Natalie hadn't exaggerated describing the docking bay. Hundreds of men and women pushed and shoved to get close to our ship's exits. Vid cameras swooped over the crowd, somehow managing to avoid colliding with each other. As bad as that was, the news vids were worse.

One newsie exclaimed, "Word on the station is those aboard this very ship stormed the base of the infamous pirate captains Caudill and Quint, slaughtering every last one of the pirates."

Another reported, "We have been told that these people from a long-lost human colony forgot all technological knowledge but may have gained powerful mental or mystic abilities. Frankly, viewers, it's the only logical explanation for how a band of barbarians could have defeated these pirates."

Callan, Rupor, and Tristan bristled at the speculation.

"Darling, did that man just call us barbarians?"

"Now, Callan-"

Laura pointed to a screen. "Look, it's David!"

An image of me in my cadet uniform filled one screen.

Martin burst out laughing. "Isn't he adorable?"

His laughter stilled when my image was replaced by one of Martin in *his* cadet uniform.

Megan wrapped an arm around Martin. "Don't worry, Martin, you look *much* cuter than David in that uniform."

Everyone had a laugh at our expense, but I'd seen all I wanted to see.

"Heidi, cut the broadcasts to the office and then get me the commander of the military base."

Several minutes passed before Heidi reported, "I've got an aide to the commander, David. It's the best I could do."

A harried face replaced Heidi's. "I have a task force docking as we speak and do not have time for civilian inquiries. You have thirty seconds."

"I am the reason the task force is docking, so you will *make* time for my inquiries."

"Look, I don't know who you are and I don't care. I-"

"I am David Rice, Scout First Class and captain of the *Aashla's Hope*, formerly the ship of the late pirate captain Caudill. I led the forces that took the base of the late pirate captain Quint. On board my ship are two future heads of state and diplomats representing a dozen other countries on the lost colony of Aashla. While you dither about your task force, my people are under siege by a mob of newsies."

I'd taken exactly the wrong approach with the aide.

"Then I suggest you stay on board your ship, Captain Rice. We'll contact you when we have time for you."

With a ridiculous flourish, the aide ended the call.

"I know too many men just like that twit," Rupor mused. "If we were back home, I could just order out some troops to clear away that rabble."

I grinned. "Then I say we pretend we're back home."

The diplomats and one hundred marines gathered in the cargo hold. The marines formed up around the civilians and diplomatic personnel and I ordered the cargo hold's airlock opened.

With the marine commander, I led the march through the airlock. Newsies surged forward when they caught sight of us.

"Commander, if you please?"

The commander's voice carried, even over the clamor of the newsies.

"Present. Arms!"

In unison, one hundred swords slid free of scabbards. The newsies ground to a halt.

"Marines. Give voice!"

A wordless roar rose from the marines behind us. The newsies closest to us began pushing backward. The commander motioned with his arm and the marines marched forward.

We stopped for no one and no one dared stand before the bared swords and roaring marines. Five minutes later, the base commander met us at the entrance to the military section. With no expression beyond a cocked eyebrow, she welcomed us into her domain.

69

MEDICAL WORKUP

ADMIRAL MCGILLIS, THE BASE COMMANDER, TURNED OUR MARINE ESCORT over to the base's marine commander with instructions to make them comfortable and debrief their commander concerning the fight for the pirate base. She led the diplomatic representatives, Martin, and me into a well-appointed reception room. The aide from my brief comm call waited within.

"I was in the middle of some rather important business when I received word of your approach." McGillis turned a steady gaze on me. "Scout Rice, you will never again bring an armed force onto my base without my express permission. Are we clear on that?"

I was prepared to acknowledge the statement and move on. Callan was not in as forgiving a mood.

"We most certainly are *not* clear on that, Admiral. Furthermore, David *did* contact your office, where this person," she waved at the aide, "made it quite clear our ship, our men, and our actions against the pirates were of no consequence when weighed against the arrival of your precious task force."

Callan folded her arms and gave Admiral McGillis her best princess glare. And it really was Callan's best. I only know of one person who could have stood against it unmoved, and Rob had been dead for nearly three years. I'll give McGillis credit, she figured out Callan was Someone Important long before her aide did.

"Admiral, I was-"

"I don't want to hear it, Smitts." The admiral's tone was so sharp the aide drew back as if he'd been cut. The admiral smiled at Callan. "With whom do I have the honor of speaking?"

Never let it be said I don't know my cue.

"Admiral McGillis, may I present Her Royal Highness, Princess Callan, heir to the throne of Mordan, and my wife." McGillis's left eyebrow rose and I turned to Rupor. "And this is His Royal Highness, Prince Rupor, heir to the throne of Tarteg."

Martin added, "Mordan and Tarteg are two of the most powerful and enlightened countries on the lost world of Aashla. Good relations with those two countries, as well as the countries represented by the rest of our diplomatic mission, will be vital if the Federation has any hope of bringing our world into the Federation."

McGillis got a faraway look for a second while she consulted her implant. "Scout Martin Bane, isn't it? I note that you refer to their world as your world."

"I've called Aashla home for eighteen years." He put an arm around Megan. "And, like David, I'll be marrying a local girl."

"My congratulations to both of you on your nuptials, past and pending. And please allow me to express the Federation's relief that both of you have returned safely after such an extended absence. No doubt you're both aware the Scout Corps wants to debrief you. Would you be averse to getting that out of the way as soon as possible?"

"Of course not, Admiral," I said

"Thank you, for your cooperation. Smitts will take you to the base scout commander now." McGillis nodded to Callan, Rupor, and the diplomatic personnel. "I'll personally see to their needs."

Smitts looked terribly uncomfortable playing escort to people he had snubbed earlier. Neither Martin nor I said anything to put Smitts at his ease. Perhaps he would learn something from this, though I doubted it.

The Scout Corps office was a flurry of activity when we arrived. Smitts attempted introductions.

"Scout Commander Collins, may I present-"

Collins cut him off. "David Rice! It's good to see you hale and hearty. And Martin, the Bane of my existence, back from the dead! It is quite a grand day for the Scout Corps, indeed."

Oblivious to Smitts' discomfort, Collins said to him, "David was one of the best cadets I ever taught during my years at the academy. And Martin was one of the best troublemakers."

With a quick nod, Smitts excused himself and fled the office.

"Now that we're free of that idiot Smitts, let's get comfortable and start that debriefing, shall we?"

Martin raised a forestalling hand. "I would suggest a full medical workup, first, sir."

Collins gave Martin a quick up and down glance. "You do look as if you've had a rough time of it, recently, Martin."

"The navy took good care of me and I'm healing quite well, sir. It's David who should receive the medical attention."

"He looks remarkably fit to me, Martin."

"I'll admit David looks great on the outside. I'm worried about possible internal damage from over-Boosting."

Collins gaze sharpened. "Is this true, David? Have you been over-using Boost?"

"I Boosted only when necessary, sir. Unfortunately, there have been times when it was necessary to Boost rather more often than suggested."

"And longer than suggested, as well. I personally watched David Boost for thirteen straight minutes." Gasps sounded from the personnel in the office and the color drained from Collins' face. "We got his heart started again, but it was a close thing."

Fifteen minutes later, Collins had me inside the base hospital and about to go under anesthesia in preparation for a full scale invasion of my body by medical nanites. I refused to be put under until Callan arrived.

When she did, worry was etched across her face. "What's going on, David? Why are you in the hospital? Are you hurt?"

"This is all just a precaution, dear. Martin has gotten the scout commander worried about the effect Boosting has had on my body. They're going to send in an army of nanites to check me out."

"Martin's not the only one who's worried about you, darling." Callan kissed me lightly. "If you know what's good for you, you'll cooperate with the doctors."

She backed away so the doctors could get started. Her lovely face was the last thing I saw as I went under.

70

THE SPACEBABE

I HOVERED ON THE EDGE OF CONSCIOUSNESS, DREAMING I WAS BACK HOME with my parents and sister. Mom was talking to a nurse about me. For a few seconds, I wondered why I was having such a boring dream. Then I came fully awake.

"According to your son's medical report, the nanites did a lot of internal reconstruction. Simple, though extensive, wear and tear from Boosting, it says. That kind of reconstruction puts a strain on the body, but it's nothing a little sleep won't fix," the nurse said.

"And you're sure he's just sleeping?" my mother asked.

"Well, I was, Mom," I said, my throat parched, "until you woke me up."

My mother, father, and sister all crowded around my bed, hugging and kissing me and generally making it hard for me to breathe.

"You should pour him some water, ma'am. He hasn't had a drink in two days," the nurse said, smiling. "And do let him come up for air every now and then."

"We've been so worried about you, David!" Tears rolled down Mom's cheeks. "You've been missing for nearly three years."

Dad clapped me once on the shoulder, a big smile on his face and tears welling in his eyes. Then my little sister pushed past him and promptly punched me on the arm.

"You had Mom and Dad worried sick, lunkhead. So don't go off and get lost again. Have you got that?"

Yes, she and Callan were going to get along famously. I sat up to pull her into a hug and then found myself simply staring at her.

"What are you staring at? Have I got something on my face?"

I shook my head. "No, Sandra, I'm just wondering when my awkward baby sister turned into such a beautiful young woman."

"Mom, something's really wrong with David. He's being nice to me."

A slight cough sounded near the door. Harris stood there, watching the scene with a broad smile. Seeing my eyes on him, he snapped to attention and addressed me in Mordanian.

"Her Highness only left your bedside to attend an appointment with a doctor." Alarm must have crossed my face as he added, "I'm told it is a routine matter. Perhaps it's associated with the implant she had installed yesterday. I've taken the liberty of informing her that you're awake."

"Thank you, Harris."

Harris nodded and withdrew.

"Who's that?" Sandra asked.

"Harris? He's a marine from the world I've been on for the last two and a half years."

"He's really cute. Does he have a girlfriend?"

"I have absolutely no idea, but I will be more than happy to introduce you." I looked past Sandra to my father. "Don't worry, Dad, Harris is as honorable a young man as I've met. We can trust him with the brat."

Sandra punched me on the arm again.

Rubbing my arm, I asked, "So, how did the three of you get here so quickly?"

"The Scout Corps brought us on one of their fastest ships," Dad replied. "We only docked at the station half an hour ago."

"Did anyone tell you anything about what had happened to me or where I've been?"

"No, son, the people we talked with didn't know anything except you'd crashed on some lost colony and had just resurfaced." Tears welled up in Mom's eyes again. "You can imagine how we felt when they brought us to a hospital."

"You always said you were going to find a lost colony someday," Dad smiled. "Looks like you're a man of your word, son."

Sandra flashed a wicked grin. "Yeah, yeah, so you found a lost world. Whoopee. I want to know if you found your spacebabe?"

A lilting voice spoke from the doorway. "What on Aashla is a spacebabe?"

Callan stood just inside the doorway, a fond smile lighting her face. Seeing Callan for the first time, Sandra's eyes went wide. "Wow, David. You really *did* meet her."

"I've got to say I'm impressed, son," Dad murmured. "That girl is beyond beautiful!"

I sat up straighter in bed. "Mom. Dad. Sandra. This is Her Royal Highness, Princess Callan, heir to the throne of Mordan and, more importantly-"

"Oh my God, are you serious? The spacebabe is a princess, too?" Sandra gave me a hard look. "You've *got* to be putting us on."

"Sandra, that was incredibly rude!" Mom blushed and attempted a curtsey to Callan. "Please forgive my daughter, Your Highness. She *has* been raised with better manners than that."

Callan laughed. "There are no apologies necessary. But the 'spacebabe' comment still intrigues me. What is that all about?"

Dad stepped in with an explanation. "When David was a boy, a retired scout lived across the street from us. He was a nice old man who filled David's head with stories of lost colonies, daring rescues, and a beautiful princess. Growing up, David swore he was going to become a scout, find a lost colony, have amazing adventures, and rescue a beautiful princess. Even if, to quote his seven year old self, it meant he had to kiss a girl."

"I see." Callan flashed her lovely smile again. "And am I supposed to be the beautiful princess?"

Sandra turned an incredulous look on me. "She's kidding, right? I mean, they *do* have mirrors on her planet, don't they?"

"Yes, we have mirrors, brat. But there's one more thing I need-"

Eyes dancing, Callan interrupted me. "And what about kissing a girl, David? Did that turn out to be as onerous as you feared?"

It was my turn to grin. "Well, I've found it rather tolerable when I'm kissing the *right* girl."

Sandra was much quicker on the uptake than my parents. "Oh my gosh! Do you mean you kissed the spacebabe?"

"Yes, brat, I kissed the spacebabe. Then I took it a step farther and I *married* the spacebabe."

Mom's hand flew to her mouth and she dropped onto the side of the bed. Dad gave me a big grin and a double thumbs up. Sandra even relented and gave me a big hug.

"I always said I wanted a sister. You done good, big brother."

Her eyes still dancing, Callan sat next to Mom and wrapped her in a big hug.

"David is far too modest to say it, but he did more than just kiss me and marry me. He has saved my life more times than I can count. His courage and conviction in the face of overwhelming odds gave me hope when there was little hope to be found. His love and compassion gave me the strength to carry on when all seemed lost. My people love him almost as much as I do." Callan kissed Mom on the cheek. "Thank you for raising such a son."

As Mom blushed, Callan took my hand in hers. "I only pray I can do half as well when our child is born."

I pulled back and looked into Callan's eyes. "*When?*"

"Yes, darling. I saw the doctor today to confirm it." Callan guided my hand to her stomach. "You're going to be a father."

I thought I could never be happier than I was on the day I married Callan. It turns out I could.

71

HOME AGAIN

NOTHING THAT HAPPENED DURING THE ENSUING THREE WEEKS CAME CLOSE to matching the joy I felt seeing my family again and learning Callan and I were mere months from having a family of our own.

My wife, Rupor, and the other Aashlander political representatives benefited greatly from their new implants. They all received diplomatic implants—which provided language translations, cultural traditions, and the governing laws of the Federation, but *not* Boost—and made good use of their newfound knowledge. An agricultural assistance treaty was hammered out, along with an agreement to provide naval patrols on the Federation side of the wormhole.

Martin became a media darling, with the newsies playing up his "mischievous boy gone bad boy gone hero" story. Martin managed to pull me into the limelight, as well, and much was made of my adventures and my romance with Callan. I was never comfortable in front of the vid cameras and, after three dreadful interviews with me, the newsies decided to get all their stories from Martin.

Megan's music proved to be Aashla's first export. A musician touring military bases happened to hear Megan performing traditional and original songs for our marines. He whipped out a pocket recorder and captured the rest of her performance on video. The musician asked permission to upload the performance to the net. Megan agreed, but only after conferring with Martin and Callan. Two thousand years of isolation from the rest of humanity resulted in a musical evolution far from anything found in the Federation. With trillions of people looking for new and different entertainment, Megan's performance was an instant hit.

Callan's captivating beauty and animated interviews made her the face of Aashla. Newsies packed into her public appearances and vid cameras flitted all around her. Harris took it upon himself to organize an escort of armed marines for Callan, keeping the newsies at bay and clearing a path for her with bared teeth and, sometimes, bared blades.

Two days after my family arrived on the station, Harris requested a formal introduction to Sandra. My sister couldn't decide whether to be offended that Harris came to me rather than her or simply relieved that Harris finally picked up the signals she had been sending. Callan explained Mordanian dating customs to Sandra, explaining Harris simply followed the customs of his home world by approaching me. I had Martin advise Harris on Federation dating customs. Their first date went well right up until Harris got arrested for brawling.

According to Harris, a group of drunken young men voiced vulgar approval of certain parts of Sandra's anatomy. They refused Harris's demands to apologize to Sandra and then compounded their error by questioning Harris's parentage. Three of the men lay unconscious when station security took Harris into custody. According to Sandra, the offensive comment was nothing she hadn't heard before, but Harris's defense of her honor surprised Sandra and, according to Callan, pleased her no end.

We turned Chapman and the pirates over to Federation law enforcement and recorded hours of testimony for use against them in their trials. Chapman made matters worse for himself, challenging Heidi's Mordanian citizenship and the divorce granted by Callan. A judge ruled the matter lay outside of Federation jurisdiction and told Chapman he would have to argue his case in a Mordanian court. The day after the ruling, Chapman and the pirates were transferred to the planet below to await trial.

After three long weeks of preparations, the navy assembled the ships necessary to clear the Aashlan end of the wormhole. I'm told the clearing operation was quite a sight when witnessed from Aashla. It also served notice we were coming home.

A huge crowd gathered to watch the *Aashla's Hope*, escorted by half a dozen Federation Navy fighters, land outside Morda. Callan and I were the first to descend the ramp from the ship. Before us stood Callan's parents. Next to them stood Kim, smiling and craning her neck to see around us. The moment we both dreaded was at hand.

Kim focused on us as we approached. Our somber expressions told her we brought bad news. Tears ran down her cheeks even before we reached her. The queen put her arm around Kim as I told her of Milo's sacrifice and gave her a heartfelt hug. Leaving Callan comforting Kim, the marine commander and I undertook the daunting task of speaking with the families of each marine who gave his life on the mission. I will never forget the haunting look of the parents who lost their child, of the wives who lost husbands, and of the children who lost fathers.

At a reception that evening, Callan announced her pregnancy to the court. It lifted the mood around the palace, where Milo had been well-known and well-liked, and even drew a smile and congratulatory hug from Kim. Callan's parents rejoiced at the prospect of a grandchild and heir. The next day, the rest of the kingdom rejoiced with them when the news was proclaimed throughout the land.

In the following months, Federation delegations took up negotiations with many Aashlander countries and the first agricultural assistance missions arrived. Nist and Kim were married in a small, intimate ceremony. Martin and Megan were married in a huge, raucous ceremony. It made news across the Federation. Callan convinced her parents to fund a medical school in Morda and put Tristan in charge of it. And, in the largest wedding Tarteg had ever seen, Rupor made good on his promise to Heidi. For the record, Heidi *does* look beautiful in Tartegian black and gold.

Nine months after we left on the *Aashla's Hope*, Callan went into labor. I sat by her side as Tristan guided her through the delivery and placed our newborn son in her arms.

"Welcome to the world, Robbill Milo Martin Edwar Rice Villas," she said to him.

"That's an awfully big name for such a little guy. Do you think he can live up to it?"

"Of course he can, David. After all, you're his father!"

Callan laid her head on my shoulder and our son caught my finger in his tiny fist. Then time went away and all was right in my world.

ABOUT THE AUTHOR

Growing up, Henry worked at the usual range of menial jobs before ending up in software development. In between the menial jobs and the IT jobs, he achieved some small fame as the writer and co-creator of the small press comic book titles Southern Knights and X-Thieves. In 2006, Henry took up the professional storytelling and has performed all across the state of North Carolina.

Henry has been a fan of science fiction for as long as he can remember. He has loved space opera and planetary romance since the beginning, that is why his science fiction novels end up in those subgenres.

Henry currently lives in Raleigh, NC, with his wife, a cat, and a host of imaginary friends clamoring to tell him of their adventures.

www.henryvogelwrites.com

ALSO BY HENRY VOGEL

Travis & Trouble

Trouble in Twi-Town

Trouble on Mars

The Fortune Chronicles

Fortune's Fool

The Scales of Sin & Sorrow

The Scout Series

Scout's Honor

Scout's Oath

Scout's Duty

Scout's Law

Scout's Training

Scout's First Mission

Hart for Adventure

The Princess Scout

Scout: The Lost Colony Adventures

Non-series books

The Lost Planet

Heart of Dorkness & Other Stories

The Connaught Family Chronicles

The Fugitive Heir

The Fugitive Pair

The Fugitive Snare

The Hostage in Hiding

The Captain Nancy Martin

The Counterfeit Captain

The Undercover Captain

The Recognition Series

The Recognition Run

The Recognition Rejection

The Recognition Revelation

Comic Books

Aristocratic Xraterrestrial Time-Traveling Thieves Complete Collection

Southern Knights Almost Complete Collection

Southern Knights Color Edition

Southern Knights: The Morrigan Wars

Southern Knights: Leaving Atlanta (prose novella)

Missing Beings

Illustrated Children's Book

I'm in Charge! and Other Stories

www.ingramcontent.com/pod-product-compliance
Lightning Source LLC
Chambersburg PA
CBHW030429310726
48979CB00009B/1681/J

* 9 7 8 1 9 5 8 3 3 3 0 4 4 *